A Game of Inches

A Game of Inches

A novel by S.R. Doss

Golden Word Books
Santa Fe, NM

Library of Congress Control Number xxxxxxxxxx

G
W
B

A Game of Inches. Copyright © 202x by S.R. Doss

Printed in the United States of America

Published by Golden Word Books, Santa Fe, New Mexico.

ISBN 978-1-948749-75-6

A Game of Inches

STOP THE PRESSES

I REMEMBER EXACTLY WHAT I WAS DOING WHEN I HEARD THE news that LBJ had bought the farm. I was sitting at a café table by the river, under a tree, drinking beer and wiping bird shit off the morning paper. Off the society pages. All alone, looking at a picture in the paper, when the waiter told me they just announced it on the radio.

LBJ. Nobody else remembers. Where they were, or what they were doing, when they heard that Lyndon Johnson died. Not like the day when JFK was shot. Hell, the woman next door, mention Kennedy and she can't stop talking. Telling how she was buying a necklace in Tiffany's when she heard the terrible news. Ashamed to come back to Texas. The day LBJ died? Mention that and she'll shrug her shoulders.

But I remember. How I looked at the picture, trying to see the faces in the background. The Secretary of the Army coming out of the officers club at Fort Sam Houston. With his aides and their wives behind him. One of the wives, her face not quite in focus. Barely enough to recognize her. Twelve years since I had seen her. Twelve years of trying to forget her.

I remember, all right. The picture and what it led to. My editor sending me to cover the funeral. That week in Washington, and another week there later on. The picture, the reunion, Johnson's body in the Capitol rotunda. The secret documents, the scandal, the accusations. Testifying in front of a Senate subcommittee. Not easy to forget that.

Not easy to forget a week in jail, either.

All because of a picture in the paper. I should have ordered another beer and turned to the obituary section. Or the Zodiac column next to the comic pages, so I could see what the prospects were that day for Libra. I have a good idea what my horoscope would have told me. It would have warned me to watch out. Call in sick, tell them you're under the weather.

Under the weather, hell. I was under the blackest of black clouds, and I had no way of knowing it.

He's up on the roof, I was told when I entered the city room. Bettelmy, almost thirty years since he flew a B-17 over Germany, that's where he goes when he's thinking about his enemies. Up on the roof, where he can look at the opposition. Where he can plot some way of dropping bombs to raise the paper's circulation. I had an idea what he had on his mind. He wanted to chew my ass out about my last interview with Lyndon Johnson.

"Nice view of the Alamo" I said as I approached him.

"You were a paratrooper, you ever jump this low, Phil?"

"This low? Six stories? Hell no, you'd never get your canopy open."

"I almost did. Once, after we were hit coming back from bombing Munich."

"I know, you told me about it. Downstairs, they said you wanted to see me, Bill."

"We're getting our butts kicked. The Sunday edition, we're behind by forty thousand."

"Look, I'm sorry. In another week or two Johnson might have. . ."

"I told you, Phil, find out before he had another heart attack. Remember?"

"He was starting to get around to it. He was already hinting at it, he. . ."

"That would have made a hell of a story. Would have blown the lid off over there."

I could see what he was looking at. Not the Alamo. A building down the street, three blocks away and three stories shorter. The home of the Light, part of the Hearst chain of papers. Bettelmy, gazing at that building, looking frustrated. For the past month planning to drop a bomb right down their ventilator shaft. With me lighting the fuse, trying to get LBJ to talk about it, this crooked business Bettelmy was so sure of he could smell it.

"I want you to go to Washington tomorrow" he said. "Cover Johnson's funeral."

"His funeral? Look, I'm not. . ."

"Pick up your plane ticket from my secretary."

"Bill, all the ceremonies, his body lying in state, that will take. . ."

"While you're there, I want you to look up someone. An old friend of mine, a lawyer with the Commerce Department."

"All right. I'll look him up. Then what?"

"See me before you leave tomorrow. I need to call him first."

"Whatever you say. Commerce. . .you think they might. . ."

"Forty years ago, you know what they used this roof for?"

"No. That long ago, I wasn't even born then."

"Homing pigeons, to bring back pictures from a hundred miles away."

"Anything else? I need to help on the obituary."

"This time, when the chickens come home to roost we'll have the Light by the balls, Phil. All of them, Hearst and that whole damned crowd of his."

Bettelmy was still looking at the building in the distance when I left him on the roof. Four floors down the elevator then, past the TV studio and the executive offices, back to the news room and back to writing. My contribution to the special edition the paper was putting together. A story about the last time I saw Lyndon Johnson, four days ago, sitting in a rocking chair on the front porch of his ranch house.

With my name in a kicker headline in italics: Phillip Dee's Farewell to LBJ.

A final tribute, more or less. But nothing about the way he looked, his face sad and wrinkled, his white hair drooping to his shoulders. Not a word about his chain smoking and the bitterness in his voice. About the way he'd been lied to by McNamara and the generals. About the way he knew he'd be remembered, not for all the good things he had done, but only for that goddamned war in Vee-et Naam.

And not a word about what I'd been trying to wheedle out of him for weeks. What he knew about a big time government swindle while he was President. What he knew about the LSI, the Lone Star International Corporation. Crooked sonsofbitches, that's all he ever said, the LSI included, all those crooked bastards feeding off that goddamned war in Vee-et Naam. Not enough for Bettelmy to run with.

Too bad. LBJ had not come through, but Bettlemy wasn't finished. Sending me to cover the funeral, hell, what he really had in mind was sending me to see this friend of his in Washington. Follow a new lead, keep tracking on the LSI accounts, he was sure the Hearst Corporation had made millions off that damned conglomerate. Nail them, he had told me once while we were drinking, win a Pulitzer, drive the Light right out of business.

Five hundred words and I was finished. My last interview with Lyndon Johnson. Good shit, the managing editor said, no wonder BB wants you to write about the funeral.

Wrong, I could have told him. He's sending me to see a friend at Commerce, and even that, that's not really why I'm going. I was going because of someone else I would look up when I got to Washington. I was going because of a picture, the picture of a woman in the morning paper.

Molly. Married. To an old friend of mine who hustled her away. Molly, the woman I might have married. Might have, hell, that's not what news is all about. Not what might have happened. News is what you'd never think would happen. Even when it does.

Wives. You work for a morning paper, you lead a zombie's life. Get home at two or three a.m., have a drink, go to bed and try not to wake your wife up. Not me. My wife stays up as late as I do. Writing cowboy novels. Victoria Lovelace, that was her name before we married. But who would read a cowboy novel written by a woman with a name like that? No one. So I never knew, when I got home, who might be waiting.

"Howdy, pardner" she said when I came in the living room that night.

"So who is it this time?" I asked. "Matt Larue or Lash Laramie?"

"Matt Larue" she answered. "Don't you recognize him, cowboy?"

I walked past her to the kitchen, poured a drink, and turned around to watch her working. Typing fast, banging away at her typewriter like she was roping a calf at a rodeo. Matt Larue, wearing jeans and boots and a cowboy hat, a black Stetson perched on top a head of hair that said forget it, pal. Forget that night you met LaRue and thought it was a wig. Forget that night you wondered if you'd lost your marbles.

Hard to forget. I had been drinking, sure, but what she did that night, how could I forget it? And Bettlemy, too, that bastard, the way he introduced us at that party.

Meet Matt Larue, he said, the famous cowboy novelist.

Howdy, Larue had said in a husky voice, why are you looking at me that way?

You remind me of someone I once knew, I answered.

Watch out for him, said Bettelmy, he used to be a paratrooper.

So who do I remind you of, Larue had asked.

A woman I once knew, I said, too bad you're not a woman, too.

You're right, too bad, Larue had said, let's have another drink and maybe I can help you to forget her.

Another drink and another drink. Larue, sizing me up. And me, drunk, wondering how in hell this cowboy in high drag could look so much like Molly.

Come on, Larue had said, I'll take you home. You were a paratrooper, were you?

I'll walk, I said.

Paratroopers, Larue had said, I heard it took a lot of balls to jump out of airplanes.

A lot, I mumbled, only a real man could do it.

We'll see, Larue had said.

So off we'd gone, in a pink Cadillac with longhorns mounted on the hood. To Larue's place. Larue, trying to drag me into bed. Me, drunk, wondering what the hell I was doing there, watching Larue get undressed. Husky voice and all, not a man in drag but a woman with a beautiful body. How the hell could I forget it?

We were married one month later.

Married, with Bettelmy giving away the bride, telling everyone how he introduced us. Some day I'll tell him how that night went. And then throw him off that goddamned roof, as soon as I get finished with this crap about the Lone Star International. Right, do that and then live off all the income from these cowboy novels she keeps writing.

"So what are you working on?" I asked when I came out of the kitchen.

"Something different" she said. "Something really different."

"You ever wonder how you got into writing Westerns?"

"I told you, I was tired of doing feature stories for the paper."

"Sure. But hell, Vicky, you never even saw a horse before you moved to Texas."

"Not true. I took a horseback riding course at Wellesley."

"And then you started fantasizing about cowboys."

"Someone like you, Phil. Someone to ride my saddle."

"You're lewd, you know that? You want to go for a ride right now?"

"Not now, I'm busy. Don't drink too much, wait until I've finished."

I poured another drink and watched her go on typing. Fast as hell, grinding out another novel. Four a year under two different names, Larue and Laramie. Plus the screenplay she's been working on, hell, she's like a damned machine at work. In bed, as well. Fast on the draw, like they say in the cowboy novels.

"This thing you're working on. So what's so different about it?"

"Negro cowboys" she answered.

"You're joking. Negro cowboys?"

"After the Civil War, a third of all the cowboys were Negro."

"I know, but nobody writes about that, Vicky."

"I'm going to. And to hell with my publisher if he doesn't like it."

She stood up and stretched, and as she did I handed her my drink. She took a sip, smiled at me, sat down and started typing again. Stubborn, when she has an axe to grind. This thing she wrote a couple of years ago, about a woman rancher on the prairie, at first her publisher didn't like that, either. Now it's going to be a movie.

"Bettelmy's secretary called this evening" said Vicky as she went on typing.

"She left a message?"

"She said they're sending you to Washington tomorrow."

"She's your friend, I know, but that woman really loves to gossip."

"I've decided to go with you."

"Vicky, look, I'll be busy with the funeral, there won't be time to. . ."

"Negro cowboys, Phil. The Smithsonian is opening a new exhibit."

She went on typing as I poured another drink. So she's decided to go with me. If that's what she wants don't argue with her, she'll go no matter what I say. So let her tag along. Maybe she'll meet Molly, too, if I can find her. Let her see how much they look alike. Hell, for all I know Molly may have read her novels.

Novels. About Negro cowboys now. So Vicky wants to visit the Smithsonian. Fine. I finished my drink and tried to get my mind on Washington, on what I'd need to do there. Write about the funeral. Look up Bettelmy's friend at Commerce. Keep tracking on the crooks who ran the Lone Star International.

Negro cowboys and the LSI. Worlds apart. Who could have guessed the two would somehow wind up being tied together? Not me.

Tommy Fry, an old drinking buddy from the sports department. That's who I ran into on the stairwell up to Bettelmy's office. Fry, famous for inventing that remark about the opera singer. It ain't over 'til the fat lady sings, he had said once when a game was coming to its close. On television. The whole damned world had picked it up. From the look on his face I wondered if she had just started singing.

"Last night" he said. "Did you watch the ten o'clock news on television?"

"No. I was busy, I. . ."

"You didn't hear what Thornton said?"

"Paul Thornton? No, I. . ."

"Just before I did the sports report. He went after your ass, Phil."

"Me? Why would he mention me?"

"He had the galley proof of your story on LBJ. He called it propaganda from the fair haired boy downstairs."

"Sure, he hated Johnson. I'll deal with him when I get back from Washington."

"He's going, too. The station's sending him to cover the funeral on television."

Thornton, that conniving bastard, keeping the folks aroused with his nightly bullshit on TV. Telling them how a zookeeper shot a baby giraffe for stepping on a worker's toes. How a Negro soldier raped a teenage girl in the back room of a grocery store. How the Mexicans have been peddling tacos filled with rat flesh. So now they're sending him to comment on the funeral. Looking over my shoulder, no telling what he'll do with that.

"Damn" I muttered as I started up the stairwell. "I'll talk to Bettelmy about him."

"Phil, wait, there's something else you might as well know."

"What else? I'm in a hurry, Tom."

"Vicky. I heard Thornton say he's going to expose your wife when he gets back."

"Expose her? For what? He's out of his mind, she's. . ."

"He was talking with the station manager. He said Matt Larue is a man who lives in Lubbock and your wife's a phony, shit like that, Phil."

"That sonofabitch. Where is he? I'll settle with him right now."

"He's up in Bettelmy's office, he's. . ."

I charged up the stairwell. To the fourth floor, where the bosses sat behind closed doors, running the paper and the TV station. When I got there I heard shouting in Bettelmy's office. I waited in the hallway. After a moment the shouting stopped and out they came, Thornton and the TV station manager, with Bettelmy standing behind them in his doorway.

Paul Thornton, old and gray, bent over at the waist. Years ago, the paper's ace reporter, ravaged now by age and alcohol. For a second I felt sorry for him. For a second I could see a kind of warning in him. Get out of the newspaper business, Phil. If you don't you'll wind up a drunk like him, over the hill and telling the world to go to hell.

"Paul, I'd like a word with you" I said, standing in front of him in the hallway.

"Go fuck yourself" he answered. "Get out of my way."

"Lay off my wife, you hear me?"

"Fuck her, too."

"Look" I said, raising my voice. "You're an old man and I don't want to hurt you, but I'll break your goddamn neck, you hear me? If you ever mention Vicky in that shit you keep spewing on TV I'll break your neck, Paul."

"You hear that, Bettelmy?" the station manager yelled. "You hear how he just threatened Thornton?"

"I heard" said Bettelmy. "Come in my office, Phil."

Thornton was still cursing as I walked past the station manager into Bettelmy's office. I closed the door behind me. I was angry as hell, and I could tell by the look on his face Bettelmy was angry, too. Still tall and thin, but looking ten years older than he had the day before, an old bomber pilot worn down by all the missions he's been flying.

"Leave Thornton alone" he said. "There's nothing we can do about him."

"I can. And I will if he gets out of line with Vicky."

"It's not her, it's you he's after."

"I know, I heard about last night. I can live with that, as long as he. . ."

"He had a copy of what you wrote. You know what's in his contract?"

"You must be joking, Bill, nobody around here has a contract. . ."

"He does. That's what we were arguing about. You want to tell him, Sarah?"

I turned and looked at Bettelmy's secretary, standing in the entrance to the room next door. Sarah Bella Bellow, still erect at damned near eighty.

Miss Sarah. I could never see her without smiling at the way she looked. Always formal, like some Daughter of the Texas Revolution serving tea at a reception, a stiff white collar around her neck, a dress down to her ankles, a wrinkled face that seemed to tell you to be careful, she knew where all the bones were buried in that building.

Legend had it she had danced with Teddy Roosevelt. Legend also had it no one ever cursed when she was present, if you did your ass was mud and you would sure as hell regret it.

"I looked it up for Mister Bettelmy" she said.

"You looked up what?" I asked.

"Mister Thornton has a contract with the television station."

"Fine, Miss Sarah. So what?"

"It requires the paper to provide him access."

"Access? To what?"

"To everything reporters write."

"So he can comment on it? Before we even go to press?"

"The contract says so he may analyze it in the evening news."

"Analyze it? You ever watch him, Miss Sarah? It's disgusting."

"Yes, Mister Dee, I find him quite disgusting."

She shook her head and walked back to her desk. Then she returned and closed the door into her office. I looked at Bettelmy. He seemed resigned to fate, his last engine gone and his plane all shot to pieces. He also seemed embarrassed.

"Let me guess" I said. "Thornton. He blew up in front of her."

"Face it, Phil. When he's on the air, everyone in town is watching."

"Watching, hell, they should be ashamed of him, they. . ."

"The paper's losing money, the TV station is a gold mine, it's as simple as that."

"So what about this contract crap? What about the funeral?"

"Whatever you write, you send it here by telegraph, we send him back a copy."

"Damn. . ."

"We'll set it up so it's automatic. Don't worry about it."

"Automatic, hell, that's larceny, Bill."

"I'll make sure that tapes are kept of what he broadcasts."

"So I can see what he said when I get back? Look, if he. . ."

"Sit down, get your mind off Thornton. There's something more important."

"All right. . .all right. . ."

"I have a letter for you to take to Washington."

He handed me an envelope. Sealed, with a name and an office number on it. A letter to his lawyer friend at Commerce.

"I talked to him last night" he said. "He's on to what we're looking for."

"Sure, something to nail the Lone Star International. Fine, I'll. . ."

"Something to nail the Light. He may have the proof we need."

"William Baxter" I said as I looked at the name on the envelope.

"He was my copilot in the Air Force."

"Baxter. . .that name, somehow it rings a bell, I wonder if. . ."

"If Vicky's going with you, have her meet his wife."

I nodded, put the envelope away, and headed for the airport. Vicky would be waiting there. Meet Baxter's wife, hell, she'd meet another wife as well in Washington. Molly, married to a colonel now. As for Baxter's wife, fine, be sociable when you get there, have Vicky meet her also. How little did I know what that would lead to.

Washington. At night, coming from the West, flying along the Potomac River, seeing the city from above, with all the lights on that can be inspiring, even for someone from Texas. The Capitol, the Lincoln Memorial, the Washington Monument, the story of a nation right beneath the window of an airplane. The White House, too, lighted for the world to see. Lyndon Johnson must have loved it.

LBJ, poor bastard, dead two days after the date he might have finished one more term in office. Except for Vietnam. Except for all the protests. No monument for him, not now, not even the funeral he deserved. A story there, as well, waiting to be written. An ex-President shouldn't die in the same week someone else is being inaugurated. The ceremonies will conflict, they just won't fit together.

So it's Nixon for a second term. Four years or more since he said he'd stop it, since he said he had a secret plan to end the war. And he's only now announced some deal to bring it to a close. Johnson's war, they used to call it. And drove him out of office. But Nixon gets a second term. There must be another story there, but I'd have to figure out how it might be written. Things like that can be damned complicated.

"You're quiet" said Vicky, looking out the window. "What have you been thinking?"

"About some things I'm going to write."

"Not tonight, I hope. We have a long day ahead tomorrow."

"Tonight. I'm going to drown that sonofabitch with paper."

"What sonofabitch? Which one do you have in mind?"

"I'll tell you when we get to the hotel."

"If we get there. You know I don't like to fly, Phil."

"Matt Larue wouldn't be afraid to fly."

"You want to know what your pal Larue might be afraid of?"

"Sure. Afraid I'll be up all night writing. Don't worry, I'm fast on the draw, babe."

After we landed and loaded our baggage in a cab I told the driver what to do. Take us by the Capitol on the way to the Hotel Washington, and wait while we look around for a few minutes. That's out of the way, he said, and I'll have to keep the meter running while you get out. Fine, I said, so that's another twenty for you and five hundred words for me. He had no idea what I was talking about. Neither did Vicky.

"The scaffolds" she said as we stood behind the Capitol. "It's really quite ironic."

"For Nixon's inauguration. They'll still be up when Johnson's body gets here."

"Why would you want to write about that?"

"I told you, I'm going to drown some sonofabitch with copy."

At the hotel desk I asked about the Western Union office. Open all night, said the clerk, six blocks away on K Street, you can call from here. No, I said, what I'll have in a hour or two can't be sent by telephone, I'll need someone to take it to them. I'll lay it on, said the clerk, an old soldier wearing a bronze star ribbon on his jacket, but first we'll get your bags upstairs, your wife, she'll like the view from the room we're putting you in.

She did. While I unpacked she opened the drapes and smiled as she looked out the window. At Lafayette Square and the White House. And then at a line of men and women marching back and forth across the street from the White House, carrying signs and shouting. I looked out, too, and nodded.

"It's almost midnight" she said. "Don't those people ever sleep?"

"Not when there's something to protest."

"Maybe you should write about that, too."

"I will, when I get around to it. Ten thousand words a day, that's my quota."

I set my portable typewriter on a table and took out a ream of paper from my suitcase. She looked at me and started laughing. Ten thousand words a day, she said, you must be joking, that's forty pages of copy, Bettelmy will think you've gone bananas.

"It's not for Bettelmy, not exactly. It's for Thornton."

"Thornton? That old fart? You'll be writing for him?"

"It's in his contract. The paper has to send him everything I write while I'm here."

"I smell a rat, Phil. What are you up to?"

"I told you, I'm going to drown that sonofabitch in copy."

"Go ahead, then. Wake me up if you feel like a break. I'm going to bed."

Fifty words a minute, non-stop that's three thousand words an hour. At three a.m. I put the carbon copies aside, stuffed almost forty pages in the envelope the clerk had given me, and went downstairs. Six separate stories, one or two worth printing, maybe. Here, I said, this goes to the Western Union office, be sure they send it right away.

Vicky was sound asleep when I returned. Too bad, but let her sleep, she would have a lot to do when she got up. So would I. And so would that bastard Thornton.

He's gone to lunch, he'll be back in an hour, I was told when I got to Baxter's office on the top floor of the Commerce building. With an hour to kill I went down to the lobby. To look for a public telephone. To call the Pentagon, to start the ball rolling on another matter. On what I had been wondering about since I saw that picture in the paper.

Molly. How had it happened? How had she wound up marrying Lamont, after she told me she was finished with him? Finished with me, finished with both of us, finished with the whole damned Army. But there she was in the picture, coming out of the officers club at Fort Sam Houston, Lamont an aide to the Secretary of the Army and her right there behind him.

Nothing personal about it, of course, what I was wondering, hell, I was married to Vicky now, but I was a reporter, too, and that's what a good reporter does, he wonders, he digs into things and finds out what really happened. Even if he has to lie a bit to get the job done. That's something else I was wondering about. If I was lying to myself about Molly.

Colonel Lamont is in a meeting, I was told when I reached his number. Please give him a message, I said, tell him an old friend is in town for a few days, Phillip Dee, I'm with my wife at the Hotel Washington, tell him to give me a ring, it would be nice to meet for dinner, all four of us, it would be nice to talk about the good old days in Germany and Fort Campbell.

Right, all four of us, I thought as I hung up the telephone. Lamont would know what I meant. No surprise in that. What surprised me, when I got back to his office, was what Baxter wanted to talk about. After I gave him Bettelmy's letter. Baxter, I'll be damned, that's what he had in mind, as well. Something that happened in Germany.

He was unlocking his door when I got there. A middle-aged man, wearing a high-price business suit and carrying a briefcase, with a woman beside him wearing a suit like his, trousers and all, carrying a briefcase also. When I told Baxter who I was she nodded. A bit dumpy, but not bad looking. Looking like she knew how to get things done, that kind of woman.

My wife, said Baxter as he introduced us in his office. Louella, this man is a friend of a friend, he said to her as he set his briefcase on a coffee table. That's nice, Bill, she replied, I don't know why you want that IRS file you asked me to get, but you have it now, so I'm going back to work, it's a busy day in the Senate. I noticed she was frowning as she left his office.

I handed him the letter I had been told to deliver. He opened the envelope and read what Bettelmy had written. I looked around the room while I waited. On a wall, a row of pictures, the standard for a government office. Faces easy to recognize, big-time politicians shaking hands with the hired help. A photograph of Baxter with the President. Not Johnson. Nixon.

On another wall more pictures, altogether different. A ten-man crew standing next to a B-17, under the nose art, an image of a big breasted nude with two grenades hanging from her nipples. Double Trouble, the name of the plane. Four rows of bombs under the pilot's window. Twenty bombs. Damn. Bettelmy had told me they went down on their twenty-first mission.

"I'm afraid he's wrong" said Baxter as he folded the letter and put it back in the envelope. He reached down and opened a drawer and locked it in his desk. Then he went to the door and locked it, too. When he returned to his desk he took the telephone off its cradle. Whatever Bettelmy was wrong about, Baxter sure as hell wanted to keep it secret.

"This is big, all right" he said. "But it won't lead back to the Hearst Corporation."

"The LSI, you mean. What have you found out about them?"

"At least a hundred million in graft, give or take a few millions."

"Enough to put someone in prison."

"Perhaps, but there's something else you'll need, and it's hidden in DOD."

"The Department of Defense, hell, that should be. . ."

"Look, I'm risking my career on this already. My wife's, as well."

"I'm sorry, I. . ."

Baxter opened his briefcase and removed a folder. He looked through the papers in it, sorted them out, and handed me a half-dozen sheets. Xerox copies, I could tell right away.

"Here" he said. "And for God's sake, don't tell anyone where you got this."

"What is it?"

"Transaction records. How much the LSI was paid for building things in Vietnam."

"But no records of what they actually built, right? That's in DOD."

"Also an IRS file my wife got through a friend she used to work with."

"And that's what clears the Hearst Corporation, their IRS records."

"Right again. You've turned out to be a smart reporter, Dee."

"Not smart enough for Bettelmy. It's the Hearst crowd he wanted to nail."

I folded the papers Baxter had given me, put them in an over-coat pocket, and assured him I would keep them secret. Thanks, I said, even if I wind up writing about the LSI, don't worry, no one will ever know where I got these records, except, of course, for Bettelmy.

"I owe him my life" said Baxter.

"I owe him, too" I said, recalling the night he introduced me to Matt Larue. But that was none of Baxter's business, and he wasn't listening, anyway. He was looking at that picture of the crew lined up beside the B-17.

"I was badly wounded on our last mission" said Baxter. "Maybe he told you about it."

"Not all the details, no. . ."

"We were hit and he ordered the crew to jump. He could have gone out, too."

"But you were too wounded to jump?"

"I was unconscious. Dead, if he hadn't gotten me back to England."

"He never told me that, he only said. . ."

"Two engines out, Dee, and he made it all the way back from Munich."

"Munich, I saw the bombing damage, when I was stationed near there after the war."

"Yes, yes. . ."

"At a place named Mambachel. You probably never heard of it, but. . ."

"My God!" said Baxter. "You don't know who I am, do you? I thought you had, but you haven't even recognized me, have you?"

I looked at him, seeing the way he was staring at me, annoyed, maybe, I couldn't tell. William Baxter, sure, the name had rung a bell when Bettelmy handed me the letter to give him, but all I had known was that he worked at Commerce, and whatever or whoever he was beyond that, well, hell, I had no idea. I certainly hadn't recognized him.

"No" I replied. "I'm sorry, I. . ."

"The Congresswoman I was with, you don't remember?"

"I'll be damned, you were. . ."

"The one who thought you murdered Negro soldiers, you must remember that."

"You were the attorney with her. . ."

"The Polaroid pictures you gave me. That's what made her a Senator, Dee."

I slumped in a chair, the first time I had sat down since I entered his office, looking at Baxter. Words, that's what I was good at. But not faces. And sometimes not too good at remembering, either. But when he mentioned murdered Negro soldiers, that had come back like a flash. I could never have forgotten that.

"I'm sorry" I said. "I owe you an apology. I've made a fool of myself."

"Perhaps I have, too, talking about the war and Bettelmy that way."

"He said I might take you and your wife to dinner while I'm here."

"All right, why not? I could tell you more about what happened after I last saw you."

I shook hands with Baxter and he patted me on the back as I started to leave his office. He stopped me before I could open the door. Listen, he said, Mambachel, that's water under the bridge, forget it, but these papers I've given you, and this business about the LSI, that's something else, so watch out, you may be dealing with real criminals.

Criminals, right. I had been called a criminal myself. By that Congresswoman Baxter had reminded me of. He had also reminded me of something else. How I feel when things start piling up that way. Bettelmy's copilot, turning out to be the lawyer I had come to grips with back in Germany. A mere coincidence? No way. No way I would ever buy that.

I stopped at a bar on K Street, halfway back to our hotel. To think about it. To sort it out and add it up, how I had come across him years ago, Baxter, this attorney who had flown with Bettelmy. Who had given me, a while ago, some stolen papers I might use to nail the LSI.

Trying to unravel a mystery, going over all the relevant details.

Eisenhower was still President when I arrived in Germany. Right.

All hell had broken out the same day I reported to an airborne unit there. Right.

The troops had dropped some dummies rigged with parachutes that did not open.

They had done it to harass some Congressmen about jump pay.

The dummies had been put together with black tape around their heads.

The Congressmen had witnessed what had happened.

Word had gotten around in Washington some Negro soldiers had been murdered.

A Congresswoman who had not been there showed up later to investigate it.

Baxter was the attorney who came with her.

I had given him some Polaroid pictures of the dummies on the ground.

The pictures proved they were only dummies, and up close they did not even look like Negros, anyway.

So that had settled it. No Negro soldiers had been murdered. They had gone away then, Baxter and the Congresswoman, leaving me to get tangled up in other matters. Thirteen years ago in Germany.

Right. Right. All the relevant details. Maybe nothing to it after all, a mere coincidence, my running into Baxter again. Another random incident in all the crap I've been involved in over the years. Tangled up, indeed. With Lamont and Molly, right after Baxter and the Congresswoman went away. Lamont and Molly. Hard to figure out what's relevant there.

I finished another beer and walked on. In the dark. Late, time to take Vicky out to dinner, get back then and write another forty pages. Ten thousand words to send by way of Western Union. Blast away at Thornton. Something else I've gotten tangled up in. Getting revenge on that dumb bastard.

She was getting ready when I got there. Changing into another dress, in a way that made me see there could be better things in store right after dinner. While she dressed, telling me about her day at the Smithsonian. About a woman Senator she had met, the lady who had sponsored the new exhibit there, some kind of Negro cowboy celebration.

Telling me, too, about something else I had trouble making sense of. Something that happened just before I got to the hotel.

"You had a call from the Pentagon" she said. "Some colonel named Lamont."

"Really. What did he say?"

"He wants to take us out to dinner. Tomorrow night. He sounded odd, Phil."

"Lamont's not odd, he's a soldier."

"The way he talked on the phone, it sounded like he thought he knew me."

"Maybe he was flirting with you."

"He asked how long we had been married. How I was getting along, what I had been doing lately. That's not flirting, Phil, that's prying."

"Forget Lamont. Let's go, you must be hungry."

"As hungry as a horse. You know what cowboys like to say, they say you have to feed a horse before you can go for a ride, Phil."

We went to dinner. First things first. That's also what old cowboys like to say.

Friday night at the Myer officers club. Packed and noisy. The Pentagon crowd at the bar, colonels mostly, drinking away their problems with the big brass. I'm up to my ass in alligators, I'd give six months' pay to get back to troops, one of them was saying as we passed the bar on the way to the dining room. A full colonel, no doubt out of the running for a star.

The dining room was not so crowded. Yes, said the maître d' when he looked in his reservation book, a table for four for Colonel Melvin Lamont, please follow me and I'll guide you to your table, colonel. I'm not Lamont, I said, we're here to meet him, if you'll show us where the table is, we'll wait. I could feel it coming. We were off to an evening of confusion.

"Your friend Lamont, tell me about him" said Vicky as we sat and waited.

"We used to be friends. He's a colonel now, you'll meet him any minute."

"A colonel. Like the one at the bar you heard talking."

"No, that fellow's a full colonel. Lamont's only a lieutenant colonel."

"So why do you call him colonel if they're not the same?"

"I don't know, see if you can spot a waiter, Vicky."

"The Navy, too. A Navy captain's not the same as an Army captain, is he?"

"No, a Navy captain's the same as an Army colonel."

"And an Army colonel's not the same as a colonel, you just told me."

"Damn it Vicky, you'll drive me to drink. If I can find a waiter."

She was in a jolly mood, no question about it. Playing Abbott and Costello with me, teasing me, I figured, about my poor performance in the sack last night. I was in no mood for entertainment, not then, not now. I was flat-out tense, in fact. Like the way I felt sometimes before a jump. Waiting to see if my parachute would open when I saw Molly.

I saw her, at least I thought so, as they approached the table. Lamont, in his dress blue uniform, silver leaves and all, two more rows of ribbons, with her in tow. The room was dark and they were late and I'd had several drinks by then, but damn it, I could see it was her, I knew it was her, I could feel myself tightening up as Lamont led Molly to the table.

But it wasn't her. It was someone else, someone who only looked like Molly.

Lamont and I shook hands and greeted each other. I could tell he had been drinking, the same as me, hell, we had gotten drunk together a hundred times before Molly came between us. I could also tell from the look on his face he was as shocked as I was. Two old paratroopers, greeting each other, both of us acting like we'd landed in the wrong damned drop zone.

"Meet my wife Madeline" Lamont said as he introduced us.

"And meet my wife Victoria" I said.

We sat down and a waiter brought us menus. A bit of feeling out between the two women, my wife asking his wife if the seafood there was any good, that sort of thing, while Lamont and I looked at each other, staring at each other, wondering what had happened with this damned reunion. I was sure as hell wondering.

"I need to go to the men's room" said Lamont.

"I do, too" I said.

"My, my" said Vicky.

"Hurry back" said Lamont's wife. "We'll need to order soon."

I followed him to the men's room. Crowded, filled with officers who had gotten loaded, but we paid no attention to them. We both had something else in mind.

"Where's Molly?" Lamont asked as he grabbed my shoulders, almost shouting.

"Where's Molly?" I asked at the same time, grabbing his shoulders the same way.

We had asked the question in unison, sounding like an echo of each other, and neither had an answer. We stood that way for a moment, Lamont with his two hands on my shoulders, me with mine on his. And then we both stepped back and started laughing, laughing so loud a drunk colonel walking by stopped and shook his head and started laughing also.

"You two act like you won the goddamned lottery" said the colonel.

"Maybe we did" said Lamont.

"Right" I said. "Maybe we did."

We were still laughing as we stood side by side at the urinals, getting rid of what we had been drinking. Getting rid of years and years of bad karma, some might call it.. Years and years of thinking the other sonofabitch had married Molly. Neither had, and that was that, and what had come between us years before was done and over. Not quite, of course. I knew, and so did Lamont, we'd get back to that question sooner or later. Where is she? And then the rest of it. What happened to her? What happened at Fort Campbell? Sooner or later, we'd want to talk about something else, too. The women we married instead of Molly. But not right now. Right now they were waiting for us to order dinner.

"Maddy recommends the lobster" said Vicky as I looked at the menu.

"Maddy?" I asked, looking at Lamont's wife. "Is that what they call you?"

"Only my friends" she said. "Mel, you should hear what Vicky does."

"I know what she does" he said. "She keeps a tiger tamed, the same as you do."

"With a rope" said Vicky. "He's not a tiger, he's a Brahma bull. Sometimes."

"She writes about cowboys" said Maddy. "She's been telling me about it."

"Cowboy novels" I said. "She's Matt Larue, Mel, right here in person."

"A fictitious name" said Vicky. "What I write is fiction."

"Fiction" said Lamont. "Hell, we know all about that, don't we, Phil?"

"Matt Larue" said Maddy. "That sounds real. A real cowboy, Vicky."

"That's what Phil thought when we met. Sometime I'll tell you about it, Maddy."

"Like hell you will" I said. "Let's order."

Dinner for four then. No lobster for me, I'd rather eat cold chili if I had to. A T-bone steak for me and one for Mel, leave the lobster to the ladies, the four of us talking and laughing, as noisy as a roundup back in Texas. My reunion with Lamont had turned into a celebration.

Two hours of that and we were still going at it. Let's get some fresh air, he said, there's a porch outside, this time of night you can see all the lights in the city. Our wives barely noticed when we got up. They went on talking. Lamont and I had a lot to talk about also.

"So you went back to being a reporter" he said as we stood outside.

"After I got out, after I left Campbell."

"You should have stayed in the Army, Phil. You would have loved Vietnam."

"I kept waiting to be called up. Johnson had other ideas."

"Johnson, done in by all the crap back here."

"I know. His funeral starts tomorrow. I'm writing about it."

"Your paper should have sent you out there. You could have seen it for yourself."

"Maybe not. Sometimes I think I can't see a damned thing going on around me."

"You could have shown that bastard Cronkite he was full of shit."

"I don't know, maybe I could have. There's been a lot of could haves in my life, Mel."

"A lot of maybes, too. That woman was poison, Phil."

I looked across the river at the monuments. Lighted up, but a different view from here, different from the way they looked when we were flying in. When I told Vicky what I planned to write, keeping to myself what I hoped to see in Molly. A woman who had calmed down since she married Mel, not the woman I had left behind at Campbell. He was right. She was poison.

"I know" I said. "She gave me hell when we got back from Germany."

"Mambachel, right, we were blind as shit back then, both of us."

"I think it was after her mother died, that's when she went to pieces."

"Gone to pieces, hell, I thought she had gone with you to Texas."

"And I thought you took over after I left. I wanted to marry her, Mel."

"Phillip Dee, old buddy, you're one lucky bastard. Forget her, leave it at that."

Lamont went back inside, to bring back a couple of drinks, he said. To leave me alone, I think, knowing I could never leave it at that. And I couldn't. What he'd said about her being poison, that had done it. I stood there, looking at the lights in the distance, thinking about her. About Molly. How she had almost ruined my life twelve years ago.

How I had fallen for her in Germany, a Red Cross worker with the airborne outfit Mel and I were in, how he had fallen for her, too, how we had come damned close to being enemies over her. How we had argued about which one would escort her back to the States.

How her mother had died the day before we left. How I had gone back and forth to her home in Nashville, trying to console her. How she had quit her Red Cross job and told me to kiss off. How I had come unglued, drinking so much they let me resign and leave the Army.

How I had gotten drunk for months on end, thinking she had married Lamont when he came back to Campbell later. No, I couldn't leave it alone. Not until he returned with drinks and started talking about something else, sounding like he was ready to change the subject.

"Your wife" he said. "She told me you're here for more than Johnson's funeral."

"I'm digging into a crooked company, Mel. You ever hear of the LSI?"

"The Lone Star International. Sure. They operated in Vietnam."

"They were paid to build things there. My guess is they stole a lot of money."

"But you're only guessing, right? You can't prove it."

"The proof I need is hidden in DOD. Hell, I'd have to steal the records."

"Maybe I can help you, Phil. You won't have to steal a damned thing."

"Look, I don't want you to get in trouble. This LSI crap could be a bombshell."

"Don't worry about it. I owe you one."

"You don't owe me shit, Mel."

"Hell yes, I do. Remember, I was the one who introduced you to her."

He had, all right, one more thing I had forgotten. Lamont, as sharp as always, talking about some secret records in the Pentagon while thinking about Molly. The same as I was.

"Sunday, in my office, Phil. The building's almost deserted then."

"All right, call me, let me know how you can get me in."

"Finish your drink. I'll drive you back to your hotel."

"Thanks, but I promised Vicky we'd walk around. Look at the cemetery, maybe"

"This late at night? Hell, she must be tired by now, she. . ."

"She's a night owl, Mel. Late at night is when she's at her best."

"You're a lucky sonofabitch, you know that? We both are."

"But there's still that question we can't answer. Maybe some day."

"Molly, whatever happened to her. Another maybe, Phil."

"Another maybe, sure. That's what it all comes down to, Mel. It's always maybe."

Lamont was laughing as we went back inside. The dining room was nearly empty and the waiters were cleaning up the tables. Straightening up things. A lot of things had been straightened up that night. Maybe. Right, as sure as hell, another maybe.

Vicky wanted to see the Iwo Jima monument. One of the Marines in that statue was an Indian from Arizona, she reminded me, telling me how she might work that in to another novel if his distant relatives had fought with cowboys. We looked at it from a distance. It was dark, and I'd heard rumors about what went on around it late at night, so we moved on.

"Rumors?" she asked. "What kind of rumors?"

"Sailors, sailors and the kind of guys they hang around with."

"The guys they hang around with? You must be joking."

"You don't know the Navy, Vicky."

"That's dopey. Come on, let's go and find the Tomb of the Unknowns."

That part of the cemetery was far away, almost two miles in the cab we found on a nearby street. You're fortunate, said the driver, the tomb is usually closed at night, you'd have to watch the soldiers from a long way off, but it's open at night this week for all the folks in town, you'll see a lot of them there, even at one in the morning.

A lot of them, true, a hundred or more, standing near it when we got there, solemn, all of them, gazing at the marble tomb and the soldier from the Old Guard marching back and forth in front of it. At a ritual that never ended. I had watched it before, standing in the rain, before I went overseas. Sacred, if you've ever been a soldier.

"Count the steps he takes" I whispered as we watched.

"I know, I read about it, twenty-one steps before he stops and turns around."

"You read about it, so tell me why it's always twenty-one."

"The same as a twenty-one gun salute, Phil."

We stood there for a while, Vicky telling me, like a tour guide, how the tomb held the body of an unknown soldier from World War I, how two more from the Second World War and Korea lay under the slabs in front of it, how there may never be another unknown soldier because of DNA, and so forth. Vicky, always on top of things. So to speak.

"Tell me about their medals" I said as we rode in a taxi back to the hotel.

"The Medal of Honor for each unknown soldier, Phil."

"And a medal called the Victoria Cross for the first one."

"So you expect me to earn a medal like that when we get back, is that it?"

"Sure, I've already sent my ten thousand words for the day."

"Not tonight, pal, I need to rest up for tomorrow."

The desk clerk handed me a stack of messages when I picked up our room key at the hotel. One from Baxter, inviting us to join them for lunch next Monday. And six from Bettelmy, one each hour, calling again and again, telling me to call him back right away. So I was not surprised to hear the phone ringing when I unlocked the door to our room.

"That has to be a crank call" said Vicky. "It's two a.m., Phil."

"But only midnight in Texas. It's a crank, all right, and I think I know why he's calling."

I took off my coat and tie and sat down. And the phone kept ringing. I smiled. Sure, the desk clerk would have told the switchboard lady we were back, she would have told Bettelmy we were in, and he wouldn't hang up until I answered. And Vicky wouldn't stop saying answer the damn phone, so I finally did. I took a deep breath first. I knew what was coming.

"I finally got you, I have something to tell you, damn it" said Bettelmy when I answered.

"And I have something to tell you, Bill. That woman who runs the society page. Tell her to get her goddamn pictures in focus."

"You must be drunk. Where the hell have you been?"

"I've been out. Doing what I came here for."

"I didn't send you there to bankrupt us. You know what Western Union charges?"

"I'll try and guess. A nickel a word?"

"Two transmissions, that's five hundred dollars a day, goddamn it."

"Charge it to the TV station, then. They're the ones who started it."

"The TV station, my butt. They're raising hell about this, too."

"Why? Don't tell me poor old Thornton can't keep up."

"They're afraid he'll have a nervous breakdown. I may, too, so stop it."

"No way. And you can tell that TV station boss I'm just getting warmed up."

"Phil, you don't have a contract like Thornton has. I could fire you."

I held the telephone at arm's length, knowing Bettelmy would not hang up. Thinking, measuring what he had just said. I had come here to see Molly, and I hadn't seen her, and that was that. So let him fire me, I could go back to Texas and write fiction like Vicky. Maybe. But then there was that other matter I had gotten tangled up in.

"Listen" I said. "Don't worry about the Western Union bill. Take it out of my bonus."

"Bonus? What bonus? What are you talking about?"

"The bonus you're going to give me for nailing the LSI, Bill."

"You've got it? The proof we need? Why didn't you tell me that before?"

"I'm telling you now. And I'm going to bed, so leave me alone. Good night."

I put the phone down and started to undress. To hell with Bettelmy. To hell with Thornton. And to hell with the Lone Star International, too.

"What was that about?" asked Vicky.

"About a man biting a dog, I think that's how they put it."

"A what?"

"Headlines, Vicky. The kind of headlines that sell papers."

"What if the dog bites back? This LSI business could be dangerous, Phil."

"Go to sleep. I've got a funeral to cover in a few hours."

She was right, of course. Baxter had already warned me about them. But I wasn't worried about it. Why should I? I was just a reporter doing my job, helping Bettelmy sell papers. I had no idea how right she was.

The flags next to the gravestones in Arlington National Cemetery, the soldier marching back and forth in front of the Tomb of the Unknowns, the horse named Black Jack, following Lyndon Johnson's coffin, its saddle empty, its stirrups hanging backwards, reminders, all, of death and sacrifice, symbols of the way a nation mourns its warriors and their leaders.

At least that's how I planned to write about it, standing there, watching the funeral column moving slowly toward the Capitol. Standing on Pennsylvania Avenue, mingling with the people who were watching. The weather was cold and they were only three or four deep along the sidewalk, not as large a crowd as I expected, but easy to walk among and listen.

What I heard made me wonder.

I heard one man muttering there goes that worthless bastard, don't ask me to feel sorry he's dead, he drafted my son and my son came back crippled.

I saw the man next to him nod and heard him say you have a

point, the kid next door came back hooked on drugs, he was drafted, too, and LBJ just left him hanging.

I listened to a couple of Negro women, one of them saying LBJ was good to us, we can vote now, but my husband didn't trust him, he would never vote for a Southerner from Texas.

I heard the other woman say she didn't trust him, either, not after the way he turned on us when he was President, ninety percent of the boys he sent off and killed were colored.

A mixed crowd at best, some of them grumbling, some of them weeping, thousands and thousands altogether, since the funeral route was several miles to the Capitol. Hard to judge what they were feeling, most of them at least respectful, it appeared, most of them silent as they watched the coffin and the rest of the procession moving slowly along the avenue.

I had no trouble judging what the little old lady I wound up talking to was feeling. She was waving a flag as the coffin went past, and out of the blue she turned to me and started talking, smiling while she told me what she was doing there.

"I've seen nine in a row now" she said.

"Nine" I replied. "Nine what, ma'am?"

"I grew up in Bethesda" she said. "I still live there."

"Yes ma'am, Bethesda. I've been there."

"I started watching when I was a little girl. I can recite their names."

"Names? What names?"

"Wilson, Taft, Coolidge, Roosevelt, Kennedy, Hoover, Eisenhower, Truman, and now Johnson. I'll bet you couldn't do that, mister."

I sure as hell couldn't. Johnson was the thirty-sixth President, I knew, but I had never bothered to memorize the names of all the rest and the order in which they served, and here was this woman reciting it, not when they were elected, but when they died, the order in which nine former Presidents had been honored with the kind of funeral we were watching.

"I have all their pictures" she said. "They're on a wall at my home in Bethesda."

"All nine, that's very touching, ma'am."

"I collect beer cans, also. That's one of my other hobbies."

"Really. Beer cans."

"Butterflies, too. You have to have a lot of hobbies if you want to stay healthy."

"Yes ma'am, I'll take that as advice."

Collecting beer cans and insects and watching Presidential funerals, putting their pictures on the wall, this little old lady and her hobbies, for a moment I stood there and thought about it. She'd be worth ten thousand words all by herself.

But Thornton would leap on it, he'd claim she was the well known Mad Maiden of Maryland. Or something like that. She was odd, but in her own way she was charming, too, and as much as I needed something to write about, she didn't deserve that. So I moved on.

On toward the Capitol, following the procession. Watching as they neared the East Wing, where the scaffolds were still standing. Watching as the most intricate part of the ceremony started to unfold, the honor guard carrying the coffin up the steps, the carriage moving away, the troops moving off in two columns to the streets nearby, the TV cameras rolling.

They would have to carry him through the Senate wing because of the scaffolds. I pinned my press badge on my coat, so I could get through the barrier separating the crowd from the procession, so I could watch a bit closer. What I saw surprised me. It shouldn't have, I knew, but it did indeed surprise me.

Amid all the television cameras and the TV crews, there he was. Thornton, getting ready to interview two men as soon as the procession had moved into the Capitol rotunda. With his cameraman recording it, Thornton and the two men, both quite tall, both of them wearing cowboy hats. I could not see their faces, but I had an idea what he was up to.

I figured he wanted a few comments about LBJ. Something he could twist around and turn into another scandal. What I never dreamed of was what they would say, the two men he was talking to, and the way it would turn out on the TV tapes they were keeping back in Texas.

No doubt I would have laughed about it, had I known at the time. Thornton, with me trying to drive him to his knees, was doing me one hell of a favor.

I met him at an entrance to the Pentagon, Lamont, in civilian clothes, with a pass to get me into the building. I had been there before, when I was still on active duty, and I remembered what it looked like then. Crowded offices and thousands of people running around in the corridors carrying papers. Not this time. It was Sunday, and the corridors were empty.

His office was small, barely room enough for a desk, a file cabinet, two leather chairs and a TV set. But big, by Pentagon standards, for a mere O5 lieutenant colonel. When I was there before I had noticed six officers sitting at desks pushed together in a room not much larger. Compared to them Lamont was in clover, working for the Secretary of the Army.

The TV set was still on, but the sound was muted. He sat down in one of the chairs and motioned to me to sit in the other. When he looked at his watch and turned up the TV volume it was clear he had something on his mind, something besides the secret papers I had come for. I looked at the screen and realized what it was. Henry Kissinger.

"Right on schedule" said Lamont. "He's announcing it from France."

"What? How he's settled things in Vietnam?"

"The Paris Peace Accords. How they've sold us out, Phil."

We listened. Kissinger, speaking with that heavy German accent, sounding like another Doctor Strangelove. I'd heard what someone asked him once, how he could wheel and deal and still have time for all the Washington night life. He had smiled when he answered. Power is an aphrodisiac, he said.

Could be. If Lamont was right, he'd sure as hell screwed someone.

"That bastard's lied again" he said when he turned the volume off.

"So you don't think it's really over."

"It's over, all right, but not the way he makes it sound."

"The way he got the North and South to come to terms, you mean."

"We've promised we'll come back if it starts again. A goddamned lie, Phil."

"You don't think we will, you think. . ."

"Hell no, we won't. My boss is so pissed off he may resign."

"Mel, listen, you shouldn't quit, not now."

"I'll stay in. This war has ruined the Army, maybe I can help to save what's left."

"Maybe."

"Right, maybe. You want to watch the funeral? Here, I'll turn the sound up."

The funeral. The network we'd been watching had switched back to the Capitol, now that Kissinger was done in Paris. To the rotunda, the cameras zooming in, showing the people walking slowly past the coffin. I had seen it already, and written about it, too, and in any case it wasn't the funeral I was thinking about. It was what Lamont had said about the Army.

I smiled as he turned off the television set and reached for the thermos bottle on his desk. A thermos bottle. Odd, how something like that can bring back memories. The Army, what it was like before it marched off to Vietnam. What I was like before that happened, when I arrived at my parachute unit in Germany. "You recall the day we met, Mel? You offered me coffee from a thermos then."

"On the road to Mambachel, I stopped you on your way to the group. . ."

"You made me watch that goddamned dummy drop."

"The dummies the Congressmen thought were Negro soldiers. . ."

"I didn't think that, I thought they were dead paratroopers."

"Until I took you to their bodies, when you saw they were only dummies."

"I was green, you said. You really had me going, Mel. Remember?"

"What I remember about that day is how you knocked me on my ass, pal."

Two old friends, drinking coffee and laughing about it. The good old days, when all we thought about was getting drunk and staying fit to duke it out with the Russians. Friends until a woman came between us.

Lamont set his cup down and went to the cabinet behind his desk. He entered the numbers on a combination lock, bent down, and took a folder from the bottom drawer. When he stood up he turned around and faced me. Ready to give me a secret file, what he said he owed me for introducing me to Molly.

"That's not the same as the records they have in DOD" he said as he handed it to me.

"So you didn't steal it from them, you. . ."

"I've seen what they have, Phil. This is even better, if you're after the LSI."

"You bet I am. I have the records on what they were paid, but. . ."

"But you need a record of what they actually built in Nam. There it is."

I looked at the file. Thirty or forty pages, a Xerox copy, I could tell, since some of the entries had been marked with ink notations that showed up faint and barely legible. I glanced at it, turning the pages. Year by year, site by site, dollar by dollar, what the Lone Star International had built in Vietnam.

"If you match this with what they were paid, Phil, I expect you'll find a big difference."

"I can see that much already. Where did you get this?"

"Long Binh. I asked the comptroller there to make me that copy."

"What for? This is what I need, but I don't understand why you. . ."

"I was the S-4 with the One Oh One. I wanted to cover my ass. As simple as that." I glanced through the file, looking for references to the One Hundred First Airborne Brigade. Places where their base camps had been located. What was built, how much it cost, where the money had gone. The Army had kept tight records. Mc-Namara had seen to that. Hell, the bean counters ran the war. And Lamont had been in the middle of their crossfire.

"This isn't even classified" I said.

"Not when I got it at Long Binh. The Army has the original. It's Top Secret now."

"So why did you keep it? This copy you had made."

"You never know, pal, you never know."

I unbuttoned my shirt and put the file next to my chest. Don't worry, he said, you'll get out of the building without any trouble, but don't let anyone ever know where you got it, and hang on to it when you're finished, in case it's ever needed to keep me out of jail. He was laughing when he said that. I don't remember, but I suppose I was laughing, too.

"Let me know how it turns out" said Lamont.

"I will, and thanks, Mel. I have your office number, I'll write you."

"Not here. I'm leaving for the War College in a week or so."

"Your being in the secretary's office has paid off, then."

"Damned right. At this level, that's what it's all about. Connections." We shook hands and I left. So Mel had been selected for the War College, the next big step to making general. And I had the records I needed, a step towards a Pulitzer Prize, Bettelmy had said, and I believed him.

I should have listened to what Lamont said, about the way he might need that file to keep him out of jail. I should not have been smiling, not when I was the one who had it now, walking out of the Pentagon as if I had nothing to fear at all.

Vicky hit it off with Baxter's wife Louella, the same way she had with Lamont's wife. The four of us at lunch in a café near the Commerce building, with me trying to say something to Baxter across the table, the two wives sitting opposite each other, their words colliding with mine. In the middle of the meal Baxter's wife decided that was enough and took over.

She nodded to her husband, stood up, took Baxter's plate, put it where she had been sitting, and traded seats with him so she could sit next to Vicky.

"Bill, you don't mind, do you?" she asked her husband.

"No, Lulu, not a bit" said Baxter.

An old bomber pilot being pushed aside by his wife, hell, I'd seen that sort of thing before. If she had asked me I would have said I don't mind, either. I wanted to talk to Baxter, and what I wanted to say was best done with a whisper, not having to shout across a table in a crowded café in the middle of downtown Washington.

"Good, now we can talk" I said. "I have the rest of what I needed."

"I have no idea what you are referring to" said Baxter.

"What I needed to go with what I had already."

"No idea at all, since I have never seen you before."

"Hell, Bill, don't kid around, you invited us to lunch, you.."

"It must have been my wife who invited you."

"Lulu, you just called her. . ."

"I believe she has read some novels written by your wife. She wanted to meet her."

"All right, so it was Lulu, then, who. . ."

"I have never met you before, do you understand that?"

I looked at Baxter, poking away at the salad he was having for lunch. Feeling dumb as I realized what he was trying to tell me. Wondering if he thought we were being shadowed. For all I knew that might be so, since half the people sitting around us looked like they worked for the government.

All right, we had never met. I had never seen him before. And if anyone ever asked, no sir, he wasn't the one who gave me the records of what the LSI was paid to build things in Vietnam. His wife Lulu? She reads cowboy novels, I heard, but I wouldn't know, I had never met her, either. Never.

No, but I could hear her chatting with my wife, once Baxter and I stopped talking. Vicky and Louella, Lulu, as Baxter called her, sharing stories, not easy to hear exactly, with all the noise in the café, but loud enough for me to tell what they were talking about. Some lady Senator, some woman Baxter's wife worked for.

"My goodness" said Lulu. "You met her at the Smithsonian?"

"Oh yes" said Vicky. "At the exhibit she is sponsoring there."

"And I work for her. It's a small world, Vicky."

"Lulu, would you believe it? The Senator said I should stay in touch. Imagine that."

"Of course. She will want to hear about this new novel you're writing."

The laughter at a nearby table drowned out their voices. I glanced around and saw where the noise was coming from, four teenagers, tourists, I supposed, laughing about something they had seen and thought was funny. For a moment I considered asking what it was. No need to. I had already filed my last ten thousand words for Thornton.

Baxter pushed his plate away and stood up, speaking to his wife in a voice that sounded casual. We must go, he said, I must return to my desk at the travel agency, I will thank our waitress for seating us at this table with this charming couple from Michigan. Not bad. In fact, a damned good cover story for anyone who might be listening.

Evidently Vicky understood. We waited a while, paid the waitress a separate check, and left through a different door. We were a block away before she started talking.

"Lulu's worried about her husband" she said.

"No wonder. The way he was acting, like he thought the KGB is after him."

"She said he gave you some papers, Phil."

"He did. Bettelmy asked him to."

"Over the weekend he had second thoughts about it, she said."

"So why did they meet us for lunch, then?"

"I don't know. These papers she said he gave you, that sounds like LSI stuff, Phil."

"Keep your voice down, babe. Someone might be listening."

I was kidding, of course. Vicky may have thought I was serious, I don't know, but we walked another block toward our hotel before she spoke again. And when she did it was not about Baxter and the papers he had given me.

"You would never guess how she got her job, Phil."

"Who? Lulu? I heard her say she's working for some Senator."

"It started when her husband gave some pictures to a Congresswoman he worked for."

"Pictures? Tell me more."

"Lulu was working for someone else, and that woman asked her to pass them around."

"The pictures I gave Baxter in Germany. . ."

"She didn't tell me that, she said the pictures turned that woman into a celebrity of sorts."

"Baxter. . .I think he tried to tell me that. . .but I wasn't listening, I. . ."

"She's Senator Beverly now, and Lulu's still working for her."

"Beverly, I'll be damned. . .Beverly Amador. . ."

"You know about her? Senator Beverly? That's what she said I should call her, she. . ."

"The way she reamed my ass in Germany, damn right I know about her."

Vicky must have realized I had heard enough. She was silent as we walked on to our hotel. Beverly Amador, I had forgotten her name, but I knew about her, all right. Accusing me of killing Negro soldiers. Until she saw the Polaroids I gave Baxter to quiet her down. And the pictures turned her into a celebrity? How in hell could that have happened?

So she made it to the Senate, did she? She was big on civil rights back then, perhaps the pictures helped, I didn't know and I didn't care, but I knew damned well I'd be in trouble if I ran into that woman again. Mean, pissed off because she couldn't hang me. And now she'd told my wife to call her Beverly. I would keep my distance, and hope to hell she kept hers.

"What time's the flight tomorrow?" asked Vicky when we got to our room.

"Early. We'll be home by mid-afternoon."

"I'm glad I came along. What I saw will help me with my writing."

"Johnson's body is on the way already, back to Texas."

"You weren't listening, Phil. You don't want to hear about my next novel?"

"I was listening, but look, I. . ."

"You're bothered about something. What? The Western Union bill you've run up?"

"To tell you the truth, I'm not sure, Vicky. . ."

"My, my. Then let's see if I can help you run up something else."

She tried. And succeeded. But later, when we went out to dinner, I still couldn't pin it down, what I was bothered about. Maybe the people jeering at the funeral. Or Bettelmy raising hell on the phone. Or Lamont showing up without Molly. Baxter acting paranoid, that Congresswoman turning up again, the records I'd collected on the LSI. Hard to tell exactly.

I settled for the records. Nothing but dates and figures. We had been in Washington a week, and that's all I really had, only a stack of secret papers. I had pored through it page by page, shaking my head and cursing out loud at some of it. But I could not see, not yet, how to shape it into a story. No wonder I was bothered.

We were halfway back before it finally dawned on me. How to add it up and tie it all together. Looking out the window, seeing the towns from up above, thinking about the way the country had been torn apart by Vietnam, wondering what the people down below would turn to next. That's when it struck me. What they'd turn to next would be a scapegoat.

Not Bettelmy. That's not what he wanted. What he wanted was something else. It would not be easy to sell him on what I had in mind.

"You've let me down" he said as he looked through the files I showed him when I got to his office. "From what I can see this won't implicate the Hearst crowd at all, and if we can't do that we can't blow the Light away. It's only numbers about the Lone Star International. This won't raise our circulation diddly squat, Phil."

"I think you're wrong, Bill. I think you've missed what's going on around you."

"What I've missed? Tell the man upstairs, he's the one I have to answer to."

I was silent for a moment. Bettelmy, turning to God? No way. When I realized who he was talking about, it occurred to me. A way, perhaps, to get him on board with the plan I had for dealing with the Lone Star International. "Upstairs, right, the publisher. I believer he flew bombers, just like you."

"So we're friends. But that won't cut it, not when we're behind by forty thousand,"

"Suppose the runways you flew off were badly built. So bad you lost a lot of planes."

"I'm talking about circulation, and you want to talk about runways?"

"Suppose you lost fifteen or twenty bombers every day because of the runways."

"You're out of your mind. What happened to you in Washington, Phil?"

"Dead crews every day, because the runways weren't constructed right."

"Okay, I'll go along. For one more minute. That's all."

"The folks back home, losing their kids, you think they'd want to blame someone?"

"That never happened. The fields we flew from were built by Army engineers."

"But not in Nam. A lot of that was built by contract. The LSI, Bill." Bettelmy looked at the papers again, thumbing through the ones Lamont had given me. The records showing dates and sites of what the LSI had built. And what it cost. He glanced at the records I had gotten from Baxter, showing what they had been paid. Bettelmy was not dumb. He knew the records would not match. I would not be standing there if they did.

"All right" he said. "I can read."

"Stolen money, enough to put some folks in jail."

"If that's all it is, you could have skipped that business about runways."

"Enough to put some folks in jail, but not enough to sell papers, right?"

Bettelmy stared at me. Nodding. Stolen money might make headlines for a day or two, but not the kind of headline that sold papers. He was silent, so I went on, knowing if I kept stabbing away at it sooner or later he would see it, what I was after.

"When you were flying, near the end of the war, you knew you were winning, right?"

"Of course we knew. That's why we kept on bombing, so we could end it."

"Winning, but what if things went wrong? Who would folks have blamed for that?"

"I don't know, someone, I suppose. What are you getting at?"

"Someone, right, anyone they could point their fingers at.

Even if they knew the war was being won. And they would want to read about who to blame."

"I'm listening. Go on."

"And it's worse, a lot worse, when a war is lost. Vietnam, Bill, think about that, think about the LSI, damn it, think about what's in those files." He looked at me. Not nodding this time. Smiling. The wheels had started turning, going full speed, Bettelmy finally seeing what I had in mind. Stir up the readers by blaming someone. Vietnam was over, but we had lost, they would rush to find out who the culprits were. They would buy a million papers if we would tell them.

"How do you want to do this, Phil?"

"Eight or ten big stories in a series, one each Sunday."

"Good, on Sunday, that's when the Light is way ahead of us."

"With a lead-in preview every Thursday, to build up interest."

"When can you get started?"

"I'll need at least a week. I'll need to do a lot of research."

"Research? You're not into research, you're a straight reporter."

"Year by year, battle by battle. A ton of research, Bill."

"So you can stretch it out, sure, so that you can make a series of it."

"So they can suffocate, the sorry bastards, before I bury their coffins."

Bettelmy handed me the files I had brought and patted me on the back as he led me to his door. With a bit of advice before he turned me loose.

"Listen, Phil, you're a good reporter, don't let emotions get in your way on this."

"I'll try not to."

"And that runway business. You should try to curb your imagination, too."

I left his office and went straight home. Tired of having to talk about a way to sell papers. Tired, after the flight from Washington and what I'd seen there. The soldier marching at Arlington, Johnson's body lying in state in the rotunda, rituals from a past betrayed.

I was tired already of what I was going to write about the LSI.

Bettelmy was right. I was not into research. Three hours and I was spent, going through the record of a single battle, trying to match the outcome with what the LSI had failed to build. The battle of the Ia Drang Valley. Not enough helicopters when it started. The launching base was incomplete. But the records showed the LSI was not involved. Three hours wasted.

Not entirely wasted. Going through the daily reports from Vietnam I had stumbled onto something else. In the corner of the microfiche screen, a story with a picture, about an argument in the Senate. A member had gotten into a debate with a newly elected lady, a debate so heated he had cursed her. But Senator Beverly Amador had stood her ground, according to the story.

I made a copy and put it in my briefcase, thinking Vicky might enjoy reading about it, the way her friend had stirred up things in the first week of her term in office. Realizing, since the microfiche was eight years old, she had been elected for a second term. That Senator who cursed her should have known better. Hell, Miss Beverly thrived on controversy.

So, what to start with next? Skirmishes, week after week, I knew without returning to the archives room. The Army, using helicopters in a new kind of warfare, and the LSI making money hand over fist. Building ports and base camps and everything else. Padding the books to hide the fraud. I could tell already it would take a lot of research to show how they did it.

I had spread out a map and was typing notes when I heard the voice of Tommy Fry, coming by from the sports department, bringing coffee with him, sitting down next to my desk and smiling like a long lost brother.

"Welcome back" he said. "Tell me about your trip to Washington."

"It was sad, Tommy, watching Johnson's funeral."

"While you were there, did you hear anything about the Senators?"

"Hear anything? Hell, Vicky met one, a lady named Beverly."

"Damn, I knew they were bad, but. . ."

"Beverly Amador, that's her name."

"What was she, a pitcher? I never heard of her."

"You're talking about a baseball team, right? The one that moved to Texas last year."

"Sure, there's a rumor Congress wants them to move back to Washington."

"Tommy, I'm talking about a real Senator, not a goddamn woman pitcher."

Fry leaned back and started laughing. So loud some others in the city room broke out in laughter too. No doubt figuring he had come up with another line as good as the fat lady singing when the game was over. They knew how funny he could be. And I knew that's why he followed Thornton every night on TV, so his wit could bounce off Thornton's poison.

"Damn, Phil, in our spare time we should work up a comedy routine."

"I don't have any spare time. Bettelmy has me all booked up."

"It was his idea, having you send all that copy back from Washington?"

"No, everything I write has to go by Thornton. He was the one who asked for it."

"Then he asked for way too much. I heard he's still back East, resting in a sanitarium."

"With his cameraman, I hope. I imagine he sent the station his usual insights."

Fry leaned forward in his chair, with his hands gripping the edge of my desk, acting like he wanted to push it away. The laughter was gone. In its place, an angry tone instead.

"Upstairs, they had to edit the hell out of it. You haven't seen it, have you?"

"Bettelmy kept the tapes for me. I'm in no hurry to watch that shit."

"He said Vicky was there to cozy up to niggers. That's the kind of crap they had to edit."

"Damn it, Tommy, even if he has to see everything first, I warned him."

"I know, but I have to admit, some of what they cut was funny."

"Funny, hell. When he gets back I'm going to throw that bastard off the roof."

"SSS, he called something you wrote. Then he winked, like it was a secret."

"That's not funny, Tom. SSS? What is that, some sort of code?"

"Sob sister shit, Phil. They had a hell of a time trying to edit that."

"That's funny? You know what FH means? That means fuck him."

"No, it's the way he said it. What he said you should do, that was really funny."

"What I should do is get a gun and shoot that sorry bastard."

"Don't laugh, he said you should write freelance for the Ladies' Home Journal."

"That's not funny, either. Piss on Thornton."

"It's the way he said it, Phil. He's a prick, I know, but look at the tapes sometime."

Fry said something more, along the lines of Thornton is too much, say hello to Vicky, welcome back, let's get together and have a drink, that sort of thing. I wasn't paying much attention. When he went back to the sports department I turned my typewriter on and started again with the notes I had been writing. And then it hit me, all at once, something he had said.

"I'll be damned" I muttered. "That's it, freelance with the Ladies' Home Journal."

I put a fresh sheet of paper in my typewriter and went at it. Step by step, all the details I wanted to include. Pausing now and then to be sure I had it right. In thirty minutes I had what I wanted. I crossed out some parts, changed the words in some other parts, read what I had put together, and typed a final copy. Final, by God, a final jab at Thornton.

Bettelmy was busy when I got upstairs. I could see through the glass door into his office he was talking with someone. So I waited. When they shook hands and the someone turned around I could see who he was. The publisher of the paper. A captain before the war and a general when it ended. A man cut out to be a boss. The type you stayed away from.

He had kind words for me, however. When he came out the door he stopped and greeted me. Excellent, he said, Bill has told me what you plan to do, do it well and you can count on me to ensure you are rewarded. Fine, I thought, we'll see about that, Bettelmy may have other ideas, he may go ape-shit when he reads what I have written.

"Phil, you're rolling now" he said when I entered his office.

"I know."

"He's pleased. I'm sure he told you when he saw you in the hallway."

"He did. Too bad, too, since I quit."

"Quit? What are you talking about? You can't quit now. . ."

"Really? Here, read this."

I handed him what I had written. A single sheet of paper. He shook his head as he read it. He sat down at his desk and read it again. I waited, standing in front of his desk, watching as he shook his head again and read it again and looked at me again, with a look on his face that said you must be joking.

"You can't do this" he said. "It's not legal."

"It's legal. Ask someone who knows. Ask Miss Sarah."

Bettelmy pressed a button on his intercom. A moment later she came through her door into his office. She greeted me, said welcome back, Mister Dee, and read quickly through the sheet of paper he handed her.

"Sarah, can that be done?" he asked her. "Can he make a deal like that?"

"I see no reason why he can't, Mister Bettelmy. It's perfectly legal."

"Legal for him to quit and force me to pay him as a freelance writer?"

"Yes, Mister Bettelmy, at a weekly rate equal to his previous salary."

"Legal for him to keep the copyright on everything of his we publish, even if. . ."

"Yes, Mister Bettelmy, with the right to sue if anyone quotes what he has written."

"You see what he's up to, Sarah? You know what it means if I accept this?"

"It means Mister Thornton cannot refer to anything Mister Dee has written."

"All right, all right, Sarah, go ahead, put together a contract for him."

She nodded, straightened her collar and smiled at me as she started to return to her office. She knew what I had done, and I knew she'd make sure it was spelled out clearly in legal terms. I could sue the paper if that bastard Thornton even mentioned my name again on television. She understood. She was as fed up with him as I was.

"Miss Sarah, wait" I said. "There's something else I'd like you to put in my contract."

"Yes, Mister Dee. Mister Bettelmy will have to sign it."

"The syndication rights. Double payment when the paper sells what I have written."

Bettelmy was not happy when Miss Sarah walked away. And with her door closed he could show it. He could curse without her hearing him. An old bomber pilot, feeling the flak as it rattled off his wings, cursing at the enemies trying to shoot him down. Except he wasn't clear who they were now. Me, the publisher, Thornton, or the lawyers who would head his way.

"I don't like this one damned bit" he said. "I'd like to fire your rotten ass, Phil."

"But you won't. You heard what the publisher said."

"I don't like it when my balls are being squeezed this way."

"Call it being caught between some rocks and a hard place, Bill. Miss Sarah wouldn't like to hear you using vulgar language."

I admit I sounded cocky when I said that. I had silenced Thornton, at least for now, and hell yes, I felt rather pleased about it. But I also knew the risk I was taking. I would be on my own, with no guarantee of anything once I finished with the LSI. And if I didn't deliver on that, Bettelmy wouldn't need to fire me, he could simply say we won't hire you back.

I knew that. What I didn't know, because I couldn't see so far ahead, was that he might not have to bother.

Bettelmy backed me up. He had to. So the Thursday lead-in to start things off made it to the front page of the paper. A one-column headline and three paragraphs there, with the rest carried over to an inside page. A modest beginning for a series I might have dreamed would bring me fame and fortune. Hell no, what I had in mind was a steady job when I finished.

A modest beginning was the way to do it. No mention of the LSI, no effort to stir up passion, even in the first big Sunday segment that followed, no hint of what I would expose in the weeks to come. Only a bit of speculation. The Army had lost in Vietnam, and why it had would surely merit investigation. Surely, but slowly, too, to build up interest,

Too slowly. After two more Sundays I still hadn't pointed fingers at the LSI. I had a damned good reason not to. Hours and hours of digging through the archives had left me empty handed. Fraud alone wouldn't do it, I knew that and so did Bettelmy. What I needed was something bloody. Proof that lives had been lost because of the LSI. And I couldn't find it.

So I was not surprised when I came out of the archives room and saw the note from Bettelmy. Stuck on a spindle on my desk, on top of two others, one from Vicky and one from an auto mechanic down the street. All right, go upstairs and face the music.

He had been patient. In his own way. All he had said was you're whining, stop whining and keep digging. Maybe his patience had run out. Maybe he was ready to give me hell now. But he wouldn't be able to curse, I could see when I reached his office. Not with Miss Sarah standing in front of his desk.

"You want to see me?" I asked. Cautious, because I noticed he was grinning.

"Not me" he said. "It's Sarah who wants to see you. Tell him, Sarah."

"Mister Dee, there is an aspect of your contract I overlooked" said Sarah.

"An aspect? So I can be let go right now, is that it?"

"No, Mister Dee, but you must leave the news room."

What the hell for, I started to ask. I held my tongue. Miss Sarah would be offended. So I waited for her to go on. With my eyes on Bettelmy.

"It is a legal matter, Mister Dee. The news room is reserved for active reporters."

"So that leaves you out" said Bettelmy, damned near laughing.

I listened while she explained. Tedious, but thorough. How management has allocated space to the newspaper, the TV station, and so forth. How they have made it a matter of law, perhaps, she said, to prevent any further squabbling. In any case, Mister Dee, since you are no longer an employee, legally there is no place here for you.

"Sarah, don't forget that one exception you told me about" said Bettelmy.

"Oh yes, Mister Dee, you may rent a desk somewhere in the building."

"Rent a desk? Miss Sarah, you must be joking. All right, what will it cost?"

"Twenty dollars a week, Mister Dee. I'm sure the IRS will permit you to deduct it."

"Thanks, Sarah" said Bettelmy. "I'll take it from here."

He watched her leave, and then leaned forward at his desk, looking at me. Whispering, even with her door closed. And still grinning.

"You know what SSS means, Phil?"

"Some code Thornton used, I heard. What about it?"

"Sob sister shit, that's what it means."

"On the tapes he made. I haven't watched them."

"You want me to find you a desk in the TV studio? So you can sit near him?"

"All right, Bill. You have something up your sleeve. What is it?"

"The only other desk you can move to is in the society section."

"You must be shitting me. At twenty dollars a week, you want me to move in there?"

"With all the other sob sisters, right. Now get back to work and stop whining."

Well, hell, what difference will it make, I muttered to myself as I walked downstairs to the news room. Let Bettelmy harass me, even if it costs me twenty dollars a week. Clean off my desk. Starting with the notes stuck in that spindle. Starting with the auto mechanic where I left my car this morning.

"Damn good thing you dropped it off" he said when I called him.

"I know, the brakes felt like they were going out, so. . ."

"They're gone. Damn good thing you weren't driving fast and had to stop."

"All right, fix them. How soon can I pick it up?"

"You could have been killed. How soon? I don't know, two weeks, it all depends."

"Two weeks to fix a set of brakes? What do you mean, it all depends?"

"Don't yell. It's not me. It's the Ass Shuns. They make the parts, not me."

"Ass Shuns?"

"Up in Michigan. If you ask me, we should send them back where they came from."

"Ass Shuns? You mean Asians?"

"The boat people. Paul Thornton, that's what he calls them, Ass Shuns."

"Paul Thornton."

"Yes sir, he has it all in focus. I'll call you when the parts come in."

All right, I said, I'll get a rental car if I have to. No point in arguing with him, not if he's the kind who swallows that crap from Thornton. Spare parts from Ass Shuns. What bullshit.

Asians. Spare parts. And I could have been killed. And Thornton has it all in focus. In focus, hell, he's blind, he's. . .

I'll be a sonofabitch, I muttered out loud. That's it. I've been as blind as that dumb bastard. I've been looking for the wrong damned thing. Spare parts and Asians and someone could have been killed? Why the hell hadn't I thought of that?

Forget this desk. Let them move it wherever they want to. It's the archive room that counts. I knew what to look for, and I knew how to pin it on the LSI.

I knew now where the bodies were buried.

The next Sunday segment went off like a hand grenade hitting an ammunition bunker. The first three weeks had been a drag, but this one drew attention. By sundown anyone who had read it was in the mood I thought they'd be in. Some were so irate they called the paper wanting to know where the LSI was located. They were ready to burn down their offices.

A simple matter, once I knew what to look for. Not at the battles and skirmishes, except indirectly. At the roads and bridges the LSI constructed, at what folks had come to call an infrastructure, all the way back to the ports in Vietnam. Built with Asian labor, so the LSI could make what amounted to a criminal profit. Built in such a way a lot of soldiers died.

Bahn Bahn, a minor firefight amid the battles in a monsoon, that's what I leaped on right away. An artillery battery, socked in by bad weather, firing away at the coordinates on a hill five miles away. After three days, out of ammunition and overrun. Because no one could get there to resupply them. Because the roads were washed away, and a bridge collapsed, as well.

Eight U.S. dead, and four missing. I double checked the records from Lamont and Baxter. The LSI, all right. When I went through the lists of KIA, digging through the microfiche, matching the lists against the records for Bahn Bahn, I remembered a list like that I'd seen before. When I was a kid, reading a magazine, reading about Murder Incorporated.

Eight murdered, that's what I wrote. By coincidence, two of the eight were Texans. Bahn Bahn had been barely mentioned in the press when it happened, only another day in the jungle, but with two Texans dead and the LSI to blame, it made a hell of a story now. A full page in the Sunday paper. And I had at least three more to go just like it.

"I hope you know what you're doing" said Vicky when she read it.

"I know what I'm doing. I'm pissing people off."

"It's all innuendo, Phil. All you're doing is hinting who's to blame."

"It's the newspaper business, Vicky."

"I'd rather write novels. At least my readers know it's fiction."

"And my readers don't give a damn."

"So you'll let them be both judge and jury."

"I'll let them run up circulation. Stop nagging like you think I have a conscience."

She stopped nagging and tossed the paper aside, ready to take care of what I had come home for. Ready to entertain her cowboy. Who was not about to confess he'd been out rustling cattle. And not about to admit she was right. It was mostly innuendo, and sooner or later I'd have to start naming the bad guys who wore the black hats. Whoever the hell they were.

Right. Whoever the hell they were. And no one seemed to know. Vanished, over the border and gone, before the posse could catch them. A billion dollar enterprise, closed when the Army announced it was standing down in Nam.

Gone, leaving no trail behind, even before I had started interviewing Lyndon Johnson. I pointed that out to Bettelmy when he called me to his office after two more Sundays in the series. He had wanted me to track on the Hearst Corporation, I reminded him, not the Lone Star International, trying to prod something out of Johnson by merely mentioning the LSI.

"So we missed that target. Forget it. What do we do now? We need names, Phil."

"The problem is the LSI was never a corporation. It was only a private company,"

"Somebody must have been running it. Who?"

"I've tracked on the names they listed in Texas. They're phony, all of them."

"Look, somebody real must have signed the contracts in Washington."

"Sure, but it's secret information, and my contact there is gone."

"Your friend Lamont. What about Baxter, he might. . ."

"Not him. I told you, he was running for cover when I last saw him."

Bettelmy pressed a button on his intercom and asked Miss Sarah to please come see him. I could hear what she said in reply. No, Mister Bettelmy, I will not, unless you promise Mister Thornton is not in there again. Hell, if Baxter's had it, he should see how his old flying buddy acts around her. Having to make a promise to get her to come in his office.

"Sarah, how many syndication deals have come through?"

"Eight so far, Mister Bettelmy. At the publication price you stipulated."

"The Washington paper, what about it?"

"It begins next week. Would you like me to tell Mister Dee, now that he is here?"

"No, I'll tell him. Thank you Sarah, and I apologize about Paul Thornton."

Syndication deals? He was selling what I'd written to other papers, without telling me? With me holding the copyright? And paying twenty dollars a week to rent a damned desk in the society section? Hell, with that kind of double handed dealing he would have qualified to run the LSI himself.

"We'll let the government smoke them out, Phil."

"What about these syndication deals?"

"When it shows up in the Washington paper, they'll start investigating."

"How much? How much are you getting for what I've written?"

"Enough to cover your Western Union bill, I imagine."

"How much, Bill?"

"Go back to work, we'll add it up when it's done. Keep at what you've been doing."

Back to work, indeed. Keep the heat on the LSI. Keep writing about murder and fraud. Get the Feds involved. Bettelmy was on the mark. Devious, too, the way he held back about the syndication income. But amusing, also, the way he apologized to Miss Sarah. God only knows what that bastard Thornton had said in front of her.

Fry knew. He was laughing about it when he came by my desk, in between his usual jokes about the ladies I was keeping company with. The bullpen, he called them, and he wasn't talking about baseball, he was hinting at their social preferences. None of my business, I had told him. What he said about Thornton and Miss Sarah, that turned out to be another matter.

"I heard about it in the studio" he said. "They're having a hard time controlling him"

"Thornton, sure, I've got that bastard throttled."

"He's been out on the street making tapes, trying to get people to do it for him."

"Do what? Talk about what I've written, since he's afraid to?"

"When the station manager told him he can't even do that, he went off the wall."

"My contract is clear about it, Tom, I'd have his ass, and the TV station, too."

"He went to Bettelmy's office about it, cursing like hell in front of Sarah."

"If he did, he's dumb. Making tapes on the street, that's even dumber."

"They edit it before they show it. They won't let him go on live anymore."

"Too bad, now you can't tease him about the latest scores, right?"

"No, but I can laugh at what's deleted. I'll get you a copy, you'll see what I mean."

You needn't rush, I said, I haven't had time to look at the ones he made in Washington. Maybe I'll get around to it when I've finished what I'm doing. This summer, I said to myself, when I'm lying on the beach in Jamaica, drinking rum and living off my syndication royalties.

I would look at them sooner than that. All because of a call to Vicky. From Miss Sarah. And when I did I wouldn't be headed for Jamaica. I'd be headed for a Federal slammer.

As Thomas Edison used to say, when he was mucking around with light bulbs, or whoever it was who said it, it's one damned thing after another. First my car, waiting to be fixed with the help of Thornton's Ass Shuns, and next the television set, also made by folks on the other side of the ocean, all of them in the business of selling high-priced junk to Americans.

As opposed to the noble business I was in. Selling papers for Bettelmy. Keeping the public informed. Trying to lure them away from the game shows they watch on television.

"It's broken" said Vicky when I got home around midnight.

"What's broken?" I asked.

"The television set. What have you done to it?"

"The TV? You want to watch that crap? Why?"

"Sarah called and told me there's a cowboy movie I should see."

"She watches movies this late at night? As old as she is?"

"She records them. See if you can fix it, Phil."

"Fix it, hell, I haven't turned it on since we came back from Washington."

"I did, remember, I was going to watch the tapes they made while we were gone."

She went in the kitchen and poured me a drink while I fiddled around with the TV set. A tape was stuck, and I couldn't get it out, and that's all I could turn on, and I wasn't too damned interested in doing that, either. I had other things on my mind when I came home at night. Like dragging Matt Larue into the old corral beyond the kitchen.

"Then I'll watch that" she said, when I explained the problem with the TV.

"That tape Thornton made? You prefer that to. . ."

"Relax, Phil. It's not your turn, or have you forgotten?"

I had. The cycle of romance. Marked on the calendar in the kitchen and I had overlooked it. Maybe some day some genius in Japan would come up with a way to cope with that. Or maybe they already had. Maybe that's what the TV sets they made were meant for.

"All right, Vicky, I'll watch it with you if that's the best you have to offer."

"I could also offer some advice. Go take a cold shower."

The drink she had brought was clearly a better option. I started the tape, reminded her which buttons to press, handed her the remote control, and settled for a sip of bourbon. Not pleased at all with the way the evening had turned out.

The tape was about what I expected. Thornton at his worst. Along the funeral route, trying to agitate a Negro sailor, starting an argument with a man he called a Mescan, growling at the camera after someone else had told him to bug off. None of it worth using on the evening broadcast, even by Thornton's standards. The tape was what the station had left over.

"Vicky, wait" I said. "Stop there, run that back."

"That part? That's just two men he's talking to. You can't even see who they are."

"Turn up the sound, I want to hear what they're saying."

"You do it. I'm going to bed, Phil."

She handed me the remote and disappeared into the bedroom. I barely noticed she was gone, running it back again and again, five minutes of tape, watching it with the volume as loud as I could get it.

"You could turn it down" she said when she returned with a robe on.

"Vicky, you know who that is, the one on the left? That's Lomax."

"It's so loud I can't sleep. Please turn it down."

"Lomax, that sonofabitch, that's him."

"How can you tell? All you can see is the back of his head."

"He'll turn around in a minute, you can see his face then."

"Fine, so who is Lomax?"

"He used to be a Congressman. A long time ago I helped drive him out of office."

She sat down on the sofa. I played it again, still loud, damned near overwhelmed by what I'd found. I had seen it from a distance when I was there, Thornton interviewing two men on the steps of the Capitol. Now I knew who one of them was. And I had a good idea of what it meant. I had found the smoking gun I'd been looking for.

"So you drove him out of office. What for?"

"For buying Negro votes. He was on his way to being governor."

"A long time ago, you said. So why are you so excited now?"

"He's tied to the LSI, Vicky, listen to what they're saying."

She listened. Thornton, facing the camera, telling the world how chickenshit it was to honor Lyndon Johnson. He had found two old friends he was certain agreed with him. He was asking questions, while the two men faced him with their backs to the camera and the voice boom overhead. No mention of their names, only loaded questions filled with poison.

The way he gave your money to the Mescans and the Nigroids, he said, you weren't fans of LBJ, were you? You've taken care of yourself without handouts, right? You're right, the one on the left answered. All my life I've worked hard, building things for the people back in Texas, and building things in Vietnam, too, we could have won that war if he hadn't been in office.

The man on the right was evasive. I'm from Ohio, he said, but I must agree with my friend from Texas, yes, there's no doubt about it, you will prosper if you do what's best for the people of this great nation.

Thornton held his microphone in front of the one on the left after that. Was he aware it was LBJ who pushed through the civil rights bills that ruined the USA? Are you aware you might as well move to another country, now that Lyndon Johnson has corrupted this one? For several minutes Thornton went on like that. And then abruptly something odd. The two men turned around, looking like they were running for cover, showing their faces. They had seen another TV reporter approaching, with his own cameraman behind him.

"That's Dan Proctor" said Vicky. "I recognize him. . .what's he doing?"

"That's Proctor, all right. He sees Lomax. He's after him again."

"Again? What do you mean, again?"

"That's how Proctor got his start. A long time ago, he helped me nail Lomax."

"So now he's a big shot anchorman. Was he an arrogant prick when you knew him?"

"Look, we were friends once, but that's not important. It's why Lomax ran when he saw him coming. You can bet on it, Vicky, that bastard's involved in the Lone Star International."

"You can't tie him to the LSI, Phil, that wasn't even mentioned."

"You weren't listening. Didn't you hear what he said about building things?"

"Yes, and I heard what he said about helping in Vietnam. So what?"

"You saw how Lomax nodded when Thornton mentioned getting out of the country?"

"Fine, but the tape ends right there...what are you going to do, watch it again?"

"I'm going to have a technician take it out of the set and save it."

"Save it? For what? That tape proves nothing, Phil."

"Save it, so I can get a picture from it to go with what I plan to write."

"Look, I know you're good at innuendo, but. . ."

"I'll make it read just right. I'm going to finish that rotten bastard once and for all."

She got up from the sofa when I turned off the set. Then she stopped, halfway to the bedroom, and turned around, with a helpless look on her face.

"You can't do that, Phil. You'll be making it up."

"Making it up? Damn, Vicky, you really don't understand how newspapers work."

Neither did the U.S. Marshall who was waiting for me, at my desk, when I arrived on an afternoon two weeks later. Wearing a bow tie, not the sort of thing they wore in Vicky's novels, but a lawman, nonetheless, proving it by showing me the badge pinned to his wallet. And by handing me a subpoena.

"What's this for?" I asked.

"Read it, you'll see."

"This is a newspaper office. You can't walk in here like this."

"I believe they want to ask you some questions in Washington."

"Questions? Haven't they heard about the First Amendment?"

"Ask them yourself, when you get there."

"Freedom of the press. I'll tear this up, the minute you leave."

"I wouldn't recommend it, Mister Dee."

He walked away, leaving me holding the subpoena. No, I wouldn't recommend it, either. But what the hell, I couldn't act like I'd fallen off a horse, not with the women in the society section watching me. All I could do was go bang on Bettelmy's door. And tell him he was right, they had come to get me, just as he had said they would.

He was thumbing through a stack of papers on his desk when I got there. All the Sunday editions since I started writing about the LSI, eight, with the first one on the bottom and the latest one on top.

"There it is, right there" he said without looking up.

"I know, I can see it from here. You want to see what I have?"

"Week by week, the circulation going up, not bad at all."

"I've been handed a subpoena, Bill. By a U.S. Marshal."

"I know, he came up here hunting you. Look at this stack, you see what it tells you?"

"I can see what this subpoena tells me. Be in Washington two weeks from now."

"And this stack tells you why. They've bitten the bait, Phil, hook, line and sinker."

He pressed a button on his intercom, the one, I knew by now, for Miss Sarah's office. Without a word from him she came through the door, ready to answer his questions, with a look on her face that said she knew I'd be there waiting.

"Sarah, you've checked on Dee's contract with the paper?"

"Yes, Mister Bettelmy, legally you cannot provide him a lawyer."

"Because legally he's not an employee. What about Thornton?"

"Mister Thornton can televise Mister Dee when he testifies in Washington."

"Because that will be in the public domain. Thank you, Sarah."

She returned to her office and Bettelmy pulled one of the Sunday papers from the stack on his desk, the second from the top. He unfolded it, took out the page I had written on the LSI, and held it up so I could see it. The page with the picture of Lomax, big and grainy, the face of the man I had named, suggesting, only hinting, of course, he was the mastermind behind it all.

"That's what did it, that picture" said Bettelmy.

"Fine, so they bit the bait. Now what do you have in mind?"

"Keep the heat on. You can do two more Sunday stories before you leave."

"Leave, right, without a lawyer. You know what that means?"

"You don't want a lawyer with you. You want to act dumb and let them ask questions."

He folded the page and inserted it into the Sunday section he had taken it from. Neat, a man in control of things, running up the paper's circulation, not bothered at all by the way he was sticking my head on a chopping block.

"Bill, what if they find Lomax? What if they subpoena him?"

"Even better. Then we won't need Thornton to do it for us."

"I know, I heard what you told Miss Sarah."

"If Lomax is hiding here in Texas, he'll hear about it from Thornton."

"So you'll let that bastard make Lomax show his face. You've got it all figured out."

"All except the other man in that picture. We don't know who he is."

"Goddamn it, Bill, I don't like it, the way you're using me. This is bullshit."

"Careful now. Don't forget who might hear you."

Right, Miss Sarah. But her door was closed, so to hell with it. Go to Washington and act dumb. I'd have no problem with that.

I'd been dumb from the start, betting I could sell papers for Bettelmy by turning the public on. And now he'd raised the ante, knowing damned well my having to testify would raise the circulation even more.

Vicky was not surprised when I told her what I had to do. She reminded me she had warned me not to write about Lomax. But like a good wife should she brought me a drink as I sat down on the sofa that night. Wearing a negligee, nice and black, and thin enough to get my mind on something else. If she hadn't felt like nagging first.

"You shouldn't trust him, Phil."

"Bettelmy, you're right, I shouldn't."

"He manipulates people, the way he's sending you off without a lawyer."

"Two weeks from now, all on my own. You want to go with me?"

"Of course. I'll stand by my man, like Tammy Wynette says in that song she sings."

"Who's Tammy Wynette?"

"She's a cowboy singer. That's one of the songs that made her famous."

"How fat is she? Maybe she's the fat lady who sings when it's over."

"She's not fat. And I'm not, either. Or haven't you noticed?

"I've noticed. Let me finish my drink and I'll show you what I've noticed."

Stand by her man or not, she wasn't in the Senate hearing room when I arrived there. She had to go to New York first, she said, to have it out with her publisher. Fine, why not? A novel about Negro cowboys might be more in line with the public sense of truth and justice, anyway. It would certainly draw more attention. With the room almost empty that was obvious.

A half-dozen Senators, looking down from the standard horseshoe perch in a hearing room. The rest of the seats around them vacant. No one else there, except for Thornton and his cameraman. Plus the sergeant at arms, ready to swear me in. I promised to tell the truth, put my briefcase down, and got ready to evade their questions.

"Do you understand why you are here, Mister Dee?" asked the chairman.

"Not exactly, Senator."

"You are under oath, I must remind you. Do you understand that?"

"Yes, Senator, I do."

"Mister Dee, do you understand why this committee has been formed?"

"Not exactly, Senator."

"We are here to ask you about what you have reported, Mister Dee."

"Go ahead, Senator."

"You are an employee of the San Antonio Express, are you not?"

"No, Senator, I am not."

"No? They have distributed what you have written, have they not?"

"They purchased what I wrote, Senator."

"So you work there, after all. Is that correct, Mister Dee?"

"Senator, I am only a freelance writer. I rent a desk there."

He had asked all the questions, the chairman of the committee. One of the other Senators had gotten bored and left, and the others looked like they were asleep. Even Thornton seemed bored, sitting in the corner behind his cameraman, looking sleepy also. The chairman hadn't done his homework, asking nothing but dumb questions.

Or maybe not so dumb. Trying to tie me with the paper, maybe it was Bettelmy he was going after. Hell, I knew what his damned committee wanted, even if the few who were there were sound asleep. They wanted to know who my sources were. And if they couldn't force it out of me, maybe they could bring in Bettelmy and force it out of him.

Another half hour of questions like that and the chairman gave up. We will recess until two o'clock, he said, since the other members of my committee seem distracted. They were. All but one had gone, to a room down the hall, where the real action was. The Watergate hearings, with Nixon's neck in a noose a hell of a lot tighter than mine.

Or so I thought when I left the hearing room. No chance to watch the Watergate hoohah, I could tell when I saw the crowd down the hallway. So I sat on a bench in front of the Capitol and waited. A warm and sleepy afternoon, no wonder I dozed off when I returned to the hearing room. Too bad. If I had stayed awake I might have realized I was about to be in trouble.

The sound of the chairman's gavel woke me up. When I looked around, still drowsy, I wondered why he was pounding away so loud with no one there. The room was empty. No other Senators had returned, and neither had Thornton. Except for the sergeant of arms standing in a corner, I was alone with the chairman. Damned irregular, it seemed, but what did I know?

I knew enough to stay away from the questions he began to ask me. Right after reminding me I was still under oath. Banging away with his gavel when I failed to tell him what he wanted to know. Going one on one, hurling questions at me through his microphone, with no one else there, damned irregular, indeed.

"Once again, the Lone Star International, you called it the LSI in what you wrote?"

"I did, Senator. I have told you that already."

"And you have charged the LSI with fraud, is that correct?"

"As I said before, in what I wrote I urged they be investigated, Senator."

"But you will not reveal to this committee how you learned about the LSI?"

"No, Senator, I repeat, I will not reveal my sources."

"But you have linked John Lomax to the LSI, have you not?"

"Lomax? Not exactly, Senator, but. . ."

"Is he the source of what you think you know about the LSI? Is it Lomax?"

"I told you, Senator, I cannot reveal. . ."

"Where is he now? Where is Lomax? This committee needs to know!"

He pushed aside his microphone and stood up, pounding away with his gavel, demanding to know where Lomax was, raising hell because I would not tell him where Lomax might be hiding. As he yelled away I realized something odd. With the microphone in front of his face I had not been able to see what he looked like. I had not recognized this Senator at all.

I opened my briefcase, looked inside, and found what I was after, a blown up copy of the picture printed in the paper. Taken from the videotape Thornton had made on the steps of the Capitol. The picture that had led me to Lomax, not knowing or even caring who the other man in the picture might be. But now I realized who it was. It was this damned Senator.

He was still banging away with his gavel, still yelling about Lomax, when I realized something else. This Senator wasn't after me. He wasn't after Bettelmy and the paper. It was Lomax he was after. He wanted to know what Lomax had revealed. This bastard had been involved in the LSI himself, by God, and he was running for cover.

"What did he tell you?" shouted the Senator. "This committee needs to know!"

"What committee, Senator? You're the only one, as far as I can tell."

"Where is Lomax? I will hold you in contempt if you don't answer."

"Senator, I don't know, and I wouldn't tell you if I did."

"I have warned you, Mister Dee."

"You have, have you? Go screw yourself, I can warn as well as you can, I. . ."

"Arrest this man! Hold him for contempt of Congress!"

I smiled as the sergeant at arms took my hand and led me away, whispering he had never seen anything like this before, and he wasn't sure it was legal, but what could he do, he could only follow orders. With the Watergate business holding center stage, no one noticed as he led me down the steps to a patrol car. To a policeman ready to haul me away.

But I was pleased. This Senator might have overstepped his bounds, and I might be off base about his role in the LSI, but one way or the other, he had handed me one hell of a story. A reporter in jail makes great copy. Damned right I was smiling.

I was not so pleased when I woke up the following morning. Even with the middle-aged lady unlocking my door and saying hello, it's time for room service, it was still a cell, and I was in it, behind bars, cursing myself for being there and wondering how the hell I might get out. Stir crazy, after a single night in the hoosegow.

"Here's the breakfast you ordered" said the lady. "Also the menu for lunch."

"I'm much obliged, ma'am. So how long have you been with the Justice Department?"

"Ten years, the last two working in here. It's really rather nice, you know."

"Sure, if you don't mind being locked up. Cowboys like me, well. . ."

"A cowboy. I see you know how to write. You've used up half that pad I brought you."

"Yes, ma'am, jotting down my latest adventures for the Police Gazette."

"But you haven't used your telephone. You want me to show you how to dial it?"

"No, ma'am. But I will, as soon as I can figure out what to tell the sheriff."

She locked the door and went away, in no mood for further horsing around with a Federal detainee. That's my status, they said when they brought me in, adding they would have to hold me here until they heard from Congress. A detainee, hell, I was a prisoner, and the sound the door made when she locked it made it clear. No need for such a nice distinction.

A need for a lawyer, maybe. She was right. I had not used the telephone. Who could I call? Not Bettelmy, I knew what he would say. You don't need a lawyer, let them keep asking questions. Not Vicky. I had no number for her, off in New York with her publisher. And what good would a lawyer be? I'd done nothing wrong. I would wait to hear from Congress.

I waited. Day two, no word from anyone. Day three, still no word, time to start worrying. Contempt of Congress? Nothing in the papers about it. Not a peep from Congress. No word from Vicky, either, wherever she was. And no bugles in the distance, no sound of the cavalry coming to my rescue. I was all alone, and waiting.

Being alone was the worst part, I realized later. No one to talk to, no one to hear my stories. Plenty to read, plenty to eat, clean sheets every morning, this was a five-star hotel with bars included, but deadly quiet. A bit of chit-chat with that lady when she came around and that was all. Looking back, I think it was the silence that bothered me as much as the waiting.

That changed abruptly on the fourth day I was there, when a man I would later come to know as Big Sal The Fixer arrived to keep me company. Around dinner time. I heard his voice before I saw his face. He was speaking to the lady in charge as she led him to a cell, and from what he was saying I could tell there would be no more silence. He was here to take over.

"Rosie, how have you been?" I heard him ask her.

"I've been all right" she said. "I see you've gained some weight."

"Living high. How's the lasagna tonight?"

"I'll order you some. You have your own wine, I suppose."

"Chianti, one bottle in my briefcase, that's all they let me bring in."

"Sal, when are you going to learn? Racketeering again, at your age?"

I saw him then, for the first time, walking back and forth between my cell and the one across the way. She had evidently left his door unlocked. A big man with a pockmarked face, getting on in years, his hair already gray, wearing what looked like a thousand dollar suit. When he stopped to stretch he saw me watching through the bars on my cell.

"Who are you?" he asked.

"Dee" I said. "Phillip Dee, I'm. . ."

"Dee. What's that short for? Difransci? Dicontesso?"

"Just plain Dee."

"Clever. How long you been in here?"

"Four days."

"You need a better lawyer."

That's easy for him to say, I thought. He'd be out in an hour or two and I would still be here. I went back to my note pad, writing some ideas about the story I had in mind. What it was like to spend time in a Federal holding cell. I could hear him talking on a telephone, asking questions and giving orders. Some big crime boss, ready to walk again, as soon as his lawyers could spring him.

When she brought dinner I heard him tell her something quite surprising. A crime boss, sure, one I started to wonder about when I heard what he said. "Rosie" he said, "give some of this Chianti to that goombah Dee. I checked him out, he's that newspaper guy who put the screws to the Lone Star International."

She unlocked my door and set my dinner on a table. Pointing to the chef's salad I had ordered, not the glass of wine he had sent me.

"Don't let him see you eating that" she said. "He thinks salads are for wimps."

"He calls you Rosie, does he?"

"I've left your door open. So you can visit with him."

"Not me. Tell him thanks for the wine. I'll keep my distance."

"He won't hurt you. Go and talk to him."

Maybe I would. I might be a wimp for eating salads, but he had mentioned the LSI, so hell yes, go talk to him. I had heard the Mafia kept tabs on every big-time gangster in the country, he might know where Lomax was. He might know something about this Senator who had stuck me in here, too. Damned right, go and talk to him.

"So you're a newspaper guy" he said, without looking up from his dinner.

"I am, I'd like to ask you a question, if you don't mind."

"Newspapers. In the old days, I had to put a couple out of business."

"The LSI. What do you know about them?"

"Non-union. We knew they were crooks right away."

"That's why I'm asking, I wonder if you. . ."

"Stealing from their own damn country, they shoulda been more patriotic."

"So what else? What else do you know. . ."

"What you wrote I read. You did good. Bunch of damned Commies."

"That's all? That's all you. . ."

"Get lost, I need to talk to my lawyer again. Take a hike."

Take a hike. Well, hell, at least he didn't call his lawyer a mouthpiece. An old-time hoodlum, really old when I saw him up close, the napkin around his neck splattered with sauce, reaching for the phone as I went back to my cell. No point in trying to squeeze anything out of him. He wouldn't rat. He wouldn't have to. He didn't know a damned thing.

I went back to my cell, finished my salad, and checked the menu for tomorrow. I was about to decide what to have for breakfast when I glanced up and saw him standing in my door. Holding his briefcase, getting ready to walk away from Federal custody.

"My lawyer said it's okay I should talk to you before I go."

"What about? Not about the LSI, I don't imagine."

"I want you should write about me. My life story."

"You're kidding. If that's what you want you need a ghost writer, not me."

"I seen enough ghosts already. Fifty G's up front, fifty more when you finish."

"A hundred grand? It must be a hell of a life you've led."

"Here's my card. Call me, soon as you get outa here."

I looked at the card. Salvatore Balderetti Imports. Some life story that would be, God only knows what he imported over the years. I put the card away, checked off grapefruit for tomorrow, and looked at the card again. A hundred grand would buy a lot of grapefruit. I would have to tell the lady concierge about that when she came by to tuck me in for the evening.

"I hope you were nice to him" she said. "He's getting old."

"But not too old to be indicted for racketeering."

"It won't stick, it never does."

"He has connections, right?"

"A long time ago they used to call him Big Sal The Fixer."

"It's Rosie, right? How do you know all this about him, Rosie?"

"He's my uncle. He lives in New York, so I don't get to see him very often."

"Wait, he's your uncle, and you're working in the Justice Department?"

"This is Washington, Mister Dee. Here it's all about connections."

She shrugged her shoulders as she walked away. Nonchalant. I looked at the card again. Connections, damn, I'd be in here forever if that's what it took, connections. Big Sal had them and I did not. All I had was Rosie's word that she'd be back in the morning. And a couple of uncertain thoughts about a hundred thousand dollars worth of grapefruit.

I had finished breakfast and was reading the paper when I heard the noise outside my cell. A man in a suit, with some sort of badge on his lapel, opening my door. And behind him Vicky, yelling and trying to push him away and get near me.

"Lady, stand aside" said the man. "I have to take him back to the Senate."

"Not before I hug him" said Vicky. "I've been waiting all night to see him."

"Give her a break" said Rosie. "It's visitor's hours, she has a right to be here."

He looked at his watch and walked away, arguing with Rosie about something. Let them argue, it was Vicky I was listening to. Calm, now that we had embraced, eager to tell me where she'd been the past four days.

"Phil, I couldn't find you. No one seemed to know where you were."

"Don't worry about it, I've been locked up, but. . ."

"That's over now, it's taken care of, you'll see when. . ."

"Time's up, let's go" said the man with the badge on his lapel.

"I'll follow in a taxi" said Vicky. "You'll see when we get there."

All I could see when I got there was an empty Senate hearing room, with no one around except for Thornton, his cameraman beside him, and the sergeant at arms who had taken me away almost a week before. Standing next to the witness table, ready to swear me in again.

"It's a different room" he said. "Not so close to that Watergate business."

"There's no one here. What is it, one on one with that Senator again?"

"The committee's been reorganized. I don't think he's on it anymore."

No chance to ask what had happened. The committee was filing in to take their seats. Reorganized, indeed, at least a dozen Senators this time. Noisy, talking among themselves as they came in.

A bit of noise in the back of the room, as well, and when I looked around I started to wonder. Not about the crooked bastard who had sent me off to jail, but what was going on here. Baxter? With his wife? What were they doing here? Vicky, sure, she had arrived, and they were talking with her, but they were on the lam, they had to be stupid to be here.

No chance to ask about that, either. Only something else to wonder about. The new committee chairman, watching as I took the oath again. Not a chairman, a chair lady, whatever they called a presiding woman.

I wasn't wondering what to call her. I knew what to call her. Trouble, big-time trouble. It was Senator Amador, Vicky's buddy Beverly, brushing the tip of her microphone so I'd be sure to hear her. What I was wondering was how many lashes she would give me.

"Mister Dee" she said. "I believe we have met before."

"We have, Senator. It would be perjury to deny it."

"Some years ago we met in Germany. You were in the Army then."

"Yes, Senator, I was. I was in the Army."

"Mister Baxter, in the back of the room. Do you remember him?"

"Baxter? Did you say Baxter? I may recall a. . ."

"He was with me then. I am sure you must remember."

Damned right, I remembered. How she wanted to burn me for those dummies dropped by parachute, the dummies she had thought were Negro soldiers. And now she was after Baxter, too, ready to nail him for smuggling secret Commerce records to me. To hell with her. I wouldn't name my sources. I would plead the Fifth Amendment if I had to.

"I apologize" she said, interrupting my thoughts on how to cope with her.

"We understand" said one of the Senators.

"I have wasted our time reviewing an acquaintance. I'll get on with business now."

"Take all the time you like" said another Senator.

"Mister Dee, I have been placed in charge of this committee. Do you know why?"

"No, Senator, I do not" I answered, and I sure as hell didn't.

"What you have written, evidently you have misled one of our colleagues."

My ass I had. The only thing misleading was that bastard posing as the head of a committee. So they were covering up for him, fine, she hadn't asked a question, so I didn't need to answer. I would let her lecture all she wanted to about her colleague.

"I shall be brief, Mister Dee. A company you identified as the LSI was charged by you with government fraud, my colleague formed a special committee to investigate these charges, and we have now learned that this investigation was unnecessary. Can you follow me so far?"

"Unnecessary? I disagree, Senator." Disagree or not, she wasn't listening.

"I know that as a reporter you believe you must protect your sources, but in at least one case that has also proven to be unnecessary. Whoever provided you with records from the Department of Commerce needs no protection. Do you know why, Mister Dee?"

"No, Senator, but. . ."

"I have been informed that none of the records in that department relating to the LSI were ever secret, that is why. Moreover, I have been assured by the Department of Defense that no further inquiry into the LSI is warranted at this time. Do you understand what that means?"

"Yes, Senator, I am starting to see."

"It means my colleague from Ohio was misled. It also means this committee can be dissolved now, as soon as I counsel you about the manner in which you offended him. Please step forward, Mister Dee, so I may give you some advice before you are released."

I stepped forward, surprised as hell by what had happened here. In a matter of minutes she had taken Baxter off the hook, given that bastard Senator from Ohio a free pass, left the door open on the LSI, announced I was going free, and not once suggested I should get out of newspaper work and do something honest. Not at all what I expected. No fifty lashes.

"You are fortunate" she said, with her microphone off, almost whispering.

"I'm not sure I understand, Senator."

"I am speaking about your wife Vicky."

"She had trouble finding me, yes, I know, she. . ."

"I assume she has told you how she called on me yesterday."

"I'm sorry, Senator, we haven't. . ."

"It is because of her I asked to be placed in charge of this committee."

"I know, she's fond of you, she. . ."

"Lulu and I were up all night, cleaning up this mess you were in."

"Lulu? Oh yes, Baxter's wife, I've met her, she works for you. . ."

"Lulu believes what you wrote is true. She thinks you should pursue it."

"The LSI? Fine, but what about this Senator who stuck me in jail? He. . ."

"Do not concern yourself with that. I will take care of him."

She was looking at me with a frown on her face when she said that. I imagined she would take care of him, all right. One tough woman, covering all the bases. She started to turn on her microphone, but paused and smiled, still speaking in a whisper.

"I do have one last question. Why are you so damned afraid of me?"

She did not wait for an answer. With her microphone turned on she said I was free to go, thanked the committee for its cooperation, and announced the meeting was over. I stood there, watching as she shook hands with the other Senators. Thinking about what Rosie had said.

When I looked around I spotted Vicky in the back of the room. Patting Lulu on the back. Then coming forward to say something to Senator Amador, Senator Beverly, as she called her. Whatever it was, the Senator smiled when she said it.

Rosie had nailed it on the head.

Washington. It's all about connections.

Bettelmy had his own ideas about connections. He would like to hitch me to a wagon load of cow shit and let the driver haul me off to Amarillo, some place far away, he said, so I would stop harassing him about the Lone Star International.

"Phil, I've told you over and over again, forget it, there's nothing left there."

"And I'm telling you again, Bill, the LSI could still sell papers."

"Wrong, damn it. You know what the Feds have told you about Lomax."

"He's left the country in his jet, fine, but that's not the end of it."

"Go ahead, go chase around in Mexico looking for him, I'm not paying for it."

"I'm not talking about Lomax, Bill. It's that Senator from Ohio I'm after."

"So he swindled a few million. Nobody gives a damn about that."

"They should, he was in deep with the LSI, Bill, he's the story."

"That's Vietnam. Vietnam and the LSI, that's back page now, forget it."

"Forget it? Drop it, just like that? What kind of paper are you running?"

Bettelmy reached for the morning edition on his desk, motioned for me to follow, and walked to a window overlooking Broadway. When he raised the shade and pointed to the people four blocks below he answered my question. Holding the paper in front of me.

"The kind they will read, goddamn it, that's the kind I'm running."

"You mean the kind you can sell. So let them read about a crooked Senator."

"One crooked Senator, hell, they couldn't care less."

"Sure, they'd rather watch Dan Proctor go after Nixon over Watergate, but. . ."

"You stirred them up with Bahn Bahn, fine, but that's over, forget it."

"Bill, listen. . ."

"Thornton. He knows how, that bastard. He knows what they want to hear."

"He's after the Mexicans again, I know, but. . ."

"Wetback pepper bellies, he calls them, Phil. You want to go after them, too?"

"No I don't, but. . ."

"Write about that, if you want to stir up those people down there."

Bettelmy threw the paper on his desk and sat down. Looking at a yellow note pad and shaking his head. I knew what was on it. The paper's circulation figures. Going down again, he had told me, the last two times I had been in his office since we got back from Washington, trying to talk him into letting me stay on the LSI. And he still wasn't budging.

"Bill, look, suppose I do it on my own."

"That sonofabitch, they listen to his TV shit and believe it."

"If I have to, I could. . ."

"The paper's losing ground and the station's getting rich because of that bastard."

"That Senator's crooked, Bill. If I have to, I'll go freelance again to prove it."

"What? You want to go after him on your own?"

"I'll work out a new contract with Miss Sarah. . ."

"She's out getting her hair done. Forget it, goddamn it."

I should have known she was out. If she was in her office Bettelmy would not have been cursing so loud about Thornton and the TV station.

To hell with Thornton, it was this bastard from Ohio I was after. In it deeper than Lomax, trying to cover his tracks in that one on one crap in the Senate. Sending me off to jail. Get revenge. Expose him. That's what a newspaper is for.

But Bettelmy wasn't with me on that. He had circulation numbers on his mind.

"What you wrote about the LSI, we closed in on the Light. But only for a while."

"So the numbers are down. This is still a big story, Bill."

"Ten weeks, that worked. But damn it, Phil, Vietnam is over and done with."

"It's not over, not with people like him around."

"Ten weeks, you picked up a lot of syndication money, too."

"I'm not in it for the money. I'm after a crooked Senator."

"You go freelance on the LSI, nobody will buy it, including me. Not now."

"Too bad. I remember when you would have said stick with it."

"Hell, Phil, you don't even remember why you went freelance in the first place."

"All right, so you've hired me back, but look, this is different, it's. . ."

"Take a few days off. And don't bother me anymore about the LSI."

He was right. I had forgotten it was Thornton I wanted off my back when I signed that contract Miss Sarah put together. Thornton. I heard his voice up above, when I went into the stairwell to return to the news room. Thornton, coming down, talking with the station manager, something about Bettelmy. Fine, let them have him. I was tired of arguing with him.

Not a bad idea, however, what he had said about taking a few days off. Good, clean up my desk and do it. Go someplace quiet and think about it. Think about what it's like to be on top of a story and have the rug pulled out from under you. Because it won't sell papers, when you know damned well that shouldn't matter.

What mattered, Fry assured me when he came by my desk, was that I was back in the ballgame. Away from those lady cheerleaders in the society section and back in center field, as he put it. Batting cleanup, where I could hit more dingers for the home team. Something along that line. I wasn't paying much attention. I was wondering what to do next.

"They're really screwing around with baseball" said Fry.

"So the season's started. Mine's about over, I'm afraid."

"This new rule they're experimenting with. The designated hitter, they call it."

"So I heard. Some guy who doesn't play, all he does is hit?"

"Right. So what's this crap about your season being over?"

"I'm a straight reporter again, and I'm not sure how long I'll last."

"If it's Thornton you're thinking about, don't worry about him."

"Thornton? Sure, I'll be fair game for that bastard again. But that's not it, Tom."

"You know what he wants to do? He wants to start writing for the paper."

"You're joking. Bettelmy will tell him to kiss off, he won't let him."

"That's the word upstairs. TV and a daily column, too."

"We'll see. I'll be back in a few days. Guard home plate, Tom."

I locked my desk and headed out of the newsroom. So Thornton wanted to start writing again. Hell, he's made the TV station rich, a daily column filled with that poison of his might sell papers, a lot of papers. Maybe Bettelmy would be forced to let him.

He wouldn't have to.

By the time I got back, some designated hitter, name unknown, would come off the bench and take care of Thornton.

Once and for all, in the worst way one could imagine.

Vicky told me what I should do, in no uncertain terms, soon after I met her at a ranch outside the city. Quit the newspaper racket. Get on a horse and follow her to Arizona. Ride into the sunset. Get out of Dodge before they lynch me. Take up fiction. I had shown, she said, a certain talent for it.

First I had to listen to her quiz me. Looking down from the palomino she was sitting on, patting the horse on the mane with one hand and me on the head with the other. Wearing a cowboy hat and dark sunglasses, Matt Larue, the master of the Western novel. Not acting at all like I'd been missed. Wanting to know what part of Texas I'd been lost in.

"You knew where I was, Vicky. I was visiting Lyndon Johnson's grave."

"You could have called last night. I waited to hear from you."

"Get down from that damned horse and give me a kiss."

"He's not a damned horse. His name is Phillip The Fantasizer."

"So you rent him and now you've named him after me. Charming."

"I don't rent him anymore. I bought him. Two thousand dollars, an hour ago."

She rode into a stable and I followed her. Impressed again with what they had taught her at Wellesley. Watching how she got down, took an apple from her saddlebag, cut it into slices, and fed it to her horse while murmuring in his ears. Nice. Then she reached for a bag of chips, gave the horse a bite, and handed the rest to me.

"Here" she said. "Now they can call you the Frito Kid."

"All right, Vicky, what's eating you?"

"I talked to Lulu. I don't want to see you make a fool of yourself again."

"Lulu. What did she say about that Senator I'm after?"

"They can't pin anything on him. He's clean, that's what she said."

"Clean, hell, he's a crook, damn it, I'm sure of it."

"And if not you'll make it up as you go along, the same way you did with Lomax."

"So you think I should give it up. Throw in the towel, just like that."

She did not reply. With her back to me she went on rubbing down her horse. Leaving me to think about it. Clean? Not in a million years. Guilty as hell, the way he shouted about Lomax, that proved it. Except it didn't prove a damn thing. Maybe Bettelmy was right. Maybe Thornton knows what sells papers.

"How long have you been a reporter, Phil?" she asked, with her back still to me.

"How long? Long enough to know better."

"There's a ranch in Arizona I've been thinking about. We could move there."

"I'm not a goddamn rancher, I'm a newspaperman."

"I can buy it outright with the money from my last novel."

"What else did Lulu tell you?"

"You could write some kind of fiction. Real fiction, for a change."

"Lulu, what else did she say?"

"I couldn't go without you. You would have to come along, Phil."

The horse made a noise and she patted him on the head as she closed the gate to his stall. Horses. I didn't know a damned thing about horses. And not much about women, either. But I followed her to a nearby table, under an awning, where this dude ranch she hung out always kept a keg of ice cold Lone Star. Beer, that was something I knew about.

"That's not his real name" she said as she looked back at the stall. "His name is Rex."

"Maybe the other name was better, Vicky. You're right, I fantasize."

"I don't want to see you hurt, Phil. Once in jail is enough."

"That's all Lulu said, that Senator's clean?"

"There was something else, about a man named Rupert Mulrock."

"Mulrock, I never heard of him. What about him?"

"Murchock, Mulldoch, I'm not sure, we had a bad connection."

"Lulu thinks he might be involved with the LSI?"

"No, he's some foreigner who goes around buying up newspapers."

"So what? If he's not a crook, why did she even mention him?"

"I don't know, I think they're afraid of what he does when he buys them."

"And Congress is worried about that? Hell, let him buy all the damned papers in the country. Including the one I work for. He couldn't make it any worse."

I drew a second glass of beer from the keg and noticed she was smiling. Figuring, I imagined, that what I'd said meant yes, we're headed for Arizona. Maybe we were, I had no idea, I needed to clear my head and get my mind on something else. Anything, as long as it wasn't the newspaper business.

"You have a couple of days left before you go back to work. Think about it, Phil."

"I'd rather think about this beer I'm drinking."

"I could buy you a horse of your own. You could ride around with Matt Larue then."

"Not me. I don't ride on anything that doesn't have an on-off switch."

"Matt Larue has an on-off switch, or have you forgotten?"

"Go get in your car and I'll follow."

"My, my, I'll have to tell Rex I'm going for a ride with someone else."

"Damn right. Tell Rex the Frito Kid is on his way."

Broadway was blocked. A week out of touch and I needed to get back. I needed to make up my mind. Decide, for Vicky's sake and mine as well, whether I would go on being a reporter. I needed to see Bettelmy. But the street outside the paper was barricaded.

Police milling around next to an ambulance, all the signs someone had been run over. I parked behind the building and went in through the back way. Let some young police reporter cover it. I'd been there, I'd done that. Not anymore.

"Life and death in the street" I muttered when I got to the newsroom.

"Same old same old" said a reporter nearby, typing away with his hat on.

"The police are all over out there" I said. "Hard to get in the building."

"Not that one. He's been blocking the stairwell for a good half hour now."

"Why? What's going on upstairs?"

"Who cares? Who needs to go see Bettelmy, anyway?"

"I do. I don't want to, but it's time for me to see him."

Time to or not, I could not get past the policeman standing at the entrance to the stairwell. He held his arms out and stopped me.

"Look" I said. "I need to see the editor. What's the problem?"

"You can't go up there. The detectives are up there."

"What for? Officer, what's going on?"

"Keep your voice down. There's been a suicide, maybe a murder."

I looked around. The newsroom, full of reporters, and no one knew about a murder right under their nose? Maybe, hell, plain-clothes folks went up that stairwell all the time and no one noticed. And the police were keeping it quiet while they investigated. Sure. They knew how a reporter could screw things up looking over their shoulders.

"The editor" I said. "Bettelmy. Don't tell me he's involved."

"Don't ask me" said the policeman. "All I know is the detectives are up there."

"Look, I just got here, I'm his special assistant."

"Fine, but you can't go up there. No one can while they're asking questions."

"Officer, trust me, I'm the one who can tell them what they want to know."

He looked at me for a moment, then nodded and let me pass. Right, reporters can screw things up. And also lie like a whore in church to get near a story. This smelled like a real one. A murder, right here in the building? Forget about quitting for now. Get upstairs and find Bettelmy, find out what happened.

What I saw, when I got to Bettelmy's office, was not exactly what I expected. Miss Sarah, standing in the middle of the room, holding her hands behind her. Bettelmy, leaning against his desk. And two men, both detectives, no doubt about it, one of them looking out the window. The other one talking to her. Why? Why was he questioning her?

"Who are you?" asked the detective, turning to me.

"I work for Mister Bettelmy. I just got here."

"Then stand over there and keep your mouth shut. This is a murder investigation."

"Right, officer, I'll keep my mouth shut."

"Lady" he said, "we've identified the body down there. You knew him, I believe."

"Yes" she answered. "I understand it is Mister Thornton."

Damn. So that's who it was in the street. Thornton. Murdered. Someone had finally gotten to him. Whoever it was, this detective seemed to think Miss Sarah knew something about it, writing notes in a pad as he asked her questions.

"Paul Thornton, ma'am. How well did you know him?"

"Oh, my, many, many years."

"He was in here a few days ago" said Bettelmy.

"I am aware of that" said the detective, turning to Bettelmy.

"He used to work for me. He was with the TV station."

"I know, Mister Bettelmy, he was famous, so what did Thornton want from you?"

"He wanted to write again for the paper."

"Yes" said the detective. "I understand he cursed you, too."

"He did, because I wouldn't hire him for the paper."

"So for that reason you threw him off the roof? No, I didn't think so."

Bettelmy had not responded. The detective wrote something in his note pad and turned back to Miss Sarah. Cool. Not letting on what he already knew and what he didn't. Standard procedure in a murder investigation. I knew, I had served my time on the police beat. What I couldn't figure was why he wanted to pester her. Miss Sarah? What could she know?

"Ma'am, you said you knew him. Did you know he was afraid of heights?"

"Well, of course, we all are."

"I suppose someone he knew might have talked him into going up there."

"Oh, my indeed, Mister Thornton loved to talk."

"Were you here when he cursed your boss about the job he wanted?"

"Yes, of course, I am Mister Bettelmy's secretary."

"Have you ever been on the roof, ma'am?"

"When I was young I used to watch the pigeons there."

"Suppose I told you someone saw you going up to the roof with Mister Thornton."

"Oh, my, I'm much too old to use the stairwell now."

"I didn't mention the stairwell, ma'am. There's a service elevator also."

He looked down and wrote again in his note pad. I watched, feeling some sort of anger boiling up inside me. I don't know, maybe it was worrying about what to tell Vicky, maybe it was worrying about what I should do, whether I should quit or not, whatever it was I had had enough of this detective's cat and mouse game. Enough of his harassing poor Miss Sarah.

"Thornton had a lot of enemies" I blurted out.

"I told you to keep your mouth shut" said the detective.

"A lot of enemies. Leave her alone."

"Enemies, you say. Were you one of them?"

"Damned right I was, I despised that bastard. I'm sorry, Miss Sarah, no one should curse in front of you, I know, but yes, detective, I couldn't stand that sorry bastard."

"So where were you when he fell off the roof?"

"Don't answer" said Bettelmy. "Do what he told you, keep your mouth shut."

I looked at Bettelmy, still leaning against his desk. I was about to answer when the other detective, the one looking out the window, turned around and faced us. I recognized him. The chief of detectives, a man I had gotten to know when I worked the police beat. Always honest. Always on top of things.

"It was an accident" he said. "I'll take over now."

"Chief, this lady should be booked and held" said the other detective.

"He fell. Nobody pushed him. I'll write the report."

"All right, chief, if that's the way you want it, it's your call."

"It is" he said. "Go down and tell them to clear the street. Tell them it's all over." He waited a moment until he was alone with the three of us, Bettelmy and Miss Sarah and me, and when he spoke it was Miss Sarah he was looking at.

"I heard Phil say just now you don't like to hear cursing,"

"I do not" said Miss Sarah. "It is not worthy of a gentleman."

"Then I will apologize in advance."

"Yes, thank you, detective."

"Accidents. It's about time that sonofabitch had one."

He walked away, smiling as he went past me. Miss Sarah was also smiling as she returned to her office. She left her door open, I noticed, and I could hear her humming. I wasn't sure, and I could only hear it from a distance, but it sounded like she was humming the Eyes of Texas. She had prevailed, not much doubt about it. There would be no more cursing around her.

I was not so sure about Bettelmy. He sat down and started marking on his yellow pad with the circulation numbers on it. I waited, not certain what to tell him, trying to remember what I planned to say, before I came up here and learned what had happened to that bastard Thornton.

"His funeral will be huge, Phil. The whole city will turn out."

"Not me, you know what I thought about him. All poison."

"You covered Johnson's funeral."

"Of course I did. What about it?"

"You cover this one, too. And don't ask me why. Just do it."

He could be devious, I knew, but this was something else. I had come up here to have it out with him, I had learned of Thornton's death, I had seen Miss Sarah vindicated, and now he was telling me to cover the funeral? pThe anger I had felt a few minutes before was gone. In its place, a feeling of downright helplessness. Like stepping out of an elevator on the wrong damn floor. Or worse. Stepping out where there's no floor to step on.

That crooked Senator turning out to be untouchable, Bettelmy telling me to cover Thornton's funeral, and don't ask why, I was being jerked around, goddamn it.

The funeral was huge, just as Bettelmy had predicted. Thousands, standing beneath the trees surrounding the grave site, watching as the pallbearers carried the coffin from a hearse and placed it underneath an awning, where a preacher waited, whispering something in the PA system to make sure it was working. A spectacle most reporters would have leaped at.

But I couldn't do it, no matter what Bettelmy had told me, no matter what the gods of print might have in store for me. To hell with fate, I couldn't write about Thornton's funeral. Not a paragraph, not a word, not even a syllable. Not after what I witnessed as I watched from the edge of the cemetery.

The crowd was quiet, some of them weeping as the preacher read a sermon from the Bible. It wasn't the way they behaved that set me off. It was what they were holding in their hands. Signs, hundreds of signs, some home-made, most of the signs commercially printed, duplicated, so the same words showed up again and again among the mourners.

Send The Pepper Bellies Back To Mexico.
Only White Boys and Girls Need Schools.
No Blackies Buried In This Graveyard.
Don't Buy From Slant Eyed Japs.

There's No Place In Texas For Jews.
Keep America For Real Americans.
Paul Thornton: The Voice Of The Country.

A few signs saying things like impeach Nixon, some urging Texas to secede from the Union, some claiming Thornton was the last real Christian. The rest of them nothing but bitter echoes of his raving on TV. Thornton's legacy. Poison printed on signs. The most unnerving of all, too big to carry, was mounted on a billboard behind the coffin. His Voice Lives On.

Unnerving and ominous. Enough to make me realize, finally, where I stood. Too far out of the mainstream to fit in. If Thornton was dead but his voice lived on there was only one thing I could do. I thought about it all the way back to the office. Vicky was right. It was time to go hide on a ranch someplace.

At least Broadway was clear this time. No bodies in the street, no barricades. The newsroom was noisy, but I paid no attention. Only a glance at a package on my desk, wrapped with a ribbon and a card saying don't open if you're sober. I was sober as hell, and fed up with what had struck me, all at once, at Thornton's funeral. TV. The devil's workshop.

Fry disagreed. When he saw me sitting there, with a blank sheet of paper in my typewriter, hearing me tell about the signs at the cemetery, hearing me blame it on the way Thornton used TV, he told me I was wrong. Not wrong about Thornton, no, he was gone and good riddance. Wrong about television.

"Listen, Phil, we'd make a great team on the nightly broadcast."

"You stick to the baseball scores. I hate television."

"Hate it or not, you'd better face up to it. You're the leading candidate."

"Candidate for what? I've had it, Tom."

"Thornton's replacement. All you have to do is say yes to the station manager."

"What I have to do is say no to Bettelmy. I'm going up there now."

"Bettelmy? You haven't heard? There's been a shake-up in management, Phil."

"What I have to say won't shake him up. Hell, it may even make him happy."

I could never tell about Fry. Always joking, sometimes funny. That joke about me replacing Thornton, that wasn't funny. That was sick. He wasn't joking at all about a shake-up in management. Bettelmy was taking pictures off his wall and packing boxes when I got there. He was moving up, getting ready to join the big boys on the top floor of the building.

Moving up, with no time to waste on me. Not even looking at me when I tried to tell him I was finished with the newspaper business. He was too busy packing boxes.

"Bill, I'm sorry. I couldn't do it."

"You couldn't do what?"

"I couldn't write about Thornton's funeral. It was too disgusting."

"Too disgusting for you to write about it."

"It did prove one thing. Thornton's TV shit poisoned half this town."

"That's why I sent you to cover the funeral, Phil."

"I did, but I couldn't write about it. I'm done for, Bill."

"Too bad. We could have printed it in the Light this coming Sunday."

"The Light? What are you talking about?"

"I'm moving over there. What the hell do you think I'm packing for?"

Some things are too damned hard to swallow. Bettelmy, trying to get the goods on the Hearst crowd and put the Light out of business, giving up on that but still trying to close the gap in circulation, and now telling me what? He surrendered and decided to join them?

Swallow it, hell, no way. I was in no mood to chew on it, either. Let him. If he wanted to sell out, fine, why should I care? I was headed West with Vicky. All he had done was give me the green light for Arizona. As soon as I could say adios, amigo.

"The London papers. Have you ever seen a London tabloid, Phil?"

"No, but listen, I. . ."

"Scandals and gossip. That's where this paper is headed."

"I'm headed someplace else, Bill."

"Damned right, we both are. Let them buy it, we're out of here."

"Wait. . .wait a minute. . ."

Bettelmy went on packing boxes. I watched, trying to recall what Vicky told me Lulu had said. Something about some foreigner buying up papers. Who knows? Maybe he bought this one. A shake-up in management, maybe that's why Bettelmy was packing to leave.

"So you quit? Because they're going to turn the paper upside down?"

"I didn't quit. I've been canned, Phil."

"You were fired? Why? Because you wouldn't. . ."

"Because I wouldn't let Thornton write a column filled with shit, that's why. "

"That was a week ago, Bill, that was. . ."

"Last night, the new owners made it official. I knew it was coming."

"You knew a week ago? You. . ."

"Hell, yes, the Light snapped me up when I told them."

"But you were fired, you just said, you waited until. . ."

"Severance pay, Phil. It cost them a fortune to fire me."

Bettelmy pushed the boxes aside and sat down at his desk, laughing like hell. I hadn't planned to listen, I had come upstairs to tell him I was quitting, but this was too rich to skip over. Bettelmy, going to the Light with a wagon load of money, and laughing as he looked at me, telling me how he'd outwitted the new owners. Too smart for me to keep up with.

"You want to hear something really amusing, Phil? What they want to do with you?"

"Screw them. I'm not staying here."

"They reviewed what you wrote about the LSI. How you stirred up the country."

"That was your idea as much as mine, listen. . ."

"They want you to take Thornton's place on television."

"You think that's funny? I don't."

"Good. Go with me. Write about the funeral. That's why I sent you there."

"You've had it all planned out, I see."

"We'll run it in the Light this Sunday. Hell, I'll give you a raise when you get there."

"No way, Bill, I've made up my mind. I'm not going with you."

"Don't be a fool. Sarah's already over there, she's. . ."

Bettelmy was still going at it when I left his office. I went downstairs, picked up some things from my desk, and left the building. Enough of this. No job, no Pulitzer, no future to speak of, but piss on it, I would learn how to ride a horse if I had to. Something else I would have to learn, as well. How to let Vicky support me.

I opened the package when I got in my car. A gift from the ladies in the society section. A blown-up copy of the picture they had run four months ago, the day LBJ died. The one with Molly in the background, or so I thought. Framed, with a magnifying glass attached. The note said don't open if you're sober. On the back, another note. Keep things in focus.

Some sense of humor they had, those ladies. I would have to send them a letter and thank them for the gift. I wouldn't tell them I had opened it prematurely, when I was sober. No need to. I was headed home to fix that right away. For now, at least, that was my only future. Getting drunk, trying to forget I'd once been a reporter.

Vicky was working at her typewriter when I got there. I slipped past her as quietly as I could, on my way to the kitchen to pour a double bourbon. Keeping the noise down so she could go on writing. So she could go on turning out novels. Right, so she could put bread on the table, whatever it takes to feed an unemployed husband.

Evidently I was not quiet enough. I heard her calling out, over the sound of the typing, all the way to the kitchen.

"You're back. You could have said hello when you came in."

"Two funerals in one day, I need a drink first."

"Two? Thornton's and who else?"

"Mine. My own damned funeral, Vicky."

"Really. Sounds to me like you're still breathing."

"Phillip Dee, the ace reporter, dead and gone."

"My, my, so who is that in the kitchen?"

"A derelict in need of room and board, babe."

I added some ice cubes to my drink and sat down on the sofa behind her, watching as she continued writing. Amazed, as always, at how she could type so fast and talk without looking up as she went on grinding out fiction.

"A derelict. So you quit your job and you're ready to head out West."

"I did and I am. I suppose you've heard about Bettelmy."

"Sarah told me. The Light. There's a real scoop for you, Phil."

"Not me, no one would believe it. What are you working on?"

"A short story. About a city slicker who winds up at a dude ranch."

"Right, there's a scoop. Stop the presses."

"He falls in love with the owner and sticks around to write about horses."

"That's only half correct. I'm through writing, Vicky."

"What makes you think this story's about you?"

"Wishful thinking, babe. You brought the mail in?"

"It's in there. You had a couple of registered letters I signed for."

She went on typing as I wandered off to my desk with another drink in my hand. Wishful thinking, hell, that story she was working on was not about me. Some dude who writes about horses? No way. I would have to settle for something less exciting. Or quit altogether. Maybe that's what she was thinking when she joined me and gave me a kiss on the forehead.

"Listen, Phil, you're not through writing."

"Travel guides, that's all I'll be good for."

"I've told you, when we get to Arizona you can write whatever you want."

"A cactus brochure, how does that sound?"

"Phil, what in the world is that picture on your desk?

"That's a going-away gift, from the ladies at the paper."

"With a magnifying glass attached? What is that, some kind of joke?"

"It's so I can keep things in focus. So I won't step in cow shit."

"You have a twisted mind, you know that?"

"Go finish your story, Vicky. Let me dig through the mail."

I pushed the picture aside, had another go at my drink, and sorted the mail into piles. Ads, bills, and the two registered letters. The ads I disposed of. The bills were another matter. With what I had saved from the syndication payoff I had enough to keep things going until we headed for Arizona. After that, hell, Vicky would have to support us.

The registered letters were both from Washington, and they looked like bills, as well. The first one shook me, before I saw who it was meant for. One thousand nine hundred dollars. From the Western Union office there, past due and delinquent. Still owed by the paper. Not by me, this was only my copy. Maybe they figured I should nudge my bosses. I tossed it away.

After I opened it and saw what was in it, the second one damned near floored me. I could not believe it. I shook my head, and then I smiled and nodded, and then I started laughing, so loud Vicky came and stood in front of me, looking at me and wondering. I held the letter up so she could see it, but I could not stop laughing.

"Phil, you're going to rupture a gut. Calm down."

"Life. . .life. . .by God, it is. . .it's a game of inches. . ."

"Life? What's in that letter? What's so funny?"

I could feel the tears rolling down my face I was laughing so hard. I tried to stop and tell her. Not easy. But I managed. She said I had a twisted mind, hell yes, but not so twisted I couldn't tell what that letter meant. And what it reminded me of.

"I knew a fellow from Brooklyn who called it that. A game of inches, Vicky."

"That sounds like baseball talk. What's so funny about that?"

"Baseball, right. Sometimes the ball rolls safe, sometimes it's foul by inches."

"I can't follow you. What does that mean?"

"It's all random, that's what it means. Life. It's all a matter of chance, Vicky."

"Like Thornton falling off that roof? That was a week ago, that was. . ."

"No, not that. It's what's in this letter, Vicky."

"Really. I'll get you another drink, maybe you can explain it."

I looked at the picture as she went to the kitchen. The photo I had thought showed Molly in it. The picture that had led me to Washington. And then one damned thing after another, all because of that picture, all random.

Vicky meeting Senator Amador by accident, random as hell, no doubt about it. Lulu working for Amador, Baxter flying with Bettelmy, no rhyme or reason to it. That Senator from Ohio throwing me in jail. My meeting Big Nick The Fixer there, one more accident.

Even the way I got involved with Vicky in the first place. By chance. Too much for her to grasp, I knew, hell, I could barely add it up myself. All I could do, when she came back, was point to the letter.

"Look at that" I said. "See the initials on the envelope?"

"R.M.B. So what, Phil? That's part of the return address, so. . ."

"Look inside at the name on the letterhead. Then read what it says."

"It's from someone named Rosetta Maria Balderetti. So?"

"Go ahead, read it, you'll see why I started laughing when I opened it."

"It says her uncle told her to send this to you. What's so funny about that?"

"It's signed Rosie. Here, look what came with the letter."

"My God, Phil, this is a certified check for fifty thousand dollars!"

"You see what I mean? It's all random. All luck, a matter of chance."

"Her uncle? She sent this check for him? Who is he?"

"An old crook I met in jail. By accident, Vicky."

"Phil, damn it, stop laughing. What does this check mean?"

"It means l have something to write about now. The Mafia."

She went to the kitchen and returned a moment later with a drink of her own. Still wondering, I could tell. But grinning, too, as she sat down beside me.

"Phil, I don't understand, but if you're happy about it, so am I."

"Hell, yes. This is something to celebrate."

"Then I had better finish my story. It is about you after all, I was only teasing."

"The city slicker who makes out big time, right."

"I'll yell when I'm finished. You'll hear the ending."

I put the check in the letter from Rosie and locked it in my desk. When I looked again at the picture from the society page I was not laughing, not any longer. Only thinking.

Remembering what Mel Lamont had said that night in Washington, when we were talking about Molly, when he told me how she was poison.

Phillip Dee, old buddy, you're a lucky sonofabitch, he said.

I was thinking about that when I heard Vicky call out. The ending of her story.

"Ride 'em, cowboy!" she yelled.

I was one lucky sonofabitch, all right. Ride 'em cowboy!

DRUNK FROM THE HO CHI TRAIL

I HELD HER HAND AND WHISPERED LOOK, I'M HERE, I'M SORRY. I knew she could not hear me, but I whispered again, Molly, look, damn it, I'm here, it's me. I watched her for a while, lying there unconscious. Breathing through an oxygen mask. Fragile. Your wife has lost weight, the doctors said, we're not sure but she may come around if she wakes up and sees you. All I could do was wait and wonder.

I closed the door to her room and stood in the hallway, smoking a cigarette and asking myself if I was really to blame. Midnight. Three hours of waiting and wondering, watching the nurses come and go, waiting for the right doctor to show up, waiting for someone to tell me what was wrong with her. Half asleep as I leaned against a wall, trying to understand what had happened to Molly this time.

"Are you Major Dee?" I heard someone ask.

"I'm Phillip Dee. You must be the doctor we've been waiting for."

"Two hours from Kansas City, I'm sorry, I had a patient to take care of."

"So you're in private practice, fine, maybe you can figure out what's wrong with her."

"I must ask you a few questions first. And please put out that cigarette."

"Listen, Doctor, this is the goddamn Army, do you understand that?"

"Yes, of course I understand, but. . ."

"You've never had your ass reamed out by a land mine."

"No. . .no, but. . ."

"I'm too damned tired to argue with you. Go ahead, ask your questions."

"All right, I will. I was told you have just arrived from Saigon. Is that correct?"

"Correct. Emergency leave. What else?"

"I was also told you have served three tours in Vietnam. Is that correct?"

"Correct. Go in there and see what's wrong with her."

"I think I can tell you already. You should have stayed home more often."

Right. Stay home and ride it out. Like all these draft dodging bastards back here. Like this doctor. Pompous. As if he could tell what the hell's wrong without even looking at her. I felt like knocking him down, but I was too worn out to do it. The nurse who joined us in the hallway understood. She was all Army.

"Keep your major away from me" the doctor told her as he entered Molly's room.

"Yes" said the nurse. "We have another place where he can wait. . ."

"Wait? Damn it nurse, I've been waiting long enough."

"Here" she said, as she led me to the hospital lounge. "Watch out for the Christmas tree."

I sat down on a sofa and looked at the tree. Still up. Another Christmas I had missed with Molly. You're exhausted, get some rest, said the nurse, let the doctor look at your wife, we'll let you know when you can see her. Right, get some rest, wait for a shrink to tell me what's wrong with Molly.

Rest, hell, I was back in the jungle in a matter of minutes. Surrounded by Cong, thousands in their black pajamas. Yelling on the radio. Lone Ranger Six, roger, fire mission, over, over, pour it on those bastards. Wake up, said the nurse, you've been dreaming, you can see your wife now, she's asleep but you will see she's breathing better.

I pushed a blanket away and found my glasses. The nurse, whoever she was, had covered me so I could sleep. I looked at my watch as I followed her to Molly's room. Six a.m. I had been out for hours, the first sleep I had since I left Saigon, thinking about Molly, wondering what had happened to her.

"Her pulse is better" said the doctor standing beside her bed, an Army colonel. "The specialist from Kansas City was not much help, so come back this afternoon, I need to go over her medical history with you. I have some questions about your wife's condition."

Questions. Right. Like what the hell am I doing at Fort Leavenworth. Like why she stayed here while I was gone, like what she's been up to while I've been off fighting the goddamned war. Like. . .

"I've been on leave" said the nurse. "But from what I've heard your wife was lucky."

"Lucky? I hadn't heard from her in months, she. . ."

"She was working as a Red Cross volunteer, you know."

"No, I was not aware of that."

"On New Year's Day, she did not show up. It's a good thing they found her."

"Found her? Where? The last I heard, she was living off post, she. . ."

"She was unconscious. She's been that way ever since."

"Nurse, that was weeks ago, and these doctors still don't know what's wrong?"

"No. I understand the Army sent for you, but they couldn't find you, they. . ."

"Where I was, hell, it's an accident they found me at all."

"Come with me. You need some breakfast, major."

Scrambled eggs. The Army lives off scrambled eggs in the morning. I pushed my tray away and lit a cigarette, looking around at five or six patients limping in for breakfast. Ambulatory, in blue hospital clothing marked CGSC. The Command and General Staff College, keeping field grade types in shape, even if the war was all but over.

"I was a student here" I said. "She stayed behind when I left again for Nam."

"New Year's Day" said the nurse. "I imagine she was lonely."

"Lonely. . .maybe. . . I don't know. . ."

"I do. I lost my husband last year in the Delta."

"I'm sorry, nurse, I. . ."

"We've put your bags downstairs. You can get cleaned up before you see the doctor."

"Thanks. . .I'll shave and take a shower. . .I. . ."

"We'll take care of you. The Army, we have to care about each other."

"Right..."

"Now eat your breakfast. Coffee and cigarettes won't do it, major."

A different nurse led me into Molly's room that afternoon. An Army captain, red haired and looking all worn out. Like me. A veteran of Nam herself, I guessed by the way she was limping. Lieutenant Truesdell was here last night, said the captain, she told me the doctor who came from Kansas City insulted you, don't worry about him, I don't trust civilian doctors, either.

The oxygen mask was gone and Molly's eyes were open. But there was no response when I asked her how she was feeling. The nurse said she's still out of it, she can't hear you, please follow me, her doctor is waiting in his office to talk to you about your wife's condition.

"She's not well" said her doctor. The same colonel, with a file in his hand.

"What's wrong with her? You have any idea yet?"

"She was once a Red Cross worker, in Germany, according to this record."

"Before we were married, yes. . ."

"So she knew about drugs and their effect."

"Drugs? What are you getting at? What about drugs?"

"On New Year's Day, she was fortunate, major. Quite fortunate."

"I understand they found her off post, yes, but. . ."

"Valium, Major. She overdosed on valium. A whole bottle, evidently."

Damn, so that's how it happened. Valium. Molly, all alone at Christmas, all alone on New Year's Day, depressed and despondent. And angry, maybe. My fault once again, not being here. Always my fault. My fault from the beginning.

"How bad is it, colonel? How bad did she hurt herself?"

"She will survive. Has she tried this before?"

"No. . .no. . .she had trouble with my being gone, I know, but. . ."

"When we move her on post you will have to watch her closely."

"On post? Doctor, I'm not stationed here, I. . ."

"You are now, major. Fort Leavenworth. Here, read this."

He handed me a page from a message pad. You can use my phone, he said, you can check for yourself, I have other things to do. I looked at the message and dialed the number on it. The Leavenworth personnel office. Stationed here? No way, damn it, I don't belong here.

"You were asked for" said a personnel officer on the telephone.

"Asked for? I'm on emergency leave, what are you talking about?"

"Colonel Woods, the commandant of faculty, he asked for you personally."

"How do I reach him?"

"Colonel Clarence Woods, wait, I'll give you his office number."

Woods. That Woods. Twelve years since I had my last run in with him. Over Molly, at Fort Campbell. Hard to forget what he said. You're making a mistake, lieutenant, if you marry the wrong woman you'll regret it. Woods, a major then, one of the first to volunteer for Vietnam, not there for the wedding. Why would he want to keep me here?

Not the kind of man to ask on the phone. A colonel now? Hell, no wonder, they must have loved it in the Pentagon, the way he handled that interview on television. Dan Proctor, no less, asking questions about Negroes bearing the brunt in Nam.

I may look black on camera, Woods had told him, but here in the jungle the only color we worry about is yellow.

Not bad. I had seen it myself and nodded. Woods, all soldier, since the first day we faced off in Germany. I braced myself as I waited outside his office.

"How is your wife?" he asked when I stood in front of his desk.

"She's unconscious, colonel. She's in the hospital here."

"Yes, I know. My wife is a friend of hers."

"That's not why I asked to see you, sir."

"I suppose you want to know why you're being kept here."

"I'm on emergency leave, colonel. I have a job to do in Nam, I. . ."

"You're not going back. No one is. Vietnam is over, major, you should know that."

Of course I knew it. We all knew it, we had guessed it would end this way, no parades, no celebration, no cheering crowds, nothing. Standing in front of a desk and being told it's over, that's all. No more war, no more reason for being gone. No more excuses. No more running from a shaky marriage. Vietnam was over.

"Move your wife on post, major. Get your life in order."

"Colonel, if I'm not going back, I'm supposed to be assigned to Bragg then."

"Too bad. You should not have shown up here on emergency leave."

"So why are you keeping me here? Damn it colonel, I have a right to know."

"Later. By the way, you're on the promotion list. Three tours, I hope it was worth it."

Woods. Mentioning Molly in a backhanded way, perhaps. Worth it? None of his business. I started to leave, but he had something else to say. He was looking at a map of Vietnam on a wall above his TV set.

"Bahn Bahn, major, I wonder if that was worth it, too."

"A village near Pleiku. What about it?"

"You don't need to know right now. Report to me next Friday morning."

I left without saluting. Remembering what he told me a dozen times before, years ago at Campbell, never salute him in his office. Remembering how I felt like cursing him, instead, when he said my life would change if I married Molly.

None of his business, not then, not now. Woods could go on looking at his map, wondering about Bahn Bahn for some reason. Fine, let him. I had no idea what was going on, all I knew was I was here because she'd had a breakdown here. Stuck here because of Molly, with no idea how long it would take her to recover.

Weeks, maybe months, maybe never. And something else I discovered along the way. It wouldn't matter.

She won't touch her breakfast, she won't eat a bite, said the part-time maid I had hired when I returned from running. Something I had learned early on as a soldier, run hard in the morning. Run, get your mind off whatever's bothering you. I was covered with sweat when I entered the kitchen. And still bothered.

I sat down and glanced at the headlines in the morning paper. Lyndon Johnson, dead of a heart attack. Poor bastard, he would not be around to see how his war came out. When the maid mentioned Molly again I looked up and reassured her.

"Clara, I know you fixed what the hospital said to give her."

"Every meal, every day, just like you told me, major."

"Colonel Woods' wife, tell her I appreciate her letting you help with Molly."

"You had better tell her, major. That lady won't listen to me."

"I know, she's a lot like him. So why do you go on working for her?"

"A colored woman like me, with two boys to raise, I need every penny, major."

She took off her apron and picked up her purse, getting ready to leave, when she said something else that caught my attention.

Telling me how she hoped my wife would get better, how Miss Molly had seemed fine on New Year's Eve, when she was at the colonel's place for lunch, fine, until she talked with the colonel's wife before leaving.

"On New Year's Eve, Clara? What were they talking about?"

"I don't know, but it looked like Miss Molly was crying when she left."

"Really. Crying, after she talked with the colonel's wife."

"I'll get along now, major. Nurse Truesdell is in there with her."

I watched as she left for her real job. Working for a colonel's wife. Ramona Woods, full of gossip back at Campbell. Asking me one night at a party if it was true, what her husband had said about me. I imagined things, he had told her, and she wondered if that was why I imagined I should marry Molly.

Years ago, telling everyone how her husband was going to be the first black general. A goddamned gossip, and still at it. No telling what she'd told Molly on New Year's Eve.

"She's asleep," said Lieutenant Truesdell as she joined me in the kitchen.

"Resting, I hope. Sometimes she seems better, sometimes she doesn't."

"You have to report tomorrow, you told me. Here, I'll show you what we've done."

I followed her into Molly's room, where she pointed to the phone next to the bed, being careful not to wake her up. And back to the kitchen, where she showed me a red button on our other phone. These were installed just now, she said, while you were out running. All your wife has to do is press the button on either phone, help will be here right away then.

"That takes a load off my mind, lieutenant. Sit down, I'll pour you some coffee."

"Fine, but as often as I've been here, you don't need to keep calling me lieutenant."

"How about Lieutenant Rebecca, then? I'll be Major Phil."

"Major Phil. You know, that's the first time I've seen you smile, Major Phil."

A good nurse, this lieutenant. Dropping by every morning after getting off work at the hospital. Telling me how she caved in when she learned her husband had been killed. But nothing like my wife, in a coma after taking valium, mumbling names and strange words, acting like she had no reason left to live.

"It's strange" said the nurse, "the way she keeps talking in her sleep."

"I know, I hear her from the other room at night. She's. . ."

"The same words, over and over. Mel, Mel, and bomb, bomb."

"She knew a Mel once. We both did. But bomb, bomb, why that?"

"I don't know. But before I go, let me see you smile again."

She patted me on the shoulder as she got up to leave, saying you have my number, call me if you need me. I lit a cigarette and sat there, looking through the open door into Molly's room. Wondering, as I had for days, each time I thought about it.

Wondering if it was my fault, off to Nam again and again, maybe to get away from Molly, I wasn't sure. Wondering if Woods was right, my life would change if I married her.

Wondering why she would mumble bomb, bomb, in her sleep. I had heard it myself, all the way in the other room, Molly calling out for Mel and shouting bomb, bomb.

Wondering what Ramona Woods had said to her on New Year's Eve, wondering what led Molly to down a whole bottle of valium.

Bomb, bomb, hell. That was Bahn Bahn she was shouting. That was Mel Lamont she was crying out about. Mel, who wanted to marry her, involved somehow in that damned village.

It wasn't me at all, not my missing Christmas once again, it was Mel and something Molly had been told, that's why she tried to drown herself in valium.

Bahn Bahn, damn it, that was during Tet, five years ago. That woman Ramona, with all her goddamn gossip, what had she heard, what had she told Molly?

I didn't know. I was covered with sweat from running. And too strung out to think about it. Leave it alone, wait until tomorrow, ask Woods what kind of crap his wife fed Molly, what she told her about Bahn Bahn.

Woods was not about to let me ask, I could tell when I reported to him. He had an open file on his desk, and he was shaking his head as he read it. Muttering something I could not hear. Not even looking up as I stood in front of him, with his head still down when he pointed to a window behind him.

"Look out there" he said. "What can you see?"

"Buildings, colonel, what am I supposed to see?"

"If you know where to look you can see the prison from here."

"The Leavenworth Penitentiary, what about it?"

"Calley spent time there, major, did you know that?"

"Calley, sure, for the My Lai massacre, what about him?"

"Sit down, I will tell you why I kept you here."

I sat down. So Calley had served time in the Leavenworth pen. He was back at Benning now, under house arrest, I heard, so what? I waited for Woods to tell me what Calley had to do with me. He seemed concerned with something else when he spoke, still looking at the file on his desk.

"You were a newspaper man before you joined the Army."

"I was, yes, a long time ago, back in Texas."

"Dan Proctor, I believe he was your friend at one time."

"Proctor? The anchorman? Sure, I knew him."

"The most powerful man in television, I understand."

"I suppose. The last time I saw him was in Germany."

"Thirteen years ago, to be exact."

"What about him? Why are you asking me about Proctor?"

"I will tell you. . .wait. . ."

Woods reached for a telephone as it rang. Yes, general, he said, he is with me now. With his hand over the receiver he motioned to me to wait outside his office. I did, wondering why some general would want to know if I was there, thinking about Proctor, puzzled why Woods had asked about him.

Dan Proctor. The biggest name in television. A long way from Houston, where I first knew him. A long way from Bavaria, where Woods and I had first been stationed together. A long time ago, but not hard to remember.

Proctor, getting his start in television then, coming to Germany to cover a speech by John Lomax, the crooked politician I had known in Texas when I was a reporter. Broadcasting live, exposing Lomax with the inside information I gave him. Proctor's first big break in television. Years ago, friends then, sure, but I had no idea why Woods would ask me about him.

I could see through the glass panel in his door he was nodding as he talked on the phone. He was looking at his watch and writing something on a note pad. When he hung up I went back in, ready to find out what the hell was going on here.

"What's this about Proctor?" I asked.

"That was General Calloway on the phone. He's in command here, major."

"Calloway? Why would Calloway want to know where I am?"

"You will find out soon enough. This afternoon, two o'clock in his office."

"Damn, colonel, he threatened to court martial me in Nam."

"I know, I heard you tried to shoot some visiting Senator."

"You heard wrong, then. It wasn't the Senator, it was. . ."

Woods held his hand up, with an open palm, as if to say shut up. Fine, let him think what he likes, it wasn't a Senator I wanted to shoot, it was who was with him. Lomax. And it wouldn't have mattered, anyway, if I shot the bastard. He had nine lives. Proctor and me, we drove him out of office in Texas, and there he was in Nam, building runways for the Army.

Proctor. Maybe that's why Woods had asked about him. Something to do with Lomax.

Wrong. Woods had something else on his mind.

"Listen carefully, major. There may have been a massacre at Bahn Bahn."

"Like My Lai, you mean. . ."

"General Calloway has been ordered to find out."

"That's why you've kept me here? To help with that?"

"A perfect assignment for you."

"And then what? What if it's true?"

"Proctor must be told at once then. You have access to him."

"So he'll know the Army has nothing to hide. Very clever, colonel."

I was sure he could sense the sarcasm in my voice. Clever, all right. Bypass the regular channels, go straight to Proctor. Except for one thing Woods left out. Bahn Bahn, after all these years, why it's surfaced now. Why? If someone stumbles onto that, hell, maybe Proctor himself, it won't matter if it's true. Another My Lai scandal. Headlines, all over again.

"What if there's a leak, colonel? What happens then?"

"This must be kept close hold. A leak? Out of the question."

Out of the question, hell. There was something else Woods had left out. Something I had been chewing on all morning, adding it up, thinking about what the maid said and what Nurse Rebecca told me. Getting more and more pissed off at Woods as I thought about it, what was wrong with Molly.

"There's been a leak already, colonel. Your wife knows about Bahn Bahn."

"My wife? No way."

"No way? She sure as hell said something to Molly about it."

"Ramona. . .she. . ."

"On New Year's Eve. Whatever it was, that's why Molly damned near killed herself with valium."

Woods slumped back in his chair. Looking straight at me, silent. Not a word, no expression at all on his face. No way of knowing what he might be thinking. But easy to guess. He knew damn well he had leaked it himself.

Screw him. He's kept me here, fine. And now I'm supposed to see Calloway, I'm supposed to dig into a goddamn massacre. With a sick wife on my hands. To hell with Woods. To hell with that gossiping bitch Ramona, too.

I walked out of his office, leaving Woods sitting there, silent.

Lieutenant General Calloway was not so quiet when I reported to him. I had barely finished my salute when he started talking, not to me or his aide, just talking, in the Southern accent the troops tried to imitate, but couldn't. GSB, they called him. The Great Southern Breeze. Hard not to like him, unless you let him down. No Southern Breeze then. All Army.

"Politicians, good old politicians" he drawled, looking up at the ceiling. "A country boy like me, bless my heart, I do find politicians hard to swallow. The way they try to run the Army, the things they worry about, like public relations, you would think we're in some kind of goddamned Miss America contest."

After a moment he looked down and came around his desk to face me. Chewing on an unlit cigar, still looking dumpy, like the last time I saw him. Short and a bit overweight, looking more like a county sheriff than the man some thought might be the smartest general in the whole damned Army.

"I see you're on the promotion list" he said.

"Yes, sir. But I'm still a major, the same as when I saw you near Dak To."

"Dak To, have you been there?" he asked, turning to his aide.

"No, sir" replied the aide, a captain whose nameplate said Reilly.

"Dee has" said the general, still looking at his aide. "Have you heard what he did there?"

"No, sir" the aide replied.

"He threatened to shoot a Senator who showed up with some friends in tow. He hates politicians as much as I do."

I said nothing. What happened at Dak To was more complicated than that. And the general knew it. I kept my mouth shut as he went on talking to his aide. About the way he had been advised I should be court martialed. Or worse, thrown out of the Army. About the reason I survived, instead. Because I hated politicians as much as he did.

"Reilly" he said. "Let that be a lesson for you. I don't imagine they taught you that at West Point."

"A lesson, general? I don't think I follow you" his aide responded.

"Of course you don't. Wait outside while I talk to Major Dee."

Calloway smiled as he watched his aide depart. Class of sixty six, he said, naïve as hell, that young captain, he's working on his master's degree, he'll go a long way in the new Army. The new Army, Dee, all public relations and television, that's why you're here, and not back at Bragg on parachute status.

He was silent for a moment. An old airborne soldier himself, wounded at Normandy with the Eighty Second. I had read the book he wrote with Ridgeway, a long time ago, about airborne tactics. Before Vietnam. Before the dawn of helicopters. Before the dawn of television.

"Bad timing, Dee" said the general. "Showing up on emergency leave."

"Yes, sir. Colonel Woods told me I'm to. . ."

"Politicians. A week before Christmas, the Secretary of the Army called me."

"About Bahn Bahn, general? Woods said. . ."

"Find out, that's all the Secretary asked. Woods was looking for someone to do it."

"And then I showed up. But why now? Bahn Bahn, that was five years ago, that. . ."

"The colonel in command, his wife thinks there may have been a massacre."

"His wife? What does his wife have to do with it? What about this colonel?"

"He was killed a few months ago. She's given his letters to the secretary."

"His letters? Why?"

He merely grunted. As he did I realized how strange he was acting. Short, clipped sentences, no longer the Great Southern Breeze. Not since Bahn Bahn had come up.

"Wives" he said. "You remember that saying about wives?"

"What saying? I'm not sure I. . ."

"If the Army wanted you to have a wife it would issue you one."

"Wives, yes sir, I. . ."

"This woman and her letters. Wives cause half our goddamned problems."

As Calloway spoke he reached in his desk and pulled out a stack of files, three or four inches thick at least. He looked in one of the files, took out a single page, put it away, and pushed the rest across his desk toward me.

"Her letters, general, I assume they're in these files."

"No. The secretary will not release them."

"He won't release them? But he's ordered an inquiry?"

No answer from Calloway, but from the look on his face it was clear he knew why I was puzzled. This woman's husband has been killed, she gives his letters to the secretary, she thinks there may have been a massacre, Calloway's been ordered to find out, and there's no way of knowing what's in the letters?

"This doesn't make any sense" I blurted out. "What's going on here, general?"

No answer for that question, either. Without a word he looked down at the files and pushed them closer to me.

"Study these records, major. The brigade and division logs during Tet."

"Fine. What I'd like to know is. . ."

"You will be talking to several people. Find out what you can."

"About Bahn Bahn, right. Find out, and then what?"

"Keep Woods informed, he's my deputy in this matter. No one else is to know."

"Dan Proctor, what about him, general? Woods said. . ."

"Proctor, that TV shithead? Woods has a bug up his ass about him."

"Maybe since that interview in Nam. I don't know, but. . ."

Calloway did not reply. Instead he reached in his desk and pulled out another folder. Thin, not many pages, but evidently one too many. He removed a page, folded it, and put it away. To go with the page he took from the files he was giving me to dig into. A three-star general, acting mighty strange.

"This is a list Woods put together" said Calloway. "People to see. Tell them I sent you. Find out what they know." He chewed on his cigar as I looked at the list, turning the pages, looking for a name not there, checking to be sure I had not missed it. A dozen names, generals down to captain. The address of the woman who had given her husband's letters to the Secretary, scratched out and barely legible. Names, but not the one I was looking for.

"Mel Lamont, sir, I thought I would see his name on the list."

"Lamont" he snapped. "Why that name?"

"A nurse. . .a nurse at the hospital. . ."

"That name's off limits. That's why it's not on the list."

"Maybe so, but my wife heard something, general."

"Off limits. I have my orders, major."

"Orders? From the Secretary of the Army, I understand, but. . ."

"I hate politicians, but I damned well know how to follow orders."

He was frowning, chewing on his cigar and looking straight at me. I waited, wondering why that woman's letters were restricted, what Calloway's orders might be, why Lamont's name was off limits. Why Calloway had not asked me what my wife had heard.

"Your wife" said Calloway. "She was in the hospital."

"New Year's Day, general."

"Too bad. If she hadn't gotten sick you would not have been on leave here."

"No sir, I wouldn't."

"So it's because of her you're now involved in this."

"Yes sir, I suppose that's true."

"Wives. That's why the Army doesn't issue wives, Dee."

He pressed a button on his intercom. A moment later his aide returned and the general told him to guide me to my new office. I saluted, picked up the stack of files and left. Thinking about a lot of things, most of all what Calloway had just said about Molly. If she hadn't gotten sick I wouldn't be involved in this.

The Great Southern Breeze, how little he knew. If it hadn't been for her I wouldn't be involved? Hell, if it hadn't been for her I wouldn't even be in the Army.

She seemed better the next morning when I came back from running. She's eaten breakfast, said the maid Clara. She's gone back to sleep, said Lieutenant Rebecca. Three women, one cooking, one sleeping, one going back to her quarters. All quiet on the home front when I left for my office.

Not so when I returned. One crying, one screaming, one shaking her head and pleading. Three women in different stages of despair and depression.

I had spent the day poring through the logs General Calloway gave me. Something puzzling about them. The way they wouldn't match, the division record showing one thing, the brigade log showing something else. Puzzling, all right, but not as puzzling as what I found when I got back that evening.

"Clara, what's going on? Why are you crying?"

"Miss Ramona, she was here, she was yelling at Miss Molly."

"Yelling? What about? Clara, stop crying and tell me,"

"I didn't know what to do, the way Miss Molly started screaming."

"Ramona, what did she say to Molly?"

"I don't know, Miss Ramona fired me when I asked her."

"Molly, what's she screaming about?"

"I didn't know what to do, I called Nurse Truesdell, she's. . ."

The screaming had died down by the time I opened the door to Molly's room. She was sitting on the edge of her bed, looking up at Lieutenant Rebecca and sobbing. I stood in the doorway, uncertain, unnerved, I suppose, by what I had stumbled into. Watching as the nurse held Molly's head, trying to calm her. Waiting, watching, not knowing what I should do.

After a moment I joined them. Standing next to the nurse I could not see Molly's face, but I could hear her saying something, words mixed with weeping. Not my fault, she kept mumbling, even as the nurse got her into bed. Not my fault, over and over again, even as the nurse stuck a needle in her arm, saying here, Molly, get some rest now.

"What's that?" I asked. "Something to calm her down?"

"Doctor's orders" said Lieutenant Rebecca. "Give her a sedative."

"What's she mumbling? Not her fault? What does that mean?"

"I have no idea. She'll go to sleep, maybe then I can get some sleep myself."

"Not her fault. . .not her fault for what?"

"I suggest you take care of Clara. She's in as bad a shape as your wife is." pRight. Clara was leaning into the kitchen sink, trying to clean some pots and pans, crying, with her back to me, when I came out of Molly's room and closed the door behind me. A nurse barking at me about my wife, a maid bawling about losing her job, not exactly the sort of thing I was trained to cope with.

"Clara, calm down" I said. "Don't worry about it."

"What will I do?" she moaned. "That woman fired me. . .

She went on crying, still fiddling around with the pots and pans. I sat down, trying to figure out how I might help her, remembering what she told me about raising her kids. And also thinking about Calloway, the job he had gotten me into.

"You can work here, Clara, full time for me. Stop crying and listen."

"Full time, oh my" she said, turning around and wiping away her tears.

"I'll be gone a lot now. You can look after Molly for me."

"I will. I don't know why Miss Ramona was yelling at her."

"Go on home, forget it. This is where you work now."

She finished cleaning up the sink and left, thanking me for being kind. Making me feel better, I had to admit. Kind, hell, I had been calculating. I would be all over the damned country, seeing the people on Calloway's list. And Clara had been fired, she could be here to take care of Molly. Add it up, maybe Woods' wife had done me a favor, no matter what she told Molly this time.

Lieutenant Rebecca was in no mood to make me feel better. She came out of Molly's room and sat beside me at the kitchen table, shaking her head. Worn out, her eyes looking red and blurry.

"Your wife's asleep" she said. "I was, too, until Clara called."

"I'm sorry. . .working the night shift at the hospital. . .you should be. . ."

"I should be in bed asleep. You have any bourbon around? I need a drink."

I poured a couple of drinks and handed her one. She sipped it slowly. Not celebrating. Silent, brooding. I said nothing, wondering how I might apologize again. For Molly. How I might ask for another favor. Because of Molly.

"I have to go away tomorrow" I said. "Clara will be here in the daytime, but. . ."

"But you need someone to check on your wife at night."

"I hate to ask, I know you're. . ."

"I'll take care of it. She's lucky she has you to worry about her."

"Lucky. . .I don't know. . ."

"It's all luck. One year ago today, I lost my husband."

I put my hand on top of hers and held it for a moment. Nothing I could say. She finished her drink without looking at me.

When she left I opened the door to Molly's room. Asleep. Not her fault, she had been saying, whatever that meant.

Not her fault. Nobody's fault. All luck. The nurse had lost her husband and I had Molly to worry about.

Right. Luck and bad judgment. I drove on, trying to get my mind off Molly.

Leonard Wood. At the entrance an MP sergeant waved for me to stop. Not a security check, he said, only a word of caution. Turn left at the next intersection, major, if you're headed for the main part of the post, if you stay on this street you won't get there, you'll wind up in a goddamned circus.

"Eight bus loads of recruits, sir, and a shit load of television people."

"TV? What's going on?"

"The draft ends at midnight, sir, you didn't know that?"

"No, I didn't. The last of the draftees, I'll be damned."

"The last of the scum, if you ask me, major."

At the intersection I looked at my watch and drove straight on. Time enough to watch a minor bit of history. Tens of thousands had gone through here on their way to Nam, and now it was over. The end of the draft, a few last bus loads making news. Posing, maybe, for the television cameras.

They weren't posing, I could see when I got there. I parked, got out, and put on an overcoat. Damned cold, but I wanted to get closer and watch. Not a circus like the MP mentioned. A mess in the making.

Young men, eighteen or nineteen years old, coming off the buses, dragging suitcases and luggage, none of them dressed for winter, shivering, wheezing, coughing, spitting crud on the street and pushing at each other.

In their midst, the TV men with camcorders on their shoulders, the reporters sticking microphones in the faces of the last draftees, asking questions, trying to get some quotes for television, shoving the drill sergeants aside when they got in their way.

The drill sergeants with their bullhorns, telling the men to line up, one of them yelling at a reporter to please step aside, the TV man falling down, acting like he'd been shoved, another one filming it so the world could see, once again, how ruthless the American Army can be.

A major running back and forth among the buses, trying to bring order out of bedlam. Behind him, near a TV van, a man who looked like a politician, speaking into a camera, making a speech, no doubt, about how he'd been against Vietnam from the very beginning.

Enough. I approached a captain who had also been watching and asked how to get to Colonel Raborn's office. Raborn, the captain answered, that's him over there, by that sedan, I wouldn't go near him, major, he's plenty pissed off at what's going on here.

"Dee" he said when I introduced myself. "I got your message. Something about Tet."

"General Calloway's orders. I have some questions I need to ask you."

"Tet. Another staff study. Calloway should come down here and watch this shit."

"It's not another staff study, colonel. It's about something that happened."

"Not now. Wait here, I want to hear what that Congressman's saying."

I waited. And watched. The drill sergeants finally getting control and moving the men into barracks. The television people drifting away, the Congressman driving off in his car as the TV van departed. Raborn, returning, shaking his head and cursing.

"That sonofabitch" he muttered. "Lying about the draft."

"There's real news for you" I replied. "A lying Congressman."

"He was one of the bastards who advised Lyndon Johnson to do it."

"To go for the draft, you mean."

"Along with all the goddamn deferments. You've seen what we got."

He went on cursing. I had questions to ask, not a good idea to argue with him. But I had seen, all right. How most of them turned out fine, proud to be in the Army. At first. Until the war went on too long. Until the protests started. Until the drugs started flowing in Nam.

"Get in your car" he said, "you can follow me to my office."

Raborn. Big, with a scar on his face. A football star at Georgia, someone told me. Ready to turn pro when Korea broke out. A battlefield commission, and a hell of a reputation. All soldier, nobody to screw with. In his office I could see right away he was in no mood for questions.

"Now, what's this shit about Tet?" he asked.

"Your division, colonel, you were engaged in a number of battles."

"Hell, yes. Tet lasted a month. VC all over the place."

"There's only one engagement I need to ask about."

"One? What's Calloway up to? You said it's not a staff study."

"It's not him, it's the Secretary of the Army. He's looking into Bahn Bahn."

He put his hands on his desk when I said that. Palms down, wiggling his fingers, quiet for a moment. When he raised his eyes it was not my face he was looking at. It was the hand I was holding my briefcase with.

"You're not West Point" he said. "There's no ring on your finger."

"West Point? No, I. . ."

"The secretary is. So was that bastard at Bahn Bahn. Tracy."

"The battalion commander, you mean. His name was Tracy?"

"Getting his ticket punched. One firefight and he panicked."

"That's what I'm trying to find out, what happened. I can't ask him, he's dead now."

"So I heard. I'll give you some advice, Dee. Tell Calloway you want out of this."

"Out of what, colonel? What happened at Bahn Bahn?"

"That bastard Tracy screwed it up, that's what, and the secretary's trying to cover for him. The Academy, Dee. Are you too dumb to see that?" Dumb. Maybe. Or maybe he had seen something I'd never seen, West Pointers covering for each other. He reached in his desk, pulled out a yellow pad and started to draw a map. Here, he said, I'll show you what I remember.

Raborn pushed the map across his desk so I could see it. The battalion on top of a hill, the village down below in a valley, a 105 battery five miles away in support, arrows showing how the Viet Cong attacked from the direction of the village.

"As I recall, the VC got inside the wire and Tracy panicked..."

"The division log shows the battery was overrun. What happened then?"

"He started screaming for air support. No way, the Air Force was socked in."

"I've got a question about the log, colonel. It says. . ."

"We were up to our ass in alligators, Dee. Five or six engagements at once."

"The log says your G4 got in there with supplies. In a Huey, colonel."

"Then it's wrong. Day six of Tet, he was wounded, just like me."

He looked down, remembering, maybe, when he was hit. I knew what the records showed. They had both been wounded, the division three and four, when a mortar round came in. But the log also said the G4 flew supplies into Bahn Bahn that very day, during the battle. And the brigade log made no mention of it. Damned odd, I had thought when I read it.

I was looking at the map when Raborn got up and went to his door. He spoke to someone in the hallway and came back, telling me he had to leave for some kind of ceremony. With that Congressman and the TV people there. So they could hear how the

Army would train its recruits, all volunteers, now that the draft was over.

"It's bullshit" he said. "If you want to wait I'll be back in a couple of hours."

"I may. I'm puzzled about something, colonel."

"Remember what I told you. A goddamn cover-up, Dee."

"It's the log, that entry about a Huey getting in there. . ."

"That could have been Lamont. Hell, that was five years ago."

"Lamont? Mel Lamont?"

"Major Lamont, the assistant G4. Maybe."

"Lamont. I'll be a sonofabitch. . ."

"Hell, yes, Lamont" Raborn said as he left. "Tell him hello if you see him."

I looked at the map. No reason to stick around, Raborn had told me all he knew. Up to his ass in alligators during Tet, he said.

So was I, five years later. The Bahn Bahn CO dead. Some West Pointer named Tracy, Raborn said. Tracy's wife giving his letters to the Secretary of the Army, Lamont's name off limits, Calloway hiding something. With me right in the middle of it.

I stopped at a motel on the way back. Heavy snow again, not a good idea to drive at night, enough was enough, I had damned near rolled over on the way to Leonard Wood, thinking about Molly.

Now I had more to think about. Why Lamont's name was secret. What Woods' wife had told Molly. What happened at Bahn Bahn. Confusing. But not half as confusing as what I found when I got back to my quarters the next morning.

Molly was standing with her back to the door when I looked into her bedroom. Barefooted, wearing a negligee, fumbling with the dresses hanging in her closet. She ate her breakfast, whispered Clara, but she's been acting strange ever since, just poking around in that closet, looking at those dresses and listening to that music.

Music. She had a record turned up loud. I recognized it right away, one of her favorites when we first met, when she tried to teach me how to dance. Nat King Cole's Mona Lisa. Two days ago she was screaming and crying, saying she wasn't to blame after Woods' wife told her something, and now she was up, trying to dance to the words of that damned music.

Mona Lisa, Mona Lisa, men have blamed you. . .

You're so like the lady with the mystic smile. . .

I turned and asked Clara if the colonel's wife had been here again. Last night, said Clara, Miss Ramona came by and said something to Miss Molly, she was here for only a minute and then she left.

Do you smile to tempt a lover, Mona Lisa?

Or is this your way to hide a broken heart?

Ramona, damn it, what had she told her now? I watched for another moment, listening to the music. Molly trying to dance, still beautiful, remembering why I stayed in the Army because she liked to dance at the officers club. Realizing once again why I kept volunteering for another trip to Nam. And it sure as hell wasn't just because I couldn't dance.

Are you warm, are you real, Mona Lisa?

Or just a cold and lonely lovely work of art?

She slipped as she took another step, staggered, and then fell against the bed. Too weak to be up dancing. The music was still playing as I reached down to help her, so loud I could barely hear what she said when I touched her. But I heard.

"Go away" she yelled. "Leave me alone." Go away. The first words she had said to me since I returned this time from Nam. Go away. I closed her door and walked to the kitchen with Clara, who was shaking her head, not knowing how to act. She had heard what Molly said. Go away, leave her alone.

"You had a big bag of mail last night" said Clara. "I put it on the table."

"Mail? A whole bag of mail?"

"The sergeant who brought it, he said it was forwarded here."

"Mail. . .sure, all the crap sent to me in Nam. I'll dig through it later."

Later. Right now, see Woods. I could still hear the words as I went out the door, the words, the music, over and over again, mixed in with what she said, go away, leave her alone.

Are you warm, are you real, Mona Lisa?

Or just a cold and lonely lovely work of art?

Report to Woods, Calloway told me, keep him informed of what I learn about Bahn Bahn. Report, hell. I had a sick wife on my hands, and it was damned well time for Woods to tell me how she got that way.

What his wife had said to Molly on New Year's Eve. What she'd said two days ago, making Molly scream it wasn't her fault. What in hell she had said last night. One way or the other, by God, Woods was going to tell me.

"Colonel Woods is not in, he's on leave" his secretary informed me.

"On leave? When will he be back?"

"I'm not sure, sir. I do know his wife went with him."

"Where did he go? I need to see him."

"Memphis, I believe he took his wife to Memphis."

Damn him, he would not get away that easy. Running off on leave, taking that woman with him, that gossiping bitch Ramona, Woods was going to tell me if I had to chase him all the way to Memphis.

General Calloway is tied up, his aide told me without my asking. Captain Reilly, sitting at his desk outside the general's office. He's meeting with some members of the faculty, said Reilly, you will have to wait in line to see him.

"I'm not here to see him. I want you to do something for me."

"Yes sir, whatever you say, the general told me I'm to help with. . ."

"Memphis, captain. Book me on a flight to Memphis."

"You're going to Memphis, major? Is that what you said?"

"Right away, Memphis, as soon as you can get me there."

Calm down, get your head straight, I told myself as I walked away. You're letting her screw your mind up again. Go away, she said. Without even looking at you. Fine. Twelve years, that's enough, listen to what she said. I turned around and went back to Reilly.

"Forget it, captain, I've changed my mind."

"Yes, sir, I was getting ready to call for. . ."

"Are you married, Reilly?"

"Me? No sir, I'm a bachelor. I'm. . ."

"Stay that way. Let me know when I can see the general."

One down on the list of people to see about Bahn Bahn. Right, get your mind on the Army, I muttered as I entered my office. Think about what Raborn said. About Lamont. About a cover-up. Look at the list, find someone who was there, someone who knew what really happened. What the big brass might be hiding.

Now, right away, before the TV people find out. Before someone like Proctor can point fingers, can twist it around so the folks who watch TV will pay attention, maybe turn it into a scandal, whatever it was that happened at Bahn Bahn.

I lit a cigarette and shook my head. The big brass versus television. With me in the middle, trying to get my mind off a wife who said go away, wondering how the hell I had wound up in a mess like this.

All I could do was carry out orders. Do my duty. I looked at the list of people to see and made up my mind. Ride to the sound of the guns. Charge ahead, damn it, no matter who gets burned, find out what happened at Bahn Bahn.

"Here" I said to Reilly a short while later. "See if you can set this up."

"Roger" he replied as he looked at the schedule I had written.

"Benning, captain. I'll start there. Fort Benning, tomorrow."

Reilly picked up his phone but put it down and leaped to attention. The door to the general's office had opened. I stood aside as a colonel came out, Woods' deputy, a man I recognized. Frowning as he walked past. Behind him, Calloway, telling me to come in, he wanted to see me.

The Great Southern Breeze then, talking about World War Two while I stood in front of his desk and listened. How he had seen the posters at dockside, before they sailed off to cross the Atlantic. Alert, on edge, watching for German submarines. Because of what the posters warned. Loose lips sink ships, keep that in mind, said the general.

I nodded, not sure what Calloway's point might be. I had a good idea when he spoke again, after a moment or so, looking straight at me.

"You will no longer report to Woods. He is out of the loop now."

"Yes, sir. Out of the loop. I understand."

"Colonel Raborn called me last night. He said Lamont's name came up."

"Sir, it looks like he was at Bahn Bahn. Toward the end of the battle."

"That name is off limits, major. You know that."

"What else, general? Did Raborn tell you about a cover-up, too?"

I waited for an answer. A mere major, looking a three-star general in the face. To hell with it. He and Woods had dragged me into this, damn it. Woods was out of it now, maybe because of Ramona, saying something to Molly about Lamont, maybe Calloway had found out and canned him. Whatever, Lamont was somehow in the center of it, no doubt about it.

If Calloway wanted to fire me also, let him. For all I knew he was in on a cover-up himself, along with the rest of the brass.

"What do you know about My Lai?" he asked abruptly..

"I know some senior officers were ruined for trying to hide it, general."

"Including a three-star like me. Reduced in rank and forced to retire."

"Calley's division commander, yes sir, I know that."

"I will not be party to a cover-up. Do you understand that, Major Dee?"

"Yes, sir, I do, but you may be involved in one already."

"Keep digging into Bahn Bahn. If there was a massacre, so be it.'

The look on his face made it clear that was final. I nodded, saluted, did about face and left his office. I had my marching orders. Lamont's name might be off limits still, I wasn't sure, but whatever happened at Bahn Bahn, that sure as hell was not off limits.

"You're all laid on" said Reilly when I came out the door. "Here's your reservation."

"Good, Kansas City at eight in the morning, I see. One way, to Georgia."

"Yes, sir, now you can stay home tonight with that wife you were joking about."

"I wasn't joking, captain. Stay single."

"Sir, it's none of my business, I know, I only meant. . ."

"You're right, it isn't. Maybe I'll tell you sometime why I said that."

Tell him what? I parked in front of our quarters and left the engine running. So I could stay warm, have a cigarette and think about it.

Dark, with the lights on and the shades up. I could see through the window, watching Clara feed Molly her dinner. After that, I figured, the pills from Nurse Rebecca. So she would be asleep by the time I entered.

Waiting outside, so I would not have to face her. Tell Reilly about that, maybe he'd understand why I said stay single. Why I was headed for Benning. Why worrying about Bahn Bahn instead of her was something I could welcome.

Benning School For Boys. Reilly might be naïve, as green as Calloway made him out to be. He was a wise old man compared to me when I first got to Fort Benning. Fifteen years ago, before the world changed. Before we had even heard of Indo-China.

Driving into Benning, seeing the jump school towers, a trip back in time, recalling what I must have thought when I enlisted in the Army.

Drunk, quitting my job on a newspaper, joining up, hoping to prove something. Maybe to see if I could match the veterans I hung around with. The paratroopers from World War Two, with all their bullshit tales of guts and glory.

Coming here to Benning, to the infantry school, an officer candidate, singing that song we sang to make a joke of what we'd volunteered for. As I drove around I could hear the words again, loud but not out loud, the way a song can stick in your mind years later.

High above the Chattahoochie, near the Upatoi, stands our cherished alma matter, Benning School For Boys.

Naïve. I suppose we were, all of us. Nonchalant, singing songs like that. Not afraid of the Russians we were training for, getting our second lieutenant bars pinned on, getting smashed in Phenix City to celebrate, too young to know what war meant. Still singing that song.

Onward ever, backward never, follow me and die. To the port of embarkation, next of kin, goodbye.

Not so naïve now, fifteen years later, the ones who stayed in the Army. Four from my OCS class I knew of, maybe more, killed in Nam. No guts and glory. No wives left behind. No parades to come home to. No longer innocent, sure as hell.

Hard not to think about it, driving on post, not with that song still rattling around in my head. I parked in front of the building I was looking for and glanced again at the name of the captain I had come here to see. About Bahn Bahn. One of the many places where the innocence had gone up in smoke and disappeared. Next of kin, goodbye, indeed.

"Captain Plunkett, let me see" said a clerk when I asked where I could find him. I waited, looking around the room. The back wall, covered with charts and names and colored push pins. One thing sure about the Army, it's damned well organized when it comes to training. Neat, everything in place. Not like the goddamned jungle.

"Range Twenty Six Alpha, that's machine guns" said the clerk when he returned, with a map in his hand and a grease pencil to mark it. "Here, major, I'll show you how to get there. Captain Plunkett's in charge, the schedule shows they'll be done in another hour."

Machine guns. From miles away, easy to hear the clack-clack-clack of M-60's firing automatic. Always reassuring in the jungle. No jungle here, only plywood mockups and a few discarded trucks for targets. Deafening, as I walked toward the range, watching the tracers from a dozen firing stations, too loud to hear the sergeant who reported to me.

He handed me a clipboard, showing me the lesson plan and the firing schedule. When I shook my head and yelled I was not here to inspect, I wanted to see Captain Plunkett, the sergeant went back to the firing line. I lit a cigarette and watched. Fifteen years since I had been on this range, a lifetime ago, it seemed like.

A few minutes later they were done and Plunkett approached me. Brushing dust off his uniform and limping. With bruises on his face, looking like he'd been in a brawl. One tough captain, not big but built like a boxer, acting like he'd rather not see me. He sure as hell sounded like it when he spoke.

"So what is it, major, an Article Fifteen or a court martial?"

"I wouldn't know, captain. I'm here about something else. Vietnam."

"No shit, maybe you can tell me, then. What the fuck were we there for?"

"Look, this is off the record, I need to know about Bahn Bahn."

"Bahn Bahn. What's that, some kind of fucking deodorant?"

"Don't bullshit me, you were there, captain."

"Really? Then up your ass, major. How's that for off the record?"

He went back to the firing line and started giving orders. Police the range, pick up the brass, clean the weapons. Pissed off big time, in trouble over something. His problem, not mine, whatever it was. He had been at Bahn Bahn, that's all that counted. When he came back he looked straight at me. Still pissed off, but he said what I wanted to hear.

"All right, I was there. My first tour. I had a platoon in Alpha Company."

"Near the end of the battle, somebody from G4 flew in. Who was it?"

"Some major. I never knew his name."

"What did he look like? Describe him to me."

"That was five years ago. Tall, that's all I remember."

"Tall. Go on, what did he do when he got there?"

"He took command, that's what. Give me a minute, let me think about it."

Plunkett looked down, stomping the dust off his boots. Faced with of an Article Fifteen for some reason. Concerned, perhaps, with another one if he didn't come up with something. Measuring his words, speaking carefully, telling me just enough to get me off his back and leave him the hell alone.

"Colonel Tracy, the commander, he was wounded. In his bunker, I think."

"Tracy. Right, I've heard that name before. What about his XO?"

"Dead, the VC got him. The bastards were inside the wire, all over."

"You were socked in, I heard. No air support. No more 105's, either."

"This major, he came in with a Huey. He was the only one who got in there."

"So he took command. What happened then?"

"He drove them back, with Charlie Company, all the way to the village. In three or four hours they were finished, no more VC. When the weather cleared, he flew off and it was over."

"Over, and he was gone. As simple as that. What about Colonel Tracy?"

"He left the next day. Medevac. We got a new commander and moved out. Twenty miles away from Bahn Bahn, back to Pleiku. End of story, major."

Plunkett went back to the firing line again, checking to see how the cleanup was going. I had noticed how he looked at the decorations on my uniform. He knew I had done my time in Nam. From the look on his face I could tell he knew about Bahn Bahn, too. I followed and asked him point blank.

"The village, captain, what happened there? I've heard rumors."

"I told you, end of story. Off the record or not, that's all I'm going to say."

"A lot of villagers were killed in Bahn Bahn, that's the rumor."

"You want to talk about massacres? Ask Calley, he's the expert on that."

Plunkett walked away, to a jeep behind the firing line. I stayed behind him. When he reached the jeep he leaned against a fender and lit a cigarette, with his back to me, not facing me as I pressed on with more questions.

"Damn it, captain, what happened in that village?"

"Ten year old kids with satchel charges. You know what it was like in Nam."

"Bahn Bahn, damn it, someone in the Army may be trying to hide it."

"The Army? There's no such fucking thing as the Army, major."

"Look, captain. . ."

"A few real grunts like you and me. The rest, nothing but pencil pushers." His voice sounded different when he said that. As if he'd given up. I had. He was not going to tell me what he knew, so to hell with it. I looked at him, with his back still to me, and started to leave. Then I heard him say hold on, give me another minute. I waited while he scribbled a note on his clipboard. When he handed it to me he nodded.

"Here, major, if you really want to know, see him."

"This address, it's near Birmingham, I gather. Who is it?"

"He commanded Alpha. He'll tell you what happened."

"Your company commander, right. . . .Renfro, that's his name?"

"He's out of it now. Disabled. I'll call him tonight and tell him you're coming."

"All the way up there? That's a long way to go to hear more bullshit."

"Bullshit? You think a massacre is bullshit, major?"

"So what made you change your mind? Why are you telling me now?"

"Read that, maybe you'll understand."

Plunkett pointed to a newspaper, lying on the floorboard of his jeep. He walked away then, back to the firing line, as I reached for the paper and unfolded it. The Columbus Ledger, with a headline and a picture on the front page, and a story that told me, when I read it, why Plunkett had bruises on his face.

The picture showed a crowd in front of the Federal courthouse, thirty or forty veterans carrying signs. Free Calley. Calley Was Railroaded. My Lai Never Happened. Underneath the picture, the headline, big and black, in italics, four columns wide, a few short words to capture what had happened. Calley Protest Leads to Riot.

An outright melee, according to the story. Most of it quotes from people who had seen it. One of them telling how it started. How some Army captain had been driving by and saw the veterans marching in front of the courthouse, how he parked his car and got out and started grabbing the signs. How a fight had broken out then.

Another witness, a woman coming from the courthouse, describing what she'd seen. The veterans across the street, yelling at the ones who were marching, rushing across the street when the fight broke out. Stomping on the signs, knocking people down, how you could see the blood on the sidewalk now that it was over.

A quote from the police chief, too. He wondered what had happened to the Army he once served in. Veterans fighting veterans over Calley, who, he pointed out, had been properly convicted and was now confined at Fort Benning. As for the unknown captain who had started it, he had no idea why, said the chief, but he was looking for him.

I finished reading the story and tossed the paper in the jeep. When I turned around I saw Plunkett, standing on the firing line, looking at me from twenty yards away. From that far off I could not see the bruises on his face. But I knew what I felt like doing, and I did it.

I stood at attention and saluted, holding my salute until he saluted in return. Then I walked back to my car and started the engine. Veterans fighting veterans, maybe Plunkett was right, the way he put it. Maybe there's no such fucking thing as the Army.

Odd, as I drove away, how I was trying to add that to the song we used to sing.

High above the Chattahoochie. . .near the Upatoi. . .stands our cherished alma mater. . .Benning School For Naïve Boys. . .

Go north from Birmingham, Plunkett's note said. Turn east on Highway 31 and look for a service station with a sign on top that says watch for UFO's. Take the gravel road behind the station. Drive six miles south to Widow's Revenge. Find the mailbox with the name J.J. Renfro on it, in front of a house with a flagpole next to it.

Watch for UFO's, right. None that I could see when I turned off and headed south, only pine trees and cows grazing by the roadside. Not much to see when I got there, either. A service station, a grocery store, and a church. A few one-story houses painted white. But none with the name Renfro on a mail box.

A mile beyond the last house I gave up and turned around. Driving slowly, stopping at each mailbox, checking again. Some of the houses had no box at all. Only one thing to do then, go back and ask. When I stopped in front of the grocery store a man came out, old, using a cane as he hobbled toward me. Maybe he could tell me how to find Renfro.

Not a good idea, I could see as I got out of my car and straightened my uniform. Not with the way he was pointing his cane at the license plate.

"You're a stranger" he said. "Where are you from?"

"It's a rental car" I answered. "I'm in the Army."

"I can see that. You know how this place got its name?"

"Widow's Revenge. No, but. . ."

"You never heard of Anna Lee Braxton, then."

"Braxton, no, I'm looking for. . ."

"Eight Yankee soldiers, that's how many she shot."

"Look, I'm from Texas, if that's what you're thinking."

He shook my hands and said Texas, good, you were on the right side, come on in, you look thirsty, you look like you could use some lemonade.

Telling me all about it as I followed. How Anna Lee's poor old husband had been killed at Vicksburg. How she got her revenge on General Sherman and his Yankee soldiers, before they caught her and hung her, on a tree out there in front of that church, she's buried behind it, I should visit her grave. And so forth.

The lemonade he handed me tasted sour as hell. But I drank it. I had to. The only way I could get around to asking about Renfro.

"Renfro" he said. "That way, on your left. The place with the flagpole."

"He's a Vietnam vet. Sounds like you didn't know that."

"Vietnam. Not worth pissing on, mister."

I got in my car and drove on. I hadn't noticed the flagpole, almost hidden in the trees. No mailbox in front of the house. Only the pole, twenty feet high, at least, with the American flag upside down. Maybe Vietnam wasn't worth pissing on, I wouldn't argue about it. But the flag upside down, Renfro had to be damned bitter to hang it that way.

He was sitting on his porch in a wheelchair. J.J. Renfro, disabled, Plunkett said. With a double-barrel shotgun on his lap. And a bottle on a table next to him, along with what appeared to be a scrapbook. Wearing a leather jacket with a half-dozen Army patches on it. Patting the shotgun, watching as I walked across the yard toward him.

"You're that major Andy called about. You want a drink?"

"Not yet, maybe later. What's the shotgun for?"

"My wife, that fucking flag, I'm going to shoot her for it."

"Damn, captain, hold on, you've been drinking."

"No shit. You can't talk about Nam if you're sober."

He handed me the bottle. Almost empty, I could tell as I held it to my mouth, keeping my lips closed. Anything to please him. Anything to get him to talk. When his wife got home I would try to grab his shotgun. But not yet. First I wanted to find out what he knew, before he passed out from drinking.

"Bahn Bahn" he mumbled as I gave the bottle back.

"Right, I'm trying to find out what happened."

"The gooks got their ass burned, that's what happened."

"You were there, you saw it, then?"

"I didn't see it, I heard it, they were shooting for an hour."

"They? Who's they? I need to know, captain, who was it?"

"C Company, when Lamont took over."

"Lamont? You're sure? You're sure that's what his name was?"

"Mel Lamont, hell yes, we went back a long way."

Bad news. Not what I wanted to hear. Renfro was drunk, but it sounded like he knew. I found a chair on the porch and sat down, not sure what to say. He took a sip from his bottle as I sat there, then opened his scrapbook and turned the pages, looking for something. He handed it to me, pointing to a picture. A picture of Renfro and Lamont together.

"That's in Saigon" he said. "In the good old days before Tet."

"Lamont. . .you're telling me he was in the village. . ."

"Fucking A. He knew how to handle those bastards."

Not the Mel Lamont I knew, goddamn it. He would not engage in a massacre or anything close to it. But that was him in the picture, all right. I hadn't seen him in years, maybe Nam had gotten to him. The way it got to a lot of us, sooner or later, fighting women and kids in one damned village after another.

Lamont. Changed, perhaps, like the rest of us. Not in the picture. The same there as he looked at Fort Campbell. Before the build up for Nam. Before Molly came between us. Before she said she'd marry me, not him, if I would stay in the Army. So here I am, because of her, I muttered to myself, damn it, get your mind off her, remember what you're here for.

"This other picture, who is that?" I asked.

"Colonel Tracy. . .getting a medal when it was over."

"I heard he was wounded, captain. How could he. . ."

"Wounded, my ass. . .hiding out. . .that's Fernhill. . .pinning it on him."

"Fernhill, the brigade commander? He was there? He knew what happened?"

"Hell yes. . .he gave Tracy that medal."

"A medal for him? Renfro, listen, can I borrow this picture?"

He nodded and raised the bottle to his mouth, draining one last drop. While I sat there wondering. What he said did not add up. Lamont wiping out a village, Tracy taking credit for it, Fernhill pinning a medal on him, bullshit, if there was a massacre at Bahn Bahn they would have tried to keep it secret. The picture, when I see Fernhill I'll show it to him and ask him.

As drunk as he was, damn it, Renfro had to be wrong. He hadn't been in the village, he hadn't seen it. He said so himself. He heard shooting when Lamont drove the VC back, that's all. Drunk, but stubborn about it, too, the way he mumbled as I pressed on, trying to get it straight, what went on in that village.

"Damn it, Renfro, you didn't see any bodies, how do you know what happened?"

"Bodies. . .an SF team. . .they counted them. . ."

"A Special Forces team? Is that what you're saying?"

"Their captain. . .black. . .damned good soldier. . .he saw them. . ."

"A black SF captain, fine, what did he tell you?"

No answer. Renfro had passed out, slumped over in his wheelchair. His face worn thin, his hair turning gray, not the same man he was five years ago, in that Saigon picture. Drunk, but it sounded like he remembered. Too bad, damn it, maybe there had been a massacre after all.

Nothing I could do about it, if that's what happened. I reached down and lifted the shotgun from his lap. Unload it, I figured, so he couldn't shoot his wife for hanging the flag that way. No need to, it was empty. Well, hell, at least wait and warn her what he said, keep him out of any more trouble, Nam had done enough to this poor bastard.

When she pulled into the driveway and got out, carrying groceries, she saw us on the porch and shook her head. I walked to the car and offered to help, but she pushed me away and carried the bags inside, past Renfro, asleep in his wheelchair. Without a word. Thin, her hair turning gray like his, worn out, it looked like, from taking care of her husband.

"You'd better put that away" I said, pointing to the shotgun when she came out.

"He's been drinking" she grumbled, looking down at the empty bottle.

"The flag, he said you put it up like that, he said you. . ."

"Vandals, they did that last night. Go away, you're not welcome here."

"Lady, look, I only. . ."

"Why are you here? What did you say on the phone last night?"

"Last night? That must have been. . ."

"He hadn't had a drink in years, until you called him."

"I'm sorry, it's Army business, I had no idea he would. . ."

"Leave us alone. J.J. has done enough for his country."

She rolled him inside the house and closed the door behind her. Sad, a worn-out wife, taking care of a crippled husband. No point in telling her I wasn't the one who called. The way she closed the door, no point in telling her anything, what I had come here to find out, what I had drawn her husband into, why that had to be the reason Renfro had started drinking again.

Poor woman. And then, at the highway, something odd, a way to make it up to her. On top of the station, next to the UFO sign, a banner I hadn't noticed before. With words on it. Tomorrow Is Valentine's Day, We Have Roses For Your Sweetheart.

Roses. For Renfro's wife, sure as hell not for mine. I went in, gave them a five dollar bill and Renfro's address, and went back to the car, trying to get my mind off Molly. Thinking about it, what Renfro said about Bahn Bahn. Another My Lai. With Lamont in the middle of it.

Not good at all. So press on to Atlanta, see Fernhill and ask him. He's next on the list, hear what he has to say about it, why he gave a medal for a massacre, if that's what he did. Why not? What I was digging into was bad enough already, it could not get any worse.

It could, it did, and I knew it would as soon as I stood in front of his desk. Worse, much worse, an avalanche of bullshit.

W.T.S. Fernhill, a major general now. Smoking a cigar, looking like he'd rather be the mayor of Atlanta, not burn it down like his namesake William Tecumseh Sherman. Talking like a politician running for office. Making a speech about the new Army, as soon as I entered his office, before I could even tell him why I was there.

I listened. For five minutes, at least, while Fernhill went on and on. About the new enlistment system, all volunteer, now that the draft was over. About his role at Fort McPherson, keeping tabs on how the program was working. About his old friend General Calloway, sending an officer to study it, the way the system would be managed.

"Of course, that is only an outline" said Fernhill. "My staff will provide the details for your study." With that he motioned to the door, ready to send me away, now that he was finished. I did not move.

"General, I'm afraid there's been a mistake. That's not what I'm here for."

"You should be, you should learn all you can about the new Army."

"Bahn Bahn, sir. That's why I've been sent here, to ask what you remember."

"Really. Then you've been wasting my time, major."

I noticed how Fernhill bit hard on his cigar. Annoyed, but maybe not because his time had been wasted. Because Bahn Bahn had come up, it looked like, the way he gritted his teeth. Too bad. I had a job to do. And I meant to do it, with or without any more speeches by a two-star general.

"Bahn Bahn, sir. During Tet. You were a brigade commander then."

"Yes. . .yes, of course" said Fernhill.

"Colonel Tracy, he commanded one of your battalions, general."

"Tracy. . .a fine officer. . . he died a few months ago, he. . ."

"Bahn Bahn, sir. He was in command there."

"Years ago. . .perhaps. . .I don't remember."

"General Calloway thinks you do. That's why he sent me."

Fernhill set his cigar in an ash tray, no longer smiling. A politician caught off guard, getting his act together. No doubt calculating where he stood. Getting up from his desk and standing in front of me. Scowling. In no more than a second or two, deciding how to act. Act innocent.

"Calloway is misinformed. I know nothing about Bahn Bahn."

"Nothing, general? That's what you're telling me? Nothing?"

"You may leave now, major, I have nothing to say."

Leave? Like hell I would. Screw him, see how he'll tap dance around the lie he just told me. I reached in my pocket for the picture I had taken from Renfro. The one showing Fernhill pinning a medal on Tracy. At Bahn Bahn. He looked at the picture and nodded. No tap dance. Only a nod.

"Yes" he said. "I suppose I had forgotten. Colonel Tracy was a fine officer."

"The medal, general, what was that for? For hiding in his bunker?"

"You are out of bounds, major. Get out of my office."

"Not yet, not until you tell me what the medal was for."

"For gallantry. . .he led his battalion to victory. . .he. . ."

"Victory. He drove the VC into the village, is that it?"

"Yes, of course. . .why do you keep asking these insolent questions?"

"There was a massacre in Bahn Bahn, general. That's why I'm asking."

Fernhill's face turned red. What happened in the village, I didn't know if there was a massacre or not, but I had sure as hell rattled him. A politician trapped in his own damned bullshit. Lying about Bahn Bahn, and Tracy, too, avoiding why he gave him a medal. Hiding something, and I would pry it out of him, by God, even if I had to be insubordinate to do it.

"Impossible" he said. "A massacre...no. . .I would have known about it."

"But you got there later, general. You weren't there when it happened."

"No. . .no. . .I wasn't there."

"The citation for the medal, that had to be approved by higher headquarters."

"Approved, yes. . .before I got there. . .a medal for Tracy."

"His letters, general. The Secretary of the Army has them."

"No. . .I was not aware of any letters."

"Colonel Tracy's wife gave them to him, general."

"The secretary. . ."

"The medal, general, he wants to know about that medal."

I was lying. I had no idea what the Secretary of the Army had in mind. Or why I was there. Or why I was lying. Or why this general was holding that picture in his hand, looking at it, shaking his head. Why he seemed more concerned with a medal than a massacre. If there was a massacre.

Lying. Looking down at the picture in Fernhill's hands. Maybe that's what did it, maybe that's what had gotten to me, the picture from Renfro's scrapbook. Renfro's wife, pushing him around in a wheelchair, saying he'd done enough for his country. He had. And Fernhill, what had he done? Pin a medal on someone.

And me, what had I done? Three tours in Nam, left with a wife who's told me to go to hell. Stuck in a goddamn investigation because of her, because she caved in at Leavenworth. Starting to lie to get the job done. Lying to a two-star general, sitting there with a picture in his hand. Lying for the sake of the Army.

The picture. Renfro's wife, saying he'd done enough for his country. And Plunkett, what had he said? There's no such fucking thing as the Army? Maybe Plunkett should have gone one step further. Maybe there's no such thing as the country, either. Vietnam, what was that for? For the country? For that old man at the grocery store in Widow's Revenge?

I reached down, took the picture from Fernhill, and put it back in my pocket. Fed up, all at once, feeling sick of what I'd gotten tangled up in. Feeling what to do now. Send the picture back to Renfro. Go back to Kansas, tell Calloway I'm finished. Leave Fernhill alone, let him worry about that medal. None of my business, not any more.

Let this two-star politician go on making speeches, let him wallow in his bullshit. If there was a massacre at Bahn Bahn, so be it. If Mel Lamont was there, so be that, too, he should have been the one who married Molly, anyway. None of my business, any of it. Not any more.

A scene from a low-budget motion picture, perhaps some kind of anti-war film. An Army officer, a major, sitting in a lounge at O'Hare, waiting for a flight to Kansas. Reading the Chicago Tribune. Reading about a place called Watergate, something going on in Washington. Reading about politics.

The terminal, crowded, travelers rushing around, loaded with baggage. A woman with two suitcases, stopping, standing in front of the Army officer, putting her luggage down, staring at his uniform, shaking her head. Cursing. Loud enough for everyone to hear. Yelling about Vietnam. Spitting in his face.

A Marine sergeant, in full dress uniform, carrying nothing, limping along with a cane, approaching the woman from behind, seeing what she's done, telling her to go fuck herself, leave this major alone, all you've ever done for the country is carry signs and raise more fucking worthless maggots like yourself.

The woman picking up her bags, cursing the Marine, stomping away and disappearing in the crowd. The Marine sergeant, sitting down next to me, holding the cane in his lap, muttering about the country going to hell. While I took a handkerchief from my pocket, wiped the spit away and cleaned my glasses.

"Maggots" said the Marine. "Fucking maggots."

"You're using a cane, I see. Where were you hit?"

"Khe Sahn, shrapnel in my hip, almost healed now."

"You've got it made then. Where are you headed?"

"Back to Okinawa. Where are you headed, major?"

"Right now, some place I can wash my face."

"Semper Fi" said the Marine as I got up.

"Semper Fi" I answered, off in search of a men's room.

Two veterans, sharing an ugly moment at an airport. To hell with that woman. We had seen her kind before, all over the country. Not worth talking about.

The woman, no doubt a veteran, also. But not on our side. A veteran of a separate war, almost a civil war, the way the protests had gone. With damned few in this crowd concerned anymore. Too busy to bother, flying away to Disney World, hauling golf clubs to California.

I cleaned my face and found what I was looking for, an arrival and departure screen in a nearby corridor. Not surprised to see my flight was delayed. For how long, no telling. I shrugged my shoulders and stood in line at a counter to find out. As I waited a lady in an airline uniform approached me. This time a woman on our side.

There's no need to stand in line, she said, my husband's in the Army also, let me help you. In a few minutes she was back. Two hours at least, a long delay, she said, if you wait in the USO lounge near the boarding gates we'll be sure and call you.

I found the lounge and joined another line, this one much shorter. Three sailors in front of me, talking with a USO lady serving coffee. I waited, so I could ask her to let me know when the airline called. An elderly woman, I noticed when the sailors moved on to the TV part of the lounge. Gray haired, a volunteer, this woman. Another one on our side.

"Yes, I'll listen for the phone to ring" she said politely.

"Thanks, I'll read a magazine" I replied. And then, making idle conversation, I asked a dumb question. How she found time to serve as a volunteer. Dumb, because a second later I realized why she was here. I saw the gold star on her uniform, pinned on her blouse above the name Flanagan.

"My son was in the service" she answered. "I take time to remember."

"I'm sorry, ma'am, I apologize for asking."

"There's no need to. I will let you know when they call."

"Miss Flanagan, is it? Is there anything I can do to help here?"

"Yes, if you wish, you can make another pot of coffee."

I stepped behind the counter and went to work. Cleaning the coffee machine, feeling good about it, even better when I heard what she told me. How an Army colonel had done the same thing a few days ago, asking if he could help, cleaning the coffee machine like me, saying it was an honor to do so.

Honor. Inside this lounge that word had meaning. The men who sat in here, waiting to fly off God knows where, for them it had to be the only thing we really stood for. Doing what's right when the time comes, even if they spit in your face for doing it. Outside the lounge, in the crowd out there, the word no longer meant a damned thing.

What it meant for me, I wasn't sure. When I left Atlanta it was clear enough, tell Calloway to turn me loose, I was through with Bahn Bahn. Hurting Renfro's wife that way, lying to that bastard Fernhill for the sake of an investigation, no more of that, I was finished. Now, hell, sitting in this lounge I was not so certain. I was not so sure what honor called for.

I would know before I got up. What I had to do, what the right thing would be. I would know as soon as I saw the evening news on television. Dan Proctor would settle it for me.

Proctor, smiling at the camera, relaxed, with the news of the day. A bill the House had passed. A Senate confirmation under way. Another Watergate disclosure. The smile began to fade as he mentioned President Nixon. It was gone completely, replaced by a frown, as he moved on to what had made him famous, exposing corruption in high places.

I knew how Proctor worked, with a carefully written script before he went on camera. The frown, that would be the lead in. To a comment about his duty as a journalist, and then some sort of revelation, a bombshell if he could manage it.

Even so, I was surprised. It wasn't Nixon and Watergate he was after, not this time. Vietnam, said Proctor, the war appears to be over. A pause then, as he took what appeared to be a deep breath. The rest of the lead in, Proctor looking solemn as he spoke.

Over, perhaps, for some, he said. As for myself and my colleagues at this network it is not over. It cannot be, for we have learned now of another cover-up by the Army, a massacre kept secret for years, one even worse than My Lai.

A bombshell, all right. I knew at once, when I heard Proctor say where it happened. In a village named Bahn Bahn. At least three hundred, he said, killed without mercy. Women and children, murdered, by order of an Army colonel named Tracy.

And then, still frowning, a hint of something more sinister. Of course, said Proctor, we have not been able to contact this colonel. He died in mysterious circumstances, soon after we began our investigation. And his second in command has disappeared also, a major named Lamont, who carried out the order for the massacre.

No, said Proctor as he ended the news, Vietnam is not over. Not for me, and not for this network. It cannot be, not until justice has been served.

Bullshit, I muttered. It's not justice he's after, it's TV ratings. And he's winging it, he's making it up as he goes along. There's no mystery about Tracy's death, and Lamont wasn't second in command. Proctor doesn't know what happened. If he did he would not be making claims like that.

I didn't know either. But I knew what to do.

Watching a young soldier shake his head, hearing him curse at the TV set, hearing the others around him cursing also, I knew what the right thing would be. Forget what I thought in Atlanta. Press on, get to the bottom of Bahn Bahn. Soldiers like them, damn it, they deserved better than Proctor.

So did the USO lady. I looked up and saw how sad she seemed, when she came to tell me the airline had called, my flight was ready for boarding. That man Proctor is awful, she said, always causing trouble on television. She didn't trust him, she added, and went back to the counter to serve coffee.

I glanced around as I got up to leave. One of the soldiers had switched the TV to another channel. A motion picture was starting, a black and white film on the movie channel. A real movie this time, not like the one I imagined, three hours before, when that woman spit in my face as I sat in the lobby.

A cowboy movie I had seen as a youngster. The Ox-Bow Incident. A story with a moral, I recalled. The tale of a rancher, caught by a posse looking for a rustler. Accused of stealing cattle, hung from a tree without a trial. A lynch mob, taking credit for it.

Innocent, as things turned out, too late for justice. Proctor must have seen it years ago, as I had. Too bad he did not remember it also.

Proctor had done more damage than I realized. Much more, I could tell when I got home that night. The television set was on the floor, shattered, with a broken whisky bottle lying in front of it. No need to guess what happened. Molly must have seen the evening news. She had heard about Lamont. The TV set, damn it, she had thrown that bottle at it.

She was not in her room. I looked around our quarters and couldn't find her. Past eleven and the place was empty. Four days away, not much sleep, none at all on the plane coming back, and now I had to figure out where the hell she'd gone, lost, maybe, wandering around the neighborhood.

She had used the phone, or tried to, I noticed when I went to the kitchen. The receiver was off the hook, lying on the counter. I hung up the phone and saw something else. Blood smeared around the emergency button on the receiver. The button Nurse Rebecca had installed, so Molly could signal the hospital if she needed help.

Damn it, that's where she'd gone. Back to the hospital, sure as hell. My fault again, being away. Maybe. I looked in the phone book for the hospital number, tired, too damned tired to know what to do about her. Call the hospital, see how she is, do my duty as a husband. Right, do my duty, as if I knew what the hell that meant.

I did not have to call. The phone rang before I could find the number. Someone calling from the hospital, saying my wife was there, they had been trying to reach me for hours, but my phone had been busy. Another voice came on the phone then. Nurse Rebecca, sounding worn out herself as she talked about Molly.

"Your wife has been in surgery" she said.

"Surgery? What for? What happened to her?"

"It looks like a light bulb exploded in her face."

"A light bulb, hell. . .how bad was she hurt?"

"How bad? Two hours to pick glass from her face."

"Damn. . .when can I see her?"

"Not now, let her sleep. You've just returned, I gather."

"I have, and I'm beat, but listen. . ."

"Get some rest, come in at six. There's something else you need to know."

She hung up before I could ask what the something else might be. Get some rest, she said. Good advice. I looked again at the TV set on the floor, broken all to hell, with pieces of glass on the sofa where Molly had been sitting. Nothing I could do about it now. I undressed and went to bed. Get a few hours sleep, I told myself, try not to think about it.

Asleep, tossing and turning, dreaming. The last dream I had, before I woke up, that would be something to think about. A damned bad dream, worse than the regular nightmares.. Sure as hell worse than dreaming about Nam.

A wedding. Molly and Mel Lamont, getting married in a chapel somewhere. . .

Plunkett, standing behind the altar, holding a sign saying Semper Fi. . .

Fernhill, coming out of nowhere, pinning a medal on Molly. . .

Calloway the best man, standing next to the bride. . .

Renfro's wife, pushing me around in a wheelchair in the rear of the chapel. . .

Woods, whispering in my ear, saying I warned you. . .

His wife Ramona, shouting her husband's going to be a general. . .

Proctor laughing as I struggle to climb from the wheelchair. . .

Molly and Lamont marching around me as they come down the aisle. . .

Molly laughing as she walks past me, spitting in my face. . .

Nurse Rebecca coming down the aisle behind them, ringing a bell in my ears. . .

The bell was my alarm clock. Five in the morning. I got up, still worn out, thinking about the dream. Not easy to shake off. I cleaned up and put on a fresh uniform, getting ready to do my duty. Check on Molly. Report to Calloway, tell him what I learned while I was away. Do my duty, hell. This mess I was tangled up in, Molly, Bahn Bahn, Proctor, a bad dream on top of that, I was in no shape to understand a damned thing.

Nurse Rebecca was not much help. When I got to the hospital she led me to Molly's room, silent, shaking her head as she pointed to the bandages on Molly's face. Her eyes and mouth were covered and she could not talk. Neither could Rebecca, evidently. Without a word she left the room and started down the hallway.

"Wait" I said. "What's going on here?"

"Ask her doctor" she answered, stopping, but not looking at me.

"On the phone, you said there was something I needed to know."

"I'm sorry, Phil, I can't be the one to tell you."

"Molly, she'll have scars on her face, is that it?"

"She'll be coming home this afternoon, you can see for yourself."

"Then what is it? Rebecca, look. . ."

No answer. I waited in the hallway, watching her go to another room, wondering what it was she couldn't tell me. Scars, maybe worse, maybe Molly's eyes had been hit by glass. In a moment her doctor came out and walked toward me. What he told me in the next few minutes was worse, all right. Like having a hand grenade go off in my ear.

"Major, this is awkward" said the doctor. "It's something we just discovered."

"What is it? Go ahead, colonel, tell me."

"I will, but only because I am required by regulation to do so."

"Regulation? What regulation?"

"You understand, I am not a marriage counselor, I am only a doctor."

"Marriage counselor? What are you getting at?"

"When she was first admitted, it was drugs we were concerned with."

"Two months ago, right, she overdosed, what about it?"

"The valium, because of that I'm afraid we missed something."

"Damn it, doctor, stop beating around the bush, what was it?"

"Major, I'm sorry. Your wife had a miscarriage, right around New Year's Day."

I leaned against the wall and stared at the doctor. Hoping what he'd said would go away. It wouldn't, I could tell by the look on his face. He knew what it meant, as well as I did. A miscarriage, and I hadn't been around in nearly a year.

He followed as I walked away to the elevator, silent, with my head down. When I got there he put his arm on my shoulder and held it for a moment, nodding, saying nothing. He knew what news like that could do to a soldier.

I rode the elevator down, got in my car, and drove away. Damn near shell-shocked, a wounded soldier running for cover.

West of Fort Leavenworth the sky was cloudy and the ground was muddy from snow. In the distance a farmer was plowing with a tractor. I stopped on the side of a country road and watched. A few hundred yards in one direction with the tractor, then back, back and forth, row after row. Simple. A hell of a lot simpler than what I was faced with.

I sat there for a while, watching the farmer, looking up at the clouds, smoking a cigarette now and then, taking my time, trying to figure out what to do. Molly would be out of the hospital sometime today, maybe we'd have it out then. Or maybe not. Hard to know what she'd say if I asked her. Hard to know what I'd say if she told me.

After an hour or so I drove back, more or less resigned to where things stood. Gritting my teeth when I thought about the irony of it. Molly, smashing the TV set, in the hospital again, her doctor checking on her, hell, if that hadn't happened, who knows? He might not have seen what they missed before. And me, I would not be trying to get my mind on something else.

On something else, right. Like Calloway. He would have heard the news last night as well. Bahn Bahn, he must know it leaked somehow. See him, find out what he wants to do about it, now that it's out in the open. Maybe he'll tell me again why the Army doesn't issue wives to its soldiers. Fine, let him remind me.

"General Calloway is not here" his secretary told me when I reached his office.

"I'll wait. Where is he?"

"He's on his way to the Pentagon. The Secretary of the Army wants to see him."

"The Pentagon. When did he leave?"

"Three hours ago. Here, his aide left you a message before they left."

She handed me a page from a memo pad. A scribbled note from Captain Reilly. The general said to tell you to leave it alone, and beware of politicians.

"Leave it alone? Leave what alone? What does that mean?"

"What does it mean? How would I know?"

Leave it alone. And beware of politicians. Why would Calloway tell me that? I went to my office and sat there, with the phone off the hook so I would not be bothered, trying to add it up from the beginning. Politicians. What Calloway's message meant.

All right, start with the Secretary of the Army. A colonel named Tracy is killed a few months ago. His wife gives his letters to the Secretary. Letters written years ago. Why did she do that? Why would she give away her husband's letters?

The Secretary orders an inquiry then. Into what happened at Bahn Bahn during Tet. Five years ago, maybe a massacre. But only an inquiry? Why not a full-scale investigation? Why? What the hell was in those letters? If that's what leaked somehow to Proctor, the letters, damn it, then what about Lamont? Proctor said he was Tracy's second in command, so he had to be mentioned in the letters. So why did the Secretary want his name kept secret?

And Tracy, what about him? Dead now, poor bastard, hit by a mortar round in Saigon, so why was General Fernhill worried about a medal he gave him five years ago? What was Fernhill trying to hide? None of it added up. I sat there, going over how I got involved in all this mess. Woods, that's how, his keeping me around so I could deal with Proctor. A full colonel, out of the loop now, after his wife spilled some secret to Molly about Bahn Bahn.

New Year's Eve, something about Bahn Bahn and Lamont. Enough to cause a miscarriage, evidently. Bad idea, thinking about that, letting it lead me back to Molly. Back to wondering, again, what the hell to do about her.

So I'm on my own. With a warning about politicians. Fine, I learned that years ago as a reporter. Maybe I should have stuck with newspaper work instead of the Army. I wouldn't be going back to my quarters now, with questions I can't answer plus a marriage I can't deal with.

Damn it, drop it, I told myself, remembering what an editor told me once in Texas. Don't look back, he said, life is full of should haves and shit if only's. How true. If only I hadn't married Molly. And if only Molly hadn't smashed that TV set. Then I wouldn't be headed home to clean up a goddamned mess now.

There was no mess to take care of when I got to my quarters. The living room was fine, a new TV set had been placed in the corner, and Clara was sitting in the kitchen filling out the paper-work I would have to sign to settle with the maintenance people. An accident, according to the form she showed me.

"Miss Rebecca told me who to call" said Clara.

"She was here this morning, was she?"

"While you were gone, while I was cleaning up the living room."

"I'm sorry, Clara. A lot of broken glass, I know."

"She said Miss Molly hurt herself, she went to the hospital with some cuts."

"Cuts, right, she's all bandaged up. But she's coming back this afternoon."

"Miss Rebecca, she said you've had an awful lot of trouble with Miss Molly."

Trouble with Molly. Damned right. She shacks up while I'm gone, gets pregnant, has a goddamned breakdown at Leaven-worth, causes me to wind up here, chasing all over the country trying to find out what happened at Bahn Bahn, running an er-rand for the goddamned Secretary of the Army, right, I'd say she's caused me a lot of trouble.

"Trouble. So what else did Miss Rebecca tell you?"

"She said I should be good to you."

"Be good. . .that's what she told you. . ."

"Miss Rebecca, she said in the Army you have to take care of each other."

Clara placed coffee and pastry on the table for me. I sat down to sign the form for a new TV set. An accident? Like hell. An-other lie. But that's what Becky said to Clara, was it? In the Army we have to take care of each other.

Really. I wondered what she'd say if I told her how Plunkett put it. Word for word, exactly as he said it, there's no such fucking thing as the Army. A few real grunts, the rest a bunch of pencil pushers. Right, so sign this goddamned form.

"Miss Rebecca, she also sorted out your mail" said Clara when I handed her the form.

"Mail? That pile they forwarded from Nam, you mean?"

"She said one of your letters was sent by registered mail, quite a while ago."

"I'll look at it later. What else?"

"A captain called you from Fort Bragg. He tried your office, but your line was busy."

"Busy. I had the phone off the hook so I could think, so. . ."

Clara handed me a note with a name and number on it. Damned efficient, this colored woman working as a maid, trying to raise two kids. She should be in the service, pushing a pencil, hell, she'd be as good as any of the other clerks who run the Army.

I looked at her note. And shook my head. I'll be damned, I muttered out loud. Captain Booker T. Malone, Fifth Special Forces Group, Fort Bragg. His telephone number, written down quite legibly by Clara. I'll be damned, I said again out loud, this time with a smile.

Booker T. Malone. Nobody else in the Army with a name like that, for sure. A corporal in my first platoon, in Germany, the biggest storyteller I ever knew, until I ran into Calloway. Malone, telling me he'd gone through jump school at the age of nine, big for his age, and a lot of other crap like that. A captain now. I'll be damned.

Malone, prying open a scrapbook full of memories.

Germany, my first day there, before I even got on post, Mel Lamont, my Company XO, making me watch from the road as four jumpers augur in, scaring the hell out of me, a naïve green lieutenant.

Four dummies rigged with parachutes that wouldn't open, meant to frighten some visiting Congressmen. Malone, the jumpmaster who pushed the dummies out, a pal of Lamont, I learn later, after I knock Lamont on his ass.

Dummies that somehow looked like Negro soldiers. And me, later, having to face a lady from Congress who came raising hell about their murders. Malone, calming her down, a black soldier himself, squiring her around, getting me off the hook.

Germany. Lamont, introducing me to Molly, the young Red Cross woman he's crazy about. So crazy we turn against each other when I fall in love with her myself. And marry her when the unit moves back to Campbell and Lamont is somewhere else.

Campbell. Where I stayed in the Army because of her.

Not the best of memories there.

Malone. Lamont. Germany. A long time ago. And Malone's a captain now, in Special Forces. So why would he be calling me? Why would he. . .

I'll be a sonofabitch. What was it Renfro said when he was drunk? About Bahn Bahn? About a massacre there? A Special Forces team had counted the bodies in the village. A black captain led the team. Renfro hadn't seen the bodies himself, he was. . .

I looked at the number on Clara's note and dialed it right away.

When Malone came on the phone we talked. A moment of greetings, but no stories now. All business. He had seen the news last night, and he knew I had been looking into Bahn Bahn. Proctor was off base, there was no massacre in that village. He was there himself, he knew what really happened. And he could prove it.

"You're sure?" I asked. "You've got proof?"

"Major, I have the photographs we took."

"And no one there was killed. . ."

"Not a single person from that village."

"Hang on, Booker. Let me think for just a minute."

I thought, all right. So what had Calloway said? Leave it alone? Leave what alone? Bahn Bahn, maybe. To hell with that. His aide's gone with him, so I'd have to buy the ticket myself, but it's time to fly to Bragg and put this Bahn Bahn crap to rest, once and for all.

Damned right. Head for North Carolina. So I won't have to face Molly when she gets back from the hospital.

"Booker, listen, I'll be there just as soon as I can get there."

"Major, I can send you the photographs. . ."

"No, we need to talk. This is a real damned mess I've gotten into."

"All right, let me know when you're arriving."

After I hung up it dawned on me, something I hadn't asked Malone. How did he know I had been digging into Bahn Bahn? Odd, damned odd, that he would know. Forget it, I would ask him later. Right now, I needed to write a note for Becky. Tell her where I would be. No point in calling Calloway's secretary, she was useless, she had no idea what leave it alone might mean. Neither did I, so to hell with it, I'm headed for Bragg. By way of Kansas City.

"Clara, I'm taking a shuttle bus to the airport, please give this note to Miss Rebecca."

"What about Miss Molly? She's coming home today, she. . ."

"You take care of her. I'm leaving my car if you want to drive her around."

"Should I give her all that mail that's been sorted out?"

"No way, it's none of her business. She's bandaged up, she couldn't read it, anyway."

I admit I had second thoughts on the way to the airport. Leave it alone? Maybe that meant Bahn Bahn altogether, now that Proctor's broken it open on TV. So what could Calloway do, put me in front of a firing squad for chasing off to Bragg? Too bad.

Something else too bad. Too bad I hadn't opened it, that registered letter sent to me in Nam. I could have been laughing my ass off. About Molly. Laughing my ass off about her, all the way to the firing squad.

Malone, thirteen years since Germany, since he left my battle group and headed for Special Forces. Speaking Russian, a real asset then, before we heard of Indo-China. I was not surprised he looked older, still tall and a little heavier, still black, of course, his grip as friendly as mine when we shook hands. What surprised me was his voice.

Weary, worn down, the way he talked about the lounge where we were meeting, the downstairs bar in Hardy Hall. The bar where the Green Berets hung out, named after an SF captain killed in Nam. Empty now, this early in the day, only the two of us at a table.

"Look around" he said. "In a few hours, this place will be packed with heavy drinkers."

"Sure, getting drunk over Nam, now that it's over."

"Trading war stories, trying to figure out what really happened, major."

"Like these pictures you're going to show me. What really happened at Bahn Bahn."

"No massacre, you can see for yourself. Proctor's full of crap."

I looked at the first two pictures he put on the table. Thatched huts, old men and women standing in mud, watching Malone and his men. A dozen kids around them, his men giving the kids what looked like candy bars maybe, I couldn't tell from the pictures.

Malone then, close-up, with the huts and the villagers in the background. Smiling, holding one of the kids in his arms. Along with a paper, the Stars and Stripes, pointing to the top of the front page.

"I had that blown up" he said. "After I called, so you could see when it was taken."

Another picture then, an enlargement, big enough to see the date on the paper. The day the Cong hit the hill above Bahn Bahn. The day Lamont flew in and took command and drove them back. The day of a massacre, if what Proctor claimed was right.

The paper, the Stars and Stripes, the date of the battle, how the hell did Malone have that paper when they took the pictures? Before I could ask, he leaned back in his chair and nodded, pointing again to the pictures of the village.

"That was Bahn Bahn, major. Right after the fight."

"Your team, you were in it then, you. . ."

"No, we were a long way off, in a heavy fog."

"So you didn't see what happened, you didn't. . ."

"No, by the time we got there it was over."

Malone set three more photos in front of me. Medevac helicopters loading the wounded. Soldiers stacking up the bodies of dead Cong, with the village in the background down below. A chaplain kneeling over a GI on a stretcher. The usual carnage left over from a battle.

"That's how it looked on top the hill, major. You can see how the fog had cleared."

"The Stars and Stripes, Booker, how did you get that?"

"They said a chopper came in with resupplies, the latest news about Tet. . ."

"A chopper, right, before the fog lifted, did they tell you what happened then?"

"What they told me five years ago, it's not easy to recall."

Malone stood up and walked around the empty bar, looking down at the floor, shaking his head, thinking, trying to remember. When he sat down again and started talking, I took a notepad from my briefcase and started writing.

Listening to Malone, matching what he said with what I'd read in the unit records, with what I'd heard from Raborn and Plunket and Renfro. And that lying bastard Fernhill. Listening to Malone as he tried to remember what they told him on the hill.

The chopper had landed in the middle of the battle, they said. . .in a fog so thick they could barely see the Cong inside the wire. Check.

Their XO had been killed and their CO was in his bunker, wounded. . .when the chopper landed, some major on the chopper had assumed command. Check.

They had rallied behind the major. . .had driven the Cong back down the hill in a heavy firefight that lasted hours. Check.

A captain, on a stretcher. . .what had he said? The major had led them to the village. . .the Cong had come from there, so the village had been burned and everyone in it had been killed. . .

Check. That sounded like Renfro, the way he talked about it, drunk, how he hadn't seen it, but that's what Lamont had done, wiped out that village. Hell no, he hadn't seen it, and no wonder. These pictures proved it never happened.

I looked at the pictures again. Too bad for Proctor, he'd have to eat what he claimed on TV. Something odd, even so, about what he reported. Tracy ordered it and Lamont was second in command? Not at all what Malone remembered hearing. How the hell did that get started?

"Booker, you went down to look, to see if what that captain said was true?"

"No, we didn't need to. That one picture I just showed you, see the village?"

"The village, sure, it looks all right from on top the hill, but. . ."

"It was my birthday, major."

"Your birthday? I don't get it, Booker. . ."

"My team wanted to take my picture there, not in the middle of all that shit on the hill."

I looked at the first three pictures again. Malone, with that kid in his arms, with the Stars and Stripes in his hands, the paper brought in on that chopper. Malone, pointing to the date of the paper. His birthday? They took these pictures because it was his birthday?

"All luck, major, these pictures. But you can see how far Proctor was off base."

"Off base, but listen, this is damned important. You know what he said on TV."

"About a massacre, sure, he claimed there were hundreds dead in that village."

"According to him, ordered by the battalion commander, Tracy."

"I know, I know. . ."

"With Lamont doing the dirty work, Booker."

"So what? Proctor's wrong, there wasn't any massacre."

"The day of the battle. Did they tell you who the major on that chopper was?"

"No, he was gone before we got there, he. . ."

Malone was silent for a moment. One by one he looked at the pictures, lining them up on the table. Staring at one of them, taken after the battle, the picture showing soldiers stacking up the bodies of dead Cong. By the sound of his voice I could tell he was annoyed.

"Lamont, if that was him, then he's the one who should have gotten that medal."

"A medal, you saw it being awarded?"

"When we came up the hill again, that afternoon, the brigade CO was there."

"Fernhill, pinning a medal on Tracy, right. I already have a picture of that."

"Why? From what I heard, Tracy was in his bunker, he was out of it."

Why a medal for Tracy? Damned good question. I'd like to know myself, I felt like saying, I'd like to know what Fernhill's covering up. And something else I was starting to feel. Uneasy. Not sure what to do with all these pictures, starting with the one of Fernhill pinning that medal on Tracy.

"Why that medal? That's one of the things I'm digging into, Booker."

"A medal, five years later? Major, what's going on here? It's not just Proctor. . ."

I shook my head. Too hard to explain. The Secretary worried about a massacre, Lamont's name off limits, the letters from Tracy's wife, Fernhill and that medal, what Proctor claimed on TV, God only knows what else. And me, I shouldn't even be here, disobeying Calloway's order to leave it alone. Too hard to explain? Hell, yes, worse than that.

"Sir, if it's on a need to know basis, I won't ask."

"Maybe that's best. Right now, I'd welcome a ride to the airport."

He was silent as we drove through Fayetteville. I was silent, also, trying to think what to do next. Go back to Kansas, maybe, do what Calloway said, leave it alone. Or take these pictures to Proctor, maybe. Make him admit he was wrong, make him say it on TV.

But maybe not, not yet, not until I could find out why he'd made that claim about Tracy and Lamont in the first place. Find out. Or go back to Kansas and forget it. Hard to be sure, what to do next.

Unsure, until a woman stepped in front of us, trying to cross the street against the light. Malone slammed on his breaks. What he said then, and what it led to, that put me on track. By the time we got to the airport I knew what to do.

"That woman was lucky" Malone said as we drove on.

"Both of us, Booker. Lucky we're still alive."

"Something else that's luck, major. How I knew to contact you."

"About what Proctor said, you mean, about my looking into Bahn Bahn."

"I had a call from Fort Benning, from Andy Plunkett."

"Plunkett? Sure, I asked him what he knew about it."

"We went through OCS together. He's a damned good soldier, major."

"That riot he started, he acted like he was ready to quit the Army."

"Not now. He said the way you saluted him, that inspired him to stick it out."

Inspired by me? Hell, if Malone only knew. A sheriff's after Plunkett, a three-star general will be after me if I don't let up, and Malone thinks she's lucky he didn't run over that woman back there. She's the one who needs inspiring. To watch where the hell she's walking.

Women. What was it Calloway said? Women cause half the problems in the Army. Molly, for sure. And Tracy's wife. . .that woman who gave her husband's letters to the Secretary and started all this mess. . .who. . .

I jerked open my briefcase as we pulled up to the terminal. Looking for a list, the people Calloway first told me to see. Her name and address scratched out, but there it was, legible enough to read. Tracy's wife. Living in South Carolina.

"Booker, thanks for the pictures" I said as I got out of the car.

"Those pictures, major, shove them in Proctor's face."

"Not yet. But listen, there's something I want you to tell Plunkett."

"Andy? Sure, I'll call him. . ."

"Tell him for me. Tell him there is such a thing as the Army."

A two-story house, in a suburb outside Charleston. The address of the widow Tracy. No way to call, evidently the telephone had been disconnected, so I knocked on the door and held my breath. In uniform, with a briefcase in my hand, looking too damned official, I knew, with a rental car parked in the driveway.

"Go the fuck away" said the man who opened the door. Young, hard core, I could tell right away. Wearing a sweatshirt with a Screaming Eagle logo on it. And words in big black letters. I Am An American Paratrooper.

Great. Another member of the airborne brotherhood. A bit of a surprise, but what the hell, with a sweatshirt like that I knew we could do business. All I had to do was look him straight in the face and act like his commanding officer.

"Stand down" I replied. "I'm here to see Colonel Tracy's wife."

"I told you, go away. My aunt's had enough of this shit."

"So have I, more than enough. That's why I'm here, soldier."

The way I said that must have worked. He stepped aside and led me into the family room. Limping, I noticed. Stopping in front of a mahogany cabinet with a row of pictures on top. Nodding at me and then the pictures.

On the left, a photo of a lieutenant with his arms around a woman. Tracy and his wife, twenty years ago, I reckoned. On the other end of the row, a picture of an older man, a lieutenant colonel, no doubt Tracy again, smiling, with his arms around this young paratrooper.

He grunted, pointing to a glass-covered frame on the wall above the cabinet, a citation with a medal attached. The wide blue band, with red and white stripes and that cross hanging beneath it, easy to recognize. The Distinguished Service Cross. Impressive. If Tracy stayed in his bunker at Bahn Bahn, by God, he must have done something really brave after that.

"Major, you can tell your general to kiss off. He can't have that."

"What general? What are you talking about? I'm not here to. . ."

"If he wants that medal he'll have to send more than a major to get it."

"Look, I don't care about that medal, I'm. . ."

"A whole damned company. With flamethrowers, that's what he'll need."

One pissed off paratrooper, for sure. Angry as hell, not listening at all. Pointing to that frame with one hand, leaning against a table with the other, sounding like he was ready to duke it out. Over what? That medal?

"Sit down" I said. "You've got it wrong. I'm not here about that."

"That's one goddamned general I'd like to get my hands on."

"Shut up and listen. I told you, I'm not here about a medal."

"No? So what do you want? Why are you here?"

"Colonel Tracy. That massacre bullshit, I want to know how it got on TV."

"What do you care? My aunt, she cares, she's had it."

"Maybe I can help. Where is she?"

"She's upstairs asleep. Help her? How the hell can you help?"

"The letters she gave to the Army, damn it. I need to know what's in those letters."

When I said that he grunted again, looking down at his legs, leaning back in the easy chair he'd sat down in. Tired, I figured, the way he limped when he let me in. Not tired, just too damned hard to stand, I realized as he pulled up his trousers so I would see. Two artificial legs, his real legs gone at the knees.

"See that, major? Hamburger Hill, three years ago."

"I'm sorry, I didn't know, I. . ."

"Three years in a VA hospital, trying to make these things fit."

"You'll be all right, soldier. Sometimes it takes. . ."

"Two legs for a Purple Heart. Fine, but they can't have my uncle's medal."

"Who? Who are you talking about?"

"That general, that's what he wanted, too, he wanted to know about those letters."

I looked down at his legs, two metal tubes with shoes attached. Patient, not sure what to say, trying to make some sense of what he was muttering about. To hell with that, right now I needed to see the letters, I needed to know why Proctor had gotten it so damned wrong, that report about a massacre at Bahn Bahn.

"Don't worry about that medal. I can prove it never happened."

"A lie, major, what they said on TV."

"Dan Proctor, right. I've got pictures, but I need. . ."

"Wait, wait. . ."

He stood up abruptly, leaning against the table, looking past me. I turned around to see what it was. His aunt, a colonel's wife for sure, the way she was coming down the stairs, poised, acting stiff and formal as she came toward us. Middle-aged, with hair turning gray. And a look on her face that made me wonder, right away, whether she was altogether with it.

"I see you have a guest" she said to her nephew.

"Yes ma'am, he says he's here to help, he wants to see the letters you. . ."

"Major, please sit down. Arnold, have you offered the major tea?"

"No ma'am, I'll bring some" he answered, hobbling off to the kitchen.

"Dee, is that what it says on your name plate? Where are you stationed, major?"

"Right now, Fort Leavenworth, I'm here to. . ."

"Leavenworth, oh my, we had a wonderful time there, my husband and I."

Damn it all, I did not want to hear about it. This woman, staring off into space, remembering the wonderful time she had at Leavenworth, reminding me of Molly and the wonderful time she's had there, too. Screwing around while I was off at war, getting sick there, causing me to chase around the whole damned country now, staring off into space just like this colonel's widow, wondering, for a moment, what the hell I was doing here.

I snapped out of it when her nephew returned from the kitchen. Not her. She seemed not to notice when he set cups and saucers on the table between us. Indifferent as he poured from a pot of tea. Gazing at that frame on the wall, it looked like, her face blank, her voice so soft I could barely hear her.

"My husband was a good man."

"Aunt Martha, have some tea. This major, he. . ."

"Not all West Pointers are. General Fernhill, do you know him?"

"We've met, yes, I know him."

"When he called, I should never have let him talk to me that way."

"Fernhill? He called you? He. . ."

"And after that, I should not have talked to that reporter, either."

She paused for a moment, closing her eyes, remembering something else, perhaps. Giving me a moment to try and add it up, to understand what she'd just said. Fernhill, that bastard, he called her? What for? Why would he call her? And then she talked to a reporter? Why? The letters, they were one thing, but all this now, damn it, this was something else.

"Do you know the Secretary of the Army?" she asked when she opened her eyes.

"No, we've never met, my guess is he. . ."

"I have met him. My husband trusted him, I know."

"I'm sure he did, but what I'd like to ask is why you. . ."

"My husband set aside some letters to send him."

"The Secretary, you mean, you sent him those letters, and. . ."

"In case he did not make it home, that is what he told me to do."

"Colonel Tracy, so he left you instructions, he. . ."

"Sometimes, oh my, it is not easy to be a good Army wife."

She looked down at her tea as she said that, her voice even softer than before. Talking to herself, it seemed. Fine, I wouldn't need to reply, and I damned sure wouldn't want to comment about good Army wives. Not with Molly creeping around inside my head. Molly, always there, even with my mind spinning, trying to get a handle on it, what this lady had let out.

"Arnold, I am going for a walk in the garden now."

"Yes ma'am, would you like me to. . ."

"You may show the letters to Major Dee, if he wishes to see them."

She stood up then, and so did I, being as polite as I could be. Behind me I could hear what sounded like her nephew kicking something, trying to open the cabinet with the pictures on it, I supposed, looking for the letters she said he should show me. For a moment I paid no attention, watching this poor woman wander away. Sad. No other way to put it.

"Here, major, look at this" I heard her nephew say, and turned around.

"That? That's a newspaper, I don't. . ."

"Read that story on the second page."

"Arnold, is it? All right, Arnold, what about it?"

"Maybe then you'll start to understand."

I looked at the headline. Two columns in italics. Decorated Colonel Dies in Vietnam. The date of the paper, four months ago, the news that Tracy had been killed. Plus an interview with the grieving widow. A dozen paragraphs, full of praise, the reporter noting how she talked about her husband's letters, how he consoled her, how he held her hands while she wept.

"So he wrote about your aunt. Fine, so what am I supposed to understand?"

"That's how he got close to her, major. You heard what she said."

"Something about she shouldn't have talked to him again, sure, but. . ."

"After that general called she went to pieces. I think she must have panicked."

"Fernhill. Damn it, Arnold, what did Fernhill say to her?"

"I don't know, I wasn't here, I was getting her some flowers."

"You said he wanted to know about the letters, right? So let me see them."

Arnold folded the newspaper and went back to the cabinet with the pictures on it. His uncle's shrine, with a stack of scrapbooks inside. He leaned over, found the one he was looking for, turned the pages, and then handed it to me. Letters from his uncle to his aunt, nearly five years old now, all of them sent from Vietnam.

I grunted as I read the first one. Tracy, telling his wife he's being transferred from a desk job in Saigon. At last he's getting a battalion of his own, and the CO of the brigade he's going to is a long-time friend, a fellow West Pointer he's played poker with. I looked at the date. A week before the start of the Tet offensive.

"Not that one" said her nephew. "It's the next three you're looking for."

"They're the ones she sent to the Secretary?"

"She made Xerox copies. I wish like hell she hadn't done that."

Damned right. I wished the same. If she hadn't done that none of this crap would have happened. No letters, no checking on a massacre that never happened, nothing to leak, no false claims on television. I wouldn't be here, a thousand miles from Kansas, sitting down to see what the hell was in these letters.

The first one, Tracy telling his wife he's taken command, his battalion's on a hill above the village of Bahn Bahn, it's been raining hard, at times the fog's so thick you can hardly see a thing, he's had to counsel his company commanders about staying alert, and p.s. he loves her. A routine letter to his wife. So why would she send it to the Secretary of the Army?

The second letter, ten days later, a bit more vivid. He's been wounded, he's in a hospital, but she's not to worry, it's not bad enough to send him home. They're calling it the Battle of Bahn Bahn, the way his battalion fought off the enemy. He's been awarded a medal, too, right on the spot, before they flew him out, so she should be as proud as he is. The third letter was the one that floored me. A few days later, twice as long as the first two put together. I went through it again and again, stunned by what I was reading. Tracy, spelling out in detail what had happened at Bahn Bahn, so his wife would understand what he was worried about. A letter five years old, leaving me shaking my head at what he'd written.

He was still in the hospital. He had talked to one of his captains, who had been hit in the legs while dragging him to his bunker after he was wounded. The captain told him what had happened then, something terrible. With the battle almost over, some major from division had flown in and led a charge into the village, killing everyone there, according to the captain.

The major's name was Lamont, he believed, and he wanted her to know he had nothing to do with any massacre. He'd been told his medal had been approved by higher command, a DSC no less. And if anything ever happened to him here's what she's to do: send what he's told her about Bahn Bahn to the Secretary of the Army, so the medal will not be tarnished.

So Tracy got the DSC for what he did at Bahn Bahn? Maybe I'd heard the wrong story from the ones who were there. Or maybe not. When I stood up and read the citation I could tell at once it was pure fantasy. For one thing, Tracy hadn't charged forward in the midst of an artillery barrage he called for. There wasn't any artillery. They were out of action.

Fernhill. Tracy's poker-playing friend from West Point. Seeing to it his buddy got a big-time medal for bravery. Taking care of Tracy's career. Nothing new there, I'd seen it happen before. To hell with it, if Tracy's widow and his nephew wanted to believe it, fine. She's lost her husband and he's lost two legs. Leave them alone.

Right, leave them alone. At least I knew now what she'd sent to the Secretary of the Army. I sat down again, closed the scrapbook and handed it back to her nephew. When I did he opened it himself and pointed to the letters, the three I had just read.

"Major, you see now why I wish she'd kept this to herself."

"She couldn't, Arnold. She did what your uncle told her to do."

"I'm not talking about the copies she sent. I'm talking about that reporter."

"The one you said got close to her? Who wrote about holding her hands?"

"I told you, after your general called she panicked. She turned to that reporter for help."

"You weren't here, right? You don't know what Fernhill said to her?"

"No, but I know what she told that newspaper guy. Here, you can see for yourself."

He turned on a TV set and pushed a videotape into the receiver. Some kind of late night talk show, local, it looked like. With a Happy Valentine's Day banner in the background and the host, a middle-aged man in an easy chair, passing out chocolates to his three guests on a sofa. I waited while Arnold kept the sound off until the tape reached the part he wanted me to see.

"The lady next door, it's her favorite program. She gave me this tape the next day."

"That young man on the sofa. That's the reporter you've been talking about?"

"It is. I'll turn up the sound so you can hear what he said."

I listened. The two women on the sofa were laughing about the Valentine cards they had received. The reporter, sitting between them, said it hadn't been such a happy day for one of his dearest friends, the widow of Colonel Tracy, the lady he wrote about a few months ago after her husband was killed.

Yes, I remember, said the host, I imagine she's still in mourning for him.

Not just that, said the reporter, today she received some very bad news from he Army.

Bad news? What kind of bad news? asked the host, leaning forward.

She's been told there may have been a massacre by a unit her husband commanded.

A massacre? Something like My Lai, you mean? That's what the Army's told her?

I saw her today, she showed me some letters he wrote from Vietnam, she. . . .

Letters, oh yes, said the host, I imagine Colonel Tracy must have denied it.

Years ago, at a place named Bahn Bahn, Colonel Tracy and a Major Lamont, they. . .

Bahn Bahn, I never heard of it, said the host, but no doubt the Army's kept it secret.

I don't know, but you can see why it hasn't been a very good day for her.

Yes, said the host, and not a good day for the Army, either, once my producer informs our network affiliate in New York of what you've just told us. Another massacre, covered up by the Army, my, my. But now, it's time for a commercial, and then we'll get back to some more stories about Valentine's Day, something a bit more pleasant, I hope.

"That sonofabitch" I muttered out loud as Arnold turned off the videotape.

"Major, the very next night, you saw what they said on national TV."

"I know, all bullshit, the way Proctor twisted it around, just like this talk show idiot."

"Damn it, sir, my uncle didn't do it, they can't take away that medal, they. . ."

"Don't worry, I told you I can prove it never happened."

Proof, right, but not something to be pleased about. Not with what I was starting to remember. Not with what I was starting to realize. Me, goddamn it, I was the one who brought down all this shit on Tracy's widow and her crippled nephew. That look on her face, I was the one to blame for that.

That sign in Alabama, coming from Renfro's place. Tomorrow is Valentine's Day, the sign said. Right, you dumb bastard, so you stopped and sent roses to his wife, another poor woman you've made unhappy, poking around the country, asking questions about Bahn Bahn, causing her husband to start drinking again.

And the very next day, that must have been Valentine's Day, what was it you told General Fernhill? That there may have been a massacre at Bahn Bahn. . .that Tracy's wife had sent his letters to the Secretary of the Army. . .that the Secretary wanted to know about the medal he awarded Tracy. . .

The medal. That goddamn medal. Fernhill must have called her right away, as soon as I left his office. No doubt thinking about My Lai. Afraid of what happened to the big brass after they tried to cover that up. A politician, worried about his own ass, giving her hell, trying to find out what was in those letters.

Maybe, but I was the one to blame for all this other horseshit. I was the one who led him to call her. And all the rest that followed. That reporter, that talk show crap, what Proctor claimed on national television. And this poor woman, out of her mind now, staring off into space. My fault, all of it.

She came in from the garden and I stood up, nodding to her. No response. Her face was blank as she went up the stairs. Her nephew had tried to stand also but had fallen against a chair. I helped him up and shook hands. Time to get to get the hell out of here. Time to try to make amends.

"Arnold, I need to make some calls right away."

"I've had her phone disconnected. There's one at a café, down the road about a mile."

"I'll find it. And look, don't worry, all this crap that's happened to you and your aunt the last couple of days, I'll clean it up. All of it. You'll see."

He braced himself and stood erect as best he could. Then he saluted sharply, holding the salute until I returned it.

A fine salute, one soldier to another. Most of the time, something to feel good about. But not today. When I got outside to my car I smashed my fist against a fender. Cursing Fernhill, cursing myself for telling that rotten bastard about Bahn Bahn, cursing out loud for what that led to.

I would clean it up? What this poor widow's had to go through? And her nephew, this young paratrooper with his legs blown off, the way he's worrying about his uncle's medal? How in hell can you clean up something like that?

The place down the road, where Arnold said I'd find a phone, I found it, all right. After getting lost and driving around for half an hour. A tavern, The Submarine Hideout, with a half-dozen Navy flags on the roof, a telephone booth outside, and motorcycles parked out front

I went inside and stood at the bar, trying to get my act together, trying to figure out what to do next. Annoyed by the sound of guitars in the back of the room. Three jerks at a table, the only ones in the bar. Singing that Barry Sadler tune, The Ballad of the Green Berets.

Drunk as hell, it sounded like. The way they were singing, enough to piss me off even more. Back at home a young wife waits. . .her Green Beret has met his fate. Full of shit, like half the assholes in every bar in the country, acting like they've been in Special Forces. Screw them.

"You're bleeding, what's wrong with your fist?" I heard the bartender ask when I turned my head and looked down. At his two arms, pushing a napkin under my hand, and then at his face, wrinkled and worn. And then back to the arms. The tattoo of an anchor on one, a submarine tattooed on the other. Retired Navy, for sure.

"An alligator bit it, chief. I'm up to my ass in alligators."

"Been there, major. Here, I'll get you something for it."

"Good. A beer and a five dollar roll of quarters, too."

He came back a minute later with what I'd ordered. Plus a first aid kit. And a brass knuckle he laid on the counter next to my right hand.

"That steel, I'll help you put it under the bandage if you say so. It's up to you."

"For those pricks with the guitars? How long have they been here?"

"All afternoon. I was about ready to throw them out when you walked in."

"Submarines, right? Looks like you run a pretty tight ship here."

"Tight? Look up there, you can see for yourself." He pointed at the ceiling, covered with sheets of plywood. Painted blue and sprinkled with holes. Hundreds, maybe. Made by shotgun pellets. I nodded and went back to wrapping my hand. First, some powdered sulfa, then a bandage. Without the brass knuckles.

"Leave the steel on the counter, major. How's your hand feel now?"

"Like it's been in a depth charge. You ever been depth charged, chief?"

"Yeah. Once. In a whorehouse in Manila."

I grunted and told him I'd be back to finish my beer, but first I needed to use the phone. With the roll of quarters in my left hand and my right hand bandaged it would not be easy to dial, but I had to. Four days away, time to call Clara and tell her I'm heading for New York.

Right, New York. To make it up to a Tracy's widow and her crippled nephew. To try and square things for my latest screw up. Latest, hell. As soon as she answered the phone I knew there was more shit coming down the pike.

"Clara, what's wrong? Why are you crying?"

"Colonel Woods, he was here a while ago. . ."

"Woods? When did he get back?"

"I don't know, he came by with Miss Ramona. . ."

"Woods? With his wife? Clara, stop crying. What did they want?"

"Colonel Woods, he wanted her to apologize to Miss Molly. . ."

"Apologize? What for?"

"I don't know, I think for all the ugly things she told Miss Molly. . ."

"Clara, wait, wait. . .all right, operator, I'm getting some more coins."

The rest of the quarters fell on the floor of the booth as I tried to stick one in the pay slot. I bent over, cursing, trying to find them in the cigarette butts and all the trash around my feet. While thinking about Woods. And that bitching wife of his. At least she wasn't the one who spilled Bahn Bahn to the network. Hell no. Not Ramona. I was the one to blame for that.

"All right, Clara, go ahead. What did they say to Miss Molly?"

"They didn't say nothing. She wasn't here, she. . ."

"Clara, calm down and stop crying. Where is she?"

"She's left you, Major Dee. She took your car and ran away. . ."

"Ran away? What do you mean, she's run away?"

"This morning, Miss Molly, she made me pack all her things in your car. . ."

"Her things? Everything she had there? Where did she go?"

"All the money in your bank account, she said she was going to take that, too."

"Damn. . .damn. . ."

"She said she's going home. To Nashville, that's what she said."

"Nashville. Give me a minute, let me think"

I held the receiver against my chest so Clara could not hear me cursing. Damn it all to hell, the whole world's falling apart. Molly's run off with my car and emptied my account, and here I am, standing ankle-deep in trash, in a goddamned telephone booth in South Carolina, trying to think what to say next.

"Clara, stop crying. Nurse Rebecca, has she been there?"

"Last night, she said she's been called in by the general, he. . ."

"General Calloway? Calloway wants to see her?"

"She said the general wants to know where you are, Major Dee."

"Damn. All right, listen. Tell her I'm going to New York, I'll call her from there."

"New York. . .I'll tell her. . ."

"And stop crying. I'm the one who should be crying."

I hung up the phone when the operator started nagging for more coins. To hell with her. And to hell with Molly, as well. What's she up to, running off like that? And now on top of every-thing else I've got a general after my ass. That figures. By the time I'm done I'll be lucky if I don't wind up in the Leavenworth prison.

Back inside then. But not to finish my beer. To have a stiff drink instead. To sort things out. This mess on my hands, Proctor and his TV crap, Tracy's widow and her nephew and that medal, General Calloway tracking me down, one hell of a mess, all right. And Molly, running away, what to do about Molly.

"Chief, you ever been married?"

"Three times. Maybe four, I'm not sure about a broad I knew in Brisbane."

"Not sure. Sounds like me. I'm not so damned sure, either."

"Women. You know what they're good for, major? Clap, that's about it."

"Clap. Right. About the only damned thing I haven't caught yet."

"That pussy back there. Stick your dong in that, you'd be dripping in three days."

I turned and looked at the back of the room. Hard to tell, with the light so dim, but he was right, one of the clowns at the table was a woman. Drinking beer, while the rest of them started up again on their guitars. Another song from Sadler's album.

Bamiba. Beer 33 in Nam. Swill, only thing worse, a dish of Montagnard blood pudding. Rotten beer but a hell of a song. Those jerks back there couldn't sing it right, but I'd heard it a hundred times in the bar at Nha Trang, so many times the words started bouncing around in my head. . .

Oh won't you help me sergeant, get me out of Pleiku jail. . .I don't know how I got here I was drunk from the Ho Chi Trail.

Drunk. No time to get drunk now, as much as I felt like it. Time to head for New York and have it out with Proctor. I finished the bourbon and nodded to the old Navy dude behind the bar. Getting ready to leave. Then I heard a couple of voices behind me, loud enough to drown out the noise from the back of the room.

"Come join us, mister, I'll have them play you a song."

"Damn right, she won't take no for an answer."

Quite a sight, the pair I saw when I turned around. The woman, straight off the cover of some hippie magazine, her hair dyed purple, holding a bottle of beer. And with her some prick wearing a shirt that looked like it came from an Army surplus store, covered with insignia and badges. Not exactly a couple you'd invite for dinner.

"No thanks" I said. "I'm on my way out."

"C'mon, have a drink with me and my woman."

"No. . .I've got business to take care of."

"C'mon, have a drink, I'm Special Forces."

The woman with him staggered back to their table. I should have walked away, as well, I know. Never argue with a drunk in a bar. But this big sonofabitch, plastered, barely able to stand,

and Tracy's nephew a mile away with his legs blown off, maybe that's what did it.

"So you were Special Forces. What group were you in?"

"Group? No group. . .Nam. . .all over Nam. . ."

"All over, hell. Where were you? What province?"

"No province. . .the Ho Chi Trail. . .on the Ho Chi Trail."

"The trail's a thousand miles long, where were you?"

"All over Nam. . .Special Forces. . ."

"No shit. How come you've got the patch upside down?"

He looked down at his shoulder, where the Special Forces emblem had been sewn. Too dumb to know the dagger in the patch goes up, not down. Too drunk to know he was being made a fool of.

And me, too pissed off to think what I was doing. Taking it out on a drunk in bar. All the crap I'd stepped into, the whole nine yards. Fernhill and that medal, Tracy's widow staring into space, her nephew with his missing legs, Molly running off to Nashville, Calloway after my ass, a pot of shit bubbling and boiling over. Waiting to be dumped on this dumb bastard's head.

"Special Forces. So you must have humped an M-16 in Nam."

"M-16. . .on the Ho Chi Trail. . .an M-16, that's it. . ."

"An M-16. What's the maximum number of rounds in the magazine?"

"Rounds...a hundred. . .no, two hundred. . .two hundred rounds."

"Thirty. You hear that? Thirty rounds."

"Fuck you. . ."

"Special Forces, hell. You weren't even in the goddamn Army."

Right. Dump that pot of shit on him. And then go to it, get it off your chest and watch what happens. This big sonofabitch, a foot taller than me, grabbing my shoulder, taking a swing and missing, and then lying on the floor, grabbing his crotch with one hand and his jaw with the other. Groaning. A scene right out of a cowboy movie.

Blood dripping from my bandaged fist, a bottle thrown by his woman sailing past my head, the two other pricks in the back of the room yelling and rushing at me, stopping as the bartender fires his shotgun in the air, in a matter of seconds the scene is over. Finished, except for the pellets still dropping from the ceiling.

"Major, you're headed for New York?" asked the bartender as he reloaded.

"Anchors aweigh, chief. Hold them off while I get on my horse."

"They're out, as soon as you're gone. Give my regards to Broadway."

Right, New York. So screw that bastard and his Army surplus medals. That gypsy bitch, as well, his pals and all their damned guitars. Bamiba. Leave the Ho Chi Trail behind you.

The pot wasn't empty yet, however. Still boiling. When I got outside I looked at the motorcycles and kicked them over.

Bamiba. Proctor, you sonofabitch, you're next.

Rebecca did not answer when I called her quarters the next morning. Then I remembered what she told me the day before I left. For the next two weeks she'd be working the day shift while another nurse was taking leave.

I called the hospital and left a message for her to give me a ring at my New York hotel. Then I looked at my hand and saw it was healing. No need for another bandage. So I could sort out the pictures Malone had given me, the ones I planned to drop on Proctor.

Proctor, sure, if that woman at the network can get me in to see him. What was it she said at first? Major, you might as well try to see the King of England? Maybe, but even a king should find time for an old Army friend from Texas. Especially if the friend says he has some inside dope, proof there was no massacre at Bahn Bahn.

"He can see you at one forty five" said the lady from the network when she called.

"You told him what I'm here to talk about."

"I did, major. He'll see you right after he's had lunch with his producer."

"How do I get in? You said before he has an office on the fourteenth floor. . ."

"I will meet you in the lobby and take you there. And don't be late, time is money."

"Proctor, he remembered me, did he?"

"Oh yes, when you were both reporters. But he seemed puzzled about one thing. He wondered what in the world you're doing in the Army."

"There's been a war on, lady. That's what I've been doing."

I could have told her I sometimes wonder myself, what the hell I'm doing in the Army. Time is money, my ass. In the Army it's hurry up and wait. I looked at my watch. Four hours to go before I'd drop a bomb on Proctor and that network. No need to hurry.

One more cup of coffee and two more cigarettes then. A soldier's breakfast. Not what Nurse Rebecca had in mind whenever we ate. You should eat correctly, she'd nag. Right, fatten me up for the kill. That's what I wanted to know as I waited for her to call. If Calloway was ready to hang me.

"What are you doing in New York?" she asked when I answered the phone.

"That crap on TV about Bahn Bahn. I'm here to straighten it up."

"You talked to Clara. . .she told you Molly's gone. . ."

"She said General Calloway called you in. Rebecca, what did he want?"

"He wanted to know where you are. I have no idea why he thought I'd know."

"Woods may have guessed you would. So what did you tell the general?"

"I told him to leave you alone. You're just doing what he ordered you to do."

"Maybe, but not exactly. What did he say then?"

"He said that's no way for a nurse to talk to a three-star general."

"Damn. . .sounds like we're both in trouble now."

"What can he do? Make me clean up bedpans the rest of my life?'

"Becky, wait. I need to answer the door."

Room service. With another pot of coffee. When I reached in my wallet for a tip I could see I was almost out of cash. Running around the country on a credit card, no Army travel vouchers to cover a damned thing, my bank account emptied by a runaway wife, hell, after Calloway's done with me I may have to hire out helping clean up bedpans.

"Breakfast, Becky. Ham and eggs, I'm eating just the way you told me."

"Really? I heard what your bellhop said. He said he's bringing you more coffee."

"Well. . .yes, that too. But listen, about General Calloway. . ."

"I've been ordered to see him again this afternoon. I'll tell him where you are."

"I'll be back tomorrow. He can do whatever the hell he wants to then."

"Phil. . .there's something else. . .I'm not sure how to tell you. . ."

A long pause on the telephone. Silence. Rebecca, no doubt choosing her words carefully before she delivered some more bad news. Maybe Calloway had told her I'd be court martialed, out of the Army for disobeying orders. Screw him, and Woods too, for getting me into this mess.

"Phil. . .you talked to Clara yesterday. About your wife."

"Sure, she was crying like hell. She said Molly's left for Nashville."

"Clara called me a while ago at the hospital. That's what I want to talk to you about."

"Something's wrong with Clara now? Becky, listen, I can't. . ."

"She said some attorney's been trying to contact you. From Tennessee."

"Tennessee. Sounds like Molly's got herself a lawyer. She'll need one."

"Clara gave me his number, Phil, so. . ."

"I'll call him when I get back. I can't worry about a damned attorney now."

"I called him for you. Maybe I shouldn't have, but. . ."

"Fine, fine. Relax, Becky. So you called him, so what?"

"He wanted to know if you ever looked at the registered letters he mailed you."

Letters? What letters? Becky waited for me to reply, aware I was trying to recall. Then I remembered. That bag of mail they set back to the States, from Vietnam to Leavenworth, after the Army finally figured out where I was. Sorted out, stacked on a table in my quarters, but never opened.

"They must be in that mail from Nam. All right, I'll read them when I get back."

"You won't need to, Phil. Would you like to know what he said?"

"Later. I've got other things to worry about right now."

"Whatever you say. But I think you'll be surprised at what he told me."

"Surprised? Hell, nothing surprises me any more. Hang on a minute. . ."

Another knock on the door. This time a different bellhop, returning my uniform. Cleaned and pressed. Ready for me to pin the brass on. And all the ribbons and hero badges. So Proctor would know where I've been. So he would know I meant business.

"That's my uniform, Becky. Clean. I need to get dressed."

"You're not dressed? You've been talking to me without any clothes on?"

"I'm in a robe. You're being nosy."

"Nothing on but a robe. My, my, how romantic."

"A robe, hell yes. It's cold in New York."

"Too bad you're so far away. I could put on a robe and keep you warm."

"Becky, you're on duty, I know you haven't been drinking, but. . ."

"You don't like my bedside manner, Phil? My my, you'll see when you get back."

I said goodbye, or something like that, I wasn't sure what to say, the way she was laughing. What the hell had gotten into her? All of a sudden, flirting like that, right on the damned telephone, after telling me she talked to Molly's lawyer. Damned odd. Flirting, after all these months of taking care of things? My God, for all I know she might be. . .

Forget it. Get your mind on what you're here for.

I looked at my watch, took a nap, got up, had one last cup of coffee, got dressed and went downstairs to hail a taxi. Dee Day, so to speak. H-Hour minus thirty. Time to parachute into enemy lines. The fourteenth floor of a network television building.

Time to settle this Bahn Bahn shit. Save Tracy's medal for that poor woman and her nephew back in Charleston. Time for Proctor to eat crow.

All business, the woman who met me in the network lobby. Telling a guard to check my briefcase. Telling me they must be careful, there had been a bomb threat a week before. Nothing there, said the guard, only pictures. Bomb, hell, if she only knew.

Beatrice something or other. Not quite middle-aged, wearing a suit. Follow me, she said, she'd take me to Mister Proctor. On the elevator she pressed the button for the fifteenth floor, not the floor for his office. I braced myself. Indian country, watch out for an ambush.

"They're working on the fourteenth floor" she said. "We will have to use the stairwell."

"The fifteenth floor, what's there?"

"Studios. Since you're early, you might enjoy seeing what they're doing."

No ambush so far. In the hallway, glass windows, twenty or thirty people on the other side, a man and a woman standing in the center of what looked like a model kitchen, surrounded by microphones and TV cameras and bright lights. And in the middle of it all, a young man in shirtsleeves, holding a clipboard and evidently running the show.

"They're on the air" said the lady. "It's live television."

"Live. What is it? Soap opera?"

"We don't call it soap opera, Major Dee. It's drama."

As she spoke the man in shirtsleeves held up two fingers and motioned to some men on the edge of the set. In nothing flat the model kitchen disappeared, the men rolled out a different background, pushed some furniture into place, and another couple stood next to a sofa and a coffee table, listening to the man in shirtsleeves with the clipboard.

"They've taken a two-minute break for commercials" said the lady.

"But you don't call it soap opera? Don't the sponsors sell soap anymore?"

"Please do not be rude, Major Dee."

"So you call it drama. Fine."

"It's drama, period. Come along, I'll take you to Mister Proctor."

Drama, my ass. And this officious network woman Beatrice what's her name, bossing me around, I felt like saying you want to see drama, lady, stick around, follow me when I get to Proctor's office, you'll see some real damned drama then.

I looked at my watch when she knocked on his door. Right on schedule, but no one answered. Wait here, she said, I have other things to do. Right, I replied, as you say, time is money. She walked away then, angry. Good, I was just getting warmed up for Proctor.

Warmed up, hell. Maybe I'd worked myself into the wrong damn mood. Maybe I'd overdone it, planning what to say when

I faced him. The wrong damned mood, all right. When he arrived and shook my hands I felt like I'd been greeted by a long lost brother.

Years since I'd helped him out in Germany. Years since we got roaring drunk in Texas, a couple of young reporters trying to make it in a tough profession. Proctor sure as hell had. The pictures around his office said so.

Proctor with LBJ. Nixon. Kissinger. With Westmoreland in Nam. Proctor, rubbing elbows with famous people. But you'd never know it, the way he grinned with an aw shucks look on his face when he greeted me. The kind of down home welcome I had not expected.

"Good to see you, Phil, we've got a lot to talk about."

"A lot, indeed. That's what I'm here for."

"What are you doing in the Army? I thought you'd gone back to newspaper work."

"Sometimes I think. . .well, hell, I got married and stayed in, and then. . ."

"And then Nam came along, I know. A rotten war, Phil."

"The war. Dan, listen. . .there's something I need to tell you."

We had sat down in cushioned chairs by then. Drinking cans of diet soda from a cooler in the corner of his office. What I had planned to say, the threats, the warnings, all of that had gone out the window. The way he greeted me, I wasn't sure what to say now.

"Something to tell me? Beatrice said when you called you. . ."

"Beatrice. That woman? All right, it's this, you're wrong about Bahn Bahn, Dan."

"Bahn Bahn. You mean that massacre story we aired last week?"

"There wasn't any massacre, damn it."

"No massacre? That's what you're trying to tell me?"

"What you said about Tracy and Lamont, not true, Dan."

"Not true? That report wasn't true? Listen. . ."

"No, you listen, damn it. The Army's had me checking for a

month, I've got proof it never happened. You want me to show you? It's right here in my briefcase."

That was it. I had told him. When he mentioned Beatrice, maybe that's what had brought me to my senses. That woman, bossing me around. So have it out now with Proctor. Friends or not, I was starting to get pissed off again. At what he'd said on national TV.

Proctor. Evidently he was pissed off, too. The way he hurled his can of soda at a wastebasket, cursing, pissed off at me, I figured. While I sat there, wondering if I'd gone too far, waiting to hear what he'd say now about Bahn Bahn.

"Damn it, I had a bad feeling about that story when they shoved it in front of me."

"What do you mean, they shoved it in front of you?"

"Right at the end of the news. A flash from an affiliate, they said."

"Who? Your writers? You hadn't even seen it and you read it on TV?"

"That's how it is when it's breaking news, but listen, you said. . ."

"I said I can prove that story was false. You should fire those bastards, Dan."

"No, but listen, Phil, I trust you, if it wasn't true I'll have to. . ."

"That talk show bastard in Charleston. Fire him, too."

"Fire someone in Charleston? Damn it, Phil, I have to move fast now."

"Fire him. He's the one who broke that woman's heart, that bastard. . ."

"What woman? I'm the one in trouble, not some woman. . ."

"He's the one who started this breaking news crap. All bull-shit, Dan."

"Bullshit, you say? Not if another network finds out. They'll have a field day, they'll laugh about it and hang me out to dry."

He sat down at his desk and pressed a button on an intercom. Two voices then, Proctor's and someone named Ron, the honcho in charge of news, I gathered. Both of them speaking calmly, working out some sort of deal about the evening broadcast.

Sixty seconds, that's all we'll need, I heard Proctor say. This major who's with me here, he has proof, we need to put this to bed before it blows up in our face. As you know I wasn't sure about that story when we aired it, that's why we haven't touched it since.

All right, it's your call, said the other voice, I'll give you a minute at the end, but what about this man Lamont? What our guys found out, it sounds like they're hiding something in the Secretary's office, you think we should stay with that?

The Secretary of the Army, no, said Proctor, I think we should focus on this Watergate business instead, Nixon's a much bigger target. But first let me wrap up this Bahn Bahn matter. Tonight, sixty seconds, good, I'll write it myself.

"Done" said Proctor when he turned off the intercom. "I'll need your help, Phil."

"Wait. What's that I heard? Something about Lamont and the Secretary's office."

"Lamont, second in command at Bahn Bahn, I think we reported, I don't remember."

"I remember, damn it, you said the Army was hiding him someplace."

"They're not. He's a lieutenant colonel in the Pentagon, married to the Secretary's niece. That's over, so forget it, help me figure out how to wrap this up."

Wrap it up, hell. I groaned and slumped backwards in my chair. Cursing myself, over and over again, you stupid bastard, you dumb sonofabitch, add it up, you can see now what you've done.

Go ahead, add it up. Lamont's name shows up in some letters, the Secretary wants a low-profile inquiry, and you've gone charging around the country, stirring up shit all over. Digging into

Bahn Bahn, with Lamont's name off limits. Because he's married to the Secretary's niece.

A low-profile inquiry, hell. You've caused Lamont to be accused of leading a massacre. The Secretary's nephew-in-law, right on national TV. No wonder he ordered Calloway back to the Pentagon. You've had it now, for sure, no matter how Proctor tries to smooth things over.

"Phil, damn it, settle down, this isn't easy, what I'm trying to write."

"Write it as a joke. That's what it is, the whole goddamn world. A joke."

"Good idea. Admit we made a mistake, but do it with a touch of humor."

"There's one thing I'd like you to include. Mention Tracy's medal."

"Tracy? He's dead, there's no humor in that."

"A DSC for valor. Just say the Army's verified it was awarded properly."

"Nothing amusing there, either. But I'll work it in. Anything else?"

"That's for Tracy's widow. Do it for her. The rest of what I've had a hand in, there's no way to make up for that."

Tracy's widow. A world of difference, the pictures in her living room and the ones on Proctor's wall. Pictures of a West Point officer and his wife. Versus famous people, Proctor with them. And no one here to take a picture now, showing him working on a cover-up.

I stood up and looked around, waiting for him to finish, and saw a picture I hadn't noticed before. Proctor with someone not so famous, not then, not yet, maybe later when they hang me at Leavenworth. Proctor and me, a long time ago in Germany.

"See, I haven't forgotten" he said, standing behind me.

"The day we nailed that crooked bastard Lomax."

"The day you helped me get started. My first big break in television, Phil."

"Lomax. That sonofabitch. He's had nine lives."

"No way. He resigned from Congress, right after I filed that story."

"I saw him in Nam, Dan. He had some sort of contract with the Army."

"Lomax with an Army contract? You may have given me another story, Phil, maybe as big as the one we started with."

A story, all right. One I'd just as soon forget. Lomax with some Senator in tow, me pointing an M-16 and acting like I was going to shoot the bastard. And then the Army, ready to court martial me for threatening a Senator. Another million dollar screwup.

A screwup, but a joke, too, in its own way as amusing as what Proctor was trying to write. If not amusing, at least ironic. Calloway, a two-star then, coming to my rescue. And now he'll have to hang me for sure, if for nothing else than to pacify the Secretary of the Army.

"I take it you're finished writing, Dan. I'll be moving on then."

"Not finished yet. I'll get Beatrice to put some polish on it."

"Her? She bit my ass for calling it soap opera, that show they do upstairs."

"Soap opera, sure, she was into that for years. She's a real pro, that's why we brought her over to the news division, Phil."

Beatrice. So she'll have a hand in what he reads. God knows what that may be. Soap opera. With a touch of humor, Proctor said. I kept my mouth shut. Worn out by what it added up to. With Proctor's help, a mere inquiry turned into a nightmare.

When I told him I was flying back tonight he hugged me, saying the next time I'm in town we'd have a drink, just like the good old days in Texas. I nodded, thinking about Beatrice, what she might write about the Secretary and Lamont. But too worn out to quarrel about it.

I should have. I should have threatened to strangle her if he let her write a word. Sitting in the hotel bar, bags packed, watching the tail end of the news, seeing Proctor smiling as he wrapped it up, I knew for sure I should have done just that. Strangled that damn woman.

And maybe Proctor, too. Almost grinning as he looked at the camera. Telling how the network always has to be on guard. How they'd been deceived, even so, by a hoax cooked up a few days ago. I admit we were misled, said Proctor, but it's left us laughing here, and you'll laugh too when you hear the whole story.

It starts in the office of the Secretary of the Army, he continued. From what we've learned it seems two women there are. . .well, how shall I put it? They're romantically involved with each other. But one of them also has her eyes on a lieutenant colonel. So this other lady is so jealous she decides she'll ruin his reputation. She's the one behind what we reported.

The Army has revealed this colonel's name is Lamont, said Proctor. It insists this woman lied, that Lamont and another colonel named Tracy were never involved in any wrongdoing, and that Tracy's Distinguished Service Cross is quite intact. So that's what it was folks, a hoax. I'm Dan Proctor, signing off from New York, with a word of warning. Beware of jealous women.

He winked when he said that, damned near laughing. Not me. I was groaning. With a good idea of what will happen next. Calloway gets ordered to the Pentagon again, and when he returns he tells me what the Secretary has decided. To send me off to Bumfuck, Egypt.

I looked at my watch, ordered another drink, and checked the time on my airline ticket. Wondering if I should go back to Leavenworth. Hell, why even bother? Right. Change the ticket, go straight there. To Egypt.

I've gone back, instead. So now I'm standing in front of a three-star general. At attention, eyes focused on the wall behind his desk. Trying not to notice how he's biting hard on his cigar and staring at the ceiling. With Woods standing beside him. Frowning at me, the look on his face telling me where I'm headed.

"Woods, by God, this major's something" says Calloway. "He's so fucked up he reminds me of a story I heard about a pecker-wood down in Georgia. He was so dumb he got lost on the way to the outhouse and the hogs et him."

I say nothing. Neither does Woods. It's GSB, the Great Southern Breeze, who's doing all the talking.

"You want to know how fucked up he is, Woods? The Secretary of the Army called me this morning. He's satisfied Lamont's in the clear, but now he has his whole damned staff chasing around, searching for a bunch of lesbians. All because of Major Dee."

I remain silent. I've made up my mind. If he ever quiets down and asks me, all I'm going to give Calloway is my name, rank, and serial number.

"And this hospital bill he's run up, how much do you think that is, Woods?"

"I would estimate twelve thousand dollars, general."

"You've got some nerve, Major Dee. Having the Army take care of a woman you're not even married to."

What's Calloway ranting about, a twelve thousand dollar bill for a woman I'm not married to? A damned good question, but I'm not going to ask. I'm not going to talk.

"Woods, what do you think I should do about this major?"

"I think you should promote him, general."

"Promote him, not a bad idea. So he can pay off what he owes the Army."

Calloway gets up, comes around in front of his desk and pats me on the shoulder. Telling me to follow him, they're waiting in my old office, he'll pin my new rank on there. He's smiling, more or less, and I'm still at attention. Shell shocked. There's no other way to put it.

"General. . .I don't understand. . ."

"You're being promoted. And then you're on your way to Bragg."

"Sir, what you said a minute ago, you said. . ."

"Take Lieutenant Truesdell with you. Get her out of my hair."

"Nurse Rebecca? You saw her, she. . ."

"She's a pain in the ass, Phil, the way she fights for you."

"Rebecca? I suppose she. . ."

"Yesterday, you know what she told me? We had no right to keep you here."

"You mean. . ."

"No right, because your wife divorced you. Before you got here, four months ago, while you were off in Nam."

I follow Calloway out of his office. With Woods beside me. He's telling me I should have read my mail, if I had I would not have been here and he could not have grabbed my ass to play detective. He's laughing. I'm not. It hasn't sunk in yet, what's going on around me.

A crowd is waiting when we get there. They're standing around a cake. I spot Rebecca. In a green velvet dress. She rushes to me and we kiss. The crowd applauds. It's starting to make sense. It's not another dream I'm having. It's real.

Rebecca. She's real, all right. I can tell by the way I feel when I touch her. One big kiss and I've forgotten Molly for good. After all these years, by God, that's over. I'm holding a woman in my arms. I'm feeling like a man again.

The general makes a speech and pins silver leaves on my shoulders. Rebecca cuts the cake, gives me a bite to taste and the crowd applauds again. Friends, celebrating my promotion. I remember what she said when we first met. In the Army we care about each other.

Calloway cares. In his own odd way. After a while he gets me aside and asks if I remember what he told me about women. How they cause half the problems in the Army. How the Army would issue you a wife if it thought you needed one.

"I see your nurse is coming to join us" says Calloway. "Tell her she's been issued."

"General, sir, I'd like to ask a favor" says Rebecca.

"No way" he replies. "I'm sending you to Bragg with this lieutenant colonel."

"My goodness, sir, you must have read my mind" she says. And gives him a hug. The crowd applauds again. No wonder. A female lieutenant hugging a three-star general, I can guess what they must be thinking. It's the new Army.

"I can't read minds" says Calloway. "But you two, you do remind me of a story I once heard in Alabama. About a farmer who found a couple in his hayloft. He thought it was his daughter and he got his shotgun. You two, you know what a shotgun wedding is? It's. . ."

We aren't listening. We're holding hands and smiling at each other. I'm thinking about the way she said she'd keep me warm. When she called me in New York. So I'm thinking about New York, as well.

New York. That Beatrice woman. What she said about soap opera. And drama.

It's drama, damn right, what's happened. What I've been going through these past few months, back from Nam, chasing around the country, getting my butt run over.

And now, after all of that, here I am, holding hands with Rebecca. And she's going with me to Bragg. It may seem like soap opera, but it's not.

It's not, by God. It's real.

CALL ME PROFESSOR DEE

Sometimes I look at Margaret and wonder. How I wound up here, surrounded by books and the kind of fools who think they're smart because they've written one. Like this woman DeLeon. One little book on the history of Portuguese pottery, that's all, and she's a flaming expert on everything. Major league baseball, how Nixon can settle things in Vietnam, how to save the United Nations, you name it, she knows.

No, that's not quite true. About DeLeon, all right. But not about my wife and how I got here. I don't wonder. I remember. An accident, thirteen long years ago, as simple as that. Sometimes I can even laugh about it, the way it happened. But not right now, not while I'm sitting in my office waiting for her. I'm in no mood to laugh at all, not when she thinks she's going to drag me off to a faculty tea.

My last one, for sure. And Margaret? She has no idea at all, what I'm getting ready to do, how I'm getting ready to spill the beans. No idea at all. If she did, she wouldn't be all dressed up and on her way here. She'd have stayed home and pulled the covers over her head. Or gone out in the yard, bellowing something from one of her goddamned operas. Wagner, maybe. Götterdammerung, would be just right. . .

So as usual I'll say Margaret, why don't you go by yourself, I've been grading papers and I have a terrible headache. And she'll interrupt and say Phillip, a break will be good for you, and anyway you need to mingle with the other faculty, that's good for you, too.

So we'll go. Together. And I'll mingle. For a while. With the crowd. That crooked Trustee who likes to run the College. The President, kissing his ass to keep his job. And his secretary, the one who stands over the punch bowl, wearing white gloves and serving crap not even Margaret can swallow.

I may even chat with DeLeon about Portuguese pottery. I may even tell her I'm an expert, too. Not about the UN or foreign policy. Not about Nixon and the war in Vietnam. About something else. Something she's sure as hell not an expert on.

What they've been gossiping about, full of rumors about it, DeLeon and all the others. The money missing from the College budget. What the President has to say about it.

Mingle, hell. I'm going to tell them what I've discovered. I'm going to dump it right in that goddamned punch bowl. And then stand back and say you'd never have guessed that, would you? So what kind of books are you going to write about it, now that you know what really happened?

Margaret won't be pleased when I say that. No more than the night we met in Germany at the opera, when I bumped into her and spilled wine on her dress. Not pleased at all then. And she won't be happy this time, either.

But this time it won't be by accident.

Accidents. Out of the blue something happens, and then something else in turn, something no one could have predicted. Like that East Coast blackout. The night the lights went out all over. The streets too dark to drive in, no radios working, no music to listen to, no TV to watch, no bars or cafes open, nothing to do. And nine months later, the hospitals, overcrowded with babies.

Or like that morning six months ago. When I was in the gym, on registration day, signing up freshmen for a philosophy course. Not by choice. I had flipped a coin and lost. And the table where I was sitting, not hidden off in a corner as usual, that was random, too. A heavy rain the night before, the roof had leaked and there I was, in the middle of the gym, parked next to the Economics Department.

All by accident, my sitting where I was, my signing up students. And not a single soul in line. While the line at the table next to mine ran halfway across the gym. Forty or fifty freshmen, waiting to get in a course dreamed up by that nosy Trustee, Ventura. The latest marketing fad, something to lure more students to the College. All bullshit, of course, even the title. Introduction To Business Management.

Bullshit, indeed, teaching eighteen year olds how to run a corporation. In the summer, trying to earn tuition, that's when they learn about business, making hamburgers in someplace like Mc-Donald's. But for now, at least, what the Trustees had in mind was evidently working. There they were, ready to make a fortune. Patient. All but one, at the end of the line and tired of waiting. Breaking away and heading for me. Frowning as he looked at the sign on my table.

"Introduction to Philosophy? What's Philosophy?" he asked.

"An effort to make sense of the world" I replied, giving my standard answer.

"That's my world, up there" he said, pointing to a basketball net at the end of the gym.

Not much of a world, I wanted to say. But not with the way he was frowning. A black kid, light skinned, one of his parents white, I guessed. Not easy to be color blind about that, no matter how I tried. And not easy to be wrapped up in basketball, either, if you're no taller than him. Not even six feet. And frowning. Like that net was all that counted.

Frowning, not satisfied with how I answered his question about Philosophy. Ready to walk away, it looked like. Fine, I was in no mood for recruiting, not then, not ever. But something, I don't know what it was, something told me here's a kid who's bright enough to see beyond that net he's looking at. If I could get him to think about it before he got away.

"You asked what Philosophy is. Ever hear of Adolph Rupp?"

"Some coach. Kentucky, I think. What about him?"

"A few years ago, his team got beat when they played for the national title."

"I remember, I was in junior high, I watched it on TV."

"All black, the team that beat him. And Kentucky was all white."

"Sure, my whole neighborhood was jumping up and down about it."

"All black, but he still wouldn't let a colored player try out for him."

"Why? What did he have against players like me?"

"You asked what Philosophy is. Maybe you understand now, it's asking questions like that. It's trying to make sense of the world you live in."

Without another word he reached down and registered for my class, smiling as I looked at the sign-up sheet and saw what he had written. No last name at all. Nothing but Tommy L. Written in some kind of elaborate script, like graffiti on the side of a railroad car.

"Tommy L. What's the L stand for?" I asked.

"That's my name. That's what I go by. Tommy L."

"Fine. But what does the L mean?"

"It don't mean shit" he answered, lowering his voice to a growl. As if mimicking some illiterate hoodlum. And then he walked away, still smiling.

Tommy L.

An accident, my being there. An accident, my table being where it was. An accident, of sorts, his signing up to take my course.

Or maybe not. Later, when I got to know him, when I found out what that letter L stood for, I wondered. I still do. How can you tell? How do you know if it's an accident or fate?

One more thing that day, something else that made me wonder, later on, why things turn out the way they do.

It was simple enough, of course, what happened. Such things usually are. The Dean of Faculty, coming by my table during registration, looking worried, asking me to grab an umbrella and come outside where we could talk in private. Where he could tell me about a problem I might be facing in the months ahead, an issue with the faculty tenure committee.

"It's Elena Bloom, Phil. The committee has elected her as chairman."

"Elena. Not exactly a friend anymore. So be it."

"You're one of the most popular teachers here, you deserve tenure."

"The student evaluations, sure, I've read them. She has, too, I know."

"I'm afraid she'll try to block your getting tenure."

"Elena's like most of the faculty, Dean, always finding someone to resent."

"I think it's the speech you made about the protest she organized."

"That antiwar rally last Spring? There's more to it than that."

"Perhaps, but if she gets the committee to vote against you, I won't be able to help."

"I know, you can't overrule them. We'll just have to wait and see."

"I wouldn't wait. I'd start looking around right now."

"That's why you dragged me out here in the rain? To tell me that?"

"I'd hate to lose you, Phil, but yes, if I were you I'd start looking for another teaching position. In case Miss Bloom succeeds."

A decent man, Dean Palmer, not the kind who would run into a burning building to save someone, but doing his best to keep the faculty from cutting each other's throats. I thanked him for his advice and went back to my table, waiting for students to sign up, but thinking about Elena Bloom. And the speech I had made after she spoke against the war in Vietnam.

Wait, I had asked, aren't we looking at this war the wrong way? Shouldn't we actually hope it never ends? All the students who've enrolled here, going to college to avoid the draft, to stay out of the war, do we really want to lose them? Do we want to lose the jobs we have because of them?

Poor Elena, organizing a march, thinking she'd make a contribution to the peace movement. Unable to cope with a bit of sarcasm from a colleague. And rattled, too, when half the faculty backed off, thought about what I'd said, thought about their jobs, and chose to stay home instead of risking unemployment.

Jobs. When the registrar started writing on a chalkboard in the center of the gym, listing the courses already filled, I knew I would soon have to get my mind off her and deal with another fact about jobs and numbers. Something else no one wanted to admit.

The requirement system, guaranteeing students must take certain courses to graduate. Guaranteeing everyone has students in their classes. Guaranteeing I'd soon be facing a line of freshmen, eager to get in a Philosophy class, now that all the other courses were closing.

In an hour or so I was done. With all six sections of the intro course complete, twenty-five students each, I could relax and survey what remained. A few last freshmen, wandering around, looking for a class still open. The floor of the gym, covered with mud and scraps of paper. And in the distance, Elena Bloom, talking with Dean Palmer.

No doubt telling him how she'd keep me from getting tenure.

Screw her. And the rest of the French Department with her.

Perhaps I should have, come to think about it. When she asked what I was like in bed, a couple of years ago when we were drinking at a faculty party. I'd have a lock on tenure now. I could spend the rest of my life playing golf, like the other tenured faculty around here.

Or playing poker. I was reminded of that when I saw who was standing in front of me. A close friend. Maybe my only real friend in this Godforsaken State of Indiana. Wearing a business suit, with his raincoat draped over his shoulders, reaching to shake hands.

"I'll be damned" he said. "I see Ventura's business course is all filled up."

"So are the Philosophy classes, Max. I'll put your name on the waiting list."

"Try to spell it right. Max Piper. That's M as in money, as in poker."

"You'll need a lot. I plan to win enough in the next few months to get out of here."

"Hell, Phil, I'm the Vice President for Finance, I have plenty of money."

"Wednesday night, as I recall it's your turn to play hostess."

"Eight o'clock. And no more of your logic shit. That's not poker, that's cheating."

I smiled as Max moved on, looking around the gym. For the other faculty members he'd recruited, over the years, to play poker. With only one house rule, never talk about the College. Maybe now he'd propose another poker rule. Make Dee drink gin instead of beer. So he can't keep his head clear. So he can't keep using logic to calculate how to win.

I smiled, all right. Thinking about what I'd stumbled onto in a logic course last year. A new way to think about games. A new insight into poker.

Smiling. About the way the game is played. Everyone figures the odds, Max and all the others. The chance of filling a flush, of drawing to an inside straight, they know the chances verbatim. And they know what to do. You play the hand you're dealt, you figure the odds, you fold or whatever. What they can't figure out is what I've discovered.

A secret way to win half the hands you're dealt. But not the secret I would like to get a grip on. What lies hidden in the deck.

The hand you're dealt. In poker and everything else in life. Whether it's really random. Whether it's a matter of chance or fate. Or part of a grand design. Or maybe, just maybe, part of some godawful cosmic joke.

Tommy L. That's one thing that made me wonder, his showing up in my class.

This tenure business, too, with Elena Bloom involved. And Max Piper, laughing about poker, talking about the money he had to play with, talking about that Trustee Blackburn, that's something else that made me wonder, later on. Whether it's all by accident, what happens.

I still do. I still wonder.

And then there's marriage. What happens when you link up with a woman. In my case, one who talked me into graduate school when I left the Army. Who urged me to press on and get a Ph.D. So I could take up the life of a professor. So I could wind up here, reading books and wondering what it all adds up to. Wondering why it's her I married.

"You're late" said Margaret when I got home.

"Really. I hadn't noticed."

"Where have you been? We've already eaten."

"I've been working on my classes, Margaret."

"Your classes don't start for another four days, Phil."

"Where's Reggie?"

"Reginald is in the basement, and please don't call him Reggie."

I grunted and went to the kitchen. To open a can of beer and make a sandwich out of something left over from dinner. When I saw what the menu had been I settled for the beer and went down the basement stairs to see Reggie. Not Reginald. Reggie.

"Look what I'm building" he said. "You think this will work, Dad?"

"Work? I don't even know what it is."

"It's the garage door opener I'm making for Mom."

"If it does work you should apply for a patent."

"Mom says you have to be twenty-one to get a patent."

"So you're nine years short, so what?"

"Grab a crescent wrench, Dad, let's see if I made it right."

A crescent wrench? What size? He was gone, up the stairs with a box of gears and cables before I could ask. With his tools arranged on pegboards, all of them labeled, of course, it was easy to find a few that looked about right. So I followed him with the wrenches in one hand and my beer in the other, watching as he climbed on a ladder to test what he'd made.

"By golly, it works, Dad. See how the door goes up when I press this?"

"That's the remote switch you designed?"

"Mom can open the door from inside her car, right in the driveway."

"From fifty feet away, like you drew it up last week?"

"You bet. This winter, she won't have to get out in the snow anymore."

The door sounded noisy, so I handed him the wrenches and he tightened a gear, opening and closing the door again. Standing on the ladder and smiling down at me. A twelve-year-old Tom Edison, proud of what he'd invented. Not his mother. She had heard the noise and wasn't pleased at all.

"Phil, get Reginald off that ladder before he hurts himself."

"He won't fall. You ought to thank him, Margaret. He made that for you."

"You two, always in the basement, what is it he's made now?"

"A new way to open and close garage doors."

"He shouldn't waste his time this way."

"When winter comes you won't think it's been a waste of time."

"He should be practicing the piano, not playing with garage doors."

Reggie climbed down and followed his mother into the house. I put the ladder away, gathered his tools and took them down to the basement, expecting to hear any second what I'd heard all summer. Chopin. Or something close to it.

Five minutes of whatever it was, followed by a pause, Margaret no doubt telling him to start again. And then a full hour of stopping and starting all over. Reminding me, for the zillionth time, there's nothing like living in a house with a kid who's practicing piano.

When he could be in the basement working quietly. Inventing new devices. A practice piano that can't be heard from ten feet away, that would be a start. Or maybe some kind of voicebox with a remote, to keep his mother silent.

"You're no help" said Margaret when she found me hiding in my study.

"You want me to take out the trash, is that it?"

"I'm talking about Reginald. He's not progressing the way he should in music."

"Neither am I."

"You don't encourage him at all. You fall asleep, every time we take him to the opera."

"It's self-defense, Margaret. Something I'm working on."

"Just keep him out of the basement, so he can concentrate on music."

When she walked away, slamming the door behind her, I gritted my teeth and thought about it. Keep Reggie out of the basement? Keep my son from dreaming up new gadgets? No way, not if I could find a book I'd thumbed through years ago and suddenly remembered.

A history of technology, gathering dust on the bottom of a bookshelf. With a chapter on U.S. patents. No age limits at all. According to the book, a girl in Kansas held the record. Eight years old when she received one for a solar-heated horse barn.

Eight years old, and Reggie's twelve.

I smiled, knowing exactly what I'd do now. Find out how to

apply. Help him get a patent for his garage door apparatus, this thing his mother scoffed at.

And then sit back and see what she says about that.

Margaret, bless her heart, not all men are as patient as I am. Now and then I read about them in the paper. Throwing wives under eighteen-wheelers. The easy way out, but not very smart, going to prison and winding up a wife yourself, sort of, at the mercy of some goon who wants a mate to hump in the shower.

There's the legal way out, of course. Get a divorce. And then cough up alimony the rest of your life, like this prof I know in the history department. Dumb, how he hasn't learned a single lesson from history, at least not his own. Married four times, broke and courting another woman. Bumming cigarettes, the last time I saw him.

And this latest matrimonial fad, wife trading clubs. Some faculty members here are into that, busy sorting out the details, like who pays the rent and who buys the groceries. Trade your wife? For a new Corvette, perhaps, but not for another wife, no sir. Anyway, Margaret would never consider it. Unless she could trade me for a grand piano.

All right, so I amuse myself by making jokes about marriage. Or maybe it's fantasizing. Sometimes I'm not quite sure.

It doesn't matter. I learned a long time ago how to cope with a wife who thinks God plays opera records. I concentrate on the one thing she can't meddle in. The courses I teach at the College. Six a year. With no wives allowed in the classroom, including Margaret. That's what I call academic freedom.

Even so, it's not easy, my escape from bondage. It's hard work. Like the intro course I put together this semester. Twenty-five freshmen, an essay each week, four months of reading and commenting on what they've written, a real workout. Meant to get them to thinking about the world we live in. That's the hard part for them. Thinking.

So I suppose I should not have been surprised, how they balked, on the very first day of class, when I set out to put their minds to work. Right away, as soon as they sat down, as soon as I'd passed out a seating chart and told them to set aside the course instructions, telling them to read all that when they got back to their dormitories.

"This is a course in philosophical reasoning" I said. "So let's start with a simple question. When you look in the mirror you notice your image is reversed from left to right, so why not upside down, as well? Why don't you see yourself standing on your head?"

A half-dozen hands went up at once.

"I have a question about the seating chart" said a young man on the back row. "You want us to print our names or sign them?"

"This syllabus you handed out" said another, "am I reading it right? A paper every week, that sounds like a lot of writing."

"I never had to write in high school" said someone else. "Would you allow a multiple choice test each week instead?"

"I have a question about attendance" said a coed on the third row. "It says here you cut class at your own peril, what does that mean?"

A few more questions like that, wasting time on matters already dealt with in the course instructions. And then a question I'd never heard before, in all my years of teaching something I had never even thought of.

"What shall I call you?" asked a young lady on the front row, sitting in front of Tommy L. Red-haired and freckle-faced, sitting up straight as an arrow, speaking in a voice with a German accent.

Wherever she came from she had caught me off guard. I thought about it for a moment. Odd, but that's the way it's always been, in class you call on them by name and they answer directly, so there's no need to know what to call you. Why would she ask such a question?

Because she's German, that had to be why. I looked at her name on the seating chart. Helga Henschel, printed neatly. German, all right. So what should I tell her to call me? Herr Professor Doktor Dee? With a couple of umlauts thrown in?

"Call me Professor Dee" I answered.

She nodded and wrote something in her notebook. I looked around at the class. Half of them dozing off, not ready to start thinking. Too bad. Time to see what they're made of.

"Now" I said, "let's get on with this question about mirrors."

No one raised a hand. Fine. I would not call on them by name, not on the first day of class. Too intimidating. Let them go at it on their own.

"Go ahead, give it a shot."

"If you break a mirror, that's bad luck" said someone.

"Like walking under a ladder" said another.

"It's like seeing a black cat run in front of you" said the coed on the third row.

"They say zombies don't see anything at all in a mirror" said someone else.

"Ghosts, what do they see in a mirror?" asked a boy wearing glasses.

"There's no such thing as ghosts" said a girl on the back row.

"What about the way you look in a funhouse mirror?" asked a boy with his hand up.

"The kind they have in carnivals" someone offered, trying to clarify the matter.

"You look fat or you look skinny, it all depends" said the girl on the third row.

"What if you lie on your side in front of a mirror like that?" asked another.

"Then you'd look really long or really short" answered someone else.

"What if you stood on your head?"

"Then your head would look fat and your legs would look skinny."

"That's a hard question, Professor Dee. What's the answer?"

Not bad, not bad at all, some of my colleagues might say. Look at the class discussion you have stimulated. The way you get them involved, it's no wonder your student evaluations are among the highest in the College.

Right. It's no wonder, either, that I told them you have done enough for today, go home and study Descartes' Meditations. And now that you've started thinking about it, here's your first essay assignment. Make it as long or as short as you like, just be sure you explain it in a logical manner, why you don't see yourself upside down in a mirror.

God only knows what I'd have to read in the way of explanations.

It would be a long semester, I could tell. Longer than long, putting up with students like them, just to keep Margaret at bay.

In fact, things settled down, once a routine set in. The students trying to make it to class on time, Monday through Friday, so they could party on weekends. The faculty giving lectures and grading exams and sitting in committee meetings, off in a world of their own. A week by week grind, something everyone could count on.

Me, too, I have to admit, letting things fall into place. Writing comments on their essays, thinking up new questions for my classes, meeting students in my office, working on a logic paper I hoped some journal would publish. A routine all my own.

Watching the leaves turn brown as summer turned to autumn. Swimming three nights a week to keep my weight down, skipping dinner, figuring Reggie would be done with piano practice before I got back from the gym.

Listening to an in-house lecture now and then, one by the chap in the history department who's been married so many times. Talking about the underground railroad, how it worked here during the Civil War. Five slaves the College got out. Almost as many wives as he's had.

Watching the news on television. Seeing the troops leave Vietnam, hearing Nixon debate McGovern about the war, noting the poll projections, hearing the experts predict who will win the coming election.

Playing poker with Max Piper on Tuesday evenings. About as exciting now as writing obits for a newspaper, or eating C rations in the Army. Not exciting at all, if you can look at the hand you've been dealt and see the pot's already settled.

Now and then I'd wonder, too, why I was here, not in the Army, not back to reporting. Why I had become a college professor instead, caught up in a question I can't answer. How it is, in just about everything, you can never know what hand you'll be dealt. Or why.

A routine without let-up, until a Sunday afternoon, halfway through the semester. When I was helping in the kitchen after lunch. And listening, more or less, to Margaret talking about what she'd heard in church that morning.

A sermon about Christian charity. I should have cleaned the sink and kept my mouth shut. But when she went on and on, telling me what her minister had said about doing right, I couldn't help it.

"How does he know what's right?" I asked.

"It's a matter of conscience, Phil."

"What if your conscience tells you what to do and it turns out bad?"

"That can't happen. If you do what's right you needn't worry."

"Margaret, it happens all the time, someone does what they think is right and it leads to an outcome no one never dreamed of."

A difficult matter, something I'd pondered many times. How you know what's right if you can't be sure of what comes next. Part of the question I'm still trying to answer. Why things happen the way they do. Whether it's coincidence or accident or fate or what.

"Something no one dreamed of" she said. "I suppose you're talking about our marriage."

"No, I'm not. It's a philosophical issue, that's all."

"You think if you'd stayed in the Army things might have been different."

"I've never said that. Maybe they would, there's no way to know."

"You think if I'd gone on singing we would both be better off."

"No, but now that you've brought it up, who knows what might have happened?"

"I should have stayed with opera, that's what you're trying to tell me."

"All right, suppose you had. Would that have been good or bad?"

"You tell me. You're the philosophy professor."

"Good, maybe, if you'd become a star. But what if they booed you?"

"And what if I hit you with this skillet? Go away, go read your papers."

I did what she said. I went to my study and looked at the stack on my desk. A Sunday afternoon of work, something Margaret could not stick her nose in. Exams and essays from my classes. And one last form for Reggie's patent application.

Reggie. Off somewhere playing soccer after lunch. Twelve now, and she would never say it, but it was true. And we both knew it. How she had given up her career because of him. Because of me. Because of one accident after another.

An accident, her being in Munich instead of Paris. An accident, my being at the opera there, bumping into her in the lobby during intermission. An accident, how we met and came to be married. And how she wound up pregnant with Reggie, by accident as well.

Exactly what I was getting at in the kitchen. How can you know what's right if you can't see what might happen later? Maybe it was wrong, for both of us, getting married. But when can you tell, if it's one thing after another? When you're eighty years old and on your deathbed?

Questions I can't answer. And essays I could not read, not then, not with my mind on things like that. And not with Margaret coming into my study with the skillet in her hand, looking like she might use it.

"The handle is loose" she said. "Can you ask Reginald to fix it?"

"Put it on the chair over there. I'll see what we can do."

"You mentioned opera. There's something you might as well know."

"It's Sunday, so there's one on the radio. Fine, what else is new?"

"I'm going to Cleveland next week for an audition."

"You're going to try out for a role? After all this time? You must be. . ."

"Fred Zimmer is driving. He's going to try out, too."

"Zimmer, the doctor? He's. . ."

"He's a baritone. We sing together in the church choir."

"Cleveland. With Doc Zimmer. . ."

I had no idea what to say. Wish her good luck, tell her to be careful on the highway, tell her I'd take care of Reggie while she was gone, or maybe tell her. . .

"If I'm selected, would that be good or bad, Phil?"

"Your audition, you mean, if you. . ."

"There's no way to know, isn't that what you just said?"

"Margaret, look, I can't. . ."

"They're doing Aida this afternoon. I'll turn up the radio so you can listen."

Nice. With a voice like that she could bring the house down. I could see her now, standing onstage in front of the curtain, holding flowers and bowing, telling the audience it was all because of her husband.

So now she'd be gone and my week by week routine would be over. Done in by Margaret's dream of singing opera. No telling how long she'd be away. Long enough, perhaps, for me to get used to cooking and taking care of Reggie, a different kind of grind altogether.

I reached in my desk for the earplugs I'd need in a few minutes. And then looked at the stack of papers waiting to be read. Essays to turn back on Monday. Good, good. At least that part of the routine would stay the same.

Good? Maybe, maybe not. How would I know?

Something else I don't understand. Why I was humming the overture from Aida while I was in the bathroom shaving Monday morning. The part where the tubas sound like elephants on a rampage.

When I realized what I was doing I stopped, of course, hoping Margaret hadn't heard me.

She hadn't. She'd gone shopping after breakfast, leaving a note that said please cash a check so she'd have money to spend in Cleveland.

Fine, I told myself while I was walking to my office. Give her whatever she wants, you'll have a great time while she's away. Swimming in the college pool, playing poker with Max Piper, watching football on television, what could be better?

Not having to deal with Elena Bloom, for one thing. That would be better. But there she was, standing outside my door when I got there. Looking almost frantic, with a package in her hands, something wrapped in brown paper.

"I need your help" she said. "I need you to look at this."

"That package? Why? What's in it?"

"I don't know, it came in the mail this morning."

"So? So open it and find out."

"You were in the Army. You look at it first."

"The Army? I never talk about that, Elena. Not around here."

"There's no return address on it. I'm afraid of what's in it."

"Somebody sent you a book, and you're afraid to read it?"

"It might be a bomb, that's what I'm afraid of."

A bomb. Great. Nine in the morning, what a way to start the day, dealing with a paranoid woman. She might be right, of course. I could think of a half-dozen reasons to send her one myself.

Still, the best thing would be to calm her down and take a look. So I opened the door and let her follow me in. Trying to recall what I'd been told in a class at Fort Bragg. How to check on explosives, the kind that come in the mail disguised as small packages.

Four steps, the instructor had said, as I remembered. First, run your fingers along the edge of the wrapper. See if you feel any wires. If you find no wires, proceed then to loosen the wrapper, very slowly.

I did, while Elena watched. Then step two. Check for wires around the cardboard box inside the wrapper. If no wires are found, but there's still room for doubt, proceed to step three. Place the box in water for five minutes and then open it.

So said the instructor. As I recalled. A long time ago, and I may have forgotten the details, but the water step seemed reasonable to me.

"Where are you going?" asked Elena.

"I'm going to the bathroom. Wait here."

"The toilet? At a time like this?"

She stood in the hallway, shaking her head as I walked away. When I got to the bathroom I remembered something else from the class at Bragg. A question someone had asked. You soak the box in water, but what if step three didn't work when you open it?

The last step, the instructor had replied. An old sergeant from Special Forces with a twisted sense of humor. After a long pause he had answered the question. Step four, he said, that's when you kiss your ass goodbye.

Step three would have to do it, then. It did. When I set the box in the bathroom sink and started the water running it came unglued in a matter of minutes. Revealing a book, paperbound, its binding loose and its pages floating in water. So much for Elena's bomb threat.

She was leaning against my desk, smoking a cigarette and looking downright frazzled when I returned from the bathroom. Dripping water from the mess in my hands, wet cardboard and book pages covered with glue.

"Where is it?" she asked. "The box, what did you do with the box?"

"This is it, what's left of it. I soaked it in water."

"Water? Wouldn't water make it blow up?"

"Blowing up comes with step four. Here, take it, it's yours."

She looked down and said nothing. While I wiped the floor with a paper towel from the bathroom. And then plugged in my coffee pot, thinking I'd offer a cup, get her to relax, and ask her point blank. What made her think someone would send her a bomb?

She was gone when I turned around. Gone, with what was left of her package. Without a word. No thanks, no explanation, nothing at all.

No explanation needed. She was batty, as simple as that. Living in a fantasy world, like half the faculty around here.

Batty, but in charge of the tenure committee, too.

I poured myself coffee, reflecting on what that meant. And then, for some odd reason, I found myself back to Aida.

Not humming, just recalling what I thought when I saw it once with Margaret. How dumb the plot was.

Maybe more than half the faculty lived in a fantasy world. All of them, evidently, the way they looked the day after the election. Gloomy. Acting disappointed. As if they had really believed McGovern could beat Nixon.

Some of the students, also, the way they were grumbling between classes. Coeds crying about their boyfriends, how they'd be drafted now for sure. A young man muttering Vietnam, Tricky Dick will keep it going forever, how far is it to Canada?

Not Helga Henschel. Vietnam was no concern of hers, she was an exchange student. Determined, it seemed, to write the longest essays I've ever seen in any of my classes. Getting longer each week, her last one nearly forty pages, enough to drive me to my knees.

"You want to see me?" she asked when she entered my office.

"It's about your essays" I said. "It must take a lot of time to write them."

"I devote my weekends to them, Professor Dee."

"Helga, maybe it's none of my business, but it sounds like you're missing something."

"The social life on campus, you mean?"

"Let your roommate show you around. You don't need to write such lengthy essays."

"I no longer have a roommate, Professor Dee. I live alone."

"Alone? What happened to the one you had?"

"She wanted football players in the room, and I would not permit it."

So much for that move on my part, trying to get her away from her typewriter. She would go on writing forty-page essays, And I would have to go on reading them, intrigued by her ingenuity, but worn down by her lack of mercy on me.

Intrigued by something else, as well. What I had noticed the first day of classes. Her red hair and freckled face, reminding me of something I'd been wrong about in Germany. A long time ago, when I still thought I could tell what was right or wrong.

"Helga, where are you from in Germany?"

"Near Munich. My parents live outside the city."

"Mambachel, that's near Munich, do you know where that is?"

"Yes, my parents lived near there when I was small."

"Your parents, could it be they came from Romania?"

"Yes, they emigrated, why do you ask, Professor Dee?"

"Years ago, when I was stationed at Mambachel, I knew a child who looked like you."

"It is Romanian, yes, my hair and the color of my face."

"Her parents lived on a farm near there, near Mambachel."

"They were farmers, yes, I understand, Professor Dee."

"She would be about your age now, Helga."

About her age now, a small child then. Who did not look German at all. With red hair and freckles, another orphan, it seemed to me, one of many left behind by American soldiers without a conscience.

A child who inspired me to act in a way I thought would be just. Make at least one soldier do the right thing, even if the others had gotten away. Looking at her now, grown up and in my office, I remembered what I had done. And how mistaken I had been.

How I had threatened to expose a fellow officer, for stealing Army money, unless he married the German woman who was mother of his child. And then discovering later, after he had done what I forced him to do, how there had been no money stolen at all.

And the child with red hair, how I'd been wrong about that, as well. Thinking she looked American, an orphan left behind. And then learning she was not an orphan, and not American, either, she was the daughter of Romanians who lived on a farm nearby.

Odd, how easy it is to remember all that in a second or so. And how easy to wonder if this might be her, years later and thousands of miles from home. By sheer coincidence enrolled in one of my classes now. Maybe more than coincidence, if it's really her.

"She would be my age now?" asked Helga.

"Your age, yes" I replied.

"My parents did not live on a farm, but perhaps I knew her as a child."

"They weren't farmers, your parents? You're sure?"

"My father was a carpenter when they came from Bucharest. He still is."

So there it was, the end of my wondering. She was not the girl I remembered. And I was not sure how to feel about it. Relieved, disappointed, or what. Embarrassed, perhaps, for all the questions I had asked about her parents.

After a moment she was the one who spoke, not me. I was silent, trying to understand what goes on inside my head.

"Professor Dee, I believe you wanted to see me about my essays."

"Your essays. Right. Your essays, Helga."

"I will try to make them shorter."

"Shorter. Fine. I'll see you in class tomorrow."

After she left I thought about it. Whether I've been living in a fantasy world, like most of the others around here. Like Elena Bloom. Imagining things.

Swimming lap after lap, soaking my head in water, so to speak, that's what I tried after seeing Helga in my office. Not troubled, exactly. Just wondering now and then whether I'd let my memories get the best of me.

All the details from the past, how I met my wife, how I ran across that child in Germany, perhaps I'd only imagined it happened that way. What I remembered, or thought I remembered, maybe that's what it was, I'd been imagining things.

Nonsense, I remember things quite well. That's what I was muttering, as I recall, the night I finished swimming, climbed out of the pool, and saw the college basketball coach waiting for me. No pal of mine, Butch Casey, not after I flunked two of his stars for cheating.

"Stop talking to your self" he said. "It's me you need to talk to."

"What about? I didn't pee in your pool."

"You're a sarcastic prick, you know that? How'd you get your job here?"

"The want ads, Butch. Lose too many games, you may want to try it yourself."

"Knock it off, Dee, it's one of my players I want to talk about."

"Who? If he's in one of my courses, don't worry, I'm sure he can read and write."

"It's Whipple. He's a pain in the ass."

"Whipple? Who's Whipple?"

"Don't you know who's in your classes? Tommy L. Whipple, damn it."

"Tommy L? You should have said so. What about him?"

"He's the best I've seen in years, but he's been ragging my other players."

"Ragging? For not winning one for the Gipper, something like that?"

"For not taking one of your goddamned classes, that's what."

My, my, so that's what Tommy L had been up to. Doing well in my course, for sure, and shooting lights out, I'd heard. Maybe growing up a bit, as well. Aggravating Coach Casey, who's too dumb to know there's more to life than playing basketball.

"It's simple, Butch. Tell him you'll have them all take one next semester."

"The whole damn team? Take one of your classes together?"

"Sure, I'll set up a special course, I'll base it on Plato."

"Plato? That Greek fart who talked about sound minds and healthy bodies?"

"Right on. He had them playing nude, that's how they did it in the Olympics."

"Nude? You're shitting me, Dee. They played basketball nude?"

"Think about it Butch. Do that here, you'll draw the biggest crowds ever."

"You're out of your fucking mind. Just tell Whipple to lay off."

He threw me a towel to dry off with and walked away, as if something had been settled. What that might be, I had no idea. In any case I had something else to think about. Something I'd never noticed. How hearing a name can ring a bell, when seeing it on paper doesn't.

Whipple. Always Tommy L on his essays. I had read his name, of course, in his file. Born in Austin, high school in Dallas, single-parent family, his mother's name Cremona Whipple. And so forth. Whipple. I had seen it on paper, but I hadn't heard it out loud.

Until just now, standing by the edge of the pool and jousting with Coach Casey.

Whipple. Whipple. Where had I heard that name before?

When I got home I said hello to Reggie, opened a can of beer, and thought about it. For quite a while, trying to remember. Then it struck me. Germany, it's up there in the attic, in an old Army footlocker, on that tape recorder I kept, that's where I'd heard it, in Germany.

It was right where I expected it to be. Under a stack of uniforms, next to a scrapbook and some Army decorations in a bag. After all these years no doubt the battery would be dead, so I carried the recorder downstairs to the basement, hoping Reggie could get it going.

Along with the scrapbook. Filled with pictures and newspaper clippings. If I was right about where I'd heard the name Whipple, the clippings would tie it all together. Not that I wanted it to. I'd rather have forgotten it altogether.

"Dad, this is really old" said Reggie. "This must be a collector's item by now."

"Made before you were born. Think you can turn it on?"

"I'll plug it into this amplifier. What's in it?"

"Something I'd rather you don't hear, if it's what I think it is."

"I'll hook up a pair of headphones then. So what is it, some kind of porno?"

"Not exactly. And I'm not into porno, wise guy."

"Me, either. I'd rather read books about machines, not about women."

"You're young yet. When you get around to it, I'll give you some advice."

"Advice, yes sir. When's Mom coming back, by the way?"

A twelve-year-old, starting to act now and then like a smart aleck. But great at fixing things. In a matter of minutes he had the recorder running so I could hear it. And had disappeared up the stairs so he couldn't.

Just what I thought it would be, when I ran the tape forward to the part I had been trying to recall. And then back again, listening a second time. Just to be sure that's where I'd heard the name Whipple.

The sound of drunks in a hotel room, telling jokes, cursing and bragging, a long time ago in Germany. One of them trying to calm the others down, complaining about the colored soldiers they'd seen die that day.

Colored soldiers, hell, said another, four dead niggers, that's what it was, right there on the ground in front of us. His voice was slurred from drinking, but I had recognized it the first time I'd heard it, years ago, and what followed was what I'd been trying to remember.

Niggers, I've been buying their votes for years, I've got a nigger mistress who passes the money around. Cremona Whipple, that's her name if you don't believe me. You dumb bastards from back East have no idea how good that nigger cunt can be.

The part Reggie shouldn't hear. Obscene. But not surprising. Typical of that rotten Congressman who'd said it. And who had paid a price for what was on that tape. Out of the running for Governor of Texas.

I unplugged the recorder and took it to my study. Along with the scrapbook I'd brought down from the attic. When I looked at the clippings in it, along with a picture I noticed, I realized something else. Why I'd just as soon I hadn't remembered it. Any of it.

The headline on one clipping, Representative Lomax Accuses Reporter of Political Slander. The reason I'd left the paper, when the publisher said apologize or be fired. The reason I'd gotten drunk and joined the Army.

The headline on another clipping, even that was one I could find no great pleasure in. Congressman Lomax Resigns, Says Farewell to Politics. Reminding me of another time in my life I'd just as soon forget.

Not because of him. Because of a woman I remembered, as I turned the pages in the scrapbook and saw that picture. The two of us dancing on New Year's Eve, a long time ago, before I met Margaret.

Still, the tape had done him in, Lomax, finishing him off in Texas. And I had no regrets about that, remembering how I'd made it happen. How I had used the tape to drive him out of office when he heard it.

How I'd been given the tape by an attorney from Congress, how I'd turned to Dan Proctor when he came with Lomax to Germany. Proctor, a friend I'd known as a reporter in Texas, starting off in TV, coming with Lomax to Germany, to cover a speech he was making.

How Proctor had gotten his first big break in television then, interviewing Lomax as he announced he was quitting politics. Because he was all worn out. Lying, as usual. Worn out, right. By what he'd said six months before, when he was drunk in a hotel room in Munich.

What he'd said about Cremona Whipple, that was enough to wear me out, as well, just thinking about it. Where it was bound to lead, now that I'd listened to the tape and remembered where I'd heard the name Whipple.

Cremona Whipple, the name of Tommy L's mother. L for Lomax. So what should I do, get Tommy L aside and ask him if he's the son of a crooked politician? Maybe. Or maybe all this was only another coincidence, like that business with Helga Henschel.

I stuck the tape in my desk, telling myself I'd best forget it, knowing I wouldn't. I could only try to. So I opened another can of beer and looked for Reggie, to tell him thanks for getting the recorder going, and maybe kick him in the butt for doing what I asked him to.

"What are you building now?" I asked when I found him back in the basement.

"It's a machine for dealing cards. See what happens when I stick this deck in?"

"I can see how it shuffles the cards, sure. Then what?"

"Notice when this arm comes out, it deals whatever game you've dialed in."

"Looks like five-card stud. Ingenious. Just don't show it to your mother."

"The way I've built it, Dad, you can never know what hand you'll get."

I went back upstairs, drinking my beer. Wishing I hadn't run into Coach Casey and heard him talk about Tommy Whipple. Wishing I'd never heard that name at all. Wishing, in a way, Reggie hadn't been smart enough to get that recorder working.

Wondering if I'd remembered it right, all that business about Lomax. Or if I'd been imagining things again. Thinking Lomax might have something to do with Tommy L and his mother. The way I imagined Helga Henschel was the child I knew in Germany.

And wondering, too, about this machine Reggie built. So you never know what hand you'll be dealt.

Tommy L. Wondering what hand I'd been dealt with him.

The hand you wind up with can surprise you, no question about it. Starting with the first card I was dealt when I entered Max Piper's office. When I heard what he wanted to see me about. Not at all what I expected, some word about why he'd changed the date for the next poker game. A word, a lot of words, instead, about the College expert on Portuguese pottery.

"Diedre DeLeon" he said. "This woman in the Art Department. You think she's loony?"

"Her? You wanted to see me about her? Maybe you're the one who's loony, Max."

"I'll take that as a yes. What do you know about baseball?"

"The perfect game. The next swing of the bat, you never know what might happen."

"I'm not talking about how it's played. I'm talking about how it's organized."

"Okay, I'll bite. A sixty-four dollar question. What does baseball have to do with Diedre DeLeon? Is that it?"

No answer. Only a grunt as he handed me a sheaf of papers. Twenty or thirty pages stapled together. Telling me to skip the details, just read the cover page and tell me what conclusion any reasonable person would come to.

"Clever" I said. "This lady's figured it out."

"You see what she's proposing? How to solve the Cuba problem?"

"Beautiful. The best way to get Castro out I've ever heard of."

"By offering him the job of baseball commissioner?"

"Sure. He's into baseball, I've read he still pitches, Max."

"You see what she's written? How she claims it would work?"

"Let him take over both leagues, right. Nationalize all the franchises."

"She even says she's certain he'd cooperate."

"He'd leap on it. Pay players a minimum salary, give the rest to the people."

"Be serious, Phil. I want your advice on how to deal with Diedre."

"Advice? On how to deal with a lunatic like her? What are you up to, Max?"

Again, only silence as I tossed the papers on his desk. And waited. Amused, and amazed as well, by this woman's ego. Next she'd be telling the Air Force how to contact UFO's, or maybe how to fly airplanes without using fuel.

"What I'm up to is this" he finally answered. "She's about to sue the College."

"Sue? What for? For not letting her give lectures on nuclear physics?"

"For not providing the funds to lobby this shit in Congress, Phil."

"And she'd sue if you don't divvy up? On what grounds, pray tell?"

"Discrimination against women of Portuguese ancestry. How's that?"

"My, my, good old Diedre, so she's an expert on civil rights, as well."

"Stop laughing. The Trustees are afraid she might win."

"Forget it. She'll never find a lawyer who'll take the case."

"You're joking. . ."

"None. Any lawyer she meets will run for cover, as soon as she starts spelling it out, how to overhaul the judicial system."

Max nodded and started writing. A note, it looked like, my guess a message to the Trustees about DeLeon. Or maybe to Castro himself, begging the Cubans to take this woman off his hands. What a scene she'd make in Havana, telling them how to run the country, how to triple the output from their sugar fields. Or make tequila out of banana leaves.

Whatever he was writing was fine with me. What I wanted to know was the date of the next poker game, so I could go back to my office. No such luck. Max wasn't ready to turn me loose. Instead he handed me another note he'd written.

"You recognize that name? He was a student here."

"K.T. Koslowski? Never in one of my courses, Max."

"First DeLeon, and now Elena Bloom. This place is a goddamn zoo, Phil."

"Agreed, but you've lost me. Koslowski? Bloom? What's this about?"

"One of the Trustees called me about him. Ventura, this morning, out of the blue."

I read the name out loud again. Koslowski. Hearing it, not just seeing it on paper, the name hit home then. Koslowski, a big bruiser, either doped out or nearsighted, I'd figured, as many times as I noticed him wandering around the campus stumbling over things.

"I remember him, Max. He was here six years and left for someplace else."

"For Canada. He says Bloom kept him out of the draft, as long as she could."

"Sure, bring the underground railroad up to date. A new College tradition."

"He admitted it in a radio program, that's how this Blackburn heard about it."

"A draft dodger, talking about it on the radio, he's crazy if he. . ."

"He came back when he discovered he's 4F, that's what he said on the radio."

"4F? So he had nothing to worry about. . ."

"Nothing, and now he says he can't get a job because of her."

"Why, because he spent six years here and never got a degree?"

"He claims he never got any education at all, and he blames it on her, Phil."

Koslowski. Could be that's who Bloom's afraid of. Afraid he learned how to make bombs while hiding out in Canada. Not likely, not if he's that dumb, so dumb he didn't know he was 4F in the draft all along.

"He wants a job, Max? Give him one, make him DeLeon's assistant."

"Damn it, Phil, I can't figure this one out, I. . ."

"One week with her, he'll quit and run back to Canada."

"Stop your goddamn jokes. There's something wrong here."

"All right, so it's not a joke. What's the problem?"

"Listen, ask yourself, why would Ventura call me about this?"

"Odd, now that you mention it, since it has nothing to do with you."

"It doesn't, and what's really odd is he refused to tell me."

He took off his glasses, rubbed the side of his head, and reached in his desk for a bottle of pills. Annoyed, I figured, by the way the Trustees pestered him. And getting no help from me, only jokes about DeLeon and this fellow Koslowski.

"Max, look, I'm sorry if I've caused you to have a headache, but. . ."

"To hell with him. Maybe I'll find out when I get back."

"Good idea. Where are we going?"

"Not you. Me, I'm heading to Minnesota this weekend."

"That's a long way to go, just to get away from the Trustees."

"Doc Zimmer arranged it. I'm going to the Mayo Clinic for a checkup."

"Zimmer? The opera singer? That's his idea?"

Max swallowed a couple of pills and looked even more annoyed. This time at me. The same look on his face I'd seen one night when he pushed me away from a fight I'd almost gotten into. In a local bar. Over Vietnam. The look of a man disgusted with a friend.

"Goddamn it, Phil, when's Margaret coming back?"

"Monday, as soon as they close down in Cleveland."

"You idiot, why haven't you told anyone what she's been doing there?"

"Singing in an opera? Nobody's business, Max, she's. . ."

"You haven't heard the gossip, have you?"

"Gossip? What about? Margaret's singing?"

"About her and Zimmer running off together, damn it."

I started to say that's dumb, the only one she'd run off with would be Giuseppe Verdi, and he's been dead for seventy years. But Max was right. I joke too much. Coming on top of what he'd just said, that he was headed for the Mayo Clinic, I kept my mouth shut.

I got up and walked around his desk, standing beside him. He was looking down at the papers stacked in front of him. Waiting for the pills to take effect, I supposed. For a moment I was silent. Then I patted him on his shoulder and spoke softly.

"You're right, Max, this place is a zoo."

"Damn it, your wife doesn't deserve this."

"I'll take care of it. Good luck in Minnesota."

Walking back to my office I thought about it. I had not learned when the next poker game would be. Or even if there would be one. I did know we'd both been dealt bad hands. Max, for sure. And me, having to deal with gossip about Margaret.

Two bad hands. And no way to know how they might play out.

Reggie was the first to notice the car when it stopped in front of our house. "Mom's back" he yelled. I opened the front door and stepped on the porch, watching as Doc Zimmer set Margaret's suitcases on the sidewalk. By the time I got there she had picked up her luggage and was walking toward me. Frowning.

"Leave your bags here" I said. "I'll bring them in, I want to see Zimmer first." She put her luggage down and looked back, watching as I walked out in the street and stood beside his car. He had started the engine and was ready to leave, but he turned it off and got out when he saw me standing there.

"Your wife has a beautiful voice" he said, almost grinning. Tall and handsome, gone with Margaret for two weeks, no wonder Max had said there was gossip. Fine, leave it at that, right now I was concerned with something else. How good he might be as a medicine man.

"Max Piper" I said. "What can you tell me about him?"

"He's a patient of mine. Why do you ask?"

"Max said you're sending him to the Mayo Clinic."

"I can't speak about that. You should know I. . ."

"Just be sure you take care of him. You understand me, Doctor?"

I knew my voice seemed threatening. I meant it to be. We stood face to face for a moment, Zimmer frowning and shaking his head, me wondering what more I could say. Nothing, as he drove off, leaving me alone in the street.

So he refused to talk about Max. Too bad. I watched as his car disappeared, then noticed the woman across the street, looking out from a second-story window. The wife of a math professor, always full of gossip. So be it.

When I brought Margaret's bags inside she was standing in the living room, her arms around Reggie and her eyes on a banner hanging from the ceiling. With two words on it, Welcome Home, and music coming from a loudspeaker in the corner. An overture from La Traviata, the opera she'd been singing in. Reggie's idea of a greeting.

"That's nice, but what's he doing home?" she asked as he took her bags upstairs.

"Margaret, school's out for Thanksgiving week, have you forgotten?"

"I suppose I had. . .but I haven't forgotten what you warned me about."

"Two weeks in an opera chorus, there's nothing wrong with that."

"When I told you I was going to audition, do you remember what you said?"

"Sure, you never know how things may turn out, you. . ."

"They may turn out bad, that's what you said."

She reached in her purse and handed me the program for La Traviata, turning the pages to a picture of the chorus. Two rows of people in costumes. I looked at it while she went to the kitchen, and found her on the back row, standing next to Doc Zimmer, both of them dressed like gypsies. When she returned with a glass of milk she took the picture and pointed to a man in the center of the front row. Big, towering over the others, dressed in a matador's costume.

"Do you recognize him, Phil? He's a College Trustee."

"Al Ventura. He sings in opera?"

"He's on the board of directors there, so they have to let him."

"He tries to run the College, too, he. . ."

"Last week we had a terrible argument, Phil, right after he telephoned Max Piper."

"Ventura, so he's the one who called about Koslowski. . ."

"Whatever it was, he said Max was rude when he talked to him."

"Rude? Max? Never, he's not feeling well, I know, but. . ."

"I told him he was wrong about Max, and then he got angry and said he'd see to it I never sing there again."

Margaret's voice was sad as she spoke. Her face was covered with tears. And all I could manage to say was don't worry about it, go rest for a while, we'll call you when dinner's ready, we're cooking up something special to welcome you back.

As she went upstairs I noticed Reggie standing in the doorway to the kitchen, looking as angry as a twelve-year-old could look. Holding a carton of eggs he had taken from the refrigerator.

"You said we'd make an omelette, Dad."

"Not yet. I suppose you heard what your Mother said."

"About not singing again, that's not fair, what that Trustee told her."

"Ventura. You're right. Not fair at all."

"You said you want to use my card machine? I'll go and get it."

Reggie's device for dealing poker hands, what we were talking about when Margaret arrived. He brought it up from the basement, set it on my desk, and placed a deck of cards in the top. While I sat there looking at his machine, trying to concentrate, trying to get my mind off what to do about Ventura.

"Reggie, do you recall what I discovered about poker?"

"Some sure-fire way of winning, you said."

"Here, read this. You can see for yourself."

I handed him a copy of the paper I'd put together, five typewritten pages. The one I sent to a logic journal. While I looked again at the letter I received in the morning mail. Nice, a tentative okay. Run one more test with a hundred different hands, send the outcome right away, and if all goes well the paper will be published.

"What's this about, Dad? It looks complicated."

"Game theory, Reggie, that's what it's called now."

"It's not as simple as breaking eggs to make an omelette, is it?"

"No, you have to know what game you're playing."

"The game I'd like is breaking eggs on that Trustee's head."

"Not bad, Reggie. You've just given me a great idea."

Crack a few eggs, right. On Ventura's skull. That conniving idiot, use this game theory I've worked out to get him off Margaret's back. And these other folks, with all their gossip about Margaret and Doc Zimmer. Try it out on Thanksgiving Day, in the College dining room, hit them with a few eggs, too.

This game theory of mine. It works in poker. If it works around here there'll be nothing left but eggshells.

Reggie begged off on Thanksgiving Day, saying he'd rather stay home and eat a can of beans or something. Margaret nodded, saying nothing. She nodded again when I said we'd better drive, we don't want to be on foot in this snowstorm that's starting. Silent, saying nothing, the way she'd been since getting back from Cleveland. Brooding, it seemed, about the way things had turned out there.

Me, too. Brooding. But not about her opera downfall. About Ventura, the way he shoves people around. About these small-town folks and how they gossip. About this faculty I'm part of, even if I don't fit in. And now, I don't know why, I'm driving in a snowstorm so we can have Thanksgiving Dinner with them. Listening to the clickity clack of the windshield wipers, wondering what I'm doing here.

"I hope it's not snowing like this at Christmas time" I said. "If it is, it won't be easy, driving to Vermont again."

Small talk. Trying to get her mind off Cleveland. On something else to cheer her up. Christmas with her family.

Christmas. One year in Texas with my folks, the next year back East with hers. When I'd just as soon stay home and write a book or whatever, anything to get a job at some other College. Something else we've argued about. Staying here, where she's happy with her church and the choir she sings in. While I'm stuck with a crowd I've had enough of.

So it's small talk now about Christmas, and still Margaret's only nodding.

She said nothing, not even about the snow, when we parked and waded through it to the College dining hall. Silent, until we entered the faculty dining room. And then she spoke, speaking softly, as if awakened by the empty tables.

"There's almost no one here" she said.

"A free Thanksgiving meal, they wouldn't miss it, Margaret."

"I don't know. . ."

"Even in this snowstorm, if it's free, take my word, they'll show up."

"You sound like you don't want to be here, Phil."

"I'd rather have a can of beans with Reggie. Let's leave."

Too late. When we turned around to go, there they were, coming through the door. The couple across the street, the Kernstadts. Werner the math prof, with his wife Flora leading him in. Werner the Wimp, the students called him, the way she bossed him around. And now she was all but pushing us back to a table.

"The Dees" said Flora. "We drove too, we followed you here."

Margaret looked surprised. Not me. Knowing how this woman gossiped, how she was always spying out the window, I had guessed already she was the one who started the rumors about Margaret and Doc Zimmer. And she had seen him take her luggage from the car when they got back. No, I was not surprised at all. She had dragged her husband here to keep it up.

"We'll join you for dinner" said Flora.

"I don't know" said Margaret. "We were just. . ."

"Sit down" said Flora. "We have a lot to talk about."

Margaret turned to me, uncertain. I nodded. Why not? I had a good idea what might happen next, so we sat down. As a waiter brought us dinner I watched Flora. Sipping a glass of wine, a wicked smile on her face. Not a bad looking woman, forty maybe, but only a fool like Werner could put up with her. I felt sorry for him, knowing what was coming.

"You two" said Flora. "It's nice to see you together again."

"Together. . .yes. . ." said Margaret.

"I suppose it did not work out" said Flora. "While you were gone, I mean."

"No" said Margaret. "It. . .well, no. . .it was a bad idea, I guess. . ."

"My my" said Flora. "Two weeks with Doctor Zimmer and you're disappointed."

Margaret said nothing, staring at her dinner. Werner paid no attention. He was nibbling at a salad. Looking at Flora, with that wicked smile on her face, I bit into a stuffed egg, remembering what Reggie had suggested. About breaking eggs on the head of that Trustee, as he put it, meaning Ventura.

That's when I made up my mind. All right, lady, let's try breaking an egg or two on your head. You like to play games, let's try this game theory I've come up with. How to stick it to another player. So I made my opening move, speaking softly.

"Flora, I suppose you've heard the rumors floating around."

"Rumors?" she responded. "What rumors?"

"About you and Doctor Zimmer, Flora."

"What?" she gasped. "What are you talking about?"

"Yes, what are you talking about?" said Werner, looking up from his salad.

"I'm sorry" I said. "I thought you'd heard the gossip, Werner."

"Gossip? What gossip?" he asked.

"About your wife" I answered, looking straight at Flora.

"Gossip? What kind of gossip about her?"

"About her and Doctor Zimmer."

Werner pushed his plate away and put his fork down. Silent, not even looking up, folding his dining napkin slowly. I watched and waited as he placed it on the table, staring at it. Flora seemed indifferent, even though she was no longer smiling.

"Flora, what have you been up to?" he asked, his eyes still on the napkin.

No answer.

Margaret had been poking at her dinner, paying no attention, deep in thought it seemed. But now she raised her eyes and looked across the table, evidently puzzled by the scene unfolding, alarmed, perhaps, by the sound of Werner's voice. Louder. Firmer.

"Damn it, I want an answer. What have you been up to, Flora?"

They were staring at each other now, Werner looking angry, Flora starting to smile again. And then she stuck her tongue out at him, as if to say kiss off, I'm in charge here, I'll do whatever I want to. At least Werner must have read it that way.

"You bitch" he said. "I've had enough of the way you treat me."

Flora reached for her wine glass. Frowning. Unnerved by what I'd said about the gossip, caught off guard by Werner's sudden mutiny. She looked hard at him. And then she leaned forward, held the glass above his head and poured wine all over him.

Werner said nothing. What he did, that said it all. He reached down for his napkin, wiped the wine off his face, then slapped her hard, grabbed her by the neck, pulled her from her chair, and dragged Flora, groaning and stumbling, toward the dining room door.

Just like that, and they were gone. Through the open door, seeing the students lining up for dinner, I wondered if they'll notice the spectacle. Kornstadt, dragging his wife out by the neck. If they do, it won't be Werner the Wimp anymore. Werner the Barbarian, maybe.

Not exactly the way I figured things would end. Something I'd have to ponder, a missing piece in the game theory I've just tried out. How to wrap it up. The way Margaret was wrapping up the pumpkin pie now, aloof, it seemed to what had happened.

"Let's leave" she said. "We can have this pie at home."

"Margaret, let me finish my dinner first."

"No. You've had enough already."

"Whatever you say" I replied, wondering for a second, the way I said that, if I was also someone married to a wife who bossed him around. But only for a second. With the Dean of Faculty approaching as we stood up I had to get my mind on him instead, knowing I'd have to answer for the Kornstadts.

"What was that about?" he asked.

"Werner and his wife, they had some sort of quarrel, Dean."

"Quite embarrassing, that sort of thing at Thanksgiving Dinner."

"They'll be all right. I think Werner's in control now."

"You should treat him well, Phil. He'll have a vote on whether you remain here."

"Werner? He's on the tenure committee?"

"He is, and by the way, Al Ventura called me yesterday about that very matter."

"That Trustee? Why? What did he want to know? If I have tenure yet?"

"More or less. You can ask him why yourself, he'll be here at commencement."

"I think I know already, Dean."

Sure, Ventura gets into a spat with Margaret, tells her she can't sing any more in Cleveland, and now he's after me for being married to her. So be it. With the mid-year commencement three weeks away I'll have plenty of time to think about it. How to polish up this game theory, how to put him away.

Even if it costs me tenure. Who needs it, anyway? It's time to get out of here, I told myself, time to get away from all these people I can't stand. Idiots, all of them, except perhaps for Werner, the way he'd finally put that gossiping Flora in her place.

They weren't back yet, I could tell when we got home. No lights on in their house, and no ruts in their driveway, two feet deep in snow. Not ours. Reggie had cleared it with the snow thrower he invented. And more. When we stopped in front of the garage I pressed a button on the remote control he had installed. The door went up, just as he designed it to.

"You see, Margaret, it works. I told you it would."

"I don't understand" she said.

"Remote control, you can try it yourself, the next time it snows."

"No, I mean back there, at the dinner table."

"Eggshells, Margaret. That's all, nothing but eggshells."

Margaret got out of the car without asking what I meant. Too hard to explain, what I'd told Reggie about eggshells. After he said what he'd like to do to that Trustee. Fine, so next we'd try it on Ventura, at commencement

Why not? It worked with Flora, even if it took a stuffed egg to remind me

Maybe, but if I'd known what Werner would do next, I would not have been so sure. I might have broken some eggs on my own head. A whole plate full.

Dean Palmer seemed ready to do it himself at commencement. Crack an egg on my skull, that is. At least it felt like that, the way he called me aside when I showed up to join the faculty procession, said he wanted to speak to me in private, and then peppered me with questions. Acting like he might want to bite my head off.

"Professor Kornstadt isn't here" he grumbled. "Do you know why?"

"Werner? No, I don't, I. . ."

"Do you know Doctor Zimmer?"

"Yes, of course, but what about Werner?"

"I bailed him out last night. He's been charged with assault and battery."

"Werner? What did he do? He must have. . ."

"What did he do? He broke Doctor Zimmer's jaw, that's what."

"Werner? He went after Zimmer? Then he. . ."

"The police said he was shouting about his wife when they arrested him."

"Flora, sure, but look, Dean, I. . ."

"What happened at Thanksgiving? You never really told me, did you?"

Palmer shook his head, annoyed and impatient, looking like some kind of Grand Inquisitor in his cap and gown. His eyes were bloodshot. Up late at night, I guessed, getting Werner out of jail. What could I say? Nothing safe, so I kept my mouth shut.

"Elena Bloom will not be at commencement, either" he said.

"Elena? What's happened to her?"

"She will not go out in public without protection. Do you know why?"

"No, I. . ."

"You should. When she called me yesterday she told me what you did."

"Me? Dean, I haven't seen her in weeks, I. . ."

"She said you defused a bomb someone sent her."

"A bomb? That wasn't a bomb, that was. . ."

"She thinks it was. What did you try to do, frighten her?"

"Look, Dean, that package she received, it was only. . ."

"That's no way to get tenure, trying to scare her half to death."

He shook his head again and said don't move, he'd be back in a minute, he wanted to make sure the faculty was lining up correctly in the hallway. I waited. Werner breaking Zimmer's jaw, Elena telling the Dean she's afraid because of me, I could only wait to see what more he had to harass me with. Much more, it seemed, when he returned.

"Something else. Coach Casey, what did you put him up to?

"Casey? The basketball coach? What about him?"

"He's been pestering me about the College dress code."

"Look, Dean, I talked to him after swimming, but. . ."

"And you suggested he should let his team play naked, right?"

"I think I mentioned the Greek Olympics, sure, but. . ."

"He's a pain in the butt. You, too, the way you've been acting lately."

Palmer walked away then, pointing to the faculty procession, telling me to get in line where I belonged. Then he stopped, looked down at the hallway floor for a moment, turned around and faced me.

"I almost forgot" he said. "One more thing before we go in."

"What now?"

"The lady who's giving the commencement address, how does she know you?"

"Who is it? Who's giving the address?"

"She wants to see you at the reception, and you don't even know who she is?"

"I'm afraid I haven't read the program, Dean. I've had my mind on something else."

"You've had your head up your butt, that's what. Get in line, you can see who it is when we get in there."

My mind had been on something else, all right. On Ventura, how to put him in his place, this time with the right ending. Now I was not so sure, not after hearing what Werner had done. The Dean was right, I'd had my head up my butt, getting ready for a pompous Trustee

And now this nonsense about Bloom and Coach Casey. Along with this lady speaker I'd been told to see, without even knowing who she was, I'd have to admit I felt uneasy as we marched into the College auditorium

Uneasy? Ambushed, I might have said when I saw her. Standing on the stage next to the College president, Beverly Amador, the axe-wielding Senator from Vermont. Over sixty now, grey haired and mean, the same as on TV, looking like she might even punch the President. How did she know I was teaching here? I had no idea. And no place to run for cover

Amador. A long time since we'd crossed swords in the Army. I could still hear her screaming, blaming me for four dead Negro soldiers whose parachutes hadn't opened. Except they weren't dead, they were dummies. Not that it mattered then. And it wouldn't matter now. The way she acted on TV, I could tell she hadn't changed. She was not a forgiving woman.

At least she wasn't yelling as she spoke. About the underground railroad before the Civil War. How the College should be proud of how it rescued slaves and hid them. How the heritage lives on, how there's still work to do, and so forth. Calm. With the TV people there, no need to shout about it. Even if half the faculty had gone to sleep in the middle of her address.

Not much of a speech, the way she cut it short and sat down. Not much of an audience, either, the auditorium almost empty. The rest of the students home for Christmas, only the mid-term graduates and their families, applauding as the President handed out diplomas. While she sat behind him, looking mighty angry. Whatever the reason, she'd be hard to deal with now.

She was. I could tell right away when I entered the reception room and saw her talking to the President. Giving him a mouthful about something. With me coming next. Might as well have a drink, I figured, a strong one before I faced her. So I headed for the bar, still wearing my cap and gown, still wondering how she knew I was here.

I never got to the bar. Ventura stepped in front of me first. With a glass in one hand, poking at my shoulder with the other. Taller than usual, wearing cowboy boots, perhaps, to go with the big Stetson cocked on the side of his head. With an arrogant smile on his face, acting like he owned the world, me included.

"Professor Dee" he said. "The man whose wife can't sing worth shit."

For a moment I said nothing. Remembering what I'd sworn, a while before, when I heard what Werner had done. Don't try that game theory on Ventura, there's no way to know how it might turn out. But I hadn't sworn to stay silent, had I? No sir, no way, not after what he'd just said.

"Maybe she can't" I replied. "But I can. You want to hear the song I've made up?"

"Go ahead. Writing songs may be your next career."

"Here's the first line. There's an asshole Trustee in Cleveland, hiding behind his dough."

"Shut up, you bastard, I'll. . ."

"The next line, no one's guessed what a prick he is, I'll make sure someday they know."

Just like that, and I had no idea where the words came from. A rhyme straight out of the blue. A suicide note in terms of tenure, I supposed, but I couldn't help it. And seeing the look on his face I'd have to admit it felt worth it.

Ventura was enraged, of course, caught off guard by a mere professor. An untenured prof, no less, insulting him and smiling about it. He grabbed my shoulder, called me a sonofabitch, and was about to say something more, but before he could go on the President of the College stepped between us.

"That Senator's impossible" he groaned.

"To hell with her" said Ventura. "It's this bastard I want you to take care of."

"Who? Dee? What about him?"

"Fire him. Right now. You understand me?"

"Al, I'm not sure I can do that, I. . ."

"You're the President, do it. If you don't I'll have your ass, you hear me?"

"Well. . .yes. . .but first he must meet with Senator Amador. She's asked to see him."

The President turned to me, with a sheepish look on his face that seemed to say his hands were tied. No doubt wondering why I was smiling. Fire me? Go ahead, I have a contract for the rest of the term, you can pay me off in full. Tell Ventura that, you're used to kissing his butt, I felt like saying. From what I could tell that's what he was doing as I walked away

Senator Amador had a few choice words about the President, too. She was alone when I reached her, so angry no one else dared approach her. The TV people were waiting for an interview, it looked like, but she motioned them away, glared at the President across the room, and started cursing as soon as I got there.

"Your President is a fucking loser" she said.

"Ma'am, if you want my opinion, I. . ."

"This was supposed to be a major event, professor."

"I'm not sure what you mean, Senator, but. . ."

"A chance to speak to a crowd on national television, that's what I mean."

"Yes, ma'am, so. . ."

"There should have been a thousand people here, but this won't even make the late night news. He let me down, this asshole you have for a President." So that's what it was. What could I say? Tell her he'd let me down, as well, stirring her up like this before I had to see her? Ask her if she's still gunning for me? Over those four dummies rigged with parachutes? If that's why she wants to see me?

"Take off that silly cap and gown" she said, before I could ask her anything.

"This? I forgot, I. . ."

"No, leave it on, Dee, but you did look better in an Army uniform."

"That was a long time ago, Senator. I suppose I'm still on your list."

"What list?" she replied, looking puzzled. Then she grabbed my arm, sounding like she'd heard a bell ring. And acting like she'd found a long lost friend.

"My list, of course" she said. "Come with me, young man, there's something I just thought of." I followed her to the back of the room. Watching as she spoke with the television people. Evidently telling them to form a circle around us, to hold the others back while she spoke with me alone. They did, keeping far enough away not to hear her.

"Thomas Whipple" she said. "He's in one of your classes."

"Tommy L? How did you know that?"

"The colored students and their professors, I asked for a list before I got here."

"A list? With my name on it, so that's how. . ."

"They were supposed to stand in front as I spoke, all the colored students."

"Including Tommy, sure. What about him?"

"Whipple, I've been wondering about that name for days. You just woke me up, Dee."

"Fine, so maybe you'll let me go now."

"Not yet. What does that L stand for?"

"Lomax. I haven't asked him, Senator, but I think that's who Tommy's father is."

"So I thought. The FBI, they're after him, Dee, they're after that bastard Lomax."

Her voice sounded hoarse as she said that. No surprise she waved to the TV crew for a glass of water. It was what she'd said about Lomax that surprised me. The tape I'd found in the attic, that was him, all right, drunk, bragging about Negro votes and his mistress. But that was years ago. Why would they be after him now?

"This kid Whipple, how well do you know him?" she asked when her voice had cleared.

"Tommy? Well enough, I suppose, but what's this about the FBI?"

"Do you remember why I came to your unit in Germany?"

"That tape with Lomax on it, sure, you thought we'd killed some Negro soldiers."

"I'm old, Dee, but I have a damned good memory. Cremona Whipple, that was the woman Lomax mentioned on the tape. That's what I've been adding up, Whipple and Lomax."

"Senator, he's been out of politics for years, he. . ."

"But not out of business, Dee. In Vietnam he swindled millions from the Army."

"Lomax? So why don't they arrest him?"

"He's disappeared. The FBI can't find him. No one can."

"Let me guess. You want me to see if Tommy knows where his father is."

"Do it. Maybe my trip to this damned College won't be wasted after all."

Why not find out? Even if it's only headlines she's really after. Lomax, what he'd done to me in Texas, pushing me off the paper there, he'd been as rotten as Ventura, trying to make the President fire me now. Right, find out, get even. With Lomax now, maybe the other one later, somewhere down the road. So I nodded and agreed.

"I'll try. If I'm still here. That's all I can promise."

"If you're still here? You don't have tenure yet?"

"No, and if it's up to the President I don't think I ever will."

"That shithead? My, my, let's see what I can do about this."

One tough old woman, the way she took charge then. Telling the TV people to come along, pushing her way through the crowd with me behind her, in a loud voice asking everyone to be quiet, waiting for a moment with a smile on her face. And then announcing she had a present for the College. I held my breath, wondering what she was up to.

"Yes, it will be a Christmas gift" she said

She paused then. A politician working a crowd. The mention of a gift had gotten their attention, all right. Mine, too.

"As you know, I came here today to speak about the underground railroad and how this wonderful College played a role in that endeavor."

Another pause. Slick, the way she said that. I could see the President squirming as she spoke. Maybe figuring the gift she had in mind was someone to replace him.

"In that regard, Professor Dee has made a marvelous suggestion, one I am happy to agree with. My present to the College will be a museum to celebrate your heritage." Another pause, while she waited for the faculty's reaction. None, only silence. So she added something else, a guarantee they'd start applauding.

"You should thank Professor Dee, for all the jobs and money that will bring."

That did it. Slowly but surely her words sunk in. Jobs and money. The faculty began applauding, louder and louder. The noise was so great I could barely hear her as she turned, leaned against me, and yelled in my ear.

"A museum, how much could that cost, Dee?

"A pile of money, Senator."

"Don't worry, I'll tack it on some bill. That's how it works in Congress."

"Money. My God, look at the President, he's jumping up and down."

"Good for him. That son of a bitch won't bother you now, Dee."

Before I could reply she was out of reach, surrounded by the crowd. Shaking hands, laughing, acting like she'd had a great day here. Moving slowly to an exit where she could head for home. A real politician, that old woman, still smiling as she disappeared.

I was more or less smiling, too, thinking about what she'd just pulled off. The way Dean Palmer applauded, the way the President joined in, the way Ventura stomped out when she mentioned my name, not bad at all

Except for one thing. Tommy L. I would have to find out where Lomax is. At least try, as we agreed. Watching Amador leave I was starting to have second thoughts about it. It would not be easy, asking this kid about a man not even listed on his College record.

I would have had no second thoughts at all if I'd known where that would lead, the search for Tommy's father. To an even bigger break than this Christmas gift she promised. Bigger, much bigger than anything I could have dreamed of

Something that crooked bastard Ventura could not have dreamed of, either.

Christmas in Vermont, with Margaret's family, it wasn't the College I was thinking about. Not about Lomax or Tommy L or Ventura or anyone else back there. It was how to put up with her relatives. Most of all, how to keep away from her mother Emma. The kind of woman they'd call a bossy bitch in Texas.

I was more or less hiding in the kitchen, all alone, listening to the radio, surrounded by leftover food from Christmas dinner, when she marched in behind Margaret's father. A sixty-year-old woman, with makeup so she might look forty. As usual, acting like a drill sergeant, the way she ordered him around.

"Robert, you cannot have another drink" she said as they entered the kitchen. Her voice was firm, but for once he paid no attention to her. Instead he grunted, opened a cabinet above the sink and brought out a bottle of whisky. An old man, his hair completely grey, fed up with her and maybe a lot more, as well, getting drunk on Christmas Day.

"What are you doing in here?" she asked, turning to me and scowling.

"Listening to the radio" I replied.

"You should be in the family room with everyone else."

"No, Emma, I'm waiting for a news report."

"You two are hopeless" she grumbled and started to leave the kitchen. And then stopped in the doorway and turned around to hear the radio. The President has ordered a renewal of bombing North Vietnam, said the announcer, a full scale resumption of B-52 strikes on Hanoi.

"Nixon!" she shouted. "That man is evil!"

"Emma, he's trying to force them back to the peace talks, that's all."

"Bombing on Christmas Day, that man is not a Christian!"

"I wouldn't know" I replied, hoping she would go away. No such luck. She came back in the kitchen, past Margaret's father with a drink in his hand, switched off the radio and stood hovering over me as I sat there. Looking like someone ready to squash a cockroach.

"Of course you wouldn't know. You don't even go to church with Margaret."

"No, ma'am, I don't, but I've read the Bible."

"You? When? When you were growing up in Texas, I suppose."

"Every word, including Deuteronomy. You should read that part yourself some time."

She glared at me, perplexed, as if the roach had bitten back. For a moment she just stood there, saying nothing. Then she shook her head, turned her back and started to walk away, out of the kitchen. Fine. As she reached the doorway I gave her one last shove, raising my voice so she could hear me.

"Chapter twelve, verse two. Maybe you'll understand what Nixon's up to then."

I wasn't sure if I remembered it right, or even if it was relevant to the war in Vietnam, but at least she was gone. A domineering woman, someone I had been uncertain how to cope with since I met her. Indifferent to the child Margaret was holding when we came back from Germany, as if Reggie was an outcast who reminded her of some great disappointment.

Margaret's father seemed to understand. "Have a drink" he said as I looked up. He was leaning against the kitchen counter, wobbly, his voice sounding slurred. I could guess what was coming. A re-run of some thoughts we'd shared before while drinking. Several times over the years, a small town banker and his son-in-law, trading jokes about the cost of marriage.

He set the bottle in front of me but I left it alone. We'd gotten drunk together in the past, but not this time, not now. No booze for me. Time to stay sober and make up my mind. How to deal with Emma, once and for all. And maybe Margaret, also, if she's too stubborn to see why I can't stand her mother.

"She's the price I've paid for lust" said Margaret's father, watching Emma leave.

"I know, you've told me. With not much collateral, you said."

"The kind you can't resist. In the banking business, a bad investment."

"So what do you get in return?"

"The next generation, Phil. That's what you get in return."

"Plus the interest paid in nagging, right?"

I helped him into a chair so he would not fall down. In the past he had laughed when he talked like that. Not now. He was silent for a while, drinking quietly, off somewhere in the past. Then he poured another drink and looked across the table at me. Angry about something, turning really drunk, trying to get his words straight.

"This boy of yours, he's all right, Phil."

"Reggie, I know, he invents things."

"This morning. . .do you know what he did for her?"

"Sure, he put a cruise control in her car. His Christmas present for her."

"Emma. . .she wouldn't even thank him, Phil, she just. . ."

"I'm not surprised. She's never seemed to like him."

"She thinks. . .she thinks he's the reason Margaret had to give up opera."

"Reggie? She blames him for that?"

"Not just him. You, too. . .she. . ."

"So Emma wanted to be the mother of a famous singer and it's my fault."

"Last week. . .she cursed you. . .when she saw you on TV. . ."

Too much to drink, and he was starting to mumble as he put his head down and passed out. But I understood what he was trying to say. Margaret's brother Rudy had laughed about it when we arrived, how the local station had shown me with Senator Amador, how I must have kissed her ass so she would give that money to my college

Rudy, another reason to stay away from Margaret's family. Close to forty, Emma's pet, too lazy to work, living off his father's wealth. Jealous and sarcastic. I was about to help his father to bed when Rudy came in the kitchen. For all I knew, sent by his mother to harass me. Along with her nephew Tom, a draft dodger who lives in Boston.

They walked past us without speaking. To the refrigerator, poking around for beer. Then they stood there drinking, with their backs to me, laughing, speaking loud so I could hear what they were saying. Like a couple of idiot kids on a playground, trying to irritate someone without looking at him.

"Uncle Bob's had too much to drink" said the nephew, almost giggling.

"Let him sleep" said Rudy. "Don't bother that cowboy from Texas, either."

"Him? I wouldn't dare. He used to be a big bad paratrooper."

"Not any more. He's a celebrity now. He was on TV last week."

"With that woman Senator, you said. You know what they call her in Boston?"

"A nigger lover, just like him. That's why they won't let him back in Texas."

"So what about him, Rudy? If he can't go back to Texas he won't know what to do."

"He knows. He'll stay in Ohio and keep on pimping for his College."

I wouldn't bite, no matter what they said. After a while they gave up and walked out of the kitchen, still laughing as they left. Leaving me to chew on something, what they said about going back to Texas. Not a bad idea, at that, getting far away from this family. Except for Margaret's father, not a decent person in the crowd.

He was still asleep, with his head on the table. It wasn't easy, getting him to his feet and out the back door of the kitchen, down a narrow hallway to the private bedroom where he slept alone. But somehow I managed. After I got him onto the bed and covered him with a blanket I stood there thinking. About what he'd said. The price of lust.

All right, so I had not been able to control myself. I had gotten Margaret pregnant and ruined her career. Reggie's turned out fine, but all these years of nagging about opera, maybe that's the price I've had to pay. Max Piper's right. Stay single, don't get married, work off all that libido by playing poker.

Max. I sat down in an easy chair beside the bed and picked up the telephone. Christmas Day, no family to speak of, no one to be away with, by now he might be home from the Mayo Clinic. You will have to wait, said the long-distance operator, all the lines are busy. So I waited. Wondering what his tests had shown.

He wasn't sure, he told me when I finally reached him. Doc Zimmer had the results, but he couldn't speak, his jaw was wired, and the prognosis he wrote was badly scribbled. Max laughed when he told me what he'd heard about the doctor's broken jaw. And the rumor about the basketball team playing its next game nude, that was something to laugh about, too

He'd be there to see it himself, said Max. If he was feeling better. He wasn't laughing when he told me that. I wanted to cheer him up and say Merry Christmas, but then the call broke off, the operator said the lines were down with ice and snow, and that was it. Not a Merry Christmas at all, the way he sounded when it ended.

I was brooding about it when I returned to the kitchen. Max in bad health, Margaret's mother Emma driving me up the wall, her brother Rudy trying to provoke me, I was in no mood for the Christmas Carols they were singing in the family room. With Margaret no doubt playing the piano.

Wrong. It was someone else at the piano. Maybe Emma, who had dreamed of playing in Carnegie Hall, Margaret's father had once told me. And had to give it up when her teachers learned that she was tone deaf. Whoever it was, it wasn't Margaret. They were still going at it when she came in the kitchen. Looking quite disgusted.

"Where have you been?" she asked. "I've been looking all over for you."

"I've been taking care of your father, Margaret. He's had too much to drink."

"He'll be all right, I know, Phil, it's my mother I'm concerned with."

"Why? Because I insulted her? She's too thick-skinned to be insulted."

I could tell Margaret wasn't pleased with what I said. The tears on her face seemed to warn me not to say another word. Too bad. She might as well know I'd had it with her mother, I'd had enough of Christmas in Vermont

Wrong again. As she went on speaking, wiping away the tears, trying not to cry, I knew how wrong I'd been. About a lot of things, no doubt. For sure, wrong about how Margaret stood behind her mother.

"I think you're right about her, Phil. We should pack and leave right now."

"Why? Because of Emma? What's she done?"

"The piano has a broken key. Reginald offered to fix it, and she slapped him."

"Your mother slapped him? So where is he now?"

"He went to his room to study. Let's go home, Phil."

I glanced at my watch. Six o'clock. Dark outside, the roads covered with ice and snow, not a good idea to drive at night. Looking at Margaret, the way she was standing there, looking lonely, wearing a red Christmas dress, I felt inspired by what she'd told me. Inspired is hardly the word for how I felt, I know, but in any case I had a better idea for how to spend the night.

"Not now, it's too late. We'll leave in the morning."

"All right, Phil. Before she gets up for breakfast."

"Here, I'll bring this radio, you bring that bottle, let's go upstairs."

"What's the radio for?"

"Music. Maybe a Christmas opera. Who knows?"

"This bottle of Scotch, you want me to take that up, as well?"

"You bet. It's time to have a drink and see how the collateral's holding up."

"Collateral? What are you talking about?"

"That's a banker's joke from your dad. You'll see, Margaret."

Collateral. She had no idea what that meant. Or what I had in mind. How I planned to celebrate it, this last Christmas in Vermont. All things considered, so to speak, Margaret was in for a surprise.

Christmas in Vermont

And except for Margaret's mother and some others in her family, a Merry, Merry Christmas to all.

Happy New Year, said the announcer over the noise of the crowd, welcome to the first game of the Spring semester. With no mention of the rumors. Or why the basketball gym was packed, standing room only, a restless mob of thousands, waiting for Coach Casey to lead his team out of the locker room. Waiting to see if the rumors were true.

I held my breath, knowing what I'd put him up to. Telling Casey about the Greeks, how they did things in Plato's day. Competing nude in the Olympics. How he'd fill the gym if he did that here. Dumb, my teasing him that way. No wonder I was uneasy. I hadn't realized Casey might be even dumber. If the rumors were right, he was going to try it.

Dumb or not, it looked like Casey knew how to tease a bit himself. When the team came out they were dressed in white togas, wearing garlands on their heads. Ready to practice with all that on, then strip down for the game

That's what the crowd must have figured. Take it off when the game starts, they started chanting. Carried away by the crowd, the College cheerleaders joined in. Take it off when the game starts! Take it off when the game starts! I sat behind the officials' table, squeezed in between a couple of visitors from out of town. "What the hell is this?" one of them yelled in my ear. "You can't practice with that crap on, you can't play basketball wearing togas." Maybe not, but Casey must have shown them how. Dribbling, taking jump shots, going in for layups, they had it down cold

The crowd went on chanting. Take it off when the game starts! While the visiting team watched in disarray from their end of the gym, so awed by what was happening they had trouble even passing the ball around.

Their coach wasn't awed. He was evidently angry, pounding on the officials' table, pointing to the togas, and shouting at the referees. Who were thumbing through the rule book, looking frantic, arguing with each other

One of them walked away, looking through the stands, calling out for someone. With all the noise I couldn't hear who that might be. When the referee came back I saw. And groaned. He had Dean Palmer with him.

I could tell the Dean was annoyed. With the officials, and what they'd dragged him into. And with me, I figured, as soon as he saw me sitting there. I was right. When the visiting coach threw up his arms and went back to his team, the Dean looked at me and started yelling.

"This is your fault, Dee! Your fault!"

"What about the togas?" I yelled back. "What does the rule book say?"

"They can wear them. Anything, as long as they wear something, damn it."

"What if they take them off? What happens then?"

"Then you'll be sorry, Dee, you put him up to this!"

I wanted to tell him the only thing I was sorry about was Max Piper, not well enough to be here. But the crowd was roaring as the players finished practice and headed for the locker rooms, so loud he couldn't hear me now. All I could do was watch as he shook his head and went back to wherever he'd been sitting.

"What was that about?" asked the man next to me when the noise died down.

"The Greek Olympics" I replied.

"You look like you need a drink. Here, have a swig of this."

He reached in his jacket, pulled out a flask, and tried to hand it to me. I said no, but I may have looked like I needed something, at that. Maybe a ticket out of town if Casey brought his team out nude to play the game. One for him, as well, if he was dumb enough to do that.

I'd know soon enough. Ten minutes to game time, said the announcer on the PA system. The gym was almost quiet, thousands of people waiting to see. And then the chanting started again. Take it off when the game starts! Take it off when the game starts!

Dumb or not, evidently Casey wasn't listening. His players were still wearing togas and garlands when they came out to start the game. And they kept them on, drawing fouls almost every time they had the ball, hitting free throws, shooting easy baskets, running up a ten-point lead in the first few minutes of the game.

While the cameraman from the local paper fired away with his flash gun, making sure the whole world could see this historic event, basketball players wearing togas. Not that the two men sitting next to me would want any pictures. They were there to root for the visiting team.

"This is bullshit!" yelled the one on my right. "Our guys are being screwed!"

"Damn straight!" yelled the one on my left. "It's those two officials!"

"It's those goddamned togas, that's what it is."

"Damn straight! All our guys do is touch them and they call a foul."

Not quite, but close. The togas were so loose they billowed out like clouds when Casey's players passed the ball around. The visiting team could not guard them without grabbing cloth, the officials kept on calling fouls, Casey's team kept on shooting free throws, the two men next to me kept on yelling, and the crowd kept on roaring.

Taking up a new chant. Togas, togas, keep them on! Togas, togas, keep them on!

By halftime five players from the visiting team had fouled out, Casey's team had a forty-point lead, the two men next to me had left, cursing as they shoved their way out, and I had relaxed. No danger of a nude show now. No need to worry about Dean Palmer, no need to think of leaving town.

No danger, and not much to entice this mob to stay here, either. By halftime the gym was almost quiet and the crowd had melted away, giving up on the rumors, giving up on seeing Casey's team play naked. I was ready to leave as well, until I saw Tommy L, heading for the locker room with his teammates, then coming back to greet me.

"I just now saw you here" he said. "I've got something I need to show you."

"You've scored a lot of points. How many? Thirty?"

"I don't know, Professor. Can you meet me when the game is over?"

"I'll wait. What is it you want to show me?"

"Something I brought back from Texas. Maybe you can figure it out."

What? A two-headed armadillo? Whatever he'd brought back, at least I'd have a chance to talk with him now, the first since I'd made that deal with Senator Amador. A chance to ask about Lomax, if I could manage some way of getting around to his father. So I waited, thinking about the right question to ask, barely watching the rest of the game.

I did watch how it ended. A blowout, hundreds of teen-age students rushing onto the floor, screaming, hugging Casey's team, grabbing at the togas, leaving three or four players with nothing on but jockstraps as they fled from the mob. A mob, indeed, leaving me to wonder, once again, what I was doing here, trying to teach them philosophy.

When Tommy L came out of the locker room, wearing a coat

and tie, I admit I felt reassured. Not the same lost kid who signed up for my class five months ago. Still playing ball, but starting to grow up, serious, making A's in his courses, trying to make sense of the world he'd been stuck in. Speaking softly as we walked through the snow to his dorm.

"Odd, Professor, the way my flight was canceled in Dallas."

"Bad weather, I heard. No sweat, classes don't start until tomorrow."

"It's not that. It's what happened when I had an extra night to spend there."

"With your mother, you mean. You spent Christmas with her, right?"

"She broke down and cried. I'd never seen her cry like that."

"Sure, she hated to see you go, Tommy, she. . ."

"No, we'd already said goodbye. It's what she told me then."

Before I could ask what it was we were interrupted. By thirty or forty students building a bonfire in front of the dorms, some of them waving parts of torn up togas, yelling "Way to go, Whipple!" when they saw him. He waved back, waiting until we were past them. When we were he spoke again, abruptly, asking a question that caught me off guard.

"That L in my name. You know what it stands for, Professor?"

"Tommy, listen, I'm not sure what to say, but. . ."

"Lomax. That's what it stands for. I never met him, but that's who my father was."

"I know, Tommy, I. . ."

"He used to be a Congressman, she told me. I never knew that before."

"Lomax, sure. Your mother, does she know where he is?"

"No, all she had is a book he left her, some kind of secret record she wants you to look at. I'll show you when we get to my room."

Some room. One side neatly organized, the bed made up, an uncluttered desk, books lined up on the shelves, the other side like trash left over from a rummage sale, including the basketball hanging from a net above the bed

I had no trouble guessing which side was Tommy's, watching as he unlocked a cabinet and brought out the book he mentioned. A ledger, the kind an accountant keeps, I could see when he handed it to me.

"It's filled with numbers" he said. "She couldn't make it out."

"It looks like a code. Your mother, why did she want me to see this?"

"When I told her I'd been studying logic with you, she said you might understand it."

"Maybe. This belonged to Lomax, did it? You're sure?"

"He told her to hide it. He beat her up when he left it with her."

"He's mean, I know, but. . ."

"She's got a gun. She said she'll shoot him if he comes back."

Tommy slumped in a chair, his head lowered. While I held the ledger, thinking fast. Amador. Call her at home in the morning, early, at the number she had given me, tell her about these records Lomax kept, have her reach the FBI in Dallas, that should do it.

"Tell your mother not to worry, Tommy. I know who to call, they'll protect her."

"She can't go the police, Professor. She's got a record, she. . ."

"She'll be all right, believe me. This ledger, can I keep it?"

He nodded. For a second I felt sorry for him. Then angry with myself. So I've got problems? Big deal. He's got a mother with a gun in her hand, he's stuck in a world light years away from mine, and all I could do was think of Amador? Not enough. Not enough at all.

"Keep it, Professor. Maybe you can figure out what's in it."

"We'll take care of your mother. Don't worry."

"Maybe you could help with my roommate, too" he said, trying to smile.

"He's on the team? His side of the room, looks like he might enjoy togas."

"After the game tonight, he asked if we could keep playing in them."

"So what did Coach Casey say?"

"He said no, it's one time only. And then something else, Professor, he said the togas were your idea. He's going to give you the game ball tomorrow."

I laughed. He laughed, too. Or tried to. Trying to laugh his way out of a world he seemed trapped in. I thought about him as I walked home, wondering what more I could do

I thought about the ledger, too. Wondering if it might be more than a mere ledger. A ticking time bomb, for all I knew. It was. In a way, the game ball, in a game a lot of crooks had been playing. One quite close to home, I would discover later.

I checked the clock when the alarm started ringing. Five a.m. Dark outside, and dark back East, I knew. Time to telephone Senator Amador. Why not? She'd said call her night or day, whenever I had something about Lomax. So wake her up, get things rolling.

Her maid, or whoever it was who answered, she wasn't pleased at all. Grumpy, telling me no one ever called that early, except President Nixon, and you sure as hell don't sound like him. Listen, I said, tell your boss I'm calling about a man named Lomax, and make it snappy. Figuring that's how Nixon would have put it. How would she know whose voice it is? Senator Amador did. She had already picked up her phone, hearing what I said, recognizing right away who was calling. Evidently wide awake and ready to do business, ready to wheel and deal.

"She's my niece, Dee, don't pick on her. Now, what's this about Lomax?"

"I've got a ledger he kept, full of numbers. I think you need to see it."

"Numbers? What is it, a goddamn arithmetic book?"

"It's all in code, it needs to be decoded, Senator."

"A piece of cake, hell, that's why I'm up, reading crap decoded from North Vietnam."

"North Vietnam? Senator, I. . ."

"The Paris peace talks, Dee, don't you know what's going on?"

"The peace talks, sure, but about this ledger, I need. . ."

I could hear her coughing, then only silence. While she held her hand over the phone and reached for a glass of water, I supposed. Not so. She wasn't looking for water, she had put the phone down and was talking to someone else.

"That's my niece, Dee. She said kiss her ass, you don't sound like Nixon at all."

"Fine, what I was starting to say, I need a favor from you, Senator."

"Damn it, I've already promised a museum, what is it now?"

"Tommy Whipple, this ledger came from his mother, she needs protection."

"Now you're starting to make some sense. It's Lomax she's afraid of, right?"

"He told her to hide the ledger, she's worried he might come back and. . ."

"Come back? If he does the FBI will catch that bastard, Dee. Where does she live?"

"In Texas. Dallas. Wait a second, I'll give you her address."

I reached for a copy of Tommy's record. As I read the address out loud, slowly, so she could write it down, I realized something I hadn't noticed before. The address. Tommy's mother was afraid, all right. Her address had changed three times since he first enrolled here.

"Good" said Amador. "They'll be watching her place within in an hour."

"Watching out for Tommy's mother, right? That's the deal. Agreed?"

"Agreed. Now, send the ledger to my office. And keep this to yourself, Dee."

"You'll let me know what those numbers mean? When they've been decoded?"

"I will. Anything else before you go back to bed?"

"One more thing. Tell your niece I'd like to meet her. She has a charming voice."

"A charming voice? Damn it, Dee, she's as ugly as I am."

Amador seemed to be laughing when she hung up. I could never be sure, the way she spoke, one minute like a slick politician, the next one like an overloaded stevedore. The only thing I was sure of was I could not go back to bed. Too much to think about. That ledger Lomax kept, what they'd find in that code he used.

At least Tommy's mother would be safe now. So I went to the kitchen, trying to get my mind on something else. Coffee, the opening class I'd teach at ten, the local paper, on the porch every morning by this time. I could wake up Margaret and leap on her after I read it. No, too early in the morning for jokes like that. Better to stick to the paper.

The front page was filled with pictures of the game last night. Beneath a huge italic headline asking Togas, Who Put Them Up To That? My name wasn't mentioned, I was pleased to see. It was a headline on the back page that made me spill my coffee

The back page, where the paper printed news from around the nation. A coal mine accident in West Virginia, an Elvis Presley concert in Hawaii, that sort of thing. And at the bottom of the page, a headline above a story about a car wreck in Chicago

Army Colonel, Wife, Die in Accident. I read the story again and again. Three paragraphs. Their names, but not much in the way of details. Only that it happened on the Kennedy Expressway, that their car had skidded in an ice patch, and that the wife had evidently been the driver.

After a while I folded the paper, placed it gently on the kitchen table, and went up to the attic looking for a scrapbook. I found it, in an Army footlocker, where I had kept some uniforms and paratrooper boots from Germany. Things I'd rather not remember. But could not forget.

I was in the kitchen, staring at a picture in the scrapbook, deep in thought, when I heard Margaret's voice. Not at first. I think she must have asked me two or three times, the same question, before I actually heard her.

"Phil, what's wrong? Why are you up so early?"

"It's like a bad dream, Margaret."

"A dream? You've been crying. What is it?"

"This picture, this story in the paper. . ."

She looked at the paper, shaking her head at the toga headline, thumbing through the pages, turning to the back, somehow finding the story about the car wreck in Chicago. When she did she read it, not aloud, more in a whisper really, and sat down beside me, leaning her head against my shoulder. Close to crying also when she spoke.

"I'm sorry, Phil. I never knew them, but I am, I'm sorry."

"An ice patch. . .a goddamned ice patch."

"This colonel, his wife Molly was driving, she must have..."

"Molly and Mel Lamont. Damn."

"Mel Lamont, I know, you've told me about him."

"We were close, Margaret. Like brothers for a while."

Close, yes. I wiped away my tears, remembering what I'd been trying to forget all these years, how close we'd been. From the first day we met, the day they dropped the dummies that looked like Negro soldiers. Two young lieutenants, wild, jumping out of airplanes, getting drunk together in Germany.

Close. Until Molly came along. Until we both thought we loved her. Until we broke up over her, over Molly, wearing a Red Cross dress and dancing the night away, coming back to the States with Mel, the two of them getting married, something I didn't even know until now, the way I'd been trying to forget it.

Margaret kissed me on my cheek. When she leaned forward, looking at the scrapbook I brought down from the attic, I remembered something else I'd been trying to forget. How we met, why I married her, how I knew, almost right away, as we marched down the aisle in the chapel, how I knew I had made a mistake I would have to live with.

"This picture you've been looking at, Phil, that's his wife?"

"Molly. I was dancing with her. One night in Germany."

"You were in love with her, I know."

"That was a long time ago, Margaret."

"Sometimes you used to say her name in your sleep."

"She's gone now, Margaret. Forget it."

"I'm sorry, Phil. I really am. I'll fix you some breakfast now."

She knew, too, I was sure. Maybe not at first, but over the years, how we'd both been mistaken. Not much we could do about it, not with a son to raise. Try to get along. Teach classes, play poker, sing in the choir. Live with it.

Right. Live with it. What's done is done.

I tore the back page off the morning paper, laid it on the scrapbook, stood up, and went to my desk. When I got there I cut out the story of the car wreck, put it next to the picture of Molly dancing with me, placed the scrapbook in a desk drawer, looked down, saluted, and closed the drawer. All very slowly, a kind of funeral ceremony, a farewell to the past.

Done. Done and over.

Now have breakfast. Try not to upset Margaret any further. Then wrap this ledger for Senator Amador, get it ready to mail. Start thinking about that class at ten.

Get my mind on other things. What's done is done, forget it.

It's not easy, trying to forget something you've thought about for years, wondering what it might have been like if things had gone a different way. If I'd said look, Molly, tell Lamont to go away, I'll stay in the Army if that's what it takes, I'm the one who'll love you forever.

Not easy to forget, how the right words might have changed your life. How the words were somehow never spoken. How a ticket to the opera did it, instead, later, after she was gone. A mere ticket, a twist of fate, whatever, bumping into Margaret in Munich.

Not easy to forget, not easy to get your mind on other things. On teaching, on a son who's growing up, on how to get along at a College you'd rather get away from. On playing poker, not easy with your mind on something else.

"I'll be damned, you lost for once" said Max a few nights later, when the game was over. When everyone else had left, while he was putting the chips away. And I was still sitting at the table, looking at the last hand I had bet on. A pair of twos, not worth holding.

"Win a few, lose a few, Max."

"Lose a few, my ass, you lost nearly every hand tonight."

"So I lost. What have you heard from Doc Zimmer?"

"Damn it, don't try to tap dance on me, what's eating you?"

"Me? I lost, that's all, forget it."

"What happened to that logic you've been winning with?"

"To hell with logic, there's no logic in any of this shit."

"Look, something's bothering you, what is it?"

"You ever been married, Max?"

"Once. You need a drink, we both do, if that's what it is."

I put the cards away and pushed the table into a corner of his living room, while Max went to the kitchen and poured drinks. Bourbon, not the beer we'd been drinking during the game. When he returned he set the glasses on a coffee table, silent, looking down at the table.

"Yes, I was married once" he said after a moment.

"I never knew that, Max. What happened?"

"Six years we were together, before I came here."

"What was it? A bad marriage, or what?"

"She was rich, loaded with money, that's how we met."

"Money, what were you, her accountant?"

"No, I was working in a jewelry store, but that's why I became one. For her."

"So she changed your life around. What happened?"

"What happened, Phil, that's how I know what's troubling you."

He reached down, lifted his glass and pointed to mine, nodding in a way that meant I should pick up my glass. I did. He held his against mine for a moment, as if making a toast. To what, I could not even guess. All I could do was wait to hear.

"The College" he said. "Here's to this College we're at."

"To hell with the College, how would you know what's troubling me?"

"You let it out that night you were drunk, when I had to drag you out of a bar."

"Sure, you kept me out of a fight, but what do you mean, I let it out?"

"You don't remember? What you said about the Army?"

"No, if I was drunk I might have said anything, so what?"

"You said you'd have stayed in if you hadn't married Margaret. That's why we're here at this damned College, Phil, both of us, it's the women we married."

He smiled when he said that. Not a happy smile. The kind that says here's something you should know. I knew one thing from what he'd said so far. Something else I never knew before. What he felt about the College. He was no more pleased than I was. Bitter, even, the way he'd started talking about it.

"All right, we're here, Max. What does that have to do with who we married?"

"You left the Army, you went to graduate school to get a Ph.D. Why?

"I wanted to study philosophy, I wanted to make sense of things."

"I don't think so. I think you did it to please your wife."

"Margaret? Please her? Why would I even try?"

"Why? The same reason I went to business school to get an MBA in finance."

"For your wife, sure, so you could take care of her money. That's not the same."

"Don't kid yourself, Phil, it is. We're not just here, it's who we are now."

"Who we are? Two poker players talking about their wives, that's all."

"No, face it, Phil, what we've become. A professor who can't get his head straight, and me, a goddamned bookkeeper at a half-fass College."

Max was no longer smiling. Thinking about what he'd hit on, perhaps. How he'd be a different person if he'd married someone else. A jewelry merchant, maybe. Fine, and I'd be a different person, too, if I had stayed in the Army. Or gone back to the newspaper business.

Or married Molly. Not something to think about, not that.

"You may be right, Max, but that's not why I lost at poker tonight."

"Really? You know the difference between you and me, Phil?"

"I'm still married and you're not, that's one big difference."

"You try to understand this shit and I don't, not anymore."

"Damn it, you asked what's wrong with me, what's wrong with you?"

"Me? I'll just watch the world go by now. Whatever happens, let it."

"You've heard from Doc Zimmer, is that it?"

"To hell with Zimmer. To hell with wives."

"All right, to hell with them all. What did Zimmer tell you?" Max would not answer. Resigned to what he'd been told, I gathered. Walking home I felt resigned, as well. To how dumb I'd been, bringing my troubles to a poker game. Talking about marriage, when I should have kept my mouth shut. Hearing Max talk about it, too.

Hearing what he said. Why we're here, why we are who we are, because of the women we married. Why I'm a dumb professor who can't get his head straight.

Maybe, maybe not. We'd have to wait and see.

Watch the world go by, indeed. Do what Max said he'll do. Just sit back and watch it happen. Day by day, week by week, whatever.

The day I heard on the radio Lyndon Johnson had died, that same day I received a letter from Germany. From Helga Henschel. Telling me how grateful she was for the course she'd taken from me. How she'd gone to Mambachel, searching for the girl who looked like her, how she would take a picture and send it to me if she ever found her.

A week or so after that Tommy L came by my office. To tell me about his mother. How she felt safe now, how she'd called to say the FBI told her not to worry, they would protect her from Lomax. How he'd been so pleased he'd scored forty points in the game last night, wearing his regular uniform.

A few days later Dean Palmer called me about my prospects for tenure. The Senator's museum gift had made no difference. A Trustee had leaned on the President of the College, the President had informed the tenure committee I would have to go, Elena Bloom and the rest of the committee had resigned in protest, and he was trying to figure out what the rules were.

In February, on a day when my classes ended early, I got home in time to watch on TV as the first POW's came back from Hanoi. Nixon's scheme had worked out, I supposed. But not Reggie's garage door contraption. When I opened the mail from the Patent Office I read how they said no, something like that had already been invented.

What no one had invented, even Reggie, was some way to make Margaret pay attention to her driving. In early March, with her mind on her mother, maybe, she skidded on an icy street, hit a brick wall, ruined the front of her car, and yelled at me about it. Saying at least she hadn't killed anyone, as Molly had.

Almost boiling as she spoke. Something seemed to be boiling in Washington, too. Watergate, whatever that was, Nixon accused of a cover-up, reporters leaping all over it. Politics. I paid no attention. Until one night when I saw my old friend Dan Proctor talking about it on TV, reminding me I might have gone back to journalism. If I hadn't married Margaret.

And so it went, another winter. The snow piling up on campus, Margaret, grumbling, waiting to have her car repaired, Reggie puttering around in the basement. While I kept at my usual grind, winning again at poker, trying to cheer up Max, teaching courses, reading student essays, offering guidance, watching to see who was listening.

Watching the world go by.

And then, on an afternoon in early April, two things happened to break the spell. A few words with Doc Zimmer, when I picked up Margaret at the church, after choir practice. And later, after we had gotten home, a telephone call from Texas. Two things that turned my world upside down.

Zimmer was coming from the church with Margaret when he saw me waiting for her. He came to my car and asked me to get out, to come back inside with him, saying it was too cold to talk out there and he had something he needed to tell me. Margaret went back inside, as well, walking off someplace where she might stay warm, not caring to hear what Zimmer had to say.

Whatever it was, he seemed too uneasy to speak about it. For all I knew, it might be about our neighbors, how Professor Kornstadt had attacked him, right after Thanksgiving. I hadn't seen him since then, neither of them, in fact, and so, as uneasy as Zimmer seemed I broke the silence myself.

"I gather you can sing again" I said. "How's your jaw?"

"I'm all right, Dee. Look. . .well. . .it's about Max Piper."

"Max, what about him? I saw him in his office yesterday."

"Yesterday. So he hasn't told you why he's been having headaches."

"No, only that they won't let up, he can't. . ."

"It's a brain tumor, Dee. A bad one, I'm afraid."

"Damn. You've told him? He knows what it is?"

"As of this morning. I shouldn't tell you about it, but look, he needs your help."

"What about surgery, Doc? What about an operation?"

"Maybe, but he said no. You're friends, you need to talk to Max."

I nodded. Zimmer waited, then nodded also and left, out the church door, his head down. Margaret, when I found her, was sitting in a pew in front of the altar, staring at a stained glass image of some angels looking down from heaven. Angels. I grunted. Max wouldn't want any help from that crowd, either.

"Do you ever pray, Phil?" she asked as we drove home. "Pray for guidance, perhaps?"

"No, Margaret, I can't say I do."

"You think you know all by yourself the path you should follow."

"I know what I need to do right now. I need to see Max Piper."

"You're playing poker tonight, I suppose."

"No, I need to pick up a book and take it to him."

"Whatever you say. I'll leave your dinner in the oven."

She went in the house ahead of me, shaking her head. When I got to my study I found the book I thought might work. Something I could take to Max to start a conversation, so we could get around to what I wanted to tell him.

I was about to leave when the phone rang. A voice from Texas, one I recognized right away. A professor I had taken courses from when Margaret and I came back from the Army, getting my grades up so I could qualify for graduate school in California.

Saying hello, laughing about the last time we'd had a drink together, reminding me he'd advised me once to teach for a while at a small college and then move on, telling me he wanted to ask some questions. About the poker paper I sent to a logic journal.

Questions that made me forget Max Piper for a moment. Questions that made me wonder if those angels in the stained glass might be looking down at me. And smiling, as if they'd like to toy with someone who would never pray for a miracle to happen.

"This paper you wrote, Dee. Have you heard from the journal you sent it to?"

"No, I added some data I was asked for, but. . ."

"They sent me a copy for comments. You've gotten into game theory, right?"

"Sure, playing poker, that's what the paper's about, I'm. . ."

"I passed it around my department, you know what they told me?"

"What, that they wouldn't want to play poker with me?"

"Game theory, Dee, they said we need to add that as a minor."

"Sure, from what I've studied lately, I'd suggest that, too."

"Suggest, hell, Dee, how'd you like to come down here to teach?"

He paused, waiting for what he'd said to sink in. While I wondered about the angels back at the church, trying to play some kind of joke on a poor, untenured assistant professor. No way. He might throw in a few good Texas curse words now and then, but he wasn't joking.

Telling me I'd start as an associate professor, with tenure, he could guarantee it, he was chair of the damned department now. Telling me to take my time, he was going fishing during Spring break, he'd be back in a week, call him then, and he'd kick my ass if I say no.

No beating around the bush with him. With Margaret, yes. She came in my study as I hung up the phone. Not the time to tell her, maybe later. She hated Texas. Too hot in the summer, she could do without the cowboy music, and she'd never eat another enchilada.

"Reginald's in the basement" she announced.

"Leave him alone. That's where he invents things."

"He should be practicing piano. Every day before dinner."

"All right, all right. I'll talk to him when I get back."

"You're going to see Max, you said. I suppose you'd rather talk to him instead."

Not quite. If I could I'd rather have stayed right there, chewing on the telephone call from Texas. On something I had wondered about, over and over again, how odd it is, the way things turn out some times.

All by chance. My playing poker, writing a paper about it, stumbling into a ticket out of here. And Max, coming down with a brain tumor he could be dying from. With only one way out for him. Another matter of chance. Let the doctors operate.

He might, if I could persuade him. After he answered my knock on his door and said come in I was not so sure. He was slumped in an easy chair, his tie loosened and his suit a bit rumpled, looking like he'd given up already.

I handed him the book I had brought, hoping a word or so about World War Two would lead around to his uncle Alex. Who, Max had told me, was shot in the head by a German, survived through surgery, and lived on for twenty years. Something to remind him of that.

It did, but not the way I intended.

"What's this?" he asked. "I don't have time to read books, Phil."

"It's about the war in Germany. Your uncle was in it, you said he. . ."

"Alex? Did I ever show you that Luger pistol he gave me?"

"Sure, you brought it out last year, when we were playing poker, you said. . ."

"I said I'd shoot your ass if you didn't stop winning so goddamned many hands."

"That game theory, Max, it's really paid off now. . .but listen, about your uncle, he. . ."

"You know where he found that Luger? In the house of a dead Nazi mayor."

"A mayor? No, I never heard that, I. . ."

"In some little town, that bastard shot himself before the Americans got there."

"The mayor, he committed suicide? Max, listen, you. . ."

"Suicide, right. The way to go when your hand's played out."

He turned his head as he said that, looking at the poker table in the corner of the room. Then he got up and went to his kitchen. Leaving me alone and lost, worried about the way he'd mentioned suicide. When he returned with two bottles of beer, I still had no idea what to say.

"Don't worry, Phil. I'm not going to use that pistol on myself."

"Max, listen, your uncle Alex, he. . ."

"I might use it on that sonofabitch Ventura, however."

"Him? Forget him, we need to talk about. . ."

"That prick Koslowski, Ventura called me about him last Fall. Remember?"

"Koslowski, sure, he spent six years here and never graduated. But listen, we. . ."

"He's Ventura's goddamn nephew, Phil."

"Fine, so they're related, like you and your uncle, that's who we. . ."

"Ventura's given him fifty thousand dollars of College money, damn it."

"He paid Koslowski off? With College money?"

"While I was at the Mayo. Going over the budget, I just figured it out today."

"Max, that's larceny, Ventura could go to jail for that."

"No, the fucking President signed off on it. Maybe I'll shoot them both."

Max leaned back in his chair, sipping beer, rubbing the side of his head, angrier than I had ever seen him. Real anger, not the kind he acted out when I had won another hand at poker. Real, as if he might do it. As if he had nothing to lose. One last act of a dying man.

"This book" he said, looking down at the table. "I can guess why you brought it."

"So I might get you to talk about your uncle. That's all."

"I know, Alex had surgery. On his head. And he survived."

"Let Doc Zimmer tell you what to do. Let him, Max."

"How long have we been buddies, you and me?"

"Ever since we met, ever since we started playing poker."

"All right, I'll talk to Zimmer. Now, finish your beer and beat it."

Driving home I wondered if Max really meant what he said. I wasn't sure whether he would talk to Zimmer or not. Whether he'd buy off on an operation. And even if he agreed, whether it would make any difference.

Too much to worry about. Whether I should tell Margaret about Max. Whether I should tell her about the telephone call from Texas.

Whether that would make any difference, either.

I never knew if Max talked to Doc Zimmer about surgery. Or if he did, what Zimmer might have told him about his chances. Or what he wrote in the letter he left for the state attorney general.

All I knew was what he said in the note he left for me. Telling me his uncle had survived, all right, blind and crippled the rest of his life. Telling me to remember an old poker maxim, the one that says you've got to know when to fold 'em.

Telling me also, at the end of his note, to keep my eyes on Ventura, the crooked bastard will screw up sooner or later and get caught, and when that happens I should show up as they haul him off to jail and shout, as loud as I could, remember Max.

The College faculty remembered, more or less, at a memorial service a few nights later. Eating and drinking, after listening to a speech by the President. Not a eulogy, only a lie, about the way he'd always worked with Max to guard the College budget.

I poured a glass of wine and wandered around. Depressed about Max. By how I failed to help him. Even more depressed as

I heard the gossip in the crowd. Rumors about Max, about money missing from the budget.

There's fifty thousand gone, said a professor I barely knew, that's fifty thousand dollars they'll take from our salaries.

Piper's work, said someone else, his secretary told me the money was used to bribe some asshole student who used to be here.

More than fifty thousand, it could be two or three times that much, you know how Piper loved to gamble. . .

Playing poker, that bastard, blowing away our salaries. . .

Las Vegas, that's where he was last Christmas. . .

Three weeks, he wasn't sick like they said, he was off gambling. . .

So he lost all that money and shot himself. . .

Hell yes, we should have shot him ourselves. . .

Rumors. Stupid gossip. Enough to make me sick. Enough to settle it, once and for all. I walked away and headed for the door, back to my office to make the telephone call to Texas, to punch my ticket out of here.

Past Diedre DeLeon, telling someone how Max had let her down, how he'd failed to find the funds so she could lobby Congress for her baseball plan, how she would show the next VP for Finance a way to make the College rich with smart investments.

Past her, but not past Elena Bloom. She was standing near the door, leaning against a wall with a drink in her hand, looking half drunk as she smiled and motioned for me to join her, saying she had something to tell me.

"Phil, I feel safe now. . .help me celebrate..."

"Celebrate? No way, not with Max dead."

"Max, he saved me. . .no more mail bombs. . ."

"Elena, listen, the package I unwrapped, that wasn't a bomb."

"That student who sent it. . . he wrote. . .he said he'll leave me alone now."

"Koslowski, the one you kept out of the draft, sure, Ventura bought him off."

"Not him, it was Max. . .he signed the check. . .I'm safe now, Phil."

She reached to hug me, spilling her drink on my sleeve. Max, so that's how they did it to him. They forged his signature, the President and Ventura. Maybe that's what he wrote the state attorney general about. I smiled. Max, raising the ante before dropping out.

Elena was smiling too, even as I tried to push her away. Whispering in my ear about something I had trouble hearing. Tenure, it sounded like. I wasn't sure, as drunk as she was, the way she was leaning against my shoulder and mumbling.

"Tenure. . .Phil. . .I can get it for you...I. . ."

"Really? I was told the tenure committee has disbanded."

"In protest. . .that Trustee. . .Ventura. . ."

"I know. He told the President to fire me. Forget it."

"He made a pass at me. . .last year. . .he wanted to get me in bed. . ."

"Elena, listen, stay away from him, Ventura's a crook, he..."

"I'll do it, Phil. . .I'll sleep with him. . .I'll make him give you tenure. . ."

She stepped back, wobbly, straightening her dress, acting sultry, brushing her hair down the side of her face like some Hollywood temptress, as if that's how she'd take on Ventura. Too far gone to hear what I tried to tell her. Trying to be as polite as I could.

"That's nice, Elena, but you don't need to do that."

"I will. . .for you. . .for you. . ."

"No, I don't care about tenure here, not anymore."

"Phil. . .take me home. . .I'll show you. . ."

"You've had too much to drink, I'll find someone to give you a ride."

"Take me home. . .please. . .for now, let's not think about Ventura. . ."

"A good idea, let me find someone who can take you home."

"No, you take me home. . .tonight, it's your turn first. . ."

Dumb me, trying to be polite. Surprised instead. I shouldn't have been. She had invited me to join her in bed before. And I'd said no. This time, looking at her, the way she was smiling, damned attractive, even if she was lushed, I felt like saying yes.

Right. Do what she's asked. Take her home. Leap in the sack with Elena. A great way to get my mind off Max. Give these bastards around here something real to gossip about. The way Margaret's been treating me, why not?

I thought about it. Tempted. Until it dawned on me why not. Bedding down with Elena, what that might lead to. No telling. And I had enough on my plate already, without having to worry about her. Too bad, having to fold a royal flush as pretty as this one.

Wait here, I told her, keep smiling, I'll be back in a minute. After I found a prof from the French department who said yes, she'd take her home, we returned and I kissed Elena on the forehead, telling her what I wanted her to do.

"Listen carefully" I said. "I want you to forget about Ventura."

"All right. . .but how will you get tenure. . .if I don't. . ."

"I want you to forget about that as well. My tenure's taken care of."

"Phil, I was only trying to help. . .I was only. . ."

"Go home now, go to bed."

"Without you. . ."

"Without me. Sleep it off, I'll call you tomorrow."

I kissed her again on the forehead. To console her, I supposed. Or maybe to console myself, for what I'd just turned down. I wasn't sure if I would call her. Too much temptation still. Right then I had another call to make. To Texas. To escape, as soon as I could.

When I got to my office and made the call it was settled in a matter of minutes. My contract would be in the mail right away. Fine. I looked at my watch. Nine o'clock in the evening, time to go home and tell Margaret what I'd done.

She wouldn't want to hear about the memorial for Max, I knew. She had a headache, she'd said, and she had heard too many farewell speeches.

She wouldn't want to hear about Texas, either. I was sure she would try to talk me out of it, saying she planned to audition for the Cincinnati opera, or something like that.

And she sure as hell wouldn't want to hear me tell her about Elena, how I'd been faithful, how I fought against temptation.

Faithful, right. Even if that's not what it really was.

I did not tell Margaret much of anything when I got home. She told me a lot, instead. How I'd failed to get her car fixed right, how my dinner in the oven had burned in because I was late. And so forth. Not happy at all. At least not happy with me.

So I kept my mouth shut and told her nothing. She could wait to hear about Texas. Dean Palmer could wait as well. He would not complain. He'd be pleased to hear I'm leaving. No contract yet, and he would not have to haggle with Ventura about my getting one.

Senator Amador was a different cup of tea. She was more than happy when she called me at my office the following afternoon. Almost beside herself as she spoke. Telling me, as she went on and on, something I could hardly believe.

"Dee, that ledger you sent, it's paid off big time."

"That record Lomax kept? It's been decoded?"

"Damned right it has. Thanks to you, we're going to nail that bastard."

"Lomax, do you know where he is? The last I heard, he. . ."

"We've traced him to Mexico. We'll find him, it's only a matter of time now."

"That ledger, you have enough to put him in jail then?"

"Not just him. Look, I know how edgy you can be. Go get a cup of coffee or something, I don't want you falling out of your chair when I tell you the rest."

Fine. I did what she told me. Rule number something or other, always do what Amador says. I went to the water cooler in the hall-way, came back, took a deep breath, picked up the phone again and tapped it on my desk, so she would know I was ready to listen.

"Dee, there's a Senator from your state who's also involved."

"In that Lomax business? The LSI, the Lone Star International?"

"He's guilty as shit. He made millions out of that crap they pulled off in Vietnam."

"Which one? There's two Senators from Ohio. . ."

"I'll let you guess. He lives in Cleveland, and he's rich as hell."

"I think I know who you mean. The Big IP they call him. IP, for influence peddler."

"More than influence, Dee. His sidekick's taken over your damned College."

"Really. I think I can guess who that is, too."

"Wait, let me check this prick's first name, we'll see if you're in the ballpark."

I could hear her shuffling papers, cursing, yelling to someone to help her find the Cleveland file. Her niece, perhaps, if Amador was calling from home. I waited. When she picked up the phone and started talking again, I knew at once I was right.

"His first name's Allen. One of your Trustees, Allen Ventura, do you know him?"

"All too well. He's this Senator's sidekick? He was in on that LSI scam?"

"Deep enough to get filthy rich. It's all in that ledger Lomax kept."

"Money, sure. No wonder Ventura acts like he owns this place."

"It's your President he owns, Dee. He has him by the balls."

"I know, he lets Ventura boss him around. That's how it is here, money talks."

"It isn't money. The FBI uncovered it, digging around. It's blackmail."

"Blackmail? Ventura's been blackmailing the College President?"

"Let's put it this way. Your President's not only a jerk, he likes to romp around with little boys."

I almost fell out of my chair. Amador had warned me I might, and I damned near did. Ventura, trying to run the Cleveland

Opera, running Margaret off, trying to run the College, trying to run me off, and now the FBI had that power hungry bastard for fraud and blackmail and maybe the President for vice, no wonder I was stunned by what she said.

"Dee, are you still there? I have some advice for you now."

"Advice? Senator, I'm trying to add this up, I'm. . ."

"Get out, before the shit hits the fan, even if they gave you tenure."

"I don't even have a contract. I'm leaving, all right, I'm heading for Texas."

"They didn't give you tenure? Then piss on them, I'll take away their museum."

"Wait. . .in place of that, you have funds for colored kids, how about. . ."

"Texas. I suppose you're taking the Lomax boy with you."

"Tommy L, you're right, if he agrees to go a scholarship would help, so if you. . ."

"I'll take care of it. And listen, Dee, keep quiet about this until Friday, that's when the FBI plans to nab these two shit heads, Ventura and your Senator. Not a word until Friday." She hung up before I could reply. Friday. The final day of classes. The day of the last faculty tea this Spring, the usual ritual to end the semester, where they can gossip some more about Max and strut around like they know which way is up.

Two days away, time to ask Tommy about Texas. Amador's right, the shit's about to hit the fan. Ventura's going to jail, and likely the President, too. They've lost their precious museum, and there's something else that may wake them up, maybe change how they act around here.

No contract, fine, I'll take the star of their basketball team instead.

Tommy L. Odd, the way we met by accident, his looking for a course to take and asking me to tell him what the word philosophy meant. And then signing up and paying attention, listening carefully to what I told them in all my courses, that philosophy, if you take it to heart, is a way to make sense of yourself and the world you live in.

Odd, too, even stranger than how we met, was the way he reminded me of that, what I'd been trying to teach. Yesterday, when he came in to talk and made me realize I hadn't listened to what I was saying in class. He had paid attention, but I had not. I hadn't been making sense of my world, I had let it get me down. I had let it make me angry.

Angry, feeling pushed around, feeling sorry for Max and how I failed him, I had let my feelings overcome my sense of how to take the world in stride. That's what Tommy made me realize when he came in, glanced at the game ball on a bookshelf, shook his head, and started telling me about his world.

"Basketball. What would you say if I told you I've decided to quit, Professor?"

"What would I say? I suppose it depends on the reason why."

"It's what I noticed when we lost in the playoffs. That's what did it."

"You think it was your fault? That's not what I heard."

"No, it's they way they cried. The whole team acted like someone had died."

"I know. A lot of folks get carried away when they lose at something."

"My roommate, he was so upset he threw all his books out the window."

"You don't sound upset yourself. So what's this all about?"

"The way they acted, it woke me up, I remembered what you said in class."

"In class? I talked about basketball in class? When?"

"Not basketball, Professor. Wisdom. When you said it's not wise to whine about water under the bridge, it's not wise to even care about things you can't change."

The Stoics, the lecture when I outlined what some ancient Greeks had claimed, that's what Tommy had remembered. How Epictetus told us it's quite simple, what's done is done, no one can alter that, the wise man stays calm by keeping his emotions in check. Tommy had paid attention and I had not. I had let my emotions get out of hand.

Not wise, my feeling angry about their gossip and a lot of other things as well. I should not have let it get under my skin. I should not have dreamed of changing the way they act around here. Ventura and the President going to jail, that might not even do it. And not some act of revenge on my part, either, taking Tommy with me when I leave here.

He had turned his back, looking at the game ball on my bookshelf. Silent, after telling me what he remembered about wisdom. When he took the ball and started bouncing it on the floor I watched, wondering why he'd decided to quit playing, wondering what I should say to him about Texas, now that I realized what I'd thought before was not wise at all.

"Done" he said as he put the ball on the shelf. "That part of my life is over."

"So you're through with basketball, what do you have in mind?"

"I've been thinking about my mom, Professor, all the trouble she's had."

"That may be over soon. The FBI's closing in on Lomax, Tommy."

"She's got other problems, too. That's why I'm giving up basketball."

"How will that help? What are you going to do, quit school?"

"No, I need time to concentrate, so I can study harder."

"Study harder, good, Tommy, you've done well so far."

"Not well enough. I need to get in line for law school, Professor."

He came around my desk, reaching down to shake hands, as if making a promise. To me, but really for his mother. Law school to help her, God only knows what record she has, after hanging around with Lomax. I looked up and nodded. Fine, I knew now what to do, and it would not be for revenge, it would be for his sake.

"If you want to help your mother, I have a suggestion."

"Whatever you say. I'll see her in Dallas, right after exams."

"Texas, if you move back you could see her more often."

"Sure, but I can't leave, I have a tuition grant here."

"How about a scholarship there? How does that sound?"

"Like I'm day-dreaming, that's how. I've quit that, too."

"I can get one for you. You can go with me if you like."

"You're going back to Texas? You bet, I'll pack my bags right now."

I got up and walked him to the door, patting him on the back, urging Tommy to be patient, he had a long haul ahead, six years, perhaps, before he could finish law school, but at least he'd be near his mother in the meantime.

He stopped in the doorway, smiling, reminding me of something else I suppose I had forgotten. "Six years" he said. "No swat, like the Stoics you told us about, what counts is how well you can endure things. I'll do it, Professor, I will."

After he left I sat down and stared at the shelf where all the books on the Stoics were lined up. Endurance. No one can change what happens, all you can do is endure it.

Endure it, right. Forget how they act around here, that can't be changed.

Forget it and head for the highway.

There's one thing I can change, by God, whether they like it or not. What I heard this morning, when I went to the basement to tell Reggie it's time for school.

What I heard on the radio he listens to, so he can know what the weather's like. The local station, predicting rain. Reporting streets closed for repair. And then, just as Reggie was about to turn off the radio, an announcement last night from the College.

An accident I heard it at all. The President plans to reveal a major crime at the College, according to the station, fraud by the late VP for Finance, Max Perkins. He will disclose the amount at this afternoon's faculty tea.

Like hell he will. He must not know the FBI is closing in. It doesn't matter. If they don't get here first I'll take care of that bastard myself. Before he can open his mouth and even mention Max.

Twenty minutes to wait now. Looking out my office window I can see them showing up already. Kornstadt, his head down, with his gossiping bitch of a wife behind him. And DeLeon, no doubt ready to bid for the VP job, now that she's heard the news on the radio.

Wives. Experts.

Sometimes I look at Margaret and wonder. How I wound up here, surrounded by books and the kind of fools who think they're smart because they've written one.

Like this woman DeLeon. One little book on the history of Portuguese pottery, that's all, and she's a flaming expert on everything. Major league baseball, how Nixon can settle things in Vietnam, how to save the United Nations, you name it, she knows.

No, that's not quite true. About DeLeon, all right. But not about my wife and how I got here. I don't wonder. I remember.

An accident, thirteen long years ago, as simple as that. Sometimes I can even laugh about it, the way it happened.

But not right now, not while I'm sitting in my office waiting for her. I'm in no mood to laugh at all, not when she thinks she's going to drag me off to a faculty tea.

My last one, for sure. And Margaret? She has no idea at all, what I'm getting ready to do, how I'm getting ready to spill the beans.

No idea at all. If she did, she wouldn't be all dressed up and on her way here. She'd have stayed home and pulled the covers over her head. Or gone out in the yard, bellowing something from one of her goddamned operas.

Wagner, maybe. Götterdämmerung would be just right.

So as usual I'll say Margaret, why don't you go by yourself, I've been grading papers and I have a terrible headache. And she'll interrupt and say Phillip, a break will be good for you, and anyway you need to mingle with the other faculty, that's good for you, too.

So we'll go. Together. And I'll mingle. For a while. With the crowd. That crooked Trustee who likes to run the College. The President, kissing his ass to keep his job. And the President's secretary, the one who stands over the punch bowl, wearing white gloves and serving crap not even Margaret can swallow.

I may even chat with DeLeon about Portuguese pottery. I may tell her I'm an expert, too. Not about the UN or foreign policy. Not about Nixon and the war in Vietnam. About something else. Something she's sure as hell not an expert on

What they've been gossiping about, full of rumors about it, DeLeon and all the others. The money missing from the College budget. What the President has to say about it.

Mingle, hell. I'm going to tell them what I've discovered. I'm going to dump it right in that goddamned punch bowl. And then stand back and say kiss off, you'd never have guessed that, would you? So what kind of books are you going to write about it, now that you know what really happened?

Margaret won't be pleased when I say that. No more than the night we met in Germany at the opera, when I bumped into her and spilled wine on her dress. Not pleased at all then. And she won't be happy this time, either.

But this time it won't be by accident.

No, and it won't be an act revenge on my part, either. Tommy L took care of that, when he reminded me of the Stoics.

All it will be is my way of saying farewell. Telling them their no good President is headed for prison, and Ventura with him. Saying farewell to them all. Telling them to kiss off, I'm out of here.

I can see them through my window, to the left, rushing to the faculty lounge. It's starting to rain, and they haven't brought their umbrellas. Too bad.

To my right, something else. Cars arriving in front of the admin building where the President has his office. Four black cars. Men getting out, wearing raincoats.

I'm watching when I hear the knock on my door. "Come in" I say, knowing that will be Margaret, ready for the faculty tea.

"There's quite a commotion out there" I hear her say.

"I know, that's what I'm watching, Margaret."

"You could at least turn around and say hello."

"Wait a second, I'm trying to see what's going on."

Nothing much. A half-dozen men in raincoats have gone in the admin building, and some others are standing by the cars, but nothing else is happening. A mystery of sorts. And another mystery when I turn around and look at Margaret.

"What do you have on?" I ask when I see what she's wearing.

"Blue jeans and a sweatshirt, what are you, blind?"

"Margaret, you can't go to a tea wearing that."

"Who said I'm going to a tea? I came by to get you."

"Get me for what? Wait a minute, I want to see what's happening."

The men in raincoats are in the doorway of the admin building, coming out, that's all I can see. That and the men outside, opening the car doors, getting ready to take on passengers, that's what it looks like when I turn around again.

"All right, Margaret, what are you up to?"

"You could have told me, Phil."

"Told you what? How I'm going to ruin their goddamn tea?"

"No, you could have told me about this."

I watch as she reaches in her purse and pulls out a cap. When she puts it on I recognize the logo on it. Dallas Cowboys.

"That cap was in my desk, Margaret. So what?"

"I know, I found it when I was looking for something to write on."

"I'm looking, too, out this damned window, so leave me alone."

What I see is hard to make out in the rain. Men coming from the admin building, the half-dozen wearing raincoats, two others with their heads down as they walk to the cars. And another car arriving, a man leaping out with a camera.

When the flashbulbs go off I see who they are, the two with their heads down. Ventura and the College President. Both of them handcuffed, trying to hide their faces from the camera as the men in raincoats shove them in the cars.

The FBI. They've arrested those crooks at last. I should be smiling, I know, but I'm not. My farewell at the faculty tea, damn it, it's blown now. By the time I can get there and tell them to kiss off, DeLeon and all the others, they will have heard already what's happened.

I turn and glance at Margaret. While I've been watching out the window she's sat down in a chair on the other side of my office. She's staring at me with an odd look on her face, still wearing my Dallas Cowboys cap for some reason.

"It's the FBI" I tell her. "They've arrested Ventura and the College President."

"Yes, I know, Phil."

"Ventura, Margaret, maybe now you can sing in Cleveland again."

"Perhaps, if that's what you would like me to do."

"You're not surprised he's been arrested?"

"No. Your friend Amador told me it would happen."

"Senator Amador? You talked to her? When?"

"She called this morning. I told you, I was looking in your desk for something to write on, here, you can read it yourself, what she asked for."

Margaret reaches in her purse and unfolds a sheet of paper. I take it, sit down at my desk and read what she's written. Senator Amador called, the note says, she would like you to send her your new address and number when you get settled in Texas.

"All right, Margaret, so now you know."

"I don't know anything, only what's in that note."

"Then I'll tell you the rest. I've signed a contract, I'm leaving."

"I'm your wife, Phil, you could have told me."

"Why? So you could argue about it? You hate Texas."

She's silent for a moment. I cannot guess what she's thinking. About me, about Texas, about my going back there. For all I know, she's getting ready to warn me I can go by myself. Hard to tell, the way she's staring at me.

"Look what I have on" she says. "Why do you think I'm wearing this Cowboys cap?"

"A joke, maybe, how would I know?"

"Do you remember the vows we took when we married?"

"Sure, Margaret, 'til death do us part."

"No, that other vow, the one that said for better or for worse."

"That's why you have that Cowboys cap on?"

"For better or for worse, Phil. For better or for worse."

I don't know what to say. She's wearing blue jeans and my Cowboys cap, ready to pack and move on. The way she's looking at me, I'm wondering whether she's the one who's really the Stoic in the family.

And now I remember what Max said. About marriage.

"Why are you smiling?" she asks.

"Margaret, do you think I'm who I am because I married you?"

"Who you are? I don't know, let's go home, Phil."

She takes my arm. We're leaving. In a few days we'll be headed for Texas. And I'll still be wondering if Max was right.

For better or for worse.

Who knows?

About S.R. Doss:

S.R. Doss has been a journalist, paratrooper, and professor of philosophy. In addition to *A Game of Inches,* he is also the author of *Blood on the Risers* and *Hattie's Pink House,* two earlier novels about the life of Phillip Dee.

www.ingramcontent.com/pod-product-compliance
Lightning Source LLC
Chambersburg PA
CBHW071739190726
48292CB00003B/809